EVELYN ROGERS

SWEET TEXAS MAGIC

ZEBRA BOOKS
KENSINGTON PUBLISHING CORP.

To Tessa Hohrath and Florence McEnery
And to Joyce Kennamer,
Special people, special friends.

ZEBRA BOOKS

are published by

Kensington Publishing Corp.
475 Park Avenue South
New York, NY 10016

First printing: April, 1992

Printed in the United States of America

"A fast-paced, sexy ride from New Orleans to Texas . . . high flying adventure combined with smoldering sensuality in *Sweet Texas Magic*."

— *Romantic Times*

PASSION'S PRISONER

They lay stretched out, Sam's hands pinning her wrists above her head, his body pressing hers down into the muck and mire. His hat lost in the fall, he stared down at her. Rivulets of water streamed down his face, and the spark in his eyes spoke of an anger that matched anything she had ever felt.

She squirmed to get away from him. With his body hard against hers, she realized right away that squirming was a mistake.

The spark in his eyes deepened to a gleam.

"Let go of my wrists," she said, lowering her voice to huskiness and putting as much suggestion in the words as she could, "and you'll find out how much spirit I have."

All she needed was one free hand. A sock in the nose would take him by surprise, and then she could get to that pepperbox.

Grasping her wrists in one hand, he brought his freed hand down her cheek and neck to her throat, loosening the string securing her cloak and pulling it aside. His fingers moved inside to touch her skin above the low scoop of her gown, stroked over the wet velvet covering her breasts and trailed down her side, past her waist to the flare of her hips. . . .

Chapter One

"I've seen enough naked men to last me a lifetime."

Smoothing a wisp of hair from her face, Lorelei Latham snapped a sheet of white linen into thirds and placed it on the shelf in front of her.

"And," she added as she reached for another, "whether you believe me or not, I've no desire to see any more."

The woman beside her, a café au lait mulatto named Delilah, sniffed in disagreement.

"No desire, *m'amie?* At the ancient age of twenty-three?"

"I didn't say I'm too old, just that I'm not interested."

"Only because the right man has not come along."

Lorelei shook her head. When Delilah got onto a subject, she could be a stubborn woman; more and more lately the subject turned out to be men.

But Lorelei could be stubborn, too. "Men come in three categories, Delilah — good, bad and indifferent. I can count on one hand the good ones I've met, and as for the others, I can't see anything to get excited about."

Delilah gave her a you'll-find-out smile. Lorelei

5

considered a retort, remembered the tasks awaiting her, and devoted herself to the folding.

The two women were working in the storage room at the rear of Balzac's Casino, the former La Chatte de la Nuit which now bore the name of owner Catherine Gase's pet cat. A week ago Catherine had promoted Lorelei from dealer to proprietor. The time was noon; when the doors opened at dusk, Lorelei wanted everything just right.

Delilah eyed the shelf of linens. "Will there be space in the gaming rooms for the food tables?"

"I'm setting up no more than Catherine used to when she ran Balzac's herself."

"It has been more than six years since she married," said Delilah. "I forget sometimes how glorious the casino was then."

Lorelei remembered, down to the last detail. Six years ago she'd met Delilah and Catherine and had seen the casino for the first time. Shortly afterward, she'd come here to live, moving into the upstairs bedroom Catherine had used before joining her husband Adam at the plantation Belle Terre.

The move had marked the end of Lorelei's nightmare. Or at least the beginning of the end. Along with a lingering sadness, a few ugly memories still remained, primary among them the image of a villainous man with a smooth, lying voice, thin face, and cold, smoky eyes.

She forced the picture aside. On this first Saturday in her job, she wanted everything to be perfect. Catherine had high hopes Balzac's would regain the popularity lost under the miserly control of the men she'd been hiring. To that end, she'd given Lorelei carte blanche.

Glittering lights and laughter, a regal feast, and coins dropping like spring rain on the gaming tables — that's what Lorelei remembered; it's what she was trying to recreate.

"You know your problem?" asked Delilah, shattering Lorelei's daydream. "You worry too much."

Lorelei smoothed her plain gray-blue gown and picked up another linen sheet. "I believe in being prepared."

"And you have another problem, *cherie,* even if you do not admit it." Delilah paused, but Lorelei kept on folding.

"As beautiful as you are," Delilah persisted, "with your golden hair and eyes the color of the sky, you have never known *amour.*"

"Now, that I can agree with."

"You speak lightly, as if *amour* is of little consequence, but you have no understanding of its power. For a woman of your spirit and your heart, it is only a matter of time."

"Ha!"

"Do not be so quick to scoff. One evening, when you least expect it, someone special will walk in the door, someone who will notice—"

"Of course he'll notice. Men look at women, and they think lusty thoughts. It is one of their obsessions, like gambling and drinking wine."

"We all have our obsessions."

"But mine isn't lust. It never will be."

"Bah!"

"It won't. I know it. Nothing you say, not even your voodoo charms, can change my mind. I'll never want a man, not in the way you speak of. Some of these dandies look all right in their clothes, but as far as I'm concerned, a naked man is about as appealing as a fresh-scraped potato."

Delilah's soft brown eyes glinted. "Not my man."

Lorelei considered the muscled, ebony-skinned Ne-

7

gro who lived with Delilah in the small house at the rear of the casino property.

"Well, no," she said, smiling, "I suppose not Ben."

Delilah and Ben had been together working at Balzac's since long before Lorelei had met them. She owed them both the same loyalty and gratitude that she owed to Catherine and Adam. All of them had helped her to heal.

They were happy couples, but Lorelei had no romantic notion that someday she would find herself similarly paired. Indeed, she had no romantic notions at all.

Lorelei had one advantage lost to other virginal young women: the close-up knowledge that while men might grow in all sizes and shapes, their sexual equipment pretty much looked the same, no matter how much they prided themselves on what some called the "third leg." The most she could say about the thing was that it was utilitarian. It gave a woman babies. And *that* made it important.

Lorelei wanted babies very much, someday after she had proven herself at Balzac's . . . someday after she avenged the tragedy of Carrie . . . after she had found the black-hearted bastard who. . . .

"I see the look in your eye again, *m'amie,*" Delilah said. "It does little good to keep returning to what has been. Didn't you learn that from the stories Madame Catherine has told you?"

Lorelei shrugged an answer. It was true that Catherine had gone through much suffering in her early life before she'd met Adam. Now she had a wonderful home, a loving husband, and two precious children, three-year-old Victor and a baby daughter Marie.

But there would be no Adam for her. "Let's get this work finished," she said. "I need to see to the food, and make sure everything is ready."

"Beware, *m'amie.* You work too much."

"The way you lecture, you'd think I was frail."

Delilah cast a sidelong glance at Lorelei's right arm. "This, you are not. No one who was here two nights ago would ever make such a mistake."

Lorelei knew exactly what Delilah meant; late Thursday she'd felled a belligerent gambler by striking him square in the nose. Acting on instinct, she'd taken him by surprise, but she'd also drawn blood. A scarlet-stained handkerchief against his face, he had hastily departed. No one at Balzac's had seen him since.

She'd been unable to resist a triumphant look at the Balzac guards moving in for her rescue. The muscled men in their incongruous black evening suits had seen she was in control.

But control meant more than just handling boors; control meant seeing to every detail, and when the last of the linens was folded, Lorelei made a close inspection of the casino's main room, which stretched the width of the building just beyond the storage area, then turned her attention to the side rooms, making certain the felt tables were brushed, the mahogany-paneled walls polished, the chandeliers washed until they sparkled.

A quick trip to the kitchen, located in a square, squat building behind the casino, told her all was as she had ordered: gumbo boiling on the stove, bread baking in the oven with a slab of peppered beef waiting to follow, fresh-caught shrimp on ice ready to be grilled. The employee she had recently elevated to wine steward assured her that there would be ample drink.

Delilah found her checking the shine on the brass doorknobs in the foyer. *"M'amie,* you must rest for a while, or you will never make it through the night."

Lorelei agreed to try, but after ten minutes of lying wide-eyed and board-stiff on her feather bed, she decided on another way to relax. She was grateful that Ben, away for the weekend helping Adam at Belle Terre, was not present to discourage her.

Quickly she changed into her riding habit; in the stable behind the casino she saddled Seabreeze, the bay mare that had been a gift from Catherine and Adam on her twenty-first birthday, then rode past the row of casinos that lined the street where Balzac's had once reigned.

The row of gambling halls was far from the heart of New Orleans, in the community of Carrollton, where Americans and Creoles could gather in the pursuit of pleasure, forgetting the animosity that often troubled them in town. Stepping high, Seabreeze carried her mistress past a mercantile store and a livery stable, and a smattering of houses. As civilization gradually thinned, Lorelei reined the bay onto a narrow, rutted trail that led westward from the main road.

She applied the crop to the mare's flanks, and the aptly named Seabreeze sprang as quick as the wind down the path, horse and rider racing as one past fields brown and stubbled on this February afternoon, past shanties that sat in their midst, with windows dark like blank, staring eyes. Ahead was her destination, the thick, bayou-laced forest that lay to the west.

She knew the countryside well, and she knew the dangers it held. In her pocket was a pepperbox pistol, and in a saddle scabbard specially designed by Adam was a .36 caliber squirrel rifle. Adam had taught her to use them both.

Lorelei prided herself on her fearlessness. Except

for an irrational repugnance to spiders, she considered herself ready to face anything or anyone—as long as she was prepared, and to that end she carried the guns. Most of the Choctaws who had once roamed the southern Louisiana countryside were removed to the Indian Territory, but renegade bands of Indians still remained, along with the more ordinary army deserters, runaway slaves, and thieves. Many of the disreputables were headed for what was called a new promised land—Texas, a republic after last year's victorious war against Mexico and reputedly rich beyond dreaming.

"Streets littered with money," she'd heard a gambler claim last week. "Woods thick with game, and out on the plains enough wild horses to supply every rider in the United States. Best of all, the soil's so rich all a man has to do is drop whatever seed he chooses and watch the crops sprout."

There were many who believed such wild tales, foolish men by the hundreds who were heading west, some with families, most alone. G.T.T.'s, the travelers were called. Gone to Texas. With so many rascals running from their unpaid debts, the term became synonymous with fugitive from justice, and Lorelei knew they could be more dangerous than any gun-waving drunk who wandered into Balzac's.

Today she stayed with the path. Long ago it had been an Indian trail, then one of the routes used by the Acadians when they first settled the area. Few people realized it eventually hooked up with the main road to the faraway Sabine River, which marked the boundary between the United States and Texas. Lorelei had explored the trail's length, but this afternoon, despite the beauty of the clear sky and the mildness of the weather, the opening of Balzac's demanded the ride be brief.

In the shadows of the forest, the air was colder, but Lorelei barely noticed, so intent was she on studying the dappled light that drifted through the leaves of the trees and onto the thick underbrush that lined the trail. She slowed Seabreeze to a walk. Around them a thousand birds harmonized. She breathed deeply; in the midst of winter she could smell a green hint of spring.

As she rode, Delilah's voice came unexpectedly into her thoughts.

The right man has not come along.

"Delilah," she whispered into the wind, "there is no right man for me."

When you least expect it, someone special will walk in the door. . . .

"I don't expect it," Lorelei said with heart-felt honesty.

The bay mare, twisting her graceful head, cast a round-eyed look at her mistress, and Lorelei's gloved hand stroked her neck.

"No, Seabreeze, I most certainly do not. What I need is a gentleman of means to propose marriage. Someone sensitive and kind who wants children but who'll find no particular pleasure in the act of mating. Someone who will respect my wishes in the matter, and forget the details of my past."

She'd once tried to explain to Delilah what she wanted.

"Might as well stay single then and keep working with those charity children you're so fond of," Delilah had thrown back, referring to her occasional afternoons helping out at the Ursuline orphanage.

"If I must, then that's just what I will do."

But, oh, how she wanted to have children of her own, to lavish on them the affection she had been denied. Those brief hours with the orphans — and the

12

increasingly rare occasions when she was able to help tend the two Gase children—did not fill her deep needs.

Lorelei had enough love stored in her to handle a dozen sons and daughters. If only she didn't have to sleep with a man.

She made fast work of the return trip, left the bay with the stable hand, and made another inspection of the kitchen and gambling rooms. This time she conferred with the dealers and guards who were already assembling in anticipation of a busy night, reminding them that all weapons were to be left at the door, assuring them she would be circulating, and in general giving them a spate of last-minute instructions they didn't need.

"Any questions?" she asked, letting her blue eyes trail from face to face.

Francois, the broad-shouldered Creole who served as the casino's greeter, responded. "No questions. All will continue to go well. We have only to say that we have great confidence in the mademoiselle."

"Thank you," said Lorelei, inordinately pleased as she hurried upstairs to bathe and dress.

She took care with her appearance the way she had cared for the polishing of the paneled walls. Whether she wanted them to or not, the gamblers noticed her all right, just as she had admitted to Delilah; she would be a fool to claim otherwise.

She felt grateful that her past was not much talked about among them, but she knew it was not a secret. Most believed she had lovers—she knew that from the comments they made—and she did nothing to disabuse them of the belief. As long as no one tried to add his name to the list, she was content. Whoever met her criteria as a husband would find out soon enough that despite her reputation

13

and opportunities, she had never lain with a man.

On this Saturday night she swept her hair atop her head in the latest 1837 fashion, wisps of honey-colored curls outlining her face and accenting her eyes.

Her dress, a rich green velvet to ward against the coolness of the February night, was cut low, draping off the shoulders, its bodice tight and slightly pointed at the waist, the sleeves long and fitted, a ruffled band of ecru lace around the wrists. The dome-shaped skirt brushed against the carpeted floor, hiding her sturdy shoes. No lightweight slippers for Lorelei. On her feet as much as she was, she needed comfort, not feminine daintiness.

Neither did she bind herself in a corset. A camisole, ankle-length drawers and five petticoats, the bare minimum sufficient to maintain the shape of her gown, lay beneath the yards of velvet. Her single piece of jewelry was a cameo, suspended from a green velvet ribbon at her throat.

As Balzac's hostess she was suitably attired. Now, if only some overbearing man did not decide she was too delectable a dish to view from afar. Lorelei had the unfortunate habit of breaking into a fiery rash when such a man tried to force his attentions on her. The rash had saved her during the darkest of her days, just as it discouraged the most forward of her would-be seducers now. But that didn't mean she liked taking on the appearance of a fresh-boiled shrimp.

Downstairs she watched with growing pleasure the number of gamblers who entered the double doors of Balzac's. Passing through the crowded rooms, she met the sounds of French and English thrown back and forth at the tables. The laughter, the excited conversations, and the clink of chips were music to her ears. She was most definitely in control, and she was doing well. Just as she'd hoped, Balzac's was once again a success.

It was late in the evening before a problem arose, a protest from one of the patrons over the casino's requirement that all weapons be left at the door. She heard the man arguing with Francois and made her way to his side.

Her demeanor cool as ever, she looked calmly at the troublemaker. "Mr. Knowles, is it not? You have been here before."

Staring back at her was a handsome man she estimated to be in his early thirties. When he had first strolled in to try his luck early in the week, she had decided he was almost pretty, with even features and brown hair and eyes. She could fault only his weak mouth and chin.

"No one here will harm you, Mr. Knowles."

"Maybe not, but where I've been residing, ma'am, a man doesn't have to give up his peace of mind."

"And where would that be, Mr. Knowles?"

"Texas."

She should have guessed. Texians considered themselves a breed apart. As far as she was concerned, they could all stay on the far side of the Sabine.

"I assure you that at Balzac's you are perfectly safe."

His eyes trailed past the crowd of gamblers in the foyer and to the beefy, stern-faced guards. At the sound of the argument, they had assembled close by.

At last Knowles shrugged and pulled from inside his coat a small pocket pistol, which he handed over to Francois.

"Now, how about some poker?" Lorelei said, waving to one of the side rooms. "I believe that's your favorite game."

"Do you notice everything that goes on around here?"

"Everything."

Within a few minutes Lorelei was seated along with the Texian and three other gamblers at one of the round poker tables, the men watching as her long, tapered fingers shuffled a freshly opened deck. Another new skill, this handling of the pasteboards. Her mother would have understood the need for the carefully nurtured talent, but her father must be turning over in his grave.

"Five-card stud, gentlemen," she said and proceeded to deal.

The betting went fast and high. At many of the gambling tables, chips were used in place of cash, but the men who chose poker preferred folding money and coins. During the next hour much of it moved back and forth.

Lorelei held her own, and one by one all but Frank Knowles dropped out, replaced by others who likewise decided after a while to try their luck elsewhere. By the time the foyer clock struck twelve, only she and Knowles were left. He won the hand with a full house, queens over sevens. The winning pot came to five hundred dollars, but while it added to his profit, it wasn't enough to put him ahead of Lorelei for the night.

Snapping his fingers for another glass of wine, Knowles fingered the coins and bills in front of him. "Shouldn't have caused so much trouble earlier. Just had it in my mind something was going to happen."

"All of us at Balzac's are grateful you were wrong," she said with a smile; then she stood.

"You'll have to excuse me, Mr. Knowles. As much as I have enjoyed the evening, my duties call me elsewhere."

"My pleasure," the handsome man said, his lips twitching into a smile as he lifted the wine. He downed it in one swallow, then set the empty glass amidst his coins. "We're both winners tonight."

She backed away from the table and turned toward the center of the room. One of her assistants, Anthony, appeared at her side and took her winnings for deposit in the casino safe beneath the staircase.

"Hell fire!" Knowles barked behind her, and a chair crashed to the floor.

She wheeled around, saw him sway to a stand, saw his brown eyes darken with fear. She followed his gaze to the open doorway leading to the foyer. Along with everyone else in the suddenly quiet room, she studied the tall, long-legged man standing in the door.

Unlike the other patrons, he was dressed informally, a brown fringed buckskin jacket over an open-throated brown shirt, fitted buff trousers tucked into calf-high tooled-leather boots. A broad-brimmed felt hat sat low on his forehead, but not so low that she couldn't pick out a shock of black hair resting over thick black brows. His eyes, brown as bark, were set in a lean and craggy face only a few shades lighter; they assessed the room and its inhabitants like a hawk stalking his prey.

He looked at the fallen chair a dozen feet from where he stood, and then on to the man standing beside it.

There was nothing weak about the newcomer's mouth and chin, she noticed with a shiver. And there was nothing weak about the stare he was giving Frank Knowles.

"Hello, Frank," he said in a deep, thick voice. "Been a long time."

He didn't speak loud. He didn't have to. In the

stillness brought on by his appearance, Lorelei could hear the tick of the foyer clock.

Knowles swallowed. "I thought you were back in Texas."

Mercy, Lorelei thought, another Texian.

"I was. But I had to come looking for you." His words cut the air like a pick piercing ice.

Lorelei could not suppress a shudder. Whoever he was, Texian or not, she recognized the man right away. He was Trouble.

Trouble with a capital T.

Chapter Two

The stranger moved slowly toward the poker table, his stride smooth and measured, his spurs jangling. The fringe on his jacket waved with each step. Lorelei found herself striding in the same direction until she and the two men stood like columns evenly spaced at the round table's edge, blocking out the rest of the room.

They formed a strange tableau, the dandy Knowles in his velvet-lapeled frock coat, this newly arrived Texian in buckskin, and Lorelei with her blond curls piled high and her green dress draped low.

His stained felt hat still in place over a pair of hard brown eyes, the stranger was the odd man out, yet he looked completely calm and very much at home. She studied him with the same care he was using to study Frank Knowles. Knowles tugged at the high white collar of his dress shirt, shifting his eyes to right and left before returning the stranger's stare.

Knowles cleared his throat. "You don't have any quarrel with me, Sam."

"I didn't come to quarrel."

Knowles laughed nervously, his thin upper lip beaded with sweat. "Then, what did you come to do, kill me?"

"Not unless I have to." Sam spoke flatly, the way a man talks about the weather, but his words carried across the casino and kept the curious, watchful gamblers silently in place.

Lorelei drew a deep breath. The air in the room hung heavy and still, like the outdoors before a storm; around her, tobacco smoke collected low as rain clouds on a winter's day.

The velvet ribbon felt tight around her throat. She raised her hand to tug at the cameo. Remembering the way Knowles had worked at his collar, she dropped her hand quickly to her side. She ought to be taking charge, an inner voice insisted, she or one of Balzac's men who were beginning to edge closer to the table.

She exhaled slowly. To let them move in so quickly, without a summons from her, would be relinquishing the authority she had so recently acquired, and she waved them off.

Sam saw the gesture. His eyes met hers, and something flickered in their dark brown depths, an acknowledgment, maybe, but nothing more—certainly nothing approaching thanks because she called off her guards.

"I left my gun at the door," Knowles said.

"Same here," Sam replied.

Lorelei felt only a momentary relief before he added, "If I wanted to take you down, you don't think I'd need anything more'n my hands, do you, old buddy?"

Whatever Knowles believed, Lorelei did not doubt the stranger could—or would—do what he claimed. Why should she doubt him when he'd brought the casino operations to a halt just by walking in?

From two feet away she felt the power of him, the physical strength as well as the force of his will. They

20

were as real as thunder and lightning, as dangerous as fire, and they carried a heat that worked its way to her bones. If he ever directed that will away from Knowles and onto her. . . . A woman given to weakness would have reason to fear. That she was considering the possibility for herself raised her ire.

It was time the stranger knew who was in charge.

"This is a business establishment," she snapped. "Please take care of your private concerns outside."

The corner of his mouth twitched once. "Fair enough," he said.

He shifted a fraction in her direction, studying her the way he had the entire room, only with more concentration—if that were possible. His perusal went from top to toe and back again, but she couldn't tell if he'd drawn some kind of conclusion about her. Not that she cared, but most men weren't so inscrutable.

He looked back at Knowles. "You heard the woman. Let's go."

"See here, Sam, I'm not going anywhere," said Knowles, "leastways not with you." He spoke with bravado; Lorelei figured he would have hidden behind her skirt if he could.

"Maybe you ought to reconsider. I've ridden a long way the past few weeks, following your trail from Texas. It was kinda like tracking a cottonmouth. I'd hate for you to slither away again."

Knowles wanted to respond with equal insults—the urge was there to read in his eyes—but it was diluted by the same weakness she'd spotted earlier in the line of his jaw and mouth. He didn't say a word.

"What's your game?" asked Sam.

"I'm not playing games," said Knowles. "I ain't going with you, and that's that."

"I'm talking about the cards." Sam shifted his eyes

21

to Lorelei. "Got a poker table going that Frank and I can join?"

Lorelei considered the question, thought about telling him to leave, and heard herself reply, "Only if I'm dealing and there's no trouble."

Sam shrugged. "That's up to Frank here. I've been looking at the ears on that old sorrel of mine for too long." His eyes dropped to the fullness of her breasts. "Maybe I ought to take in another pair for a change. Can't do any harm."

Lorelei felt a tremor down her back, and the skin on her arm began to itch. Sam was Trouble, all right, the kind of man to feel special pride in his third leg, the kind to put it to use whenever he could.

"Pick up your chair, Frank," said Sam. "Poker it is."

Knowles opened his mouth to speak, thought better of it, and did as he was instructed. His eyes were clouded, but whether from wine or fear, Lorelei could not tell. Sidling into place across from Sam, he brushed at the matted lapels of his black suit, then sat in silence, like a prisoner in the dock.

Lorelei took her own place and signaled Anthony for an envelope of currency, along with a new deck of cards. While she waited for him to return, she again studied the man who had seated himself on her right.

Up close he looked granite hard, weathered by days in the sun and by nights spent sleeping in the cold. The creases around his mouth and eyes cut deep into his flesh, as though they had been carved by the same cobbler who had tooled the leather of his boots. The bristles covering his lean cheeks were short and stiff and as black as his thick brows, and the slight curve of his mouth echoed the contempt she read in his eyes as he stared at Knowles.

She'd seen men on wanted posters who looked more benign.

Slowly he removed his gloves and shoved them in the pocket of his coat, emptied a small pouch of gold coins on the table in front of him, then leaned back in the chair and rested his hands on his thighs. Blunt and broad, the hands looked powerful enough to crush the life from a man. For a moment Lorelei allowed herself to consider the body beneath the brown shirt and coat and the tight buff trousers — a broad chest, fine black body hairs, strong thighs and calves.

There wouldn't be anything resembling the scraped potato she'd talked about earlier in the day. She decided against imagining further details.

It was a good thing Delilah was overseeing things in the kitchen, or she'd have been close by nudging Lorelei in the ribs and rolling those wide eyes to show she knew just what was running through her mistress's mind.

Impatient for the game to begin, Lorelei drummed her fingers against the felt table top. Outside the casino the night had grown cold, but the air immediately around her continued to heat fast. Even draped low off her shoulders, the velvet gown lay heavily against her skin, and she cursed the layers of undergarments women were compelled to wear.

A trickle of sweat ran between her breasts, and she had to force each breath. For her efforts she took in the Texian's scent of sun and leather and the faint aroma of sweat. Everything about him contrasted with the cologne-scented gamblers scattered about the room, especially his hat. He was no gentleman, that was for sure, but then she'd known that the moment he walked in the door.

She'd made a mistake in letting him stay. The

23

sooner he was gone from the premises, the better, and she grabbed for the deck Anthony offered. Her hands worked expertly at riffling the cards as the sounds of the casino picked up again—the spin of the roulette wheel, the scrape of chairs, the fall of the chips. Conversations started in around her, most of them in French and often punctuated by laughter, but at the poker table no one spoke.

Pulling a stack of folding money from the envelope Anthony had brought, she tossed a five-dollar bank note into the center of the table. Knowles did the same, and she looked at Sam. "You'll have to ante, Mr. —"

"Delaney."

She nodded once. Sam Delaney. The name meant nothing to her, but she hadn't supposed it would.

He flipped in a gold coin, his lean body still slanted away from the table, the contemptuous expression on his face still in place. She thought about asking him to remove his hat, which she regarded with greater irritation the longer she looked at it. She kept silent. He could damn well sit there and look like a crude and rude frontiersman if he chose.

Truth was, everything about his presence unnerved her more than she liked to admit. He had such a cool look about him, even while she knew that inside he was fired up about something. Something that made him dangerous. Except for an occasional glance at her bosom, he showed no appreciation for her charms. She didn't care a fig about being appreciated . . . and yet he irritated her.

So looking at her was better than staring at the ears of his sorrel, was it? She would delight in seeing him broke.

She dealt the hand. Ignoring the five cards splayed upside down in front of her, she watched Knowles,

24

then Sam study theirs. Knowles blinked once, twice. He'd hit on something; with Sam she couldn't tell.

"Your bet," she said to Knowles, who threw out another five-dollar note.

Sam matched the bet and raised it twenty. Again Knowles blinked, and Lorelei pulled twenty-five dollars from the stack of money in front of her. She hated matching wits with a new player, couldn't tell when he was bluffing. Her instinct told her this one seldom bluffed. Or maybe it was just that he seldom needed to.

Knowles stood pat, Sam asked for two cards, and at last Lorelei picked up her hand. The three and five of diamonds, the ace of spades, the six and seven of clubs. A pitiful lot they were, and she felt reckless enough to try for an inside straight. Tossing the ace, she dealt herself the top card. It was the four of hearts.

She looked at Knowles. "Your bet." He threw out a twenty. Sam raised him fifty, and it was seventy dollars to her. She called, and it was Knowles' turn.

"You always did play wild, Sam," he said, fingering his cards.

"I play to win, Frank, that's all. I'm not the one who turned on an old war buddy. Now, that's what I call playing wild. Bet or fold."

Knowles thought a moment, his thin mouth working, then threw down his cards in disgust.

"Seven high straight," Lorelei said to Sam's profile.

"Beats me," Sam said without showing his cards, without checking hers. He didn't seem overly concerned.

"I paid to see your hand," said Lorelei, irritated.

Sam dragged his attention away from Knowles long enough to give her an assessing look, including another glance at her half-exposed breasts.

"That you did."

He spread his cards on the polished table. Three queens, a jack and a deuce. So he didn't bluff. Or at least he hadn't the first round.

Knowles signaled for a refill of his wineglass.

"I've always heard," Sam said, "that a bad conscience gives a man a thirst."

The glass shook as Knowles brought it to his mouth.

Lorelei dealt another hand. Again Sam kept pumping up the bet; this time he won.

And so the game went for an hour, Lorelei holding her own with Sam, Knowles stacking up losses that the look in his eye said he could ill afford. Sam seemed not so concerned about winning as he did in seeing that his "old war buddy" lost, and lost big.

The only sounds at the table were the slap of the cards, the rustle of bank notes, the clink of gold.

And an occasional comment from Sam, always eased out in that deep, digging voice of his and always to Knowles.

"You've got a lot of money to lose, Frankie. Never knew you to have so much cash."

No response.

Later, "Looks like your luck has run out."

And later, "You're not looking too well, old buddy. Why not call it a night and step outside?"

Always, no response. Knowles seemed deaf to the words, seemed nailed to the chair. At one point, after dropping two hundred dollars on a full house that was topped by Sam, he asked for another deck of cards.

"Maybe we ought to stop for a while," Lorelei suggested. "There's food along the side."

"How about it, Frank?" asked Sam. "We could have our talk."

26

Knowles shook his head.

"Suit yourself. If it's later you want, it's later you'll get."

The fresh deck was brought. Shuffling, Lorelei looked from one man to the other. She might be dealing regulation poker, but the two of them were playing a different game. In theirs, the stakes were high, and Sam was way ahead—at least if his aim was to get his opponent pushed to the edge. At the rate Sam was working on him, by the time they got around to having their talk, Knowles would be blurting out whatever Sam wanted to hear.

One of Balzac's other dealers stepped close. "I will relieve you, Mademoiselle Latham."

One glance around the room told her several of the casino's men were staying close by. At the surrounding tables more than one of the gentlemen gamblers threw a curious look toward the poker table, as they had been doing since Sam walked in. Despite their interest, despite the amount of money stacked in front of her and Sam, not one had asked to join in the game. They must feel the tension, too. It surrounded the poker table like a fence.

She looked at Sam, whose eyes burned with the same intensity they'd held from the start. How eyes could be hot and cold at the same time, she had no idea, but with Sam Delaney she was learning to expect the unusual.

She looked at Knowles. His once-stiff collar lay limp around his damp neck, and he chewed at his lower lip. No longer the dapper handsome gentleman who'd strolled into the club, he looked a wreck.

With a shake of her head she declined the dealer's offer. Like Knowles, she felt nailed to the chair.

If only she could slot this Texian into one of her categories of men. She doubted he could ever be con-

27

sidered a good person, and he was hardly indifferent. But was he bad? His insolent glances at her, his goading of Knowles, his relentless play of the game certainly said so. He was the kind who liked to get his way; he didn't mind the cost, especially since he'd have already figured out how someone else would pay.

Knowles picked up the cards she'd dealt from the new deck, then threw them down in disgust. His hands shook, and he pressed them hard against the table.

"Can't put it off much longer, Frank," said Sam.

"Why don't you just shoot me here and now?" said Knowles, his voice rising to a shout. "Or stomp me or whatever you've got in mind."

"Choking is what I hinted at before," said Sam, calm as ever. "At least that's the way I remember it. But if you'd rather be stomped—"

"Gawd damn!" Knowles cried and ran his hand through his hair.

"Such a threat," a nearby gambler said, his disgust loud and clear. "Mam'selle Cat would never have let such a scene take place."

He was right. Catherine would have thrown the two Texians out on their ears long before now. Lorelei felt an icy dread inside, a realization that she had indeed let things go too far.

"You never used to be so loud, Frankie," said Sam. "Must be getting tired." His thumb worked at his own stack of cards, which he held unstudied in his strong brown hands. "Or maybe it's your conscience that's giving you trouble."

"Leave me alone, you bastard. I didn't do nothing wrong." Knowles shoved away from the table, the chair legs scraping against the hardwood floor.

"So tell me why you ran."

"I ain't telling you nothing." His voice was a rasp. "Here," he said, leaning forward to shove the notes and coins toward Sam, gathering them not only from his own fast-dwindling stack but from in front of Lorelei as well, his arms swooping out like the wings of a hawk. "Take it all. Then get the hell out."

"That I can't do."

A desperate cry rang from Knowles's throat. Lorelei took one look at the wild light in his eyes and decided to call in the guards, but before she could raise her hand, he sprang to his feet, the chair once again crashing to the floor behind him.

"I'm not gonna die! Not at your hand!"

From inside his coat he pulled out a snub-nosed gun already half-cocked. Waving it around in the air, he leveled it at Sam.

"You've been threatening me ever since you walked in. Everybody heard it, only you're wrong, you bastard. You're the one who's gonna die."

Chapter Three

Sam leaped across the table, grabbing for Knowles's gun hand, and with a crash the two men rolled to the floor.

Lorelei panicked.

"Stop!" she cried, but she might as well have been screaming at a pair of battling stallions.

Gamblers deserted their tables fast, pedaling backward from the scuffling men, and Lorelei cried out again, this time in frustration because she hadn't prevented the fight. Unable to do anything more forceful, she kicked at Sam's fallen hat as though his head were still inside.

The two men struggled, the gun out of sight between them, and the casino's troops moved in. A shot rang out.

"Mon Dieu," a voice yelled.

For a second all was still in the room; then slowly Sam pulled away. Kneeling, he stared down at the red stain spreading across Knowles's once-white shirt. Knowles lay still, sprawled at an awkward angle beside an overturned chair.

"Damn!"

The single word was drawn out from deep inside Sam, and his head dropped to his chest. When he looked back up, Lorelei caught an expression of anguish on his face so strong that for a moment she forgot Knowles, forgot her own distress as she wondered what could have aroused such a raw and terrible look.

No one else moved. No one except Lorelei, who knelt beside Knowles and felt in vain for a pulse, ignoring the fringe of Sam's jacket which brushed across her arm.

She looked up at him. "He's dead."

Sam stared back with tormented eyes.

"Knowles was threatened, all right," someone from another table called out. "Been pushed all night, just the way he claimed. I heard it. He pulled the gun in self-defense."

"Non," one of the Creoles put in. "This was not the way I saw it. The *gendarmes* must settle this unfortunate affair."

A chorus of argument erupted in the room, half siding with the dead gambler, half with the man bent beside him.

Sam seemed not to have heard the debate over his guilt. Reaching for his hat, he stood and slapped it against his thigh, then wedged it low on his forehead as he turned toward the door.

A Balzac guard came up fast and clutched him by the shoulder. Sam shook him off. Stumbling backward, the guard grabbed for an inside pocket of his coat. Without warning, Sam jerked Lorelei to her feet, at the same time his free hand reached inside his boot. Suddenly she was yanked hard against him, her back to his chest, his arm tight around her throat. He pointed a gun at the guard.

"Drop it," he barked. Like the dead man, he carried his pistol half-cocked.

The guard let his own weapon fall to the floor.

Sam's gaze drifted slowly around the room.

"Sorry, gentlemen," he growled. "Much as I'd like to get this matter cleared up, there's always the chance that things will go against me. I've got other business calling me back home." He glanced at the table. "Expensive business."

Holding the gun close to Lorelei's head, he grabbed for the poker money, thrusting notes and coins into his coat pocket. The casino's cash went in along with his.

The sight of all those riches disappearing fast wrenched Lorelei out of her shock.

"That's mine," she cried.

"Consider it a loan."

She exploded with anger, twisting her body away from the hated strength of Sam's hard frame. She pounded with feeble fists at the arm crushing her throat, but she could not ease his hold. Caught beneath the buckskin sleeve, the cameo dug into her skin. Blood pulsed in her ears.

Sam's lips brushed against her hair, which had fallen in a mass of tangled curls against her shoulders. "Honey, keep on fighting and you'll wind up with a broken neck."

Lorelei wouldn't have minded if in return she could have broken his, but for the moment he held the upper hand. Seething, she forced herself to hold still.

Sam turned his attention to the room. "Let's keep the lady safe, shall we?" he said, his voice calm and deep as ever.

Lorelei's mind raced in time with her pounding heart. If she could manage to gain enough leverage, she could adjust the aim of her fist and catch him in the nose.

The trouble was, she was having difficulty breathing, and she fought for air, her fingernails scraping

32

against the leather sleeve. For a moment he relaxed his hold, and she kicked backward. She caught him on the shin above the protection of his boot, and his arm tightened once again. With little more pressure he could indeed break her neck.

Movement from the side caught his eye. "Call off your dogs," he ordered.

She managed a cough, and his arm eased.

She looked at the nearest guard. "Shoot hi—" she began weakly.

He squeezed the rest of her command to an unheard whisper. "Now, that's not the smartest thing you've tried tonight. Someone's likely as not to do just that and send a bullet through us both. We'll find ourselves down there with Frank."

The image he suggested was all too real. Swallowing bile, Lorelei blinked that she understood. Again he eased his hold. Greedily she forced air into her empty lungs, air that seemed filled with her captor. If violence had a smell, it was Sam's smoke-and-leather scent she breathed in now. His own breath was hot on her cheek, and when she shifted her gaze to his face she could count the creases around the corner of his eyes.

She'd like to gouge in a few more with her nails.

"Care to try again?" he said.

She nodded once and managed to get out a hoarse, "Back off," before a wave of dizziness overcame her. For the first time in six years, she was experiencing real fear, and she hated it as much as she hated the man who caused it.

Sam moved away from the table until his back was against the wall close by the door. "Clear the foyer," he ordered to no one in particular, "and I'll let her live."

Lorelei was certain that he lied.

From somewhere out of the blurred sea of black-suited men, Delilah appeared. She moved toward Lorelei, stopping when she was within a dozen feet, her round dark eyes darting from Sam to Lorelei and back to Sam. Speaking loud and clear, she ordered, "Do what he wants."

Lorelei heard the shuffle of feet in the long, wide hallway that led to the front door of the casino.

Sam spoke to Delilah. "If you want her unharmed, make sure the way is clear."

Delilah shot Lorelei a look of encouragement. "I want her unharmed."

Gripping the black skirt of her gown, Delilah hurried past Lorelei and Sam. "All clear," she called out from the foyer.

With his hold still tight, Sam edged through the door and down the long hall, his back to the wall. Overhead the sparkling chandeliers sent out a bright and cheerful light, but Lorelei felt as though she were traveling down a bleak tunnel. In the midst of all this splendor, she knew only the dark taste of terror. Her hands flailed out as if she could grab the air and stop their progress, but Sam dragged her with him, unmindful of her gasps.

Hearing the whimper that escaped her throat, Lorelei turned her hate to herself.

They backed onto the veranda and down the steps to the hitching posts, halting by a sorrel gelding. Sam thrust the gun into a coat pocket already heavy with cash, then freed the reins.

As suddenly as he had grabbed Lorelei, he sprang into the saddle and pulled her up in front of him. She sat sideways across his hard, spread thighs, her own legs caught in a tangle of underwear and velvet, her skirt belling upward over the five petticoats. Sam unceremoniously crammed everything downward and wedged it between her legs.

The idea of him poking wherever he wanted! She found no word to express the jumble of anger and humiliation tearing at her.

Sam slapped the reins against the sorrel's flanks, and they took off down the street, past the casinos, past the stables and mercantile store, past the row of houses and the last post with its oil lamp casting a pitiful glow onto the edge of town. Overhead a sprinkling of stars emitted an equally inadequate light.

Down the dark, deserted road, they moved like a ship in full sail. Lorelei struggled against him, but between the jostling of the ride and his ironlike hold, her desperate efforts proved useless.

A quarter of a mile into the night, he reined to a halt. The stop caught her by surprise, and she ceased her struggles. "What are you doing?" she asked, alarmed at what he might have in mind for her now. She already knew he was capable of anything.

"Honey, it's time we said goodbye."

She stared up at the inky outline of his hatted head. "You're not kidnapping me?"

"I could swear I'm hearing disappointment in that lovely voice."

"Oh!" She clawed for his face.

He caught her hands by the wrist. "I do like a woman with fire. The trouble is, if I let you go along, you'd be more trouble than I can deal with right now. Hop on down like a good girl."

Lorelei could imagine the mocking light in his dark brown eyes as he spoke, could picture the twisted grin on his lips. She shook with rage.

"You're . . . you're bad!"

Sam let out a loud, gusty laugh.

"I've been called a hell of a lot worse than that. Come to think of it, there is one thing you can

35

do before you leave. Give me a little luck."

She opened her mouth to tell him what he could do with that luck; but his lips covered hers, and his tongue slipped inside before she could speak. The intimacy of the invasion shocked her into stillness, and she could think of nothing except the firmness of his lips as they moved over hers and the rough saltiness of his probing tongue.

A strange sensation washed over her, a feeling unlike any in her experience, a response that tempered her shock into something warm and not totally repulsive. Far from it. . . .

His murmur of satisfaction chilled the warmth and jerked her back to reality. Like a victorious warrior, he was invading her conquered body. He didn't know the battle wasn't won. Enraged into action, she took to her struggles once again, legs flailing. Just as she tried to bite him, he slipped his tongue from her mouth, and her teeth jarred together.

The sorrel sidestepped nervously in a circle, his head bobbing. Sam held her tight with one arm and loosened a boot from its stirrup, imprisoning her thrashing legs beneath one of his hard thighs. His movements were fast and sure, and she found herself caught tight against his third leg.

He shifted. "Now, that's what I call giving good luck." In the dark she could see the white of his smile.

His free hand brushed against the side of her breast. An accident? She knew it was not.

Lorelei's skin blazed with a rash that must surely light the night. It was as if the heat of her fury was eating out through her pores. Sam Delaney was everything she hated in men, everything she had sworn to avoid, right up to the day she was lowered into her grave.

"You son of a bitch!"

"Now, that's getting closer to the truth."

She reared back to butt him with her head, the only weapon left to her, but Sam released all hold on her so quickly that her momentum sent her sprawling to the ground. Her unprotected hands dug into the hard dirt, but she felt no pain. She was far beyond such minor discomfort.

Scrambling to her feet, she whirled to look up at the dark figure sitting high on horseback, a tall, lean silhouette against the fading stars. She knew it was the devil himself who returned her glare.

"I'll see you burn in hell," she rasped.

"Don't put yourself out. I'll get there all by myself."

Gone was the mocking edge to his voice, and for an instant she remembered the look on his face when he had realized Frank Knowles was dead.

He tipped his hat.

Then he looked over his shoulder toward the lamps of the city street. From this distance they were no more than pinpricks of light.

"Get on back to the casino," he ordered. "Tell your men to give up any thought of catching me."

"Don't tell me —"

But he did not hear. With a slap of the reins, he was gone, leaving her in a cloud of dust and a whirlwind of fury. She scooped up a rock and threw it into the swallowing dark. What kind of fool did he think she was?

Lorelei rubbed fiercely at her lips, but she could not rub away the tingle of his mouth against hers. She spat into the dirt, but she could not remove the taste of his tongue.

Her rage knew no bounds. In a short span of time Sam Delaney had taken more liberties with her than any man had ever dared, then demanded that her guards leave him alone. As if she were of little consequence. As if only men presented any danger to him.

She drummed her fingers against her skirt. Sam Delaney didn't know Lorelei Latham very well. But he would.

From neck to knees, every inch of her skin had erupted into one large maddening itch.

Oh, yes, he would.

She took a quick step in the direction of Balzac's; a stockinged foot came down on the sharp edge of a rock, painful evidence that she had lost one of her boots. Limping and scratching, she strode back toward the dark houses and store, toward the oil lamps on the street posts and the lights of the casinos.

With each step her determination grew. Her hair had long ago gone into wildness, her entire complexion showed her ready for a leper colony, and her lips were swollen from his kiss. Not to mention the bruises that must be at her throat. But she didn't care what she looked like, or what any onlooker might think.

So she was to call off her men, was she? Poor defenseless woman, she herself couldn't do anything to bring him to justice.

Sam Delaney was a jackass, as well as a brute.

Shouts came from the front of Balzac's, and she heard hooves striking against the hard dirt road that ran in front of the casino. As she moved into the city lights, she saw a half-dozen men on horseback, Anthony in the fore. Spying her lost boot in the street, she scooped it in her hand and struck the sole against her thigh as she continued her march.

Men poured out of the casinos lining the streets. They stood in silence, their eyes on her as she limped and scratched, limped and scratched past them. She

38

caught sight of one man in particular, the man she had socked in the nose. He grinned at her from the porch of a rival casino. If she hadn't needed her shoe so badly, she would have thrown it at him.

Fury continued to consume her, but it had settled into the cold kind that let her mind work out a revenge. It was a kind she knew well.

Forgotten was the fallen man inside the casino; she remembered only Sam. He had humiliated her, had stolen the casino's money, and had dared to take liberties with her.

She thought of those terrible times long ago when another man had schemed to ruin her, but for once the present was far more substantial, far more tormenting. Sam Delaney was a name to suppress all others. His mouth . . . his tongue . . . they were all too real. Worst of all, the stroking of his fingers lingered on her breast, aggravating the inflammation of her skin all the more.

He had ruined the one night she wanted to be perfect. More, he had set off turmoil deep inside that would not abate. She brought the shoe down hard against her thigh again. She would delight in making him pay.

With her feelings in hand, Lorelei considered what to do. He wanted luck, did he? The jackass. He'd see what kind of luck that kiss would bring. He had business at home, and that meant Texas. He'd be heading out the main road, certain he had enough of a lead to escape anyone who might follow.

Brushing the loose curls from her face, she thought of the trail she had ridden that afternoon, the little-traveled route that cut miles off the long journey to the Texas border.

Approaching the front of Balzac's, she watched Delilah push through the crowd on the veranda, rush down the steps, and hurry to her side. "Are you all right, *m'amie?*"

"I'm fine," she said, her voice sharp and strong. "Perfectly fine." She glanced at the nearest guard. "Saddle up whatever horses are left in the stables. We're riding after him."

"Lorelei Latham, you will do no such thing."

Lorelei shot a look of determination at Delilah. "I don't have any choice. Long ago I quit being the victim of a man. Any man. We'll get this Sam Delaney when he least expects us."

She lifted her head high and announced where all could hear, "I'll get him, all right. I'll see him drawn and quartered before the sun is high."

Chapter Four

Lorelei made a quick trip to her upstairs room to trade four of her five petticoats for the pepperbox pistol, then hurried down the back staircase and through the rear door of the storage room toward the stable. The sky was already streaked with the promise of dawn; she wanted to be well under way by the time the sun shed its light on the Louisiana wilderness through which she planned to lead the searchers.

Her men might not be trackers and scouts in the traditional sense of the terms—they'd been hired for their ability to maintain order discreetly indoors—but at least they knew how to use their guns. She estimated that with hard riding they could be lying in wait at the side of the main road long before Sam Delaney came riding by.

Moving into the cold fresh air, she realized she felt much better. No longer did she itch, and no longer did she burn with humiliation. The reason was clear: A woman with a purpose, she had no time for weaknesses.

From the looks of the crowded, noisy lawn separating the main building of Balzac's from the stable, Lorelei figured that none of the gamblers had departed for home. But neither were they inside losing their money as she might have hoped. The profits from this first Saturday under her leadership would fall short of her expectations; they would not come close to her dreams.

Most likely right now the gamblers were laying bets as to how the night would end; she doubted that much money had been laid on her.

Milling amongst them were Anthony and ten more of Balzac's men mounted and ready to ride. They still wore their formal evening suits, but they'd added an incongruous accessory—a holstered gun. They had also equipped themselves with rifles, which they carried across their laps, braced against the saddle horn.

As she hurried through the throng, her stride purposeful, her gaze straight ahead, the way parted for her. The talking ceased, but she could read the thoughts of everyone around.

A man would not have let himself be captured, they told themselves. A man would not have let Delaney escape.

And Lorelei Latham could never bring him back.

They were wrong.

Lorelei kept her head erect. Her unbound hair flowed loose about her bared shoulders, and her skin still held faded remnants of the rash. Her once-belled skirt dragged in the grass, and she had to hold the front high above her ankles to keep from tripping. To the onlookers she must have looked like a poor opponent for Sam Delaney, but they did not know the warrior's heart that beat beneath her breast.

They also didn't know about the pepperbox hanging heavy in an inset pocket, or of her ability to hit whatever target she chose. If there was one thing she was sure of, it was that Sam Delaney would not abuse her again.

Delilah met her in the stable door. "Ben will never let you out of his sight again if you do this," she said sharply.

Lorelei held her ground. "Probably not."

Delilah changed her tone to one of gentleness. "What you plan is worse than foolish, *m'amie*. It could bring you great harm."

The gentleness got to Lorelei for a moment, and she squeezed her friend's hand. "Please don't worry about me. I don't plan anything foolish. It's true I was terrified when he carried me down the road like that, but you must believe that I am not afraid any longer. Nor should I be. He thinks I am a weak woman, and of course that will be his undoing."

"This Sam Delaney is not an ordinary man."

"He's everything I despise." Lorelei spat out the words.

Delilah's brown eyes rounded with dismay. "What did he do to you, child? There was hardly time out there in the dark to do much, even for a man like him."

"He did nothing."

"Now is the wrong time to lie."

Lorelei hesitated. "He kissed me," she said, keeping her voice low where only Delilah could hear, "and . . . and he touched me."

"They are poor reasons to risk your life."

"For me, they are the best reasons in the world. But I'm not in danger, my dear and faithful friend. He is the one at risk." She saw that Delilah remained unconvinced. "All I want to do is guide the

43

men to where they can stop him. I won't take part in the actual shooting if that will put your mind to rest. But I can't let someone just stomp in off the street, threaten one of our patrons, and then hide behind my skirts so he can take off with our money. Word would spread that at Balzac's, anything goes."

Having said all she could, Lorelei hurried around the mulatto. She saw that Seabreeze was saddled and waiting for her deep in the lantern-lit stable.

"At least take this," Delilah said behind her. She removed the brown wool cloak she was wearing and draped it over Lorelei's shoulders. "Your anger has made you forget the cold."

Lorelei whirled, gave Delilah a brief, hard hug and, with the cloak held tight against her, signaled for the young stable hand to bring her the mare. When he came running with Seabreeze in tow, she was gratified to see that the scabbard close to the bay's neck once again held the rifle she always carried on her rides.

The youth helped her to mount. Settled in the sidesaddle as comfortably as she could manage, she tied the hood of the cloak around her head. Her fingers brushed against a small pouch that had been sewn to the lining resting just below her throat.

She glanced at the solemn woman who remained close to the stable door. "Delilah."

Delilah shrugged. "The gris-gris can do you no harm."

"But I don't believe in voodoo."

"Is there anything, *m'amie,* in which you do believe?"

The question stung. "I believe in justice."

"And retribution."

"That, too." To her own ears, she sounded defensive.

"These harden a woman's heart. Is this what you truly wish?"

"I also believe in loyalty and gratitude and the inherent innocence of children, Delilah."

Delilah stepped close and gripped the rein draped along the horse's neck. Her eyes were darkly pleading. "Then, these are what you must remember now. Not retribution. Your thoughts stray to a man long ago, but Sam Delaney is not that man."

Lorelei shook her head impatiently. "He's little better, and besides, he's the one I'm dealing with now. I'll grant the killing of Frank Knowles was an accident, but that's not true of anything that followed. He must be brought back to face the charges I will lodge against him." She listed them on the fingers of her hand. "Theft. Assault. Threatening with a gun. Kidnapping."

Delilah listened in silence, and a sliver of doubt worked itself into Lorelei's mind, a sensation that perhaps she was letting her personal anger and humiliation carry her too far, but she brushed the feeling away. The charges were not frivolous; too well did she remember Sam's arm around her throat, the gun waving in the air close to her head, the way he thrust her money in his coat. Mostly she remembered the ride in the dark. She remembered his lips and his hands and everything they had done.

As if her memories weren't enough, there were a hundred men waiting outside the stable to see if she would actually have the nerve to follow him, and her own employees waiting to see if she could lead.

The stable hand stepped close. "Beg pardon. Maybe these'd do you some good."

45

His upstretched hand held a pair of riding gloves. Lorelei took them gratefully and, avoiding Delilah's eye, put them on. Some warrior she was proving to be.

"Let's go, Breezy," she said, clicking her tongue against her teeth, and as she leaned forward the mare trotted regally into the open air.

A cheer went up. To the gamblers this was all a game, no matter how their wagers were laid. One look at the faces of Anthony and the other mounted guards told her they were very serious indeed. She could hardly wait to see them surround Sam Delaney.

Anthony reined his horse beside the bay mare. "The men wish to convey their regret over allowing such armed ruffians into the casino tonight."

"But I'm the one who let the game go on too long. Tell them to turn their regret to anger. I want Sam Delaney captured and returned."

"He will not escape."

"No, he will not. Now follow me."

He seemed about to say more, but Lorelei was through talking. She lost little time in guiding Seabreeze onto the street and, with the guards behind her, began the pursuit at a brisk clip.

In short order she had left the road and was galloping once again down the rutted trail that wound through the low, dead grasses of winter, her destination the forested bayou land directly west. This time a single row of riders loped behind. The air was brisk and dry, as it had been for this first half of February, and the fingers of predawn were fast brightening the indigo sky.

Cold air stung her cheeks, but she welcomed the feeling. With her cloak billowing around her and

46

the sound of horses' hooves echoing across the fields, she felt like an avenging angel swooping across the countryside. It was a foolish and fanciful thought, but then she was going after a devil, was she not?

And Lorelei was a fanciful name, in German lore a siren who lured the boatmen of the Rhine to their deaths. Her mother had read her the story when she was a very small child; her mother had read her many such stories before a fever struck her down.

Perhaps if she had lived. . . .

It was another fanciful thought that must be ignored. The real Lorelei was anything but a siren, and she concentrated on the barely visible trail. She was grateful that Seabreeze knew the route as well as she, especially after it led into the cluster of oak trees that marked the beginning of the forest. Here, precious little of the early light penetrated, and she had to slow her pace.

She rode steadily for a half hour, giving Seabreeze her head, and watched as the first illuminations of day gradually filtered through the trees, highlighting stands of fern and mushrooms close to the path, and an occasional bright wild flower that failed to realize it was not yet spring. Farther back began the tangle of vines and shrubbery covering that portion of the landscape not already taken over by moss-draped oak and cypress and the countless bayous lacing the southern Louisiana woods.

She would not let herself enjoy the beauty. That would be for the return ride when her mission was done.

Once Anthony rode to her side. "Mademoiselle Latham has ridden this way before?"

She gave him a sharp look. "Many times."

"It is not that the men doubt the mademoiselle."

But of course they did. Riding a dozen yards behind her, they must have been wondering if the puny female guiding them knew what she was about.

"Tell them that once it is lighter, we can pick up the pace. In perhaps an hour or so we will be on the main road again, far ahead of our quarry. They'll have their chance at him, I promise."

Anthony nodded. "I will tell them."

He dropped back, and Lorelei concentrated on the path, which she admitted to herself was sometimes almost overgrown and hard to follow. After another half hour, she signaled for the men to halt. "There's a stream not far away. We'll water the horses and take a stretch ourselves."

No one argued.

Just as she'd promised, they found the pebbled stream out of sight down a slight incline to the right, its banks thick with winter grass for the horses to crop. They kneeled to take a drink at the water's edge upstream from their mounts, and one by one the men waded across to the thick brush on the far side to relieve themselves.

Waiting for their return, Lorelei paced along the bank. She knew the path they rode well enough to know that she and her party had not strayed from its winding course, despite the men's apprehensions, but the slow pace was gnawing at her. One look at a pinkish blue patch of sky told her that soon the sun would give them the light they needed to hurry along.

The stream took a sharp bend to the left. She came to a halt. Something was wrong. She listened but heard nothing except the trill of an early-morning songbird and the rustle of a slight breeze in the trees. She looked around and saw only tangled greenery and the fast-moving water.

Yet she knew something was wrong. Perhaps she had heard a rustling not quickly identified in her mind; perhaps it was a scent that seemed out of place. Or perhaps it was some sense not yet fully developed in her that told her to beware. A tingle rippled down her spine, and her breath became shallow and quiet.

Footsteps sounded behind her, and with a start she whirled.

"Mademoiselle Latham."

She heaved a sigh, part relief, part exasperation. "Anthony, don't ever sneak up on me like that again."

"Pardon, mademoiselle." He bowed crisply. Even stalking in the wilderness, her assistant was ever one for politeness. "I became worried about you. The men are ready to leave."

"Wait a moment." She gestured for him to be silent. The seconds moved by slowly, marked by the bird's song and the sound of the breeze. "Do you feel it, too?" she whispered.

His expression remained bland. "Feel what, mademoiselle?"

"Something. I don't know."

"Mademoiselle Latham has many things on her mind."

"Many imaginary things, is that what you mean?"

She immediately regretted the remark. Sounding waspish was the last thing she wanted, and besides, there was always the possibility he was right. Perhaps she was the victim of an overactive imagination, and not the prey of a marauder lurking in the wilderness. If that's what she had been thinking was out there. The trouble was, she couldn't put her suspicions into words since they were not all that clear in her mind.

Except to say that something was wrong, which would get her little more than a few knowing nods behind her back.

"Let's go," she said, walking past him toward where the men and horses awaited.

Back on the path, she couldn't shake the feeling that had assailed her beside the stream. Something or someone had been watching; she rather thought it was someone rather than an animal of the forest.

Her hand fell to the gun in her pocket, and she eyed the rifle close to her knee. She knew how to use both well enough; she didn't need a coterie of armed men to keep her from harm.

Pulling back on the reins, she waited for the men to catch up. "The way is visible enough here," she said, her gaze taking in the broad, tough faces of the guards and settling on Anthony's finer features. "I need to stop for a moment."

None of her listeners asked why, but she could read their thoughts: Why hadn't she taken advantage of their stop as they had done? It was something they'd chalk up to the different ways of women; for once she didn't mind.

"We will wait," said Anthony.

"Keep riding slowly and I'll catch up. Don't worry. I won't be long, and we don't want to waste any more time than is absolutely necessary."

"But, mademoiselle—"

Lorelei asserted herself. "That's an order, Anthony."

Reluctantly he nodded.

She waited until the men were once again in a single line and heading away from her before reining Seabreeze off the path. The shrubs were thinner here, and she was able to guide the horse through them, her destination a wall of vine-draped cypress trees that marked the edge of a nearby bayou. Always her eyes darted around looking for a clue as to what had disturbed her; whatever it was, it continued to haunt her senses.

Someone was out there. As impossible as it seemed, she couldn't shake off the feeling that it might be Sam.

The last time she had seen him, he was heading down the main road of town well past the shortcut, but there was nothing to say he couldn't have doubled back, a possibility that occurred to her only just now.

Quickly she untied the hood of the cloak and let it fall to her back. Her fingers brushed against the gris-gris sewn in by Delilah. She squeezed the pouch briefly, then shook her head to let her hair fall free against her shoulders. Heart pounding, she once again took up her vigil. Through the shrubbery she caught a movement in the distance, close to the edge of the trees. A brown buckskin jacket? Impossible.

No, she thought, very much possible.

"Let's go, Breezy."

She had only to click once and the horse responded with a forward surge. It took all of Lorelei's riding skills to guide the mare through the maze of shrubbery and tall grass that tugged at her cloak and skirt, but she didn't think of stopping. Her blood flowed fast in her veins, and in a rush of excitement, she forgot her promise to

Delilah to stay away from any actual shooting.

He was over there. Not fifty yards away. She knew it. Surely he could hear her pounding approach; what he didn't know was that she was armed and dangerous. She would capture him all on her own.

At the very least she would fire her gun into the air as a signal to her men. One way or another, Sam Delaney would not get away.

Seabreeze gave her all to her mistress, her long strong legs twisting and turning around the thick bushes, then covering a stretch of open land in an easy stride. So intent was Lorelei on the pursuit, she did not see the sudden drop-off, or the deep, wide chasm yawning directly in front of her. The mare shied, rearing back. Her front hooves came down sharply, catching in a narrow fissure at the edge of the incline.

The horse buckled and pitched forward, tossing Lorelei over her head. She heard the snap of bone behind her, even before her shoulder hit the ground and she tumbled down the slope.

Stunned, she managed to roll out of the way of the floundering horse that came skidding after her. She fought for breath; the world spun around her, and she felt a sharp pain shoot down her left arm.

Seabreeze whinnied, struggled, then held still. Lorelei cried out, focusing her eyes until she saw only one horse lying close by and not the several that had seemed to be circling before her. The two of them lay at the bottom of a broad ditch, on cold, damp ground littered with rocks; overhead a cloud moved in to shadow the sky.

Lorelei forgot her own pain as she pulled herself to her knees, tugging at cloak and gown, her horrified gaze on the mare. Seabreeze lay on her left side, her mighty head raised above the dirt and grass. Her rounded eyes turned to Lorelei, and she struggled once again to rise, the hind legs kicking, fighting for purchase against the sloping wall of the ditch.

She managed to get halfway up, her hindquarters beneath her; but the front right leg would bear no weight, and down she went again. The head lowered, and the struggles gradually ceased. The rounded sides of the horse heaved with heavy breaths; life pulsed strong within her, but Lorelei, staring at the ominously bent foreleg, knew with a terrible surety that Seabreeze would not rise again.

Her eyes blurred with tears, and she felt a sickening twist in the pit of her stomach. She crawled closer and cradled Seabreeze's head in her lap, stroking the white patch of hair between the wide-set eyes and, as she had done so many times before, scratching behind the twitching ears. The tears spilled onto her cheeks, and her body shook with anguish; but the only sound she made was to whisper "Breezy" again and again.

She fancied she could hear the pounding of the mare's mighty heart, or maybe it was just her own, beating to the time of the words that drummed in her head: *my fault, my fault, my fault.*

A pebble skittered down the wall of the ditch closest to her and came to a rest against her cloak. She shifted her gaze past the horse and on to the top edge of the incline, to a pair of tooled-leather boots with their silver spurs, her line of sight continuing on up the length of the buff-clad legs, across the expanse of brown fringed buckskin and

Chapter Five

Lorelei stared up into the darkened face, too numbed by grief to feel shock or fear, or even elation. Every force within her was given to the mare and to the condemnation of her stupidity in taking off with such reckless abandon across an unknown field.

She bent her head once more to Seabreeze.

From the corner of her eye she could see Sam's booted feet digging into the slant of the ground as he hurried down to kneel at her side. Pulling off his gloves, he worked his hands over the horse's front flank and down the limp, twisted leg. Probing and stroking, they moved like knowing hands, long used to treating animals.

Seabreeze flinched once under the examination, then drew still. Lorelei brushed at her tear-streaked cheeks with the back of her gloved hand and waited for his verdict, hoping against all reason that he would tell her she'd been wrong about the mare's fate.

He took off his hat and dangled it at his knee, rubbing his coat sleeve over his brow.

"The leg's broken. She'll have to be taken down."

Lorelei nodded once. The tears dried, and with all hope gone the inner anguish settled into a cold resolve. She bent her head to kiss the patch of white.

"Goodbye, girl. I love you."

Gently she shifted the mare's head from her lap and rested it on the ground. Standing proved awkward, and she found her legs weaker than she had supposed; but she refused the offered hand of help extended by Sam.

As she yanked her heavy cloak and skirt from beneath her, an object in the grass caught her eye. It was the cameo, its clasp still threaded by a narrow strip of velvet ribbon; it must have fallen from her throat when she'd tumbled beside the horse. She let it lie. She had no need for adornment now.

Her balance regained, she slipped the rifle from its scabbard, along with the shooting bag and other paraphernalia that had been tied to the pommel.

"What are you doing?" asked Sam.

"I'm taking her down."

"The hell you are."

For an answer, she propped the rifle butt on the ground, measured and dumped a load of powder down the barrel, and pulled a square of ticking out of the bag. Spitting on the patch to provide lubrication, she brushed a wisp of hair from her eyes and glanced at Sam, who watched her actions with a mingling of surprise and admiration.

Patch and ball went into the barrel next, poked down by the ball starter from the bag, and last by the ramrod. Satisfied the ball and patch were in

56

place, she snapped the ramrod back into the brass fittings under the rifle barrel.

"You act like you've never seen a weapon charged before," she said.

"Not by a woman." His eyes narrowed. "Especially one who looks like you."

"What have looks got to do with anything?" she said, drawing the hammer back half-cocked and slipping the percussion cap into place.

"Good point. Now give me the gun."

"Mr. Delaney, this is a squirrel rifle, but it can shoot two-legged squirrels as well as the other kind."

She shifted the rifle upward, aiming it at a point just below his belt buckle. "Now back off. I know what I have to do."

Their eyes met; the gaze held. The morning had turned gray, losing its promise of brightness, but she could see him very well, see the hard glint in his narrowed brown eyes, see the stubborn set of his lips. With his black hair lying thickly disarrayed down to the collar of his buckskin jacket, and his stubbled cheeks as taut as his mouth, he appeared as dangerous as he had the first moment he strolled into the casino.

Again she felt the power of the man, the potential for violence, but this time she was unmoved. Her finger itched. If he gave her trouble now. . . .

He slapped the hat back on his head and stepped aside. "It's your show. I'll catch you when you fall."

"No need."

Lorelei forced herself to look down at the injured horse, which lay still, sad brown eyes staring

57

blindly into space. The mechanics of charging the gun had taken her mind off her purpose, and she took a deep, slow breath to steady her nerves.

A fine mist was beginning to fall, but she gave no thought to the weather. She must not be faint of heart, not now when her duty was clear. Seabreeze needed her as never before, and she prayed for the strength to meet that need.

Bracing herself, she rested the tip of the barrel behind the mare's ear, anchored the stock against her uninjured shoulder, and pulled the trigger.

The force of the shot slammed against her, and she held her ground. But only for a second. With the roar of the gun resounding in her ears, deafening her to all else, she dropped the rifle and turned into Sam's strength. Her head reeled, and she could not clear from her mind the last trusting glance that Seabreeze had cast up at her.

She shuddered. Sam's hands rested lightly at her back, and she touched her forehead to his shirt.

Pain ripped through both shoulders now, but it was nothing she could not endure. The one thing she could not manage was to look at the results of what she had just done.

With a start she realized what the shock of events had driven her to. She shoved away.

"I need no consolation from you!"

"My mistake," Sam said, his hands raised to show he would not touch her again.

The mist had quickened to rain, and she hurriedly fastened the hood of the cloak over her damp hair. Separating herself from this terrible place became all she could think of. A quick glance at the overcast sky told her the shower was likely to continue for some time.

She settled her gaze on the shrubbery at the edge of the rise. She could not look at Sam, and she could not look at the dark, still shape that had been Seabreeze. She shivered once and made her awkward way out of the ditch.

A shot rang over her head. She threw herself to the ground.

From somewhere out in the brush she heard one of her men yell, "We see your horse, Delaney. We're coming in to get you."

She yelled back at him to hold off, but a barrage of gunfire drowned out her words. Bullets bit into the ground around her and joined with the splatter of the rain. Suddenly Sam was there jerking her back down into the safety of the ditch. Together they huddled in the dirt that was fast turning to mud.

"Your brown cloak," Sam yelled close to her ear. "Must have thought it was me."

Lorelei shook her head. "I can't believe this is happening."

"You'd better believe it. What you've got is a lot of trigger-happy men over there. Fools. Probably heard the rifle and decided I got the drop on you."

"That's absurd."

But of course it wasn't. She had ridden off, and as far as her men knew, she had disappeared.

Damnation! Just when she thought things were as bad as they could be, they got worse.

The gunfire continued sporadically, but each time Lorelei decided it was ending, it started up

59

again before she could make herself heard over the sound of the rain.

A clap of thunder rent the air, dying out in a winding roll.

"We're getting out of here," Sam announced.

"But—"

"Keep down and do what I say."

Crouching low, he motioned for her to move away from the gunfire to the far back edge of the wide trench.

Rebellion rose like bile, but she forced it down. Now was not the time to make a stand. With the lifeless shape of Seabreeze lying a dozen feet away in the downpour, and bullets ringing overhead, she would have walked into hell to put distance between her and that ditch; what better way than to have the devil himself act as guide?

Half walking, half crawling, the two of them scurried in the direction he had indicated. He grabbed her hand. She yanked it free, but he grabbed it again and scrambled up the side, dragging her beside him over the rough ground toward a copse of bushes a dozen yards away. On the far side of the thick shrubbery, the frenzied sorrel jerked at his tethered reins.

Freeing the gelding, Sam sprang into the saddle and pulled her up in front of him, just as he'd done outside the casino; only this time she knew the routine, and she anchored her sodden cloak and skirt for herself.

No sooner had she gained her balance than he spurred the horse away from the gunfire.

The roar of the rifles came to a sudden halt. "He's getting away," one of the men yelled.

Sam tugged on the reins, and the sorrel reared, almost sending Lorelei to the ground.

"I've got the girl," he shouted at the same time he brought the mount under control. "Back off, or she's dead."

They were not words of comfort.

"Hold your fire!" one of the men shouted, and the sorrel was off again, racing through the early-morning storm as though he did not bear two rain-soaked riders on his back.

Lorelei barely managed to hang on with both arms wrapped around Sam's waist. For self-preservation she buried her head against his chest. Her arms and shoulders ached close to the point of drawing tears, but she had no choice except to hold on tight . . . and to consider the mess she was in. Again Sam was riding off with her, away from her people, only this time she had willingly bounded up into his lap.

As she bounced along over the uneven field, her buttocks pounding against the hardness of his thighs, her body chilled to the bone, she wondered if she wouldn't have been better off walking into the rifle fire.

Just when she thought that every organ in her body must surely have been jarred out of place, Sam slowed the pace, enough so that he could bark another order.

"Put your arms under my coat and hold on tight," he shouted over the rain.

"Why?" she asked into a mass of wet fringe.

"Damn it, woman, are you going to question everything I say?"

61

"Tell me we're riding back to the casino and I'll be quiet."

He muttered an obscenity she hadn't heard in years.

"Ever the gentleman, aren't you?" she muttered back.

He bent his head, and she trained her eyes onto his lips only inches from hers.

"About as much as you're a lady. Now get those arms under my coat and hold that tempting little body of yours close. I'm after sharing some heat right now, and if you weren't so determined to be disagreeable, you'd be wanting the same."

Reluctantly, Lorelei decided it was time to be practical, and once again she found herself doing what he wanted. Her hands slipped easily inside the coat and made their way to his back. He was right; his body *was* warm. And hers was heating up fast.

Holding him tight like this, she knew what she had suspected before: He was in great physical condition, all hard muscle contoured into a broad chest and tapered waist. Just as there had been no softness in his features, no gentleness in his eyes, she could detect no corporeal weakness in him now.

Not that she gave a tinker's damn how well built he was, but she couldn't help but notice. Never in her life had she held a man in such an intimate embrace.

No longer did the rain bother her; she was consumed with hating the way her body rubbed against him. She absolutely hated it. Not yet had she felt an irritation pop out on her skin, but she figured she would before long. It was only in the interest of keeping warm that she did not let go.

They rode the better part of an hour, far longer than necessary to get away from Balzac's gun-happy men. Their route took them through brush and forest, along the bank of the bayou and across the rising waters of a creek. Lorelei suspected they were going generally parallel to the path she had planned to ride, only some distance to the north.

There was no sun to serve as proof of her guess, for the rain continued unceasingly. Sam rode in silence, his hands on the reins, the sleeves of his jacket brushing against Lorelei's left shoulder and her right. When she wasn't thinking about the friction generated from their closeness, or the strong beat of his heart, she considered the pepperbox he did not know rested in her pocket.

Somehow just having the gun kept her at least partially in control of the situation. Or so she told herself.

The downpour settled into a fine, gray mist, but Sam showed no signs of halting and letting her down. Lorelei seethed. The situation was intolerable. When the sorrel slowed down to a plodding pace through a field of mud, she pushed away from him. Her hip dug painfully into the pommel, but it seemed a minor complaint given everything else that was wrong.

"We're out of rifle range, don't you think?"

His dark eyes flicked down at her. "Yep."

"Then, put me down."

"Nope."

"What do you mean, *nope?*"

"Just what it sounds like."

She sighed in exasperation. "I don't know what you're up to. You can't be kidnapping me. I'm too much trouble, remember?"

"There's just one complication. Your men know I've got you."

"So put me down and ride on out of here. I'll set up such a howl, they're bound to hear me."

"If I let you go, you're liable to get pneumonia or get yourself caught by wild animals or fall into the hands of some cutthroat heading for Texas. You die and I'm charged with murder."

She couldn't believe she heard right. "I die and you suffer, right?"

"Right."

"How unfortunate for you."

He had the nerve to grin. "Glad you see it my way."

It was the grin that finally sent her over the edge. Enough was enough. She exploded against him, pummeling him with her fists, twisting and kicking, trying any way she could manage to break his hold. She enjoyed a dubious success when the sorrel bucked under the struggle and dumped them both into the mud.

Sam fell on his back, and Lorelei landed hard on top of him. His breath came out in a whoosh. As he sucked in air, she tried scrambling to her feet, but the weight of her drenched cloak and velvet gown held her down like an anchor. Crablike, she crawled through the ooze, putting a couple of feet between her and Sam.

She shifted to face him and frantically clawed for her gun. Sam was on top of her before she could find the pocket where it rested.

They lay stretched out, Sam's hands pinning her wrists above her head, his body pressing hers down into the muck and mire. His hat lost in the fall, he stared down at her. Rivulets of water streamed down his face; his black hair, made blacker still by daubs of mud, lay plastered to his head, and the spark in his eyes spoke of an anger that matched anything she had ever felt.

"You tired of living?" His lips were inches from hers, and his words came out a growl.

She squirmed to get away from him. With his body hard against hers, she realized right away that squirming was a mistake.

The spark in his eyes deepened to a gleam.

"Bastard!"

"I do like a woman with spirit."

"Let go of my wrists," she said, lowering her voice to huskiness and putting as much suggestion in the words as she could, "and you'll find out how much spirit I have."

All she needed was one free hand. A sock in the nose would take him by surprise, and then she could get to that pepperbox.

He shook his head. "Have you ever seen a couple of crawdads mate in a swamp bottom? That's what we'd look like. I'm partial to a woman with spirit, all right, but I'd just as soon she not be covered in slime."

His eyes flicked to the hood covering her head. "Or look like a monk. Now, we get to a shelter—"

Lorelei spat in his face. It wasn't the most effective of actions, given the general condition of him, but he caught the insult.

65

Grasping her wrists in one hand, he brought his freed hand down her cheek and neck to her throat, loosening the string securing her cloak and pulling it aside. His fingers moved inside to touch her skin above the low scoop of her gown, stroked over the wet velvet covering her breasts and trailed down her side, past her waist to the flare of her hips.

His hand was in and out of her pocket so fast she had no time to react. He raised the pepperbox gun in the air. "A nice toy."

Lorelei stared in disbelief at the weapon, then squeezed her eyes closed to tears of frustration. He would take them for a woman's weakness, not a warrior's rage.

"That toy can kill a man," she said between clenched teeth.

"In the hands of someone who knows how to use it."

A painful memory struck her. "Remember the rifle. I knew how to use that well enough."

"I'll keep that in mind," he conceded with a nod of his head.

Tucking the gun inside the waist of his trousers, he released her wrists, stood and pulled her up beside him, then whistled for the sorrel, which came bounding toward them out of the mist. Scooping his hat out of the mire, he slapped it against his thigh, then stuck it back on his head. It sat lower than before, stained with black Louisiana mud, misshapen, and altogether ridiculous.

In truth, the whole picture was ridiculous—the two of them standing toe to toe in the middle of a field and angrily trying to get in the last word, their clothing hanging filthy about their bodies, and all around them air so wet and gray it was indistinguishable from the sky and, at the edge of the field, an expanse of moss-draped oaks rising high and tight like the walls of a jail. She fought an urge to laugh.

The urge passed, and she credited it to hysteria. There was nothing funny about their situation, nothing funny at all. Whether Sam meant to or not, he had killed a man, and he had most certainly of his own free will assaulted her and taken the casino's money.

She wasn't much better. Proud of being in control, she had reacted to him recklessly; because of that recklessness, she had lost the mare that had served her so faithfully. And now she was under Sam's power.

Robbed of her gun, she had no real defense against him, no way to protect herself from anything he might decide to do. Gone was her desire to bring him to justice. She just wanted to go home.

He mounted, then reached down to grab her by the waist and lift her up once again in front of him. His movements were fluid and sure, and Lorelei felt herself settled once again on top of his spread legs, wedged between his body and the saddle horn.

He studied the sky, and she could not keep her eyes away from the shape of his jaw and the long line of his strong neck. Up close he did not look ridiculous at all.

"My guess is it's going to start raining again. There's a cabin a few miles up ahead. Off any path your men might take, assuming they can find a path. I got the feeling from the way you were leading the hunting party that they're not exactly scouts."

"You, on the other hand, seem to know this land very well."

"I've been across the South more times than I've lived years. We'll get to that cabin and get out of these wet clothes."

Lorelei suppressed a shiver. What Sam proposed seemed sensible enough, yet she knew without doubt that her troubles with him had just begun.

Chapter Six

The cabin lay tucked away near a creek far off any path Lorelei had been able to detect. Surrounded by trees and tangled undergrowth, it was everything she had expected. Which meant it wasn't much.

In the dim gray light drifting through the open door she saw one small dusty room with a dirt floor, clapboard siding, a boarded window, and no furniture in sight. Cobwebs hung like moss from the rafters of the low ceiling, and the damp, stale air held the unsettling scent of a thousand rodents that had sought shelter there through the years.

And there were most certainly spiders lurking somewhere in the shadows. Instinctively she lifted her cloak and gown above the hard ground and concentrated on the two features that made the structure beautiful: a roof solid enough to withstand the pelting rain, and a stone fireplace filled with kindling and dry logs. For good measure, a stack of firewood rested on the hearth.

Standing beside her close to the fireplace, Sam explained he'd stayed there on his way from Texas to New Orleans and had left the logs awaiting his return.

Lorelei pulled her stare of admiration away from the hearth and looked at him. "So you were planning on coming back this way. You think of everything, don't you?"

"Nope. Not everything."

He did not elaborate, and she thought of Frank Knowles. No matter how much she blamed Sam for her troubles, she knew he had not planned to kill Knowles. Wanting to ask him what had been the trouble between the two men, she swallowed her questions. She had too much to worry about in the present to concern herself with someone else's past.

Again she studied the room. High on the wall over the doorway she saw a dark shadow. The shadow moved. She screamed and threw herself at Sam.

"What the—"

She gestured wildly toward the door.

He chuckled.

She pushed away and forced her gaze back to what had frightened her. Again she saw the moving shadow. It seemed to separate itself into a thousand spindly parts.

She stifled a cry.

"Daddy longlegs," he explained. "They like to huddle up like that in these old cabins."

"Spiders," she said in a horrified whisper.

"They won't hurt. You leave them alone and they'll stay right where they are, but if you're worried, just come back on over here and let old Sam protect you."

Lorelei would have run from him, except that

70

her path would take her directly under those creatures. Her fear of them wasn't rational, but it was very real.

Her wariness of her human companion, however, was definitely both. It was time he knew the way things were.

"Old Sam got me into this predicament in the first place," she said, chin held high despite the heaviness of the wet wool hood.

She ignored his harsh laugh. "You most certainly bear part of the blame," she said. "If you think I'm going to give in to your lust so easily, think again."

"My what?"

"You heard me. Your lust."

His eyes roved toward the partially opened door, then moved about the room before settling on her damp, bedraggled figure. "That's all I've got on my mind, all right."

She stared right back at him. He could be as sarcastic as he wanted, but he didn't fool her for a minute, not when it came to his ultimate plans for the night. If there was one thing Lorelei understood, it was the nature of men.

He winked, and she edged backward, careful not to look where she stepped in case she spied something crawling about the room, something that would propel her into his arms once again. This time he might not let her go so readily.

With several feet of distance between them, she watched as he kneeled to start the fire. Thumbing the woebegone hat to the back of his head, he struck a spark with the aid of a sulphur stick he'd kept in a leather pouch inside his coat. The smallest of the kindling caught fire. She stared in anticipation as the infant flames spread and grew into a full-fledged fire. The resultant glow flickered across Sam's face, lighting the angled planes of his cheeks and reflecting in his eyes.

The snap and crackle of the burning wood played against the pounding of the rain on the roof and beckoned Lorelei to draw close. She shivered from the cold. Unable to resist the lure, she sidled toward the warmth and, cramming her gloves into a cloak pocket, spread her hands above the flames. Her cheeks, long numbed by the outside air, ached at the onslaught of the heat waves, but it was a welcome and short-lived discomfort.

Sam tucked the pouch back inside his coat and straightened to a stand. He gave her a sideways glance. With his hat resting on the back of his head and an unruly lock of hair falling across his forehead, he appeared almost boyish.

His eyes met hers, and the dark gleam in their depths reminded her he was every inch a man.

He grinned, as though he could read her mind.

"I'll be back," he said. Spurs jingling, he went out into the rain.

Oh, how she despised her fears of him. Despite the spreading heat from the fire, Lorelei could not contain another shiver. Her cloak lay wet and heavy against her skin and her equally wet velvet gown, but she held it close and told herself she could handle any predicament she found herself in during the next few hours.

The seconds crept by. What was Sam up to? She

forced herself to step toward the doorway until she could catch sight of him. He was tending to the sorrel. Wrapped up as she was in her own worried speculations, she still should have known.

Sadness took hold of her as she watched the shadowed movements of man and animal in the evening downpour, and she forgot the daddy longlegs. When he led the gelding out of sight toward the creek alongside the cabin, she retreated to the far side of the room and stared into the fire, remembering yesterday's happy ride in the woods. She was still standing thus minutes later when he returned and tossed the saddle and the rest of his gear onto the dirt floor in a corner near the hearth.

"What's his name?" she asked.

Kneeling to untie a bedroll, he looked over his shoulder at her. "Whose name?"

One of the burning logs collapsed and sent up a shower of sparks. "The horse. What do you call him?"

"Horse."

She shifted her gaze from the fire and looked down at him in surprise. "That's all? Surely—"

"I don't name animals. Any horse I've ever owned I called Horse."

"And any dog was named Dog."

He stood. "That's right."

"Why?"

He paused, the first sign of hesitancy she had seen in him. "That's the way I am."

Again he strode from the cabin, leaving Lorelei to stare after him. She would bet he didn't use

73

names because he didn't like to form attachments. Much as she refused to think of him in a personal way, she couldn't keep from wondering what he had lost to make him feel that way.

Despite all that had happened to her, she retained the need to hold something close.

She warned herself not to feel too sympathetic toward him. He claimed she was not the victim of a kidnapping, but she wasn't in an abandoned cabin alone with a lusty man of her own free will.

What was he up to now? Impatience set her to pacing in front of the fire. Her shoes squeaked with each step, and she took them off, placing both shoes and stockings close to the flames. Quickly she pulled off her petticoat and added it to the pile just as Sam returned.

This time he toted two buckets filled with water from the creek. He set the buckets on the hearth close to the shoes, then exited the cabin once again. She remembered he did not like his women covered in slime. Since the rain had washed away most of the filth they'd both picked up, she was struck by an urge to go wallow in the mud.

Nor did he like them looking like monks.

The boor, setting out standards like that as though if she improved herself, he'd let her enjoy his glorious body.

Monk, indeed. She loosened the hood of the cloak and shook her hair free over the rising waves of heat emanating from the fireplace; at the same time, she warmed her toes. Running fingers through the long, matted curls, she waited to see what Sam would do next.

74

She did not have to wait long; in less than a minute he returned with a large tin tub he'd dug up from heaven knew where. Setting the tub close to the flames, he emptied the buckets and went outside to refill them.

He made two more trips, and after the third, he closed and bolted the door, then knelt in front of the fire and set the buckets on the hot stones near the burning logs. Standing, he shrugged out of his coat and hung it on a nail close to the fire. His dark brown shirt and buff trousers, soaked from the rain, lay molded like a second skin to his — well, to his everything.

Not that Lorelei cared or was impressed. But standing as she was, only a couple of feet away from him, she couldn't keep from noticing.

He took a moment to brush and block his hat, then hung it over his coat.

"Take off your clothes," he ordered.

She jumped. "What did you say?"

"Take off your clothes."

"I will not."

He removed the pepperbox from the waistband of his trousers, holding it loosely in his hand.

"Oh, yes you will."

"If I don't, are you going to shoot me?"

His lips twitched. "Don't tempt me. Miss —" He shook his head. "This is stupid. Here we are about to strip down to the altogether, and I can't even call you by name. I'll just have to settle on one that seems appropriate to the situation. How about Bubbles? I once knew —"

"Lorelei Latham."

75

"That's more like it."

"I can't see what it matters. Why don't you just call me Woman?"

For the first time she saw a smile on his face. Faint though it was, and as fleeting as his few moments of despondency, it lightened his features.

Backtracking to the wall behind him, he reached high to lay the pepperbox on one of the cobwebbed rafters, then unbuckled his own holster and gun and added them to the place of safety far out of her reach. His body was stretched long and lean while he worked.

Arms dropping loose at his sides, he walked back close and stared down at her. She forced herself to stand her ground.

"Lorelei Latham, is it? That has a nice sound to it. Now take off your clothes."

She gritted her teeth. Sam had to be well over six feet tall, and she gave him credit for being broad shouldered and long of limb—long of *muscled* limb, she amended—but he didn't frighten her.

"Are you hard of hearing, Mr. Delaney? I will not."

"I get it. You want me to take 'em off for you."

"I do not!"

"Honey, one way or another, if we're going to warm ourselves by the same fire, that cloak has got to go."

Lorelei had been thinking much the same thing about the damp wool, the odor of which had overpowered the traces of rats, but she'd throw herself into the flames before she let him know.

76

When he reached for the tie at her throat, Lorelei's hands curled into fists.

His fingers encountered the pouch of gris-gris Delilah had sewn into the cloak's lining. "What's this?"

"Poison. An ancient voodoo mixture from the islands. It seeps into the skin of whoever touches me and brings on a horrible death."

He shook his head. "I should have guessed. You certainly think men are after your lily-white little body, don't you?"

"I think *you* are. I've seen you looking at me often enough."

"I tend to look at fine fillies, too, but I don't hop on every one of 'em, even for a quick ride."

"You really are a bastard."

"That's what I hear. But that doesn't make me interested in rape."

Lorelei didn't believe him for a minute.

Keeping her head high, she finished taking off the cloak and tossed it toward the far side of the room, away from his saddle and gear. The dress she had put on so carefully twenty-four hours before was in little better condition than the cloak, stained as it was with traces of swamp mud that had ground into the fabric, the green velvet pile matted beyond repair, and the skirt hanging limp over her drawers and trailing against the dirt floor. But at least it didn't smell.

She blew a curl out of her eyes. "That's as far as I plan to go."

"We'll see." His broad, tanned hands began to work at the buttons of his shirt.

She smirked. "Undress if you have to. I don't care."

"Good. Can't stand a woman who pretends she's bashful when I know damned well she's not."

He tugged the shirt free of the waistband and eased his way out of it.

Lorelei did not look away. "You ought to wear something more during the winter, or do you think that pelt of hair on your chest will keep you warm?"

"You have an eye for detail, don't you, Lorelei?"

Pulling off his boots, he tossed them aside by his shirt, then unbuckled his pants. Lorelei decided she was only encouraging him by watching, and she shifted her eyes to the fire. She would have liked to tell him she was especially bored by naked men; but he would demand to know why, and that particular period of her history was one she shared with no one other than those near and dear.

Which Sam Delaney certainly was not.

Goodness but she was beginning to itch, and he hadn't so much as touched her.

She heard his trousers hit the floor.

She scratched at her right arm.

With his back to her, Sam moved into her line of vision to get the heated buckets of water and add their contents to the tub.

Her fingers dug at her waist. She tried to think of the disparaging things she had said to Delilah about the naked body of a man, but not one came to mind.

"If you don't want to clean up first, then I'll go ahead."

78

Ever the gentleman, was Sam.

She listened to his splashing.

"Not quite as warm as I'd like," he said at last, "but it feels good all the same. If we squeeze real close together, I think we both might fit. We can keep each other heated, the way we did on Horse."

She whirled on him. He sat leaning back, his long legs bent, his arms resting along each side of the tub's rim. His hair was plastered back, and there were droplets of moisture caught in his thick lashes. Bristled cheeks, a strong neck, contoured shoulders and chest—down her gaze traveled . . . down, down. The tub water was muddied but not so much she couldn't see into its depths. She jerked her eyes back to his face.

He was grinning . . . teasing her, of all the nerve.

Lorelei planted her hands on her hips. "You are a stubborn, self-centered, egotistical. . . ." She broke off, unable to think of the exact word. "You couldn't get Frank Knowles to do what you wanted, and now you're thinking I—"

He came out of the water after her, and she broke off.

Naked and dripping wet, he caught her by the shoulders. "Know what I think? You've done a lot of protesting about what you think I want and what you don't want. Seems to me you're protesting a little too much. Like maybe, you can't quit thinking about me. About wanting something so much you have to keep bringing it up every time I get to thinking about something else."

79

She stared up at him in disbelief, making sure her gaze fell no lower than his neck. "You can't believe that."

"Can't I? You were mighty quick to throw yourself at me over those silly daddy longlegs. A woman like you who bosses men and deals a mean game of poker and rides around the country in the middle of the night. You're not afraid of anything. Except maybe yourself."

He glanced down at her bedraggled gown. "I wanted you out of this thing so that you wouldn't come down with pneumonia and die on me. Now I'm thinking maybe I want you out of it for something else."

He set to work at the front closures, sometimes working them loose, sometimes tearing them apart. He seemed to know just where to grab and tear, and before she could come up with a defense, he had her stripped down to her undergarments, which were wet and all-too transparent.

The cold had caused her nipples to pucker; Sam paused to stare. She took advantage and socked him on the chin. She should have aimed for his nose because all she got for her efforts were a painful fist and the sharp reminder that the muscles of her shoulders were still strained.

"I do like a woman with spirit," he said.

He came at her again, this time removing her chemise and drawers, dragging them from her squirming body with the same expert and determined skill he had used to take off her dress. Scooping her in his arms, he bent over and dropped her into the tub. Water splashed onto the dirt floor and sizzled at the edge of the fireplace.

She let him have a sampling of the imprecations she'd picked up through the years.

"Thank God you're not a lady," he said. He stood with his legs apart, black hairs curling wetly on his thighs.

She kept her eyes at a level with his knees. A little knobby, she thought with satisfaction.

One of his broad hands flattened over the crown of her head, and he pushed her under. She came up sputtering.

"Don't ask for soap. I can't think of everything."

Lorelei counted to ten in English, and then in French; by the time she came to *dix,* he had spread a blanket between the tub and the fire.

He pulled her out of the water and set her on her feet at the blanket's edge. "That'll have to do."

She lifted a hand to slap him. He caught her by the wrist and twisted both arms to her back. It took only one of his broad hands to hold both of hers.

"Still protesting?" he said.

She kicked him as hard as she could. Her bare toes caught him on the shin, but she was the one who yelped.

"That'll teach you," he said.

"I'll charge you with rape. I'll see you hung in the city square."

"Honey, I'm already hung — in case you haven't noticed."

"Oh! You'll regret ever—"

His mouth covered hers, forcing her to abandon

81

her threats. His lips were firm and insistent, as was the tongue that forced its way past the teeth she tried to clench. No matter how much she tried to pull away from him, to shrink from his embrace, he was unstoppable, relentless in his quest to claim her.

For the second time since they'd met, he was kissing her, and for the second time she found herself unable to fight him. His lips caressed hers; she wanted to feel repulsion, but no matter how much she summoned up feelings of hate, all she could think about was the press of those lips, the roughness of his tongue as it stroked against hers, the overpowering strength of his will as he crushed her naked body to his.

That will wrapped around her with the same devastating effect as his arms, and she felt the familiar irritation spread fast over her skin.

His hold on her eased just enough to allow her hands to fall free. She worked her arms around and tried to shove him away, but he pulled her back into his unyielding embrace, her bared breasts rubbing against his chest, her fingers pressed against his shoulders. She heard him groan, sensed the tightening of his sinewed muscles, felt the hard wall of his chest against her taut nipples.

Most tantalizing of all was the pressure of his erection against her abdomen. The urge to stand on tiptoe, to thrust her hips forward, built hot within her.

He broke the kiss long enough to pull her down to the blanket. The fire was to her back; she felt its heat race along the length of her body, but Sam put out a warmth that made the flames no more comforting than a winter blast.

Lorelei's mind was in a whirl. What was happening to her? What were these strange sensations rippling through her? She should be thrashing about on the ground and fighting him with her last ounce of strength; instead, she lay stretched out beside him, trembling in his embrace.

So many times had she witnessed scenes of men grappling with women, but never had she thought to be in such a position herself.

He broke the kiss. She knew too well the condition of his body: He wanted to impale her on the blanket; he wanted to use her for his satisfaction; he wanted what she had sworn never to want.

And he claimed to believe she felt the same way. In truth, she was doing little to discourage him.

"No!" The word tore from her throat, and even Sam, caught up in his passion, heard her despair.

He loosened his hold on her, and she scrambled to her feet, her legs trembling, hated tears staining her cheeks.

She stared down in shame at her naked, rash-covered body, then forced her eyes back to his.

"Look at me," she said. "Do you see it? Do you see the redness? It happens when a man gets near. I don't want you. I don't want anyone. I just want to be left alone."

Sam looked at her arms, at her neck and shoulders, at her breasts, and slowly down her hips and thighs and at last on down to her feet.

Slowly his eyes moved back to lock with hers.

83

"Whether you know it or not, you were sending out more than one message. Looks like I picked the wrong one."

He stood. She edged away.

Without a word he stepped around her and picked up a second blanket from the pile of gear he'd tossed into the corner. Shoving it toward her, he said, "Cover yourself. I keep looking at you long enough, I'll forget all about that rash."

The blanket pulled to her chin, Lorelei settled on the far side of the fire from Sam and forced herself to breathe deeply, but she could do nothing about the pounding of her heart. If only the tub that sat between them were six feet high, she wouldn't have to see him at all. As things were, it didn't block her vision in the least; she could see him as easily as he could see her.

With his own blanket wrapped around his waist, he opened one of his saddlebags and tossed her a paper-wrapped package. Inside were several strings of jerky and a half-dozen biscuits as hard as the floor. Realizing just how ravenous she was, Lorelei tore into the food.

"I see you haven't lost all your appetites," he said from his position across the room. "Save a little for me."

Guiltily, she struggled to her feet and padded over to return the food, saving only a small portion for herself. He took it without a word.

Like a couple of pugilists, they settled once again into their respective corners and ate in silence. Both had drunk from the creek before entering the cabin, but she couldn't help wishing she had something to wash down the dry food.

Sam must have been thinking much the same thing, for he said, "Wasted all that water taking a bath."

She didn't respond.

After a couple of minutes devoted to chewing, he reached again into the saddlebag, this time for a leather pouch which he emptied onto the ground. Bank notes and gold coins fell into the light from the fire.

He counted out the notes and pitched a good portion of them over to her.

"Back in the casino, it didn't seem like the smart thing to sort out what was yours and what was mine."

He took her by surprise. "I thought you were stealing everything you could," she said.

"I'm not a thief, no more than you're much comfort on a rainy night." He let his eyes roam over her so slowly that she was certain he could see through the blanket. "Damned waste, too."

Any kind feelings she felt as a result of the returned money died as fast as they had been born.

"You're a real bastard, aren't you?"

"So you keep saying. What I am is a little stupid for not riding by when you fell into that ditch. I saw you and the horse roll out of sight and forgot one of my rules."

"And what's that?" she asked, hating herself as she did so.

"To ride on by. People are as tough as they have to be. Leave 'em alone, and they'll work out their problems. You did with that lame horse of yours."

"You're right I did," she said, stung by his words. "At last we agree on something. You should have kept riding."

For once he didn't have a ready comeback.

Her movements rendered awkward by the blanket she kept wrapped around her, Lorelei squeezed the water from her chemise and underdrawers and placed them by her petticoat as close to the fire as she dared. Shaking the dirt and moisture from her cloak and dress, she hung them on nails. For a moment she considered doing the same with Sam's shirt and trousers, then decided they were problems he could take care of for himself.

With a folded arm serving as a pillow, she settled herself as comfortably as she could on the hard dirt floor. Ignoring Sam's steady breathing, she forced herself to concentrate on the drum of rain on the roof as she waited for the night to pass.

Minutes passed, long torturous minutes. Try as she might, she couldn't relax. Memories of Seabreeze, of the snap of bone and of the sudden tumble, hung heavy in her thoughts. Maybe Sam had the right idea. Maybe if she hadn't given the mare a name. . . .

No, that wasn't right. No matter what the horse was called, she would have cared. Unlike Sam. If he ever did have children, would he call them Boy Number One and Boy Number Two?

For all she knew, he had a houseful of boys and girls both waiting for him in Texas. And a woman he no doubt called Wife.

Across the room he shifted about on the floor.

She reconsidered. Somehow she doubted that any woman had domesticated him enough to get him in front of a preacher.

She chewed at her lower lip. There he was lying naked and wrapped in a blanket just the way she was, and only a few yards away. If only she weren't so aware of him, maybe the itching would fade and she could go to sleep.

She went over the whole day in her mind, beginning with Sam's pulling her up on his horse after the casino guards got it into their heads to start shooting, and ending with the return of her money. Out of all the things that had happened to her, one thing ate most at her mind. He thought she wanted him.

He was wrong. Lorelei did not want any man, not in the way he meant.

And she never would.

Chapter Seven

The rain had softened to an occasional drizzle by the time Lorelei fell asleep. She drifted into troubled dreams of falling horses and blazing guns and of a frantic, naked dash through the forest with a mud-draped skeleton close at her heels.

A bony hand clasped her throat, and she jerked to consciousness. Heart pounding, she lay still and struggled to recognize the strange world to which she awoke.

Her clues were few—a hard floor, a scratchy blanket clutched tight against her neck, a flickering light cast onto a raftered ceiling over her head—but they were enough, and the particulars of her situation came back in a rush. Except that one thing had changed during her hours of sleep. She sensed the change as soon as she was fully awake.

She was alone.

She raised up, her weight on her elbows. The sight of her undergarments and shoes on the hearth encouraged her. She looked past them and, in the dim light cast by the fire, saw that the corner once occupied by Sam was empty. Gone were the saddle, the saddlebags, the blanket. His boots had disappeared from where he tossed them beside the tub. Likewise his jacket and hat from the nail on the wall, and the trousers he'd left in a tangle on the floor.

A glance over the doorway and then into the reaches of the small room told her even the daddy longlegs had departed for more solicitous quarters.

She truly was alone.

She fought a fluttering panic. Sam must have decided that if he couldn't satisfy his manly needs, there was no reason to hang around. Of course that was it. Right from the moment he walked into the casino, she'd never expected much good from him, although leaving her out here without food, without a horse, without any indication of exactly where she was did seem excessively harsh.

People were as tough as they had to be; let them work out their own problems—one of his rules, he'd called it, one he'd forgotten for a while. Too bad he remembered it now.

She glanced at the fire. At least he had thrown on a few logs before he left, and the room was adequately warm.

A thought struck her, and she glanced up at the rafter over what had been his bed. No longer was the holster visible. He had also left her without any way to defend herself.

No way to defend herself. . . . The enormity of her situation hit her.

"You bastard," she whispered into the quiet air.

Then she saw the pepperbox lying on the ground by the tub, along with the package of food.

All right, he wasn't a complete bastard, but he came close.

She scurried from under the cover long enough to slip into the warm chemise and drawers, then huddled under the blanket once again and stared into the fire. What was she to do? Tears burned her eyes; at least Sam wasn't here to see them.

She brushed the tears away. Sam said she was tough, and so she should be. So she would *have* to be if she were to survive.

And he was right about something else. She shouldn't have been so frightened by those harmless creatures that had huddled over the door last night. Shouldn't have been, maybe, but that didn't mean she could reason away her fear. They reminded her of the first time she'd ever seen Louisiana.

From the deck of the ship plowing up the Mississippi, she'd stared in awe at the overgrown riverbanks, the air around her sweet and salty and so heavy she'd felt she could hold it in her hand. Strange birds with wide, white wings had soared overhead, but she'd been fascinated more by the trees. She'd thought them draped with giant southern spiderwebs.

She'd found out later the webs were really Spanish moss, but associating them as she did with everything bad that happened later ashore, she had developed a fear of spiders which remained with her through the years.

So much she'd found out later, she and Carrie. Lorelei let out a long, painful sigh that came from her soul. Dear Carrie with her flashing brown eyes and wild black hair. Memories of a bright, shining face—and of the dying of that brightness—hurt as much as ever. More, even, than the memories of her parents.

Lorelei held herself tight beneath the blanket. How strange it was that she could call up an image of her friend but fail so completely when she tried to picture her mother.

She remembered the softness of Ravinia Latham's voice, however, and the ripple of her laughter. They were the important things, mingling with the rantings of her merchant father, Hezekiah, on the wages of sin. Which was all wrong, since he hadn't taken to such preaching until months after her mother's death, but that was the way they lingered in her mind.

He wasn't the only one who had changed. Once she'd been filled with trust, with laughter, with a feeling that all was right with the world, an only and very much beloved child used to comfort and care. Loving Lorelei, her mother had called her. Her more taciturn father had concurred.

Then came Ravinia's fever and her death when Lorelei was seven. Demanding explanations for his loss, Hezekiah turned from the daughter.

"You look just like her," he'd mutter, and she felt as though somehow the resemblance must be a shameful thing.

He sought his answers in religion, and when those answers weren't forthcoming, he formed his own sect. The Church of Latter-Day Puritans, he called it. Within a year after Ravinia's death, he had sold his Boston wholesale business and taken to preaching around the Common.

A butt of jokes was what he was, with his hair

91

wild, his clothes hanging on his skeletal frame, and his blond-haired, skinny-legged daughter tagging after him.

"God will provide," he told her when she asked why they were moving from their home. She found out later that whatever provisions were granted by her father's deity, taxes had not been among them, and their home had gone to satisfy his public debts. They sought shelter wherever they could find it — often as not at the side of a Boston street.

The years passed, and somehow they survived, the objects of charity. Eventually Hezekiah got his own church building, a ramshackle abandoned structure near the Charles River, and a few members who saw that they did not starve.

But it was an existence without love and nurturing. When Carrie came along — mischievous young Carrie with her quick grin and her imagination — Lorelei readily accepted her as friend.

Like Lorelei, Carrie was motherless, but she was also cursed with a father very unlike Hezekiah. Instead of ignoring his daughter, he paid her far too much attention. She never told Lorelei exactly what he did, but she hinted it was terrible and forbidden, something that could never be put into words.

"He visits me sometimes in the night."

That was the most she ever said, and Lorelei did not ask to know more. Instead, they spent much of their time talking about the lives they would someday lead, the families they would have, the places they would see. Gazing upon the tall-masted ships in the Boston harbor, they let their imaginations take them where their feet could not yet go.

When they were both sixteen, Carrie came to her with a plan.

"I've met a man," she whispered as the two girls walked along the Common. It was September, 1830, a month Lorelei would never forget.

She knew little about the ways of men, despite her years on the streets, and even though Carrie had tried to explain to her how babies were made, she found the whole procedure too improbable to believe. Like Ravinia, Carrie could weave fanciful tales.

This time she appeared very serious.

"He says if we are skillful with needle and thread, he can give us employment."

Lorelei's interest grew. Having been taught first by her mother and later by one of the women of the church, she had for a long while been sewing the few clothes that she owned. She wasn't sure about Carrie's competence, but she figured that she could teach her friend what she didn't already know.

"Tell me more," Lorelei said.

"The wages aren't much, at least not right away, but, oh, there's opportunities you won't believe."

Lorelei was immediately skeptical. "He's making promises. I think we'd be smarter to ask for money."

Carrie waved aside her advice. "We'll be working in a fancy boutique. That's a French word. It means—"

"I know what it means."

93

"Mr. Jacobs says if we can make fine little embroidery stitches, we'll have all the work we want; if we prove ourselves, then the women will come from miles around to buy. We'll get the money, all right, only not right away."

Lorelei could indeed make fine little embroidery stitches, although she'd had precious little opportunity to practice the skills. And she couldn't imagine the women of Massachusetts caring much for the handiwork of a couple of young girls, no matter how delicate the embroidery was.

She tried to tell Carrie just that.

Carrie grinned. Years later Lorelei could still see that smile; it lit up her dear friend's face better than any candle could have done.

"That's the best part. We wouldn't be working here. We'd be in New Orleans!"

"New Orleans?"

"That's way far away where all the Frenchies live. They just love pretty things. That's what Mr. Jacobs says."

She stared at Carrie in wonderment. Her friend might as well have been talking about flying across the sea.

"This boutique is needing all the seamstresses it can get. He says it's a real problem, what with the girls finding themselves rich husbands all the time and leaving their jobs."

"Says this Mr. Jacobs."

"He's willing to pay our passage down there, so I suppose he knows what he's talking about. Oh, Lorelei, think what a grand adventure it will be. We've always wanted to sail far away. And maybe we can find ourselves one of those rich planters he keeps talking about."

Lorelei had never seen Carrie so excited, and she couldn't keep from feeling a little of that excitement for herself. She was skeptical, puzzled, afraid—any number of things that kept her from agreeing right away to the proposal—but she was also young and lonely, and except for Carrie, she felt very much unloved.

Her father wouldn't miss her; lately he'd barely seemed aware she was alive. He'd taken to doubting the Bible, said he had visitations in the night that told him he must write a Scripture of his own. To that end, he devoted much of the daylight hours to preaching in a cold and often empty church and, when the sun fell, to scribbling on scraps of parchment he picked up wherever he could, a single candle lighting his work while she lay on a cot in the dark.

No, he wouldn't miss her.

But New Orleans. It was so far away. She told Carrie she just wasn't sure what to say.

The next day Carrie came to her and started in again, and the next day and the next, a fine edge of desperation creeping into her pleas each time she spoke. When it was time for the ship to sail, Lorelei took her place beside Carrie on the dock, her pitiful store of worldly possessions tied in a bundle at her side. The only thing she'd left behind was a brief note telling her father she was leaving and not to worry, although she doubted worry over his only child would be much of a problem for him.

Even more than she remembered Carrie's smile, she remembered the cold, smokey cast to William Jacobs's eyes when she saw him for the first time.

She'd sent samplings of her work to him through Carrie, but she did not meet him face to face until an hour before they were to sail. A fancy dresser in a fine-tailored suit, he was thin with slicked-back, pale hair and a gaunt, sharp-nosed face. His complexion was as pale as his hair, and she wondered how often he came out into the sun.

His manners were polite enough, to the point of being courtly as he bowed to the two of them and proclaimed how glad he was they had decided to help him in his predicament.

"I am desperate for upstanding young ladies like yourselves," he said with a smile, but Lorelei noticed the smile was not reflected in those eyes. She got the feeling he wasn't really seeing anything or anyone around him. It was as though his look was inward, himself being the center, beginning and end of his universe, and then she decided she was being as fanciful as Carrie, only her fancies were taking a far gloomier turn.

Standing close to them on the crowded dock, he apologized for the poor quarters they would have to share below deck and warned them not to strike up an acquaintanceship with anyone else.

"Can't be too careful. People of all sorts journey on these ships. I feel responsible for seeing you get to New Orleans in the good health you're enjoying now."

He gave them each a packet of food, said it

would have to last them for a while, and added that they didn't have to refund the cost until they received their first pay.

"We must keep all our arrangements business-like, you see," he explained.

Both girls told him that they considered him perfectly fair. They had never been more wrong.

The voyage was ill-fated from the start. The quarters turned out to be one narrow, pillowless cot set in the midst of a hundred other such cots in the women's section of the lower deck. At first they tried to lie side by side, then reached the conclusion that taking turns sleeping was better.

Except that neither was able to get much rest, not with the storms that came one after the other as the ship made its way down the eastern coast. It was debatable as to which of the two was the more seasick. Lorelei celebrated her seventeenth birthday with her head over a pail.

Despite the sounds of retching all around them, and the cries of women and children that never ceased, they held onto their hopes for the city that awaited. Somewhere in one of the upper cabins, Jacobs was quartered. They would trust him to take care of them. They had no one else.

The storms ended after the clipper ship rounded the tip of Florida, and the journey across the Gulf went fast. It was with great enthusiasm they crowded onto the deck to watch as the ship, sails snapping in a brisk breeze, made its way past the islands and sandbars scattered about the delta of the Mississippi River and on up the river itself.

Here in the bright light of an autumn afternoon

Lorelei got her first look at Spanish moss. On the busy New Orleans dock she got her first hint all was not as William Jacobs had said.

The first surprise came when she realized that there were four other potential seamstresses who had come aboard in Charleston, young girls like herself. Jacobs had not mentioned anyone else, and she asked herself just how many imported embroidery experts New Orleans could possibly need.

The second came when he informed the six of them they were to pick up their belongings and follow him down the crowded street that ran east parallel to the river. Something about the sharpness of his voice, of his warning that they were not to stray, set off a warning inside her. He hadn't spoken to them this way back on the River Charles.

The Louisiana air was filled with languages from all over the world and with a thousand wonderful scents that reminded her she had not eaten an adequate meal in weeks. None of those sounds or scents—not even the singsong of the street vendors with their strange, beautiful way of announcing their wares—could still her apprehension. Too many men stared at the girls as they trooped along; too many grinned.

"Jacobs," one snaggle-toothed man in tattered coat and trousers shouted out. "Ha' ye been out huntin' agin?"

Carrie tried to question Jacobs, but he told her to keep quiet and stay in line. All courtliness gone, he did not attempt a smile. Lorelei, the quieter of the two but usually the more skeptical, took her friend's hand and squeezed a false encouragement.

Two blocks from the wharf he hired a wagon and told them to climb aboard. They had to help each other up and, a short time later, help each other down when the wagon came to a halt in front of a two-story frame structure on a dirt street just out of sight of the river.

The building sat in the middle of a row of taverns, none of which had seen a coat of paint in years. It had no sign indicating exactly the kind of business transacted within its dingy walls, but Lorelei knew it was not a boutique.

Inside, Jacobs led them down a dimly lit corridor, past a gaudily furnished parlor and into a small room at the back, where he turned them over to a rotund Negress dressed in red.

"Aurora," he said in a crisp, businesslike voice, "tell Emile I'll be back to collect my money tomorrow." Then he was gone.

The girls tried to talk all at once, but Aurora said one word from them and she would get the whip.

Carrie made a dash for the door. Aurora backhanded her and sent her sprawling to the floor. Lorelei helped her to stand, and the girls trembled together.

"Strip those clothes off your bodies. Need to see what we gots here an' get you into somethin' a mite fancier. Or maybe not. Some of the mens don't want to fool with no clothes."

One of the Charleston girls began to whimper.

Aurora's eyes narrowed until they sank into the

dark folds of her face. "I can gets some of the mens in here with those whips. They'll beat those dresses off your backs if that's what you're wantin'."

The whimpering stopped.

"White slaver," Carrie mouthed to Lorelei, her lip bleeding where she had been hit.

Ignorant as she was of so many things, and stunned by the horrible turn of events, Lorelei understood, or at least she thought she did. Years later she could see that they should have fought more; they should have screamed and scratched and taken the beatings, never submitting to the abuse that was heaped on them . . . never, never, never. But they were all so young, virtually homeless in the world, and they were frightened and weak.

And they did not know how bad things would be.

Many details of the early weeks would forever remain a blur; much of the time Lorelei was kept drugged.

"I'se savin' you for M'sieur Laverton," Aurora explained as she thrust a cup of laced tea at Lorelei the second morning after the ship docked. "With special ones, he likes to be the first. The yellow-haired young girls with a little meat on 'em and skin like mothers' milk."

Aurora grinned as she talked, and her teeth were stark white against her round, black face. "Likes to put the marks on for hisself. You're a little on the puny side, but old Aurora will fatten you up."

It was during this period that Lorelei developed

the rash. Each time the owner Emile Laverton approached, she broke out in ugly red welts, and he turned from her in disgust. Eventually he seemed to forget about her, and she later found out he had troubles of his own, troubles with the law.

Throughout the six months she remained at the brothel, she worked as servant and cleaning woman. She saw the whores flirt with the customers, saw them undress, saw the naked men. Even the once-innocent Charleston girls learned the trade. Some of the men asked that she watch everything they did; if they were willing to pay and vowed not to touch her, Aurora demanded she comply. It was during those times of moans and cries, of naked bodies twisting and thrusting on the bed, that she knew her greatest shame.

Of all the lechers who frequented the place, she saw Jacobs only twice more; each time he brought more girls. She never heard of him using one for himself. When Laverton was captured and eventually killed for his misdeeds, all of the confederates in his criminal endeavors were eventually brought to justice. All but William Jacobs, who disappeared and, as far as Lorelei had been able to learn, was never seen in New Orleans again.

A Louisiana lawyer named Joseph Devine heard of her plight. Investigating her background, he found that her father, Hezekiah, had died and she was truly alone in the world. When he called her to the attention of his friends Catherine and Adam Gase, they made sure she was cared for, even taking her into their home. Adam taught her to shoot and to ride, and Catherine allowed her to pour out her love to the two Gase children. Gradually the shame died.

Catherine also taught her to gamble. Six years later, she was put in charge of Balzac's.

Carrie was not so fortunate. She did not live through the first month. A sailor who liked to hurt his women went too far. One of the Charleston girls reported that shortly after the fatal beating he had been knifed on the streets. It was the one moment of satisfaction Lorelei experienced during the long six months.

As for the Charleston girls, after the brothel closed, she never saw them again. Rumor was they'd gone to work as whores on the New Orleans streets, but she never knew for sure if the rumor was correct.

When she first started helping out at the casino, she'd told Delilah a few of the details of those terrible times, more than she'd ever confessed to Catherine Gase.

"I'll see that William Jacobs dies in agony," she had said.

"Don't let him get you, too, *m'amie*. A man such as you describe must be forgotten."

"A man like that must *never* be forgotten."

She had vowed to find him. Not for herself alone, but for the Charleston girls and for all the others harmed in such inhuman ways. And mostly for Carrie.

Lorelei did not regret the loss of romance from her soul; she figured she had substituted knowledge of the ways of the world, a trade that was more than fair.

With all that knowledge, surely she could get herself out of the latest catastrophe that had befallen her.

The sound of hooves on the wet leaves outside the cabin thrust the memories from her mind. She sat up and reached for the gun. Checking to make sure the shot was in the barrel, she had it trained on the door when Sam burst in.

"You!" she said. A mixture of elation and relief rushed through her.

Sam stared at her from under the low brim of his hat. Once again he was wearing the fringed jacket and tight buff trousers, to which he had added a light brown shirt, and the pistol was strapped to his side. He seemed to be eight feet tall.

"Still in bed? I was hoping you'd have caught us some fish and be frying 'em up for breakfast by now."

Oh, it was Sam, all right. The elation died, but the relief remained. "I thought you had gone for good."

Slamming the door closed behind him, he jangled his way into the room and threw a bundle by her side. "Put down the gun and see what I brought."

Curiosity—and not his order—caused her to do just that. Untying the string, she laid back the paper and inspected the contents: a coat, trousers and shirt, all in dark colors, all made for a boy. And there was also a hat, smashed from the packing but otherwise closely resembling Sam's.

"Put 'em on while I rustle us up some breakfast.

103

Picked up a few supplies along with those duds. Had a taste for ham and eggs before we set out this morning. Took a lot of care to get 'em here. It'll be the last good meal we have, more than likely, before we get to Texas."

Lorelei dropped the shirt. "Texas!"

Sam shook his head. "Not too smart in the mornings, are you?"

She rose up on her knees, forgetting she wore only a thin chemise and drawers. Hands on hips, she declared, "My place is running Balzac's. It's what I'm paid to do, and it's what I want to do. I'm not going to Texas."

He tossed his hat onto one of the nails by the fireplace and ran his fingers through his hair. "I'm not too pleased about it, myself. We got enough troubles over there without importing more."

"See here, Mr. Delaney—"

He whirled and knelt in front of her. He made no move to touch her, but he leaned close—so close she could count the bristles on his cheeks and see the fire in his eyes.

"You'll do what I say. I'm trying to keep us both alive, and I can't do that by fighting you and the rest of this damned state."

"I don't—"

"Listen for a change and maybe you'll learn something. I went into a little community not too far from here and found out there was already a price on my head. Dead or alive. I'm to be shot on sight. Seems the brilliant folks you run with got the idea I grabbed you and then most likely

104

did you in. After having my way with you. We both know that's a fat lie."

Lorelei swallowed. "How did you find this out?"

"Listening to some talk in the saloon. Keeping out of the light. I got the idea they'll be shooting at any dark-haired stranger under the age of sixty and ask later if he's the right man. Had to break into the store to get what few supplies I could. Don't look so shocked. I left more than enough money to pay for 'em."

He dropped his gaze to her scantily clad body. "Can't swear to the fit of those clothes, not having inspected you the way I should have. Put 'em on anyway and get that hair tucked up under the hat. Don't know if you can manage it or not, but try like hell to look like a boy."

He stood and went for the saddlebags he'd brought with him along with the bundle.

"But Texas—" she began.

"Anyone ever tell you you're hard of hearing? Don't worry, little Lorelei. I don't plan to keep you there. But I sure as hell don't plan on staying around here and getting shot. Once I get home, I'll figure out something to do with you."

If nature hadn't called, she might have continued to argue. As it was, she needed first to get on those ridiculous clothes and head for outside. When she could concentrate, she would tell him what she thought of his plan.

The pants turned out to be tight across the seat and loose in the waist, but the shirt and coat fit just fine.

"Don't forget the hat," he said when she reached

the door. "And take one of these," he added, gesturing to the buckets close by his side. "Make yourself useful for a change and bring back some water to wash down the grub."

Lorelei could think of several useful things she could do, beginning with banging him in the head, but she refrained. When she grabbed for a bucket handle, he put a gloved hand over hers. "One more thing."

His dark eyes assessed her, and she remembered the way he had looked at her when he stripped her naked by the light of the fire.

"You owe me five dollars."

"What?" she asked.

"For the clothes and your share of the food. I don't mind providing the transportation, Lorelei, but you're going to have to pay a fair portion of everything else."

Lorelei gritted her teeth. She'd never had the habit before yesterday, but now it seemed to be all that she did.

"You want your payment now?"

"I'll put it on your account."

Cramming the hat on her head, she spun away and banged her way out of the cabin. A tangle of trees and vine-covered shrubs met her. The rain had ceased, but the air was cold and damp. Underneath an ominously gray sky, water dripped from every leaf in sight.

Texas! And she had to pay her way.

She forced her jaws to relax. It was going to be a long ride, and she couldn't stay tense this way the entire time. There was only one course open to her that she could see. She would have to make Sam Delaney so absolutely miserable that he would abandon her long before they reached the Sabine.

Chapter Eight

With the sound of the slammed door still bouncing from wall to wall, Sam poked at the fire, pulled a tin skillet from his gear and set it on a bank of glowing embers. Easing a knife from the sheath at his waist, he hacked at the slab of ham he'd taken from the town store, threw the pieces into the pan, and watched them skitter across the hot surface.

He felt a little like that meat, the way things were heating up in his life, and not in any way that would give him pleasure.

Just what in hell did he think he was doing, dragging a woman like Lorelei Latham through the woods? Didn't he have enough troubles? He tried to tell himself he'd had no choice, but that wasn't true. He could have ridden away from town this morning and headed west toward Texas.

Hell, he could have done more than that. He could have left her in the ditch with her horse.

Should have, he told himself, but he remembered the way she'd looked, a mixture of defiance and misery peering out at him from a monklike hood, and before he knew it he'd found himself right down there beside her. Dumb fool thing to

108

do, as though he could have helped the bay mare to stand. But he hadn't been hurrying down to the horse; he'd been heading toward the woman.

Now she'd become a part of his journey, his well-being dependent on hers as much as the other way around. He'd decide how to get her back home when they were in friendlier territory, namely Texas, but right now the Sabine seemed a long way away.

He shook the pan, his callused hand unbothered by the heat of the handle. The smell of the frying meat filled the small cabin.

Resting the pan on the hot stones, he carefully unfolded the square of chamois he'd used to transport the half-dozen eggs over the long, wet miles from town. Not one was cracked. He knew how to treat delicate objects, given the right motivation.

For no reason that came readily to mind, he thought of Lorelei's breasts under his fingers and the feel of her round bottom when he'd lifted her out of the tub.

The door creaked open, and he set to breaking the eggs on top of the pork, using the knife to stir and pitching the shells into the back flames. Fat bubbled around the edges of the skillet. From the corner of his eye he saw Lorelei set a bucket of fresh stream water on the hearth.

She took care not to get near him, and Sam fought the urge to reach out and grab whatever body part came closest. Just to shake her up, not to do anything about it. She deserved a little shaking up, all the trouble she was causing riding out after him the way she had. Who could have figured a city woman like her would do such a crazy thing?

Having undertaken crazy things a time or two in his thirty-plus years, he could almost admire her, but any admiration was overridden by an urge to give her bottom a healthy swat.

Shifting away from the fireplace, she began to fold her blanket, then turned to do the same to the dress and cloak she'd been wearing on her ride from the casino.

"Leave 'em," he said. "They're still wet."

With her back to him, she kept folding.

He shrugged. "You take 'em, you sit on 'em."

She did not respond, and despite himself Sam looked straight on at her bent figure, at the tangle of blond hair that fell loose beneath a gotch-angled hat, at the buttocks and slender legs outlined too damn well underneath the boys' trousers he'd picked up for her. They'd looked shapeless, lying there on the general store table, but they sure as hell didn't look shapeless now. Good thing women weren't in the habit of wearing trousers. A man would never get his work done.

He turned back to breakfast. He ought to leave her here, take care of himself the way he always had and let her fend for herself. But sure as rain came to the swamps, she'd get herself in real trouble, and somehow that trouble would be visited on him. It looked like he was stuck with her for a while.

She'd better learn fast not to tease him the way she had yesterday, twisting that hot little body against him, talking about having sex and about

110

not wanting it so much he'd figured out soon enough she didn't always tell the truth.

The rash was a puzzle. Maybe it was something she could turn on and off just to keep a man on edge. A neat trick if she could manage it, but not one that a man could put up with for long. Sam liked his women spirited, but he also liked the ones who showed up without trouble and went away the same.

Little Miss Lorelei from the fancy New Orleans casino came labeled trouble from the fancy curls piled on top of her head down to her wriggling toes. Once she attached herself for real to a man, she wouldn't leave until she decided on the time.

Such was not for Sam. He was a loner, had been for years. How he'd managed to accumulate a half-dozen men at his former camp in the East Texas woods he couldn't say. They'd just ridden in and stayed. Drifters, most of 'em, wanted by the law. Even though he'd moved into new quarters—and was fighting like the devil himself to stay there—they were about as close to family as Sam had known since he was a boy in Georgia. At least family was what Preacher liked to call 'em, but then Preacher was an inventive man at times.

Sam thought of Frank Knowles, who had never been a part of that camp. The poor, dumb bastard would never be a part of anything anymore. The memory of Frank brought him to his real troubles. A glance around the cabin made him long for his own place. It had taken him years of wandering to realize a man needed somewhere to belong; he'd found that somewhere, only it wasn't

111

coming to him easy.

A restlessness ate at the pit of his stomach. He'd made a mess of things at that casino; he couldn't afford to do so again. Too much was at stake.

Using the flat edge of the knife, he downed half of the eggs and ham. Behind him, he heard Lorelei still rustling about.

He set the skillet at the edge of the fire. "Eat up," he said. "I'll go see to the horse."

"I'm not hungry," she said to his back.

"Suit yourself." Without looking her way, he grabbed for his hat and settled it low on his forehead. "Might not get another chance at grub before dark."

Water sloshing onto the dirt floor, he dragged the tub with him as he went into the gray morning, emptied it into the brush and left it propped upside down against the rear clapboard wall. After giving the gelding one last chance at a drink from the fast-moving stream that ran alongside the cabin, he went back inside. Right away he noted the pan had been emptied and cleaned in the bucket of water. He hoped it was a sign she wouldn't obstruct him every mile of the long ride.

It took less than a minute for him to bundle his gear. Emptying the water bucket onto the fire, he sheathed the knife, then adjusted the pepperbox at his waist and his pistol in its holster.

"Think you're armed enough to handle me?"

Slowly he shifted his gaze to Lorelei. Hat in hand, she faced him stiff-backed at the side of the room, a mass of honeyed hair falling against her

112

shoulders, her slender legs slightly apart. For a woman who was little more than average in height, she had legs that went on forever.

The jacket he'd brought hid some of her feminine attributes. Nothing could completely hide the curve of her hips, however, or the fawnlike neck and the smooth white skin that stretched across her fine features. And no boy ever had such thick black lashes or deep blue eyes.

He moved beside her. She held her ground, chin tilted, lips slightly parted. From a distance she looked delicate and inviting to a man used to the harshness of the world, but up close he saw the fighting light in her eyes. A spirited woman asking to be tamed.

He leaned closer, his lips inches from hers. "Honey, I've got weapons you haven't seen yet."

"I can only hope that I never do."

"More denials. Starting to itch?"

"Only when I feel threatened. You don't threaten me."

"Then, you're not as bright as I took you for."

"I could say the same for you, Mr. Delaney."

Sam could think of several ways of cutting off the smart-aleck retorts, starting with covering her mouth with his own.

"Put your hair under that hat and let's ride," he growled as he spun toward the door.

Outside he secured his gear tight behind the saddle, pulled himself astride the gelding and, when Lorelei finally joined him, reached down and pulled her up behind him. The damp clothing was clutched under her arms.

113

"Sit on it," he said and was surprised when she did exactly that. "Hold on," he added, and with a click of his tongue set the horse in motion.

Lorelei jerked backward, and he felt her hands grabbing for his coat. Holding on to the buckskin fringe, she settled herself more firmly into place, and with dark clouds low over the treetops, they were off for another day in the woods.

Setting out on a narrow, overgrown trail that meandered in a generally westward direction, they hadn't made much more than a mile when she tugged at his sleeve. "I need to stop."

"Tough. It's too soon."

"I can't help it; I need to stop."

Sam glanced over his shoulder into a pair of wide blue eyes. Peering out at him from beneath the floppy brim of her felt hat, they had an innocent look about them, but he knew they were about as innocent as a passel of cottonmouths nesting in a log.

He turned back around. "Tough," he repeated, and touched the sorrel's flanks with his spurs. The horse responded with a quickening trot, and Lorelei held tight to his fringe.

"I'll have an accident," she said, her voice wobbly as she bounced on her bundle of damp clothes.

"You'll live through it."

She hit him on the arm. "You better hope, Mr. Delaney, that you live through the day."

"You better hope I do, too."

With that, he spurred the horse even faster. Clinging to him, she kept to herself whatever dis-

114

comfort she was feeling, but she didn't mind complaining about everything else that came to her mind. Most of her ramblings centered on men and their arrogant ways, but she didn't let the weather, the trail, even the absence of songbirds escape her discourse.

If she was trying to discourage him from taking her west, she was closing in on success. After the first hour, he wouldn't have minded a half-dozen bounty hunters riding up, guns blazing, just to break the monotony.

As best he could, Sam concentrated on keeping to the overgrown trail. He had no urge to wander into one of the thousand bogs that lay like hidden veins across the southern Louisiana landscape. The air was cold and clammy, and the surrounding wall of oak, cypress, and river birch, massed with a hundred other species of plant life he couldn't begin to identify, kept the going slow.

Throughout the morning the rain held off, and by noon she had worked in three more demands to stop, only one of which he gave in to, and that because both he and the sorrel needed a rest. No need in spoiling her, he figured. She'd get used to the luxury.

It was jerky and hardtack for lunch, washed down with cold water from the bayou he'd been following most of the morning. Lorelei disappeared into the brush while Sam filled the canteens. Grateful for the rest from her harangue, he gave in to unease when she didn't return within a reasonable time. He told himself there was nothing to worry about. Lorelei hadn't been reasonable since she'd laid down the cards back in the city.

Ten minutes crept by; worry edged into impatience. She was trying him, hiding out like that in the woods. He'd warned her against straying too near the mud banks of the bayou; never could tell when a log might turn out to be a hibernating alligator, and water moccasins and rattlers had been known to come out even in February if they felt threatened. Surely she was bright enough to heed his words.

Then again—He took time to load the pistol, then eased it half-cocked back into the holster.

A gunshot had him reaching again for the gun and hurrying toward the sound. Swift and sure, he moved through the brush, only the jangle of his spurs making noise that couldn't be attributed to the wind.

"Don't you dare raise that gun to me."

Lorelei's high-pitched and very determined voice rose out of the wilderness to his left, and Sam altered his course in that direction.

"Lady," a man grumbled deeply in return, " 'pears to me you ain't in a position to be giving orders."

Sam's mouth twitched, and he slowed his pace. The two speakers weren't ten feet away, behind a tangle of high shrubs and vines, and he was in no hurry to interrupt the confrontation.

"There are a dozen men who'll back up my orders. I'll bet they've got you surrounded right this very minute."

Lorelei had nerve, Sam had to give her credit. It took someone familiar with her voice to catch the

116

edge of forced bravery.

He'd have to remember how boldly she could lie.

Stepping through the brush into a small clearing, he saw her whirl toward him. Behind her stood a giant of a man, more bearlike than human with wild black hair falling to his shoulders, his cheeks and chin covered by a scruffy, gray-streaked beard. He was dressed in buckskin shirt and trousers, and he gripped a shotgun at his side, the business end of which was pointed at Lorelei.

Sam didn't miss the warm relief in the pair of blue eyes that greeted him.

"It's about time you got here," she said.

There was nothing especially warm in the words. "Didn't realize you were craving my company."

"I suppose the others are right behind you."

Stubborn woman was resolved to keep up her bluff. He looked to the man. "She giving you any trouble?"

"Yep." The man spat into the damp dirt beside his oversized moccasins. "Just about had me a squirrel for dinner when she comes tearing along. Shot went wide. Swamp is gettin' just too damned crowded."

"Guess you need to thin the population a little."

The man's dark button eyes blinked within the mass of wrinkles and hair that was his face. "It's somethin' to consider."

Sam holstered his gun. "Do what you think best."

Without a glance at Lorelei, he retraced his steps. He didn't stop until he was back at the

117

makeshift campsite where they'd eaten lunch. Untethering the sorrel, he was already mounted when Lorelei came tearing up beside him.

"You bastard."

Hands on hips, she stared up at him. Her cheeks had taken on a rosy tint, her eyes were dark with fury, and a half-dozen curls had worked loose from beneath the slouch hat — a good-looking woman, all in all, even with the smudge on her upraised chin.

"Son of a bitch is what you called me back in the city, but it's been bastard since then. Can't tell if I'm going up or down in your estimation."

"Down. Way down. You left me out there, and I thought you were worried about keeping me alive."

"Hard thing to do when you don't seem too concerned."

"Then, leave me here with the pepperbox. I'll be all right alone."

"Don't tempt me." He reached down. "Time's wasting."

She growled; but she slapped her gloved hand in his, and he yanked her onto the horse. "Hold on," he said. "We've got to make good time if we're going to make it to the Sabine before tomorrow night."

"Tomorrow!"

"That's what I said."

He slapped reins against the sorrel's neck and they took off with a jerk. She wrapped her arms tight around him, but Sam couldn't remember when he'd been held by a woman with

118

such reluctance.

With the sky beginning to clear and occasional stretches of clear, flat land opening before them, they covered more ground than Sam had figured on. When night showed signs of coming on, they made camp in a clearing by a small creek. He risked a small fire, threw down the blankets to one side, and opened a can of beans, which he dumped into the tin pan. Hardtack followed to soak up the juices, and he gave Lorelei first choice at the feast.

Almost gracious, she accepted the pan with a nod. *Hunger must be making her polite,* he thought, and he followed her example, looking away as she awkwardly balanced her food on the blade of the knife. She left most of the beans, and he downed them quickly, then washed the pan and boiled some coffee.

While he worked, she sat cross-legged beside the fire, her feet tucked under her thighs, and stared into the flames. She'd discarded the hat, and the light caught in her long, thick hair. When he settled beside her, he felt almost at peace, his private worries pushed to the back of his mind.

As they passed the lone cup back and forth, she broke the silence. "How much do I owe you for dinner?"

"Two bits ought to cover it."

"Add it to my account."

"Already have."

She stared at him. "You knew that man, didn't you?"

Sam had wondered when she would figure it

119

out. "A trapper. Been in these woods since before the Choctaw got sent up to Indian Territory."

"You also knew he wouldn't hurt me."

"Lorelei, I wouldn't swear what any man would do after he's been in your company more than a minute or two."

He couldn't keep from looking at her. Her lips were parted, all full and rosy and damp from the coffee, her eyes were bright, and he could see all too well through the opening of her coat the outline of her breasts which pushed against the boys' shirt. She'd have soft pink nipples that would tighten up if he ever got his tongue on them.

He shifted to ease the fit of his trousers, but his eyes kept moving, down to the flat abdomen and the bent legs. Didn't she know what it did to a man sitting cross-legged like she was with her thighs apart? Even a man who wanted to strangle her more often than not.

With a growl, he stood. Damned if she didn't set down the cup and stand, too. The top of her head came level with his chin as she tilted her face up to his.

"I rode after you, Sam, because I was angry. You'd ruined a wonderful night at the casino, you'd stolen money, and you'd humiliated me."

"Honey—"

"Let me finish. I'm not angry anymore. That's not to say I like you, but for some reason I'm not afraid of you. And since you've returned my money, there's no real reason to have you thrown into jail."

"You sure know how to sugar talk a man, don't

120

you?"

She waved his words aside. "I'm just trying to tell you the way things are." She lowered her thick lashes, then raised them again, her eyes wide and innocent. Sam was immediately on the alert.

"Why don't you take me to the nearest town? I could go in first and explain that you've done me no harm."

"Bounty hunters won't listen to such talk."

"But there won't be a bounty; that's what I'll explain."

"Several things wrong here. First, they get one look at you, they'll figure I'm not far away and be riding out, guns cocked. Second, there's no way I would trust you to go in praising my innocence. You'd have the law on me quicker than flies on dung. We both know it."

All the softness fled her expression. He caught her wrist just as she was about to land a blow square on his nose. He jerked her hard against him, both arms twisted behind her.

"So much for peace between us, Lorelei. You better know right now that I'm no more trustworthy than you. Bat those lashes up at me and twist that body up close and you're liable to find yourself down on the ground, and I won't be worrying about how much dirt you picked up on the trail."

"You—"

Sam covered her mouth with his, swallowing her breath along with his own, tasting the food and the coffee and most of all the sweetness of woman.

He'd kissed her to shut her up, but that wasn't

121

why he kept on kissing her. For a moment he forgot she wasn't willing, and he ground his body
against hers, bending his knees just enough to
push his hardness between her trousered thighs,
sharply aware of the throbbing and the insistent
needs that were both pleasure and pain. She
seemed to soften against him, and he let go her
wrists to cup her buttocks and stroke their soft
roundness; at the same time he thrust his tongue
between her teeth, roaming in the moistness,
brushing against her own tongue before probing
deeper.

Without warning, she went from woman to
wildcat, her hands pounding at him, then pulling
at his hair, her fingernails raking across his face,
her body twisting and turning, and he felt the toe
of her heavy shoe land squarely against his shin.
He was grateful she hadn't had much leverage, but
as a discourager of his amorous intentions, the
kick sufficed.

He let her go and rubbed where his face was
stinging, then looked at the blood on his hand.
Grimly, he stared at her; she stared right back.

"Still can't decide whether you want me or not."

She scratched at her arm.

"One thing about the dark," he added, "it's
kinda hard to see that rash you're so all-fired
proud of."

She kept scratching. "You snake, you spider,
you—"

"How about daddy longlegs? You didn't seem
overly fond of them."

"I hate you."

"Maybe you do and maybe you don't. The problem is, we've got to stay together for a couple of days more, one to reach the river, and the second to cross and get on to my place. Now, I can tie you up and throw you across old Horse's rump, and most of all I can gag you; or we can ride as peaceable as the two of us can manage and get on with this journey and get it behind us."

"You refuse to take me into a town? Even if I swear on my mother's grave I won't bring the law down on you?"

"Even if I knew you had a mother who'd passed on, and even if I believed such an oath meant something to you, I couldn't agree. Truth is, there's no town left between here and Texas. Just miles of swampland and woods and men a mite more dangerous than that trapper. You might hate me, but honey, right now I'm all that's keeping you safe."

Chapter Nine

As they broke camp early the next morning in a gray light, Sam and Lorelei came to a kind of truce. Standing to one side of the campfire, she was poking hair up under her hat while he knelt to pack the gear. Behind them mist rose off the creek into the cold, windless air, and the surrounding woods lay silent, as if waiting for winter to end.

"I won't try to run off again," she said, "if you promise to let me go as soon as we get to Texas."

Sam remembered the way his scratched face had stung while he was shaving. "Nothing to worry about there." He ambled over to secure the roll of blankets and supplies on the saddled sorrel.

"One thing more."

He turned to hear her latest demand. "You must never kiss me again." She looked him in the eyes as she spoke. Neither of them so much as blinked.

"Control my animal urges, is that what you mean?"

"Exactly."

Spurs jangling, Sam walked past her, close enough to hear an intake of breath, then moved

124

on to the campfire, where he kicked dirt onto the dying embers. "You must have been doing some thinking during the night," he said, turning to face her. Purposefully he let his gaze roam over her figure.

Despite his intention to intimidate her, he felt himself reacting to the way her neck rose slender and graceful above her collar, the way the boys' shirt and coat rested very unboyishly against the curves of her breasts, and especially the way the trousers outlined the long sweep of her legs.

His gaze slid slowly back up to her face. She stared back with eyes as blue as a summer sky, her skin smooth and satiny, her lips pink. He didn't know how she managed it, wearing coarse clothing and a ridiculous slouch hat the way she was, but she was as desirable a woman as he had ever seen.

The urge to kiss her hit him hard. Even if she did turn into a wildcat, scratching and kicking and rubbing her body against his as if she thought that would discourage him. He blamed the urge on the wildness of their surroundings and the challenging gleam in her eyes. Then, too, he'd been living a celibate life for too damn long.

"You want me to control my animal urges?" He stepped close. "Tell you what. I'll control mine if you control yours."

She held her ground and lifted her chin a notch. "My urges? You flatter yourself."

He watched her lips as she spoke. "Liar."

Her only response was a muttering that Sam couldn't quite make out. She was, indeed, a stubborn woman, he thought as he strode past her.

"I've come to a decision, too, Lorelei." He drawled out her name as he checked the sorrel's bridle. "I've said from time to time that I like a woman with spirit, but with all the trouble you've put me to, I'd just as soon kiss old Horse here."

"I guess you have to kiss something. Just don't do it while I'm watching."

Ignoring the smirk on her face, Sam mounted and extended a hand. She pulled herself up behind him. He waited for another smart-aleck remark, but for once she kept her thoughts to herself.

Lorelei was a cool one, all right, as well as stubborn and sexy. The combination kept her too damned much on his mind. Slapping reins, he took off down the narrow trail, ignoring the body that rubbed against his back and the thighs that nestled close to his.

The rest of the day went as fast as the previous afternoon, Lorelei keeping her mouth shut more often than she complained. Only one incident slowed the journey, and that occurred in early afternoon when they came upon the camp of a dozen Choctaw renegades. Sam had seen their kind before on his rides across Louisiana. Given the wildness that had been bred into them, they had chosen to go their own way rather than settle on the reservation drawn up by the white man.

A tightness around Lorelei's mouth told Sam she was nervous, but he gave her credit for standing quietly aside while he talked to the Indians in their own language. He ended up trading them her cloak for a slab of fresh beef. Carved off a rustled cow, he figured, but that wouldn't hurt the taste any.

The Indians took special interest in the pouch that was sewn into the neck of the cloak. Lorelei had told him it was a voodoo potion, but since he didn't have a handle on the translation, he said only that it was "white man's magic. Keeps away the spirits of evil." They seemed pleased to have it in their possession.

When they were once again on the trail, Lorelei came up with a criticism.

"That cloak belonged to a friend of mine. Since it wasn't yours or mine to give away, we'll have to pay her as recompense. For your share, consider the money I owe you as already paid."

Sam admitted that seemed fair, and for the rest of the day they made good time, stopping just shy of the Sabine as night was falling. After checking out the area, Sam put the beef on a spit over a low fire while Lorelei saw to a little personal cleaning in a nearby creek. With the sky clearing, the air had turned even more wintry than it had been at dawn. He knew the water would be colder than the looks she'd been throwing him, but he didn't hear one squeal as she splashed at the stream's edge.

The beef went down as easy as he knew it would, and so did the coffee they shared afterward. He was especially glad she held off talk. With each of them huddled in blankets on either side of the fire, they settled down for the night.

Maybe it was the satisfaction of a good meal, or the starry sky overhead, or just the anticipation of getting home tomorrow, but when she asked him exactly where they were headed in Texas, he heard himself answer, "To the prettiest piece of land God ever put on this earth." He wasn't normally given to revealing his feelings, but the words seemed to come out of their own accord.

"Tell me about it."

"You'll see it soon enough," he said tersely.

With luck, they'd both be sleeping in the cabin this time tomorrow night.

He thought about the small, blue lake that was his, and the home he was building on the rise overlooking the water, and the rich, red soil that would grow corn or peas or cotton or whatever he decided to plant. He wouldn't grow more than a few crops; cattle and horses figured primarily into his plans. With the fields of grass to feed them during most of the year and switch cane for the winter, he saw Dogwood County as prime stock country.

Pine trees—a million of them, it seemed—formed a border around his acreage. Newcomers to the Republic talked about cutting them down for timber, and about the fortunes they would make. Sam wanted to leave the forest just the way it was.

Mostly he wanted the title to all of that beauty and richness back in his possession. He'd earned it fair and square, coming to Texas March 3, 1836, the day after a rabble of farmers and merchants and lawyers had declared the vast territory independent of Mexico. Only problem had been the Mexicans under President Santa Anna had disagreed.

Caught up in the struggle, Sam joined the Texas Army, fighting at Goliad against the Mexicans and coming as close as a whisker to losing his life. More than three hundred of his fellow Texians did make that final sacrifice in a massacre that would haunt him the rest of his days. Sometimes in the night he could hear the volley of rifles and the agonized death cries echoing all the way from Goliad through the East Texas woods.

For service such as Sam performed, Sam Houston and the fledgling Republic of Texas government had agreed to give each soldier six hundred and forty acres. The amount was doubled if a man had a wife, but Sam had no intentions of forsaking his freedom, not even for something as dependable as land. He'd be satisfied with a single soldier's allotment.

Then Frank—his good old buddy Frank, who'd come near death beside him at Goliad—lied under oath about what had gone on during the brief revolution, and Sam's current troubles began.

Damn the sniveling Board of Land Commissioners, and most of all damn Bert Jackson, who'd sat as its head. Jackson owned most of Dogwood County, including the property on which the county seat of No Pines rested, and he showed a proprietary attitude toward the rest.

He'd play hell getting Sam's. To keep the title in his name, Sam had hired himself a lawyer to file suit in the district court out of San Augustine. The case would take some time to get settled, especially with his chief witness lying in a Louisiana grave.

Sam had already scouted around for other survivors of the battle. He'd even tried to find Consuelo, but not knowing her last name or exactly where she lived had hampered the search.

What to present as evidence was eating at him now. After hours of shifting about on the hard ground, the only thing he knew for certain was that if he expected to get his land back in his name, he'd have to come up with a plan.

Dawn found them riding north through the brush of the Sabine's high, red-dirt bank. Across the wide, swollen river lay Texas and home, and Sam was itching to get across. Using Hickman's Ferry, not more than three miles to the south, was out of the question. With the way it was used to transport cattle and goods to Alexandria for shipment to New Orleans, the ferry would be crowded, even this early in the day. Sam needed to avoid crowds until his troubles with his riding companion were past.

But just as there was more than one way to carve a cow, there was more than one way to cross a river, and he kept on moving north.

"How far is the bridge?" asked Lorelei after they'd ridden half an hour.

"You don't know much about this land, do you?"

"I know about eastern Louisiana, and about some places farther east."

"How far east?"

"About as far as you can go and still be in the

United States."

"You're at the other end of the country. There's not a bridge to be found. It may take a little co-operation on your part to get across, which there's no doubt in my mind you'll be willing to give."

"You don't have to sound so sarcastic."

Sam hushed her into silence. They were nearing the destination he had in mind, and there was no guarantee he wouldn't find a waiting party in the woods. The path they'd been cutting through the brush suddenly ended in a narrow, rutted wagon trail that meandered to the left toward the river. Sam sat still, looking to right and left, listening for signs of trouble, but all he heard was the cry of a mockingbird somewhere in the trees.

"There's a ferry a few hundred yards to the west," he whispered.

"Why are we whispering?" she whispered back.

"No reason. I hope." He reined the sorrel back into the woods and dismounted. Lorelei dropped to the ground beside him.

"You do understand that the kind of men who'd be after me aren't likely to treat you with a lot of respect."

"Men like you."

Sam squinted at her. "They'll yank every stitch off of you, and before long you'll be wishing that all they had on their minds was rape. Do you want me to get specific?"

"That won't be necessary."

"Good. Now take off those clothes."

"I will not!"

"Keep your voice down and do what I say. They

131

get a closeup look at the way those britches fit, you'll never pass for a boy."

"I'd have a better chance than if I rode down to the river naked."

He thumbed his hat to the back of his head. "Anybody ever complain about the sassy mouth you've got on you?"

"No one. Ever. They have said that I have a way of seeing into the heart of matters." As usual, her chin was tilted up at him as she spoke.

"Lies are going to get you in trouble someday," he said with a shake of his head. "Now, listen and do what I say, and maybe we can cross that river without either of us getting hurt."

He proceeded to tell her what he had in mind, handed her the pepperbox, then pulled himself back in the saddle. He threw down a rolled blanket. "Get back in the woods and try not to go crossways with any bears. I'll be back shortly."

Riding down the rutted trail, Sam wished there was some way he could make himself look different from the description that had gone out with the reward notice. Women had it all over men in the way they could resort to disguise. Best he could do was slump in the saddle and put a lovesick, worried look on his face.

He suspected he looked more like someone who had got hold of bad oysters than a man concerned about his woman, but he was doing the best he could.

The trail dropped sharply as it ended on the riverbank. Tied up on this side was the ferryboat, little more than planks of wood bound together by

132

rawhide. A low rail ran down each side, and a steering pole angled upward at the nearest end. The boatman, a slight man in faded, filthy homespun, a wary look on his bristled face, came slowly up the incline to Sam.

"Howdy," he said.

Sam attempted a foolish grin. "Shore am glad to see the likes of yew. My wife's ailin' back aways, and new to the area as I am, I warn't sartin jest how far I'd have to ride afore I come t' the river."

The man kept his wary stare. "Going to Texas, are you?"

"Yep. Come from Tennessee, just like ole Davy Crockett, may he rest in peace. Plan to get me some o' that land they're giving away. Land of milk and honey, or so I've been tol'."

"And bears, panthers, cutthroats and thieves. Not to mention the wolves."

Sam pretended to be studying the land across the bank, but in reality he was taking in the terrain around him. No one in sight, but that didn't mean there wasn't someone lurking in the woods.

"A wife, you say," the ferryman said.

"Yep. How much you charge to take us across?"

"Fifty cents apiece and double for the horse."

Sam furrowed his brow, thinking awhile. "But that comes t' two dollars."

"You can always swim."

The shuffle of footsteps to the rear sent Sam's gunhand edging toward the holster.

"Don't give the man a hard time, Gabriel."

Sam glanced over his shoulder at the speaker. He stood in the middle of the road, his burly body blocking the way, his hand loose at his side near his holstered gun. Sam came up with a quick assessment: a sharp-eyed, whiskered scoundrel, the kind who would pick up on news about the bounty and not hesitate to bring in his quarry stretched stomach-down over the rump of his horse. He'd use the woman, then claim she'd never been found.

Tipping his hat with his left hand, Sam kept the right near the gun. "I'm beholden t' yew, mister, for the kind words. The little woman's right porely. Lost our wagon a few miles back to some Injuns, along with most ever'thang we had." He looked back at the ferryman, Gabriel. "Some folks back up the road apiece tol' us about this here crossin'. I'll ride back to get 'er. I guess we c'n come up with the money."

He edged the sorrel around the second man and rode slowly up the incline away from the river. Once out of sight, he tethered the horse off the trail and quickly made his way back on foot, keeping well in the woods.

The two men were having a confab in the middle of the trail. "Think he's the one, Zeke?" asked the ferryman.

"Could be. Had a kinda stupid look about him, though. I heared tell this feller we're lookin' for is right smart."

"He's got a woman with him. That'd fit."

"We'll see if she's ridin' willing or not. He don't look like the kind that'd poke a woman and make her want it agin."

Gabriel snorted. "That would depend on what

134

he's got hanging a'tween his legs, now wouldn't it?"

"He ain't got much," said Zeke with a thin laugh. "Maybe we ought t' find out."

"You'll have the law down on me for sure, something happens close by. I got to deal with both sides of the river and I'm makin' a right tidy sum with this here ferry."

Zeke glanced toward the lean-to on the far side of the trail. "Yep. Yore livin' in luxury, that's for sure."

"Don't see you with no regular roof over your head."

Slowly Zeke shifted, trailing his eyes along the woods by the road, past where Sam crouched, and on up the road. "Anything happens, I'll make sure it's away from here."

"Now, don't get me wrong. I don't want to be cut out of anything."

"Then, you'll by Gawd do your share."

"If they're the ones. If not, swear you'll leave them to go on their way."

Zeke growled an assent.

Sam debated whether to take them both down right away, but gunshots might bring more trouble, and tying them up would only alert every bounty hunter in the country that he and Lorelei had come this way.

Retracing his steps, he untied the horse and made a fast ride to collect his charge. He found her pacing impatiently in a small clearing a dozen yards off the road, the pepperbox clutched at her side. This time beneath the coat she wore the

135

green velvet gown, which hadn't fared too well during the past few days. Her hair was knotted roughly at her neck, and she had thrust what must be the boys' shirt and trousers and at least one of the blankets underneath the front of her dress. She looked as though she were about to populate the Republic of Texas all by herself.

More than that, she looked. . . .

Sam searched for the word, but the best he could come up with was *vulnerable*. Their eyes caught and held. Sam saw she was glad he was back, and he also knew he was glad to see she was all right. The realization surprised him, and he felt an urge to say something encouraging; but she spoke first.

"About time you got here. I can't decide whether to wear the hat or not. What do you think?"

Sam couldn't suppress a grin. Here was the Lorelei who was always so free with suggestions. He liked her asking for advice. "Slap it on. It'll match the coat."

It took some planning to get her into the saddle. She'd removed her gloves—he figured they were part of the supplies she was wearing across her stomach—and her hand felt small and warm when she placed it in his. They debated whether she should ride astride; but Lorelei insisted that was something a respectable woman would never do, especially one about to give birth, and after some maneuvering she sat precariously with both legs dangling in his face, the pepperbox gripped under the folds of her skirt.

Something about the brightness in her eyes puzzled Sam. "You know much about women in the family way?"

"I've never had a baby, if that's what you're asking. It's just that—oh, never mind. Let's get on with this farce."

Sam could see she was struggling with private thoughts, and for the first time in their brief relationship, he felt a kind of kinship with her, one that didn't depend upon sex.

More, he felt protective toward her, a first for Sam, except for Blue, of course, and this didn't seem at all the same. He also saw the way of things from her perspective. She had ridden after him in a surge of anger. She surely hadn't asked for her horse to go down, or for her own men to start shooting at her. And she hadn't wanted to be dragged across the width of Louisiana any more than he had wanted her along for the ride.

Thus far he'd kept her away from harm and adequately fed and sheltered, but things were different now. This morning they were riding into what could easily be danger, and she had a right to know it. As they made their way back to the road, he described the scene at the river.

"It may get ugly down there," he concluded. "If we return to Hickman's Ferry, there's the risk of running into a trigger-happy bounty hunter, but there could also be enough tradesmen and families crossing to keep us from being noticed."

She stared down at him, her blue eyes widening. "You sound as though you're leaving the decision up to me."

137

He shrugged. "Guess I am."

"You've kept me alive thus far, Sam. I trust you will get me to Texas, if only because you know I don't want to go."

He could have kissed her for the smile on her lips; instead, he gave her one last warning. "If things don't go right, it'll be just me against them."

"*Us* against them," she said, lifting the pepper-box. "I promise I know how to use this."

"Could you shoot a man?"

"If I had to. I will not let myself be a victim."

"I've noticed that about you."

This time they shared a smile.

"Hold on," he said as he took the reins and began to lead the sorrel back to the river. "Look as though you're in pain."

"It would be hard not to."

"The hard part for you will be keeping quiet. Just moan if the occasion seems to warrant it."

She let out a cry of pain. Sam whirled. "What's wrong?"

"Just practicing. I don't want to let you down."

Sam stared at her for a minute, shaking his head.

He turned his attention to the road. Affecting a wearied slump and woebegone look on his face, he was grateful that his ersatz mate could see nothing more than his back. Shuffling in the dirt, he tried to forget her as he wondered what mischief was on the greedy but not-so-bright minds of Gabriel and Zeke.

Chapter Ten

Gabriel was waiting for them by the ferry. Spindly as he was with dirt-brown eyes set in a thin and weathered face, he showed no more animation than a tree as Sam led Horse down the narrow, rutted road. He didn't look like much of a threat, but such quick judgments could get a man killed if he accepted them without question. Sam had no intention of getting killed.

Behind him Lorelei rocked back and forth in the saddle, one hand on the pommel, the other buried in the folds of her matted velvet skirt. Only the sorrel made any noise, snorting disapproval at the whole scene, his hooves marking the passage of time as they struck the dirt.

Zeke didn't make an appearance until Sam came to a halt just where the ferry met the land.

"See you got the little woman. You said she was feeling poorly. Didn't say nothing about her bein' in the family way."

Sam turned a sheepish look onto the burly speaker, wondering at the same time how he managed to get his big body out of the woods and into the center of the road so close behind without Sam's ever hearing a sound.

"You knows how wimmen folk is," said Sam with an apologetic shrug. He ventured a glance at Lorelei, who stared back at him in bemusement. She had never seen him humble before, and he could see it took her by surprise.

"No, can't say as I do," Zeke snarled. "You tell me."

Sam grinned stupidly. "Don't like t' have sartin conditions spoke of. Better t' keep 'em private."

"Can't hardly keep it to herself, not sticking out that way like a mare about to foal. Could be she ain't too bright."

Ignoring the insult, Sam prayed his wife would do the same.

"She's a game 'un, that she is." He patted the hand on the pommel. "Don't hardly complain."

Lorelei groaned. "Husband, you want this here young'un borned in Texas, we better get acrost that there river."

This time when Sam looked up at her, he caught a gleam in her eye. The gleam faded as she studied the ground, a look of pain settling on her face, so realistic that he wondered if she weren't really suffering some kind of cramp. Then he remembered the practice groan.

"Wife—"

She looked back up at him. The glance that passed between them was one of understanding and brought him encouragement. They were working together, and Sam could see that short of a natural catastrophe, they would soon ride up the far bank, both of them safe and sound. Zeke and Gabriel didn't have a chance.

140

"Wife," he began again, "yew jest hold on up thar. Got t' give these good men some money first."

Gabriel spoke up. "Might have to charge extry fer the young'un. You said two people. 'Pears to me to be three."

"You got a point there," said Zeke.

Lorelei groaned. "Husband, we ain't got much time."

Sam glanced from one man to the other. "Either of yew ever done any birthin'? I'm gonna need some he'p."

Lorelei groaned louder. A panicked look settled on Gabriel's face, and Zeke took on a decided flush beneath his whiskers. "Get 'em on across," Zeke said. "Quick."

Gabriel stepped aside to allow his passengers to get on the ferry. When Sam pulled at the sorrel's reins, the horse jerked forward, almost throwing Lorelei to the ground. Sam shot her a quick appraisal to make sure she was all right. What he saw brought a moment of panic. The "baby" had shifted to an odd angle, its resting place close to her knees.

"The young'un's a-comin'," she squeaked.

"Lord a-mercy," Sam said, but he did not stop yanking at the reins until the sorrel was standing in the middle of the ferry. Gabriel jumped on board and grabbed for the steering pole, shoving off from the bank at the same time. Zeke remained in the center of the road.

"Yew ain't a-comin' to he'p?" yelled Sam.

"None o' my bizness," Zeke yelled back.

141

The current caught the flat-bottomed ferry, and they shot over the surface of the Sabine like a hog on ice, Lorelei moaning, Sam patting the "baby" while he tried to anchor it in place. Gabriel concentrated on steering them across.

They landed in Texas with a thump. Gabriel grabbed for a rope that was twisted around one of the rails, jumped on the bank, and secured the ferry to a post sunk in the red dirt. "Give me the money and ride on off, mister. I done what you hired me to do."

Figuring he had pushed the pretense far enough, Sam pulled a couple of coins from his trousers pocket, tossed them to the ferryman and, with Lorelei bent double in her precarious side-saddle position, led the sorrel onto land. Striding rapidly up the sharp incline, he halted at the top of the rise and glanced over his shoulder. Gabriel was already halfway back home. Zeke was not to be seen.

He looked up at Lorelei, who stared back at him from under the misshapen hat, a light of triumph in her eyes.

"I'm right proud o' yew, Wife," he said.

She took off the hat and placed it on the pommel, then worked her hair free from its knot at the back of her neck. The wind stirred the wisps that outlined her face. "I'm right proud o' yew, Husband."

Looking up at her like that, with her eyes sparkling, and her lips bent in a smile, Sam felt a twist in the pit of his stomach.

"Can you hold on just a little longer? I'd like to

142

get us out of sight. In case Zeke decides to ride over and check on the baby."

"I'll be all right," she said.

Neither of them spoke until he had guided the sorrel well off the road through thick, spiny shrubbery that pulled at his jacket and at Lorelei's velvet skirt. He came to a halt in the center of a protected bower. Fallen leaves, brown and dry, formed a natural carpet, and a stand of oaks rising tall out of the surrounding bushes shaded the small, dark clearing, letting through occasional shafts of light from the morning sun.

Sam looked around him. He had expected to feel good about just being in his own country, but he also found himself enjoying the knowledge that he'd brought Lorelei here safe, just as he promised to do. He wasn't used to considering other people in such a sympathetic way—he'd never had much cause to, and when he had, they'd turned on him—but right now he had to admit to a kind of peaceful pride.

It was easy to forget the hard words they'd thrown back and forth when they were breaking camp early this morning. They were two of a kind, that's what they were, bent on their own problems, thinking of themselves. But when they worked together, they made a hell of a team.

When he turned back to her, she had already removed the pouch from under her skirt. She extended it toward him, and their eyes met. A summertime kind of warmth slipped over Sam; the unexpectedness of it, together with its potency, shook him more than he liked to admit, but he

143

wouldn't have looked away for the world.

"Here's your child," she said. "Born in Texas, just the way you wanted."

The moment was strangely touching. He could tell from the softness in her voice that Lorelei shared the feeling.

He set the bundle aside, along with his hat and gloves, then turned to help her to the ground. He reached inside the jacket and took her by the waist. Without the padding, she was not much bigger around in the middle than the span of his two hands and she weighed no more than a whisper. How something so insubstantial could put a weakness into his knees, he couldn't understand.

Her shoes crunched against the brittle leaves as she stood in front of him. She made no move to put distance between them, and neither did Sam. A bird sang somewhere in the trees, and a breeze rustled the leaves; but he concentrated on the slight sounds of her uneven breathing.

Her skin was smooth and soft, with not a sign of redness except for a tinge of pink across her high cheeks. Her mouth was pink, too, and slightly parted, and he fought an urge to brush his tongue against hers.

His eyes trailed to the short, honey-colored curls that rested against the sides of her face, then down to the finely shaped chin, the slender neck, and to the curve of her breasts that rose and fell with each breath.

Looking back at her lips, he recalled the vow to kiss Horse before he kissed her. It was one vow he intended to break.

144

"This calls for a celebration," he said, his voice husky.

Something flickered in her eyes, but she didn't look away.

He let go of her waist. She tugged the jacket close to her body and watched as he reached into one of the saddlebags.

"Brandy," he said. "I've been carrying it ever since that trip into town."

While he searched the gear for the tin cup, she spread one of the blankets over the leaves and sat down, her back supported by the trunk of a tree, her legs stretched out in front of her.

After tethering the sorrel near a clump of grass just outside the clearing, he sat cross-legged beside her. A host of birds set up a chorus in the trees. Through the oak leaves he could see patches of blue sky, and a cool breeze, no more than would stir a feather, brought in scents of pine.

Sam glanced at Lorelei, and at the mass of yellow curls resting against her shoulders. Sunlight caught in the strands, and he found he couldn't look away. It seemed to him the curls were putting out the golden light all on their own instead of merely taking it in.

He poured two fingers of liquor into the cup, glanced up at her, then doubled the amount. He held out the drink. "You first."

"It's your country, Sam. I'll drink to your return after you."

He swallowed a goodly amount and, with the sharpness trickling down his throat, handed her the cup. Her fingers brushed against his; the warmth was a jolt stronger than the brandy. She must have felt something akin because her eyes flew to his and the pink of her cheeks deepened. It was nothing like the rash, nothing at all.

She took a sip and then another before returning the cup. Sam studied a trace of liquor on her lower lip. He felt a powerful urge to taste it and see if she gave the brandy an added sweetness. He held back.

"We had them going, didn't we?" he said.

Lorelei picked up right away what he was talking about. "Gabriel and Zeke didn't have a chance."

She smiled, studying a shaft of light as if there were something funny floating in its brightness, but Sam knew she was reliving the crossing.

He took another swallow of brandy; the liquor warmed his blood, but no more than sitting close to Lorelei was doing. Refilling the cup, he handed it to her.

She stared at the offering, then slowly lifted her gaze to him. "I shouldn't."

"Then don't."

She accepted his words as a challenge; he figured she would. Even when they were getting along, they always seemed to be on the edge of a fight.

She took a healthy swallow. Her eyes teared, and he could see her struggling with the burn in her throat. She set the cup down on the blanket; it tilted, and Sam grabbed the handle just in time to prevent a spill.

Lorelei giggled.

"What's so funny?" he asked.

"The look on Zeke's face when the baby fell."

"I wasn't too happy myself. If that bundle of clothes had fallen from under your skirt, they might have taken offense."

"They wouldn't have laughed?"

"My guess is no."

"I'm teasing, Sam," she said. "I know they wouldn't have."

Sam considered warning her about the dangers of looking at him like that, her eyes gleaming with a touch of the devil, her mouth curved into a kind of pouty smile. He decided she'd have to take her chances.

"You realize we haven't argued over anything for more than an hour?" he said. "Must have set some kind of record."

Her smile grew tentative. "You haven't done anything to argue about."

Not yet. The words were implied.

She fell silent, and Sam figured it was a good time for him, too, to keep quiet.

"Tell me a little about yourself, Sam."

He shrugged. "There's not much to tell."

"You wanted to get back to Texas so much, you must have been born here."

"Nobody outside the Indians was born in Texas," he replied. She kept looking at him with that concentrated way she could have at times, and Sam found himself rambling on. "I'm originally from Georgia, but I haven't been back since I was a boy. I'd never call it home."

"What about your parents?"

147

"Dead. Worked themselves into the grave." He hadn't meant to sound so sharp, but she didn't seem to notice. He grew uneasy talking about himself this way.

"No brothers or sisters?"

"Nobody. What about you?" he asked, turning the questions to another subject.

"The same as you. There's no family left."

"So what brought you to dealing cards in a fancy New Orleans casino?"

Her eyes flashed pride. "I was . . . *am* the proprietor. How I got there, well, when I needed a job, the owner hired me. I worked my way up. And," she pointed out before he could ask, "the owner was a woman, not a man."

He got the feeling she was leaving out a detail or two that might add flavor to the story, but then he'd been shortspoken, too. He picked up the cup. "Here's to being boss."

She drank after him. He liked the way she put her lips where his had been.

"You're different today," he said.

"I guess I am. I finally saw the truth in a few things."

"Care to give me a list?"

"I—" She stared at the woods as if she were counting the leaves. "I guess I could do that. The liquor seems to have loosened my tongue. I decided that you were forced into this situation even more than I was. After all, I rode after you very much on purpose. You could have escaped, only you returned when you saw I was in trouble."

She had begun the confession slowly, gradually

148

picking up speed, not slurring more than a word or two. "I don't suppose I've thanked you for that," she said softly.

"I didn't do it for thanks."

She shifted her gaze to him. Even with a little brandy under her belt, she had a strong, steady stare to her that he liked, not the sly-eyed, out-of-the-corner glance of some women he had known.

"And you came back to the cabin, too. Whether you would ever admit to it or not, Sam, you've got an instinct for good in you."

Sam shook his head. "You may know a few things about me, but you really don't know me very well," he said in truth, thinking about how he was hoping this sojourn in the wilderness would end.

"I know you've got troubles here in Texas, and that you were hoping Frank Knowles could help you settle them. I saw the look in your eyes when you realized he was dead. If there's any question about the shooting, you can be sure I'll testify on your behalf."

"I don't much like the sound of 'testify.' Sounds like I might end up in court, and there's no jail can hold me long enough for a trial."

She studied his face. "You mean it, don't you?"

"They'll have to shoot me to hold me. I've been a traveling man for most of my life. Only when I came to Texas did I decide to quit the riding and settle down. But that means out in the open air. Or at least where I can get to it when I want."

"With a wife?" Her voice was barely above a whisper.

He shook his head. "I'm not the marrying kind."

"I guessed as much."

He set the cup aside and shifted to sit close where he could face her. "That doesn't mean I don't appreciate what a woman can bring to a man."

"I know." She loosened the collar of her dress and fanned herself with her hand.

He brushed his fingers against her hair, tangling them in one of the long curls that fell against her breast. He leaned close, watching the way her lashes shadowed her cheeks.

"But I'm not certain you appreciate what a man can bring to a woman."

Chapter Eleven

Lorelei opened her mouth to respond, but Sam kissed her and the words were lost. The kiss was tender. He was going slow, just as he'd told himself he had to, but he had a tightening inside him and a heat that threatened to explode.

"Do you have any idea what I'm talking about?" he asked.

"Oh, Sam," she said in a whisper. "I'm beginning to understand, a little, but we had that agreement, remember."

"Maybe it's time we came up with another one."

He kissed her again, this time letting his hands slip under the jacket and remove it from her body.

He felt the dampness at the nape where the hair fell thick, and a special kind of warmth. He gave in to the urge to know that warmth better, and his lips trailed down her throat. Her head tilted to one side; lifting her hair, he kissed the back of her neck.

She had a rich taste to her. Kissing an intimate part of her body like this, he wanted to put his lips everywhere.

She sighed. He let one hand brush her throat and then down the front of her gown, his palm touching the tip of one breast and then the other. Her nipples hardened.

"Stop," she said, managing to sound innocent and aroused at the same time.

He licked the lobe of her ear. "You don't want me to."

She didn't try to deny it, and he worked at the closure of her dress. Once before, he'd done the same thing, tearing a few of the buttons in the process; to hold the front together she'd fashioned a kind of tie that took him a minute to unravel. But determined man that he was, unravel it he did, and he found to his great pleasure that she hadn't bothered to put on the chemise.

He shifted them both until they were lying side by side on the blanket, Lorelei on her back, the bodice of her dress naturally falling open to Sam's gaze. Her breasts were full and firm and pink-tipped.

Her skin was smooth against his rough palm, and her breasts swelled to fit into the curve of his hand. He stroked his thumb back and forth across the hard tips; her sharp intake of breath told him what he was doing to her.

He tasted the hollow of her throat and felt the pounding of her heart. His tongue trailed lower, over the rise of a breast and onto where his thumb had been. He sucked gently, then harder, and when she cried out, he softened his motions.

With his mouth taking in the delights of her breast, his hand tugged at her skirt until it bunched around her waist. She was wearing under-drawers, thin cotton that didn't disguise the

152

warmth emanating from her body, or the shadowy patch of hair between her thighs.

He held off undressing her completely; instead stroked her abdomen and the outside of her thigh, slowly shifting to the inside, parting her legs just slightly.

"No," she cried softly.

Sam persisted, moving his lips back to cover hers while his fingers continued their exploration. She parted her legs wider, giving a lie to her words of denial.

"Tell me you don't want me to stop."

"I . . . don't stop." The words came out slow as if she'd had to drag them from somewhere deep inside her. And then, "Oh, Sam." His name was close to a sob.

He felt her body tighten, then arch so that she could press herself against his hand. Soft little mewing sounds escaped from her throat.

It was exquisite torture, just knowing how she was feeling as she moaned and drew him to her, her legs parted to his exploration, her tongue responding to his.

Caught by her rapture, he worked magic with his fingers matching the rhythmic thrust of her hips, the heat between them building to the flash point of fire. With a sharp cry, she stiffened; then with an untamed shudder she came against his hand, the hot waves of ecstacy spilling over her.

He held her tight until the shudder died, then eased the embrace, but she continued to lie in his arms, her body pressed to his, her head bent against the crook of his shoulder, her only movement the rise and fall of her breasts as she drew in ragged breaths.

He kissed the hair matted against her face, then moved onto her cheeks. Tasting a salty dampness, he brushed aside the hair and lifted her chin. What he read in the depths of her eyes came as a shock. He'd expected to see smoky satisfaction; instead, he saw misery.

"I didn't really understand . . ." she said haltingly as she stared at his shirt. "I didn't know. . . . The women . . . they said they just pretended. I thought it would be the same with me."

Running a hand gently down her arm, he leaned to kiss her throat. Her pulse pounded against his lips. He could feel her softening, and then she was pushing him away, freeing herself of his embrace.

She moved with unexpected strength, as though demons possessed her, and when she had shifted free of him, she covered her face with her hands. He pulled them away, and there was the misery again, stark in her eyes and in the trembling of her lips. Sam let her go and then he poured himself another drink of brandy.

She closed her eyes, and he could see teardrops glistening on her lashes. He hadn't seen her in such a state since her horse died; he didn't take it as a compliment to his sexual skills.

Lorelei sat up, straightened her clothing as best she could, and stared at the twisting hands in her lap.

A thought hit him. "What happened to the rash?"

"I don't know." She finally looked at him again,

154

and what appeared to be genuine puzzlement flashed across her face. "I really don't know. Whenever a man gets close—" She hesitated, then said in a rush, "Sam, no man's ever got this close."

He wasn't sure he believed her, but he didn't bother to argue.

She let out a long, slow breath. "I lost control, and I thought I never would. Things have happened to me—" Her voice broke.

"Some man force himself on you?"

She shook her head.

"I just never thought a man could get me to . . . open myself up to him the way I did to you."

"I wouldn't call what you let me do exactly opening up."

She stared at her hands, then back up at him. "For me it was. I've never . . . well, *been* with a man before."

"You're a virgin?"

"It's not a dirty word," she snapped.

The pride was back in her voice, and so was the stiffness in her back.

She hurried on. "We can blame all of this on the river crossing and the brandy."

Sam stood. "Do we need an excuse?"

She started to speak, then swallowed her words as she pulled herself up to face him. Brushing the leaves and grass from her clothes, she finally looked him in the eye.

"Whatever it was, I'd appreciate your not mentioning it again."

"Happy to oblige."

155

She blinked once, and Sam caught the look of hurt in her eyes. Somehow she'd maneuvered him to be in the wrong. He wouldn't understand her if he tried for a thousand years.

"I'm going for a little walk in the woods," he said. "While I'm gone, you change back into the boys' clothes and be ready to ride. We're not more than a few hours from home, and I've a craving to get there as soon as I can."

He timed the walk carefully, allowing for a necessary cooling of his various parts and for an assessment of what was going on with Loving Lorelei. Okay, he'd accept that she was as innocent as she claimed. And that she had demons in her past, just the way he did. The trouble was, she chose the most unfortunate occasions to set them loose. The sooner he could make arrangements to get her back to New Orleans, the better off they'd both be.

By the time he got back, she was dressed and ready to go, the sorrel once again in the clearing, all the gear in place. She'd even tucked her hair back under that ugly hat.

What she didn't do was look him in the eye. He settled his own hat back on his head, pulling it low on his forehead, and without a word they both mounted. Lorelei didn't bother to hold on; instead, she grabbed the edges of the saddle skirt.

Throughout the morning, neither of them spoke, not even when they made a stop for water and relief. It was back on the horse, Lorelei holding on as little as she could. Sam didn't mind in the least; he contented himself with working out the

156

particulars on sending her home. Preacher could help him out there.

His gut tightened the moment he rode onto his own land. It *was* his land, no matter what the government said.

They rode through the stand of towering pines that marked the easternmost boundary, the ground covered with needles and scattered cones, the sky blue as paint overhead. He breathed deeply of the sweet scent, and letting the reins fall slack, he welcomed the contentment he'd felt no place else on earth.

"Sam!"

Lorelei's voice cried out at the same time she grabbed hold of his coat and threw herself to the right. Taken by surprise, Sam fell with her just as the crack of a rifle echoed in the trees. The two of them landed hard against the ground, Sam on top of Lorelei, the horse taking off at a gallop into the woods.

Sam rolled away while Lorelei hugged herself and gasped for breath.

"You all right?" he asked. She nodded, but he could see she was unable to speak. Keeping low to the ground, he tried to hold her, but she pushed him away, still struggling for air. At last the breaths came in short gasps and then one long intake of air.

"I saw a glint of light," she managed. "I thought it was a gun."

Sam reached for their two hats, settling his in place and holding hers in the air. He poked a finger through the bullet hole in the crown.

157

"I'm not one to say this very often," he said grimly, his eyes casting about for signs of the shooter, "but it looks like this time you were right."

Chapter Twelve

Lorelei stretched out flat on the ground, her eyes on the hole in her hat. "Is somebody out to kill you?"

"Just out to rob me. At least, that's what I thought when I left." Close beside her on a bed of pine needles, Sam shifted his eyes slowly around the horizon, but all he could see were trees and more trees.

"Maybe it's someone trying to collect the reward."

He gave that a little thought. "Could be, if the word's spread up this way, but the odds are against it. We're pretty far from New Orleans for a random bounty hunter. If they're after me in particular, not too many people outside the county know I've settled here. Probably just a hunter."

He glanced around the shaded area where they lay. Spying a fallen pine branch, he grabbed for it, stuck the hat on one end, and waved it aloft. Except for a breeze ruffling the leaves, all remained silent and still. Even the birds had scattered after the gunshot. Slowly he stood, continuing to wave the hat.

159

"Be careful," said Lorelei.

Sam grunted, unmoved by her concern. Lowering the branch, he hooked a thumb and forefinger between his teeth and whistled for Horse, who came bounding out of the woods a couple of minutes later. "Good boy," said Sam, stroking the sorrel's lathered neck. Grabbing the reins, he mounted and extended a hand to Lorelei.

She slapped the hat back on her head and took the offer of help. He could tell from the set of her mouth that she was making a strong effort to hide her fear. He'd tasted a little of it himself when he heard the gunshot and then felt himself falling.

"I don't imagine there's any danger, but we'll try another route," he said. "It's unlikely we'll run into anybody, but if we do, keep your mouth shut and try to look like a boy." He'd decided she couldn't fool a bat, but at least the pretense would give her something to concentrate on.

Without a protest or suggestion, she settled down behind him. Backtracking, Sam chose a wide sweep around the pine forest, this time coming at the cabin from the rear. This part of his land was rolling and covered with brown grass marked with the green shoots that foretold an early spring. Here he planned to run his cattle. The crops he finally settled on were destined for the far side of the lake.

Topping a hill, he saw in the distance the place he'd been picturing in his mind ever since he started on his search for Frank Knowles a month ago. He reined the sorrel to a halt. Lorelei kept quiet, which showed she had a real sense of how to take care of herself. One word of criticism and she'd have been walking to the house.

The first view wasn't much by city standards, but it brought a wave of satisfaction to him. One room made of rough-hewn logs, oak shakes forming the roof, it sat high on a treeless rise, square and stark against the horizon. He'd chosen the site because of the view and because up high like that a man could catch the summer breeze.

Inside were a puncheon floor, rock fireplace, a bunk, and a couple of tables. And a big rocking chair in front of the fire. He was especially proud of that chair.

Working alone throughout the autumn and winter, he'd built everything—walls, roof, even the chair. There'd been offers of help from the men at camp, but it had seemed important for him to do it all. He'd never owned anything he couldn't ride, wear or carry, and this first possession had to be right.

He planned to add a lean-to for storage, and of course a barn and maybe another room beside the first with a dogleg passage in between. He'd fancy it all up if he ever saw the need, but to his way of thinking a single man ought to keep things simple.

It looked beautiful to him, sitting high like that, surrounded by lower, rolling fields of grass and a scattering of trees, and then the mass of forests that covered much of East Texas. Right now the lake would be blue, reflecting the clear sky as well as the cabin with its welcoming curl

161

of smoke drifting out of the chimney.

Smoke—Sam cursed himself.

"Someone's there," said Lorelei. "I had the idea you lived alone."

She'd caught the problem right along with him. "I do."

He urged the sorrel to a slow descent, and they crossed the undulating sweep of land toward the cabin. Eyes cutting to right and left, he made sure the pistol was loose in his holster, but he saw nothing that looked suspicious. Except for the smoke.

"Give me my gun," Lorelei said.

He hesitated, then did as she asked. If she was the shot she claimed to be, she would be good for something. At least she was keeping quiet right now.

By the time he was making the final ascent up to the cabin, he could see the men—a half dozen by his count, edging around both ends of the cabin on foot, each of them armed with a rifle or a pistol, every gun pointed at him.

Even without the weapons, they had an unsmiling, threatening look to them. Hats low over weathered faces, most of them days from the last shave, their clothes a mixture of buckskin and homespun and store-bought and all of it dirty and crudely made.

They were divided evenly on both sides of the cabin, as if they'd discussed just who would go where before strolling out to greet him. Between them stretched the wall of logs he'd laid so carefully one over the other, patching the gaps with clay and grass. The stone fireplace rose from the center of the wall; he stared up at the ribbon of smoke.

"Sorry," he said where only Lorelei could hear. "Looks like I made a mistake."

"Do you know them?" She didn't put much force behind the question. He knew she was scared, but then he wasn't exactly riding easy himself.

"Seen most of 'em in town. They work for a man I've met a time or two."

"Who?"

"You're about to find out."

As Sam spoke, the men to the right parted, and another figure emerged on the rise. He wasn't more than a dozen yards away, but Sam would have recognized him from a distance of a mile. They'd last met at a meeting of the Dogwood County Board of Land Commissioners. Bert Jackson had been sitting at the head; Sam had been standing on the other side of the table, listening to the judgment that took away his land.

Sam didn't much care for being on the downside of the hill and having to look up at Jackson, but there wasn't much he could do about their unequal positions, at least not right away.

He reined the sorrel to a halt. "Hello, Bert. See you got the home fires burning for me."

Bert Jackson was taller than most of his men and better dressed. He made an erect and dignified figure, but the black suit didn't disguise long, thin arms and legs, and the paunch that kept his coat from meeting in the middle. He was

163

hatless, as if proud of his bald pate. Full jowls and cold eyes behind a pair of thick-lensed, wire-framed glasses didn't improve his looks overly much.

"You're a stubborn man, Mr. Delaney. You know the land isn't yours."

Lorelei gripped the fringe on Sam's jacket sleeve, but she kept her silence.

"That's for the court to decide," said Sam.

"Already has. Didn't you get the word? We posted notices and finally decided you just didn't care anymore."

A cold fist gripped Sam's gut. "Maybe you better tell me exactly what that word was."

"The judge ruled against you. Said the evidence showed you ran long before the first bullets were fired at Goliad, leaving those unfortunate soldiers to die like dogs. And then you had the nerve to claim you'd fought beside them. You're a disgrace to the Republic, Delaney. You've got no land coming to you."

"Frank Knowles lied. We escaped during the massacre. He was right there beside me the whole time."

"So you said, but when you questioned him at the board hearing, Mr. Knowles refused to recant his testimony. It was a transcript of that testimony that the judge relied upon."

"Frank was paid well to stick to his story. He had more money in New Orleans than he's ever had in his life."

Sam liked the look of alarm on Jackson's face. "You saw him?" Jackson asked.

"Yeah, I saw him."

"And?"

"And he's still there." There were some details Jackson didn't deserve to know. Let him worry about whether Frank would clear up his lies.

Behind him Lorelei remained still and quiet, so much so that he wondered if she had been frightened out of her breath. No. She was just behaving, for a change.

Jackson took on a calculating look. "If he's still there, and you're here, that can only mean he refused to lie for you."

Sam kept his mouth shut.

Jackson went on. "Or could it be he can't? You have a temper, Mr. Delaney. I still remember how you attacked me at the hearing." He rubbed at his jaw. "Did you shoot the man down in the street?"

Sam rested his hand near his gun, his anger like a glowing coal, ready to burst into flame at the slightest provocation. Several of Jackson's men stirred, but he ignored them. "My temper is something for you to remember, Bert. You're not keeping this land."

"Come now. What can you possibly do?"

"I'll go to the state land commission."

"I'm afraid it will not sit again until summer. President Houston sent out word. Besides, the court has decided your case. The decree was no different from the decision rendered by the Dogwood County board. You shouldn't be surprised."

Sam felt a frustration that matched his rage. "I was supposed to be at the trial."

"So we told your lawyer."

"He was there?" Sam hated the sound of his voice, bringing up points this way and having them knocked down.

"As soon as we heard the judge would be arriving, we let the gentleman know. Unfortunately he departed town before the first gavel fell."

"Under his own power?"

"I wouldn't know. He was, I believe, given to drink, an affliction he had kept to himself. With no one on your side in the courtroom—"

"The saloon, you mean."

"It is, unfortunately, the only structure in town large enough to hold court. If I'm elected county judge, I intend to see that deficiency rectified."

"Land commissioner and now judge. Is there an office you don't hold?"

"I found it necessary to resign from the former post, and the latter is, until an election can be held, merely a fond wish."

Sam's rage flashed cold and hot, and he wanted nothing more than to smash his fist into Jackson's fat face. "You've got the title, haven't you?"

"As you pointed out before the board, this is a fine piece of land. When it became available, I simply did what the law allowed. I bought it for the taxes owed."

"You stole it, you mean. You're a thief and a liar, Bert. And a coward." Sam dragged his eyes over the gunmen flanking the cabin. "Care to discuss this matter in private?"

"I don't care to discuss it at all. Now, you and that youth you've picked up ride on out of here

166

and there will be no trouble."

The "youth" growled deep in her throat. Sam's trigger finger was itching, but he steadied himself. If he were alone, he might be handling this confrontation differently. And maybe he'd be stretched out on the ground as dead as Frank Knowles.

Hell, maybe he ought to open fire and let Lorelei demonstrate the shooting she'd been bragging about, but he kept his sanity and his control. Somehow he'd beat Bert Jackson, but not by facing down a half dozen of his armed men. And not when he was carrying only a couple of single-shot guns.

Then, too, there was the woman hanging on to his coat.

"This matter isn't settled. You lie awake nights wondering what I'm up to, Bert. If you're smart, you'll keep your dogs here close by your side. Night and day."

He reined the sorrel away, wishing he had Lorelei sitting up front rather than to the rear, exposing her back to a bullet. He didn't think Bert would order anyone to shoot at them, but then someone already had. He figured it had been a warning shot, but maybe the gunman had been a sorry marksman.

He'd had his fill of riding slow. "Grab hold," he barked and slapped reins. The sorrel sprinted down the hill and kept on going at a healthy gallop even after they were out of rifle range.

Sam was too caught up in his troubles to give thought to anything else. That bastard Jackson was beating him at every turn; the knowledge ate at him like lye. He'd take great pleasure in bringing him to his knees, in seeing him snivel and whine. He'd take that smirk off his overstuffed face if it was the last thing he ever did.

"Sam!"

He realized Lorelei was yelling at him. From the urgency of her voice, she must have been at it for a while, and he slowed the pace, altering his course to a creek in a stand of cottonwood trees.

Lorelei slid to the ground right after him. "I was afraid you'd ride the horse to death," she said, catching her breath. And then, "You've got troubles."

"They're just temporary." He tied the horse close to the stream, kneeled to splash water on his face, then stood.

"They sounded permanent to me." Lorelei took off her hat and shook her hair free. Gone was the animosity in her voice, and she had a calculating cast to her eye as she considered him.

"Is there anyone besides Frank Knowles able to testify you didn't lie about Goliad?"

He liked her believing him about his part in the war. He'd needed her kind on the board.

"I've heard others escaped," he said, "but I can't find 'em. And chances are, they wouldn't remember me. No one but Frank. He must have been paid a hell of a sum to lie like that. Anyway, it's my problem. You'll be away from it soon. There's a camp between here and town where I used to stay. We'll go there and see what can be arranged."

She didn't respond at first, and when she did, she took him by surprise. "The man back there. Bert Jackson, you called him. What's his full name?"

"Never asked. Bertram, maybe. Burton. Could be most anything."

"Wilbert?"

"Could be. Why ask a dumbfool question like that?"

"I don't ask dumbfool questions. If he's Wilbert Jackson, he'd have the same initials as someone I used to know."

Her voice was hard, and Sam could see something was eating at her the way Bert was eating at him.

"William Jacobs was his name." The cold, faraway look on her face managed to take Sam's worries away from himself.

"Didn't you say you hadn't been raped?"

She leveled a stare at him that would have flattened a weaker man. "There are all kinds of ways for a man to hurt a woman."

"Can't see you being left at the altar."

She stared past him, looking at devils he couldn't see. "That's not where I was left."

"So what has he got to do with Jackson?"

"I think they're the same man."

Sam figured the days of riding and the little set-to between them this morning had affected her senses more than he'd been suspecting, but he tried to treat her words with respect.

"How long ago did you see this Jacobs?"

"Six years."

169

"You must have been a child."

"I'd grown up by then. I grew up fast."

Being reasonable was getting harder, but still he tried. "It's a long time to remember what someone looks like."

"They don't look the same."

Once again, she was taking him by surprise. Right from the start of their little adventure, she'd had the knack.

"Did I hear you right?" he asked. "They don't look the same?"

"William Jacobs was leaner and had a head of slick, pale hair."

"But the face was similar."

"No." At least she had the good sense to look apologetic. "Jacobs's jaws didn't stick out that way, and he didn't wear glasses."

Sam shook his head. "But they're the same man."

"They have the same eyes."

"You could see that behind those glasses?"

"Well enough. I've been picturing his eyes for a long time. And they have the same voice. I've been hearing that voice, too."

"All this riding has got you hallucinating. Once you get back to New Orleans—"

"That's what I need to talk to you about. I've changed my mind."

Sam took a long time to respond, kicking at the dirt, staring at the way the breeze played with the cottonwood leaves, telling himself he wasn't going to hear what he knew damned well she was about to say.

170

"You've changed your mind about what?" he asked at last.

"About returning to New Orleans right away. And there's no need for you to carry on and on about it. Balzac's will have to get along without me a little longer. I'm not going back."

Chapter Thirteen

Lorelei stood her ground, stared straight at Sam and waited for him to explode. Seeing the fire in his eyes, she knew the wait wouldn't be long.

"I don't know what you're up to," he said, punctuating each syllable with a pointed forefinger, "but you're going home, and that's that."

He threw the words at her, his body slanted forward as if he would drive her into the ground by the very power of his determination. In a less important situation, she might have given in, but not now, not with the opportunity she'd been thinking about for more than six years suddenly opening up for her.

"I can't leave, and I won't," she threw right back.

"I don't know what's eating at you," he ground out, "but I said I'd get you home safely and damn it, that's one promise I intend to keep."

Hands on hips, she held her ground. The position was awkward, considering his proximity, but she could not allow herself to step away.

"Don't sound as if you're doing me a great big favor. I'll go back, all right. Believe me, I can't wait to say goodbye. Just not yet. Not until Jacobs lies in his grave."

Sam was the one to retreat, waving his hand in disgust; she took it as a victory.

"Jackson, not Jacobs," he said. "And from what you say, they don't look anything alike. Besides, leaving Louisiana wasn't up to you, and neither is your return."

With the first flood of fury subsiding, Lorelei saw he was resorting to reason, at least the Sam Delaney version of reason, which meant that he was always right. She had to agree with him in part: his Jackson really didn't look much like the Jacobs of her memory. Except for the eyes and the voice. She knew they were the same man, and at the same time she wasn't sure.

Erasing all doubt, one way or the other, was imperative; she could never rest until she did. Once she determined the truth, she would figure out how to proceed.

Sam wouldn't understand. He dealt with nothing but facts and desires as he saw and felt them. Well, she had a fact he could chew on for a while. Maybe it would make him forget his desires.

Running fingers through her hair, she tilted her chin at him. "You haven't got the full picture here. I've said for a long time there won't be charges brought against you. I've changed my mind. You try to make me go back right away, and I'll tell everyone who will listen that you kidnapped me, raped and beat me."

"That's the stupidest idea I've ever heard. It'll come out sounding like lies."

"Oh, no it won't," she said, moving beyond all

caution. "I'll inflict wounds on myself if I have to. And there's not a jury in the world who'll believe you over me." The disgust in his eyes goaded her on. "Come now, Sam. You keep saying you like a woman with spirit. That's what I've decided to be."

Sam's hands tightened into fists at his sides.

Never could he know how she was trembling inside. She was handling this all wrong. She was handling *everything* all wrong.

She forced her voice down a pitch. "All I'm asking is that you cooperate with me. I won't get in your way."

"Ha! You've been in my way since you started dealing those cards."

The words cut like a whip. "You didn't think so this morning when I helped you get across the river."

"I wouldn't have needed to play the part of a fool if you hadn't been along."

"The way I remember it, you were feeling so good afterward you wanted to celebrate."

"Some celebration!"

Lorelei forced down the lump in her throat and stared at Sam's lips, scant inches from hers. Were these scornful lips the ones that had brought her such pleasure a few hours ago? They had brushed against her body in places no man had ever seen, much less touched. She'd asked him never to mention what happened between them, but that didn't mean she could forget.

"You haven't always thought I was in the way." She spoke in a whisper, forcing her eyes to his.

174

No longer brown, they were the color of storm clouds, but she saw in their depths more than anger; she saw arousal. He wanted her now, in the midst of this horrible quarrel. He hadn't forgotten the passion after all.

She could feel the sparks between them. Having discovered the power of rapture, she understood and shared his hunger. Her hands burned to touch his face. She knew no shame.

"Sam . . ."

His stare ate into her. She parted her lips.

"What in hell are you doing to me?" he asked.

He might as well have slapped her. Something died inside. "What am *I* doing to *you?* Why, I'm laying traps. Forcing you to want me so that I can have my way."

His sigh bared a bitter exasperation. "I've got more troubles than I can handle—a drunk for a lawyer, a squatter stealing my land—and now this, a woman to torment me until I can't think of anything else." A rapid tic worked fast at his temple. "If I didn't know better, I'd say Jackson sent you to drive me loco."

Behind them the sorrel bobbed his head nervously and stomped in the damp grass beside the creek; overhead a couple of birds set up a squabble in the trees.

Head reeling, Lorelei took a steadying breath and turned away from the contempt in Sam's eyes. Determined though she was to remain with her newly chosen course, she found fighting like this the most difficult thing she had ever done.

Her downfall had begun as soon as they got to

Texas, when she had let him do those things to her. Each touch had affected her more than she had ever imagined . . . more than he knew . . . more than she could dare let him know.

For the first time in her life she hadn't been repelled when a man got close. Instead of the rash, she'd felt hot and tingly and . . . and lustful. There was no other word.

She'd felt like a woman, and then she had felt like a fool, exposing such private sensations to him the way she had with those trembles, those tears. He had led her to pleasures she had no idea anyone ever felt . . . not like that, not so deep. The passion had penetrated all the way to her soul.

Now she was threatening him with terrible lies, and he was letting her know how little she meant to him. After these dealings with Sam, she doubted her spirit would ever soar again. In truth, she didn't like herself very much right now, but neither did she like him.

She forced herself to face him once again. "I wish more than anything in this world that I had never ridden after you." She raised a defensive hand. "Don't say it. I know you feel the same way. I also know only too well that once something is done, nothing can undo it. But some things can be revenged."

His dark eyes narrowed as he stared down at her. He looked hard and immovable with his grim, weather-lined face and rigid body so close, so overwhelming that he seemed to block out the sun. Muscle and bone, that was Sam, wrapped in leather clothes and leather skin. Nothing soft like flesh and blood, nothing that would include a heart.

"Is that what this is all about?" he asked. "Revenge?"

She thought of Carrie with her sunshine smile and remembered the way the smile had died; she also remembered her own months of fear and humiliation. And the villain who had caused all that suffering could very well be less than a mile away, still stirring up trouble, still getting his way.

These were the thoughts she must hold to. A cold resolve settled in her heart and in her mind. She would never allow Sam or Jacobs or any other man to intimidate her, not ever again.

"You've got something against revenge?" she said. "Call it justice if you want. To me, they amount to the same thing."

"Just what did the man do to you?"

"William Jacobs murdered an innocent, trusting girl. A girl who was my friend at a time in my life when I found myself very much alone. For that he must pay."

"I get the feeling you're leaving out as much as you're telling."

"I've told you everything that's important."

"Nope. I don't believe you have."

They stared at one another for a long moment of silence. At last Sam looked at the surrounding trees, then back at her.

"Seems to me we've come to what's called an impasse," he said.

"Seems that we have."

In one swift motion Sam removed the gun she'd

crammed inside the waist of her trousers. "Let's get out of here pronto. No telling where Jackson's men have scattered. Just because he let us ride away once doesn't mean he will again."

Lorelei crammed the hat back over her hair. She didn't say a word, not when Sam mounted the sorrel and pulled her up behind him, and not when they headed out at a steady pace through the East Texas woods. Wherever they were going, she knew the argument between them would begin all over again.

Two hours later Sam guided the sorrel through thick, protective brush into what appeared to be a small settlement. It wasn't much more than a shaded rectangular clearing in the woods with a clear, ten-foot-wide pond along the border to the left and a small cabin to the right. A scattering of oak trees along the edges provided shade; behind the trees impenetrable vegetation much like the thicket they had ridden through formed a natural outer fence.

A large hole had been dug in the center of the clearing for a communal fire, with rocks lining the bottom and sides and firewood stacked close by. Banked embers glowed red in the middle of the rocks.

The cabin was made of logs, the way Sam's had been; only this one had a more ramshackle look to it, and it wasn't sitting high on a windy hill. She could see a couple of tents deeper in the trees, and closer to the water, at the far end of the camp, someone had furrowed a patch of ground for planting. On beyond, a rickety fence surrounded a small corral, its inhabitants a swaybacked mule standing impassively in the center and a milk cow chewing cud at the far side. Beside the corral, a couple of chickens scratched in the dirt.

There were no trails to be seen leading in or out, and the thought struck her that riders could pass by within a few yards of the camp and, unless they heard a suspicious noise, never know it was here.

The occupants weren't visible right away. Only after Sam whistled did they emerge from the woods.

The first was a tall, gaunt figure in a worn, loose-fitting suit that a decade or so ago had been black. With gray hair uncombed and hanging to his shoulders, his face lined and bristled with more gray, he appeared to be in his early sixties. He came to a halt near the furrowed ground; from the hoe in his hand, she took him to be the farmer of the settlement.

He stood still as a statue, but across the clearing, a distance of some twenty yards, she could see a welcome in his pale eyes. "Hello, Samuel," he said. "Welcome back."

The words were brief and to the point, but they rolled out deep and rich, as if the speaker were used to addressing crowds.

"Preacher," Sam returned with a nod.

The man turned polite eyes to Lorelei. "Miss," he said.

A preacher, she thought as she looked away,

wondering if she would be given a sermon on the disgraceful appearance she made as she sat astride the horse, the outline of her legs shockingly revealed by the tight trousers.

Two more figures emerged. Shorter, squatter, dirtier than the first, they had a tough, grizzled look to them with their shaggy hair and beards and with the watchful look in their eyes. They paid special attention to her; but she couldn't say their looks were offensive, just curious, and for that she could hardly blame them. Except for a difference or two in their rough clothes, they looked alike; Lorelei couldn't begin to guess their ages. Anywhere from twenty to fifty would be as close as she could get.

"Howdy, Sam."

"Howdy, Sam."

"Al," he returned to one, then "Cal," to the other.

Twins? It seemed probable.

For a moment Lorelei thought she saw another man in the woods, a Negro, but the image was gone so quickly, she wasn't sure she'd seen anything other than the wind in the trees.

Sam dismounted. Without his help, she dropped to the ground beside him.

"Jet anywhere around?" he asked Preacher.

"We haven't seen him for days. You know how he is. We weren't expecting you. Were you successful in your search for Frank Knowles?"

"I found him."

"You do not look pleased. Forgive my prying, Samuel, but we had hoped you would return with

180

him."

Instead of with a woman. Lorelei could read his thoughts.

"He wasn't in any condition to travel," said Sam. "And he won't be. I'll explain later."

Preacher shook his head slowly, his long gray hair brushing against his faded coat. "An unfortunate setback. I suppose you've heard about the judgment against you."

"I heard."

"Then, you must have gone by your place first. Our esteemed land commissioner didn't waste much time in taking over the title once the mockery of a trial was complete."

"That's what I figured."

Lorelei cleared her throat, but Sam paid her no mind. Instead, he tossed his hat and gloves beside the fire, rubbed a sleeve against his forehead, and grabbed the sorrel's reins. Without a word about her or to her, he led the horse toward the water and proceeded to untie the blanket rolls and the rest of the gear.

She felt like a fool, standing there in the clearing with Preacher and Al and Cal staring at her and no one saying a word. Preacher dropped the hoe and walked to her side. "Pardon our manners, Miss—"

"Latham."

"Miss Latham. It has been a while since we had a lady in camp."

She knew she didn't look much like a woman, much less a lady, but she appreciated the preacher's attempt at manners, even while she admitted to an uneasiness in being around him.

Taking off her hat, she shook out her hair and tried to look as though she dressed in trousers every day.

"I hope I have not offended you in some way," he said. "I sense that something about me has upset you."

"Forgive me if I seem rude, but I heard Sam call you Preacher. My father was also a minister of the Lord. Or so he called himself."

"I see. It is a profession with which you are uncomfortable."

For the first time since early morning, Lorelei smiled. After being misunderstood for so many days, it was comforting to meet a man who understood her feelings and responded to them with courtesy. She glanced over her shoulder at Sam. He was rubbing tufts of grass against the flanks of the sorrel as if no one else were around.

Preacher introduced the other two, Aloysius and Calhoun, no last name. "They prefer Al and Cal. Twins, as you might have suspected," he said. Searching for a way to tell them apart, Lorelei settled on a difference in the fullness of their beards. Al was the shaggier man.

"Could I offer you some refreshment?" asked Preacher. "It's early yet for the evening meal, but I believe we have some cold cornbread in the cabin."

Lorelei tried to remember when last she'd eaten and realized it had been before dawn. "Yes, thank you. That would be wonderful."

He disappeared inside the structure. Al and Cal kept to their positions, their eyes on her. She shifted, smiled, and shot a few ugly thoughts toward Sam. In lieu of another fight, he was making this arrival as difficult as possible for her. If he thought a little discomfort was going to change her mind about staying in Texas, he didn't know her very well.

She stepped toward the pair. "I'm sure you're wondering who I am, and why I'm dressed this way. Mr. Delaney decided it was necessary to kidnap me outside of New Orleans."

Their eyes registered surprise.

"Don't sound like Sam," said Al, scratching his beard.

"He's a good 'un," said Cal with a nod.

Lorelei didn't waste time arguing. She caught them staring at her clothes. "He thought I should wear the disguise of a boy."

"Don't disguise much," said Cal, and Al agreed.

Behind them Preacher had emerged from the cabin to hear the brief exchange. A moment's distress flashed across his face, but the expression faded as he hurried to her side. Along with the square of bread, he had brought her a cup of warm milk.

"Blue milked the cow this morning. It's fresh," he said.

"Thank you," she said and made quick work of the repast.

When the last drop of milk had been drained from the cup, she looked up to find the three men staring at her. "Sam doesn't like to stop for meals."

"Would you care for more?" asked Preacher.

"No, thank you."

An awkward silence settled over them, and she looked back at Sam. Having finished tending to the horse, he was staring into the pond. Separated from him like this, she could notice little things, like the way his black, thick hair had grown during the past few days until it covered his neck. Too, he appeared to have lost weight since that night he walked into the casino. The night he changed her life.

It was strange, but he didn't look nearly so formidable as he had when she'd confronted him with her decision to stay, not nearly so intimidating as he was when he stood near. What kind of thoughts tortured him? She doubted they included her.

No, he was thinking about his land and about how to get it back—and maybe if he ever would. He might not phrase it just this way, but he had to be hurting inside.

Fool that she was, she felt a wave of sympathy for him. She knew she was trouble, more than he needed with his worries about this Bert Jackson. But how did he know she couldn't help him? What if she found a way to prove that Jackson and Jacobs were really the same? Surely a man who had dealt in white slavery would have charges still pending against him, even after all these years. Surely such a man could be thrown into jail.

And that would be for starters only, jail being the mildest thing she wished for him. What she really wanted was to remove him from the face of the earth, a wish that was pretty close to how Sam must feel about his own enemy. Couldn't he accept the possibility that they wanted the same thing?

As she watched him, she was transported back to early morning, to that grove of trees, the flush of a successful arrival warming her blood along with a drink or two of brandy . . . and along with the nearness of Sam. The remembrance of the kidnapping faded in importance when compared to what he had proceeded to do. It was a brief moment in her life she would never forget.

She wanted to hate him for stirring up hungers that must have been buried deep all her adult life. Hungers that Delilah had tried to tell her about, desires that she'd thought were only a sham. She surrendered to a moment of honesty. She had loved everything that he had done to her . . . while he was doing it. And she had yearned for more.

But when the passion had faded, she had never felt more alone.

Lorelei sighed. She must put this unwanted knowledge of herself out of her mind, as well as any sympathy that might weaken her cause. She turned back to the men. The twins had disappeared, but the man called Preacher remained to watch her as she watched Sam. Had her face revealed her thoughts? She blushed at the possibility.

"Would it be possible for me to clean up a bit? I don't have any clothes to change into, but at least I can wash my face and hands."

"Of course," he said.

He directed her inside the cabin. "Are there any

185

belongings you would like to bring with you?"

She thought of her bedraggled dress and under-garments wrapped in one of the blankets Sam had dropped beside the pond. Right now she would have given a Saturday night's profit from the casino for a simple homespun gown.

"I'll keep on what I have," she said.

"Maybe I can help you there."

The cabin interior was dark, with only a little light coming through the open door and around the edges of a buckskin flap that covered a lone window at the side. Beneath the window rested a long cabinet; a bunk had been built against the opposite wall.

The only other furniture in the room was a leather-bound chest by the door; above it on the wall hung a small tin mirror. The fireplace at the back was cold, and the room, with its hard-packed dirt floor, had a musty, unused smell.

She raked her eyes over the scene, looking for spiders, then pushed the worry aside. She had too many other things to think about right now.

"We prefer to sleep outdoors or use the tepees, in the style of the Indians," Preacher said, "but you will want to spend the night in here."

"Are you really a preacher?" she asked, studying the unkempt look he had about him. She knew enough about the profession to understand that they came in all kinds.

"Not anymore. I have retained nothing but the title."

Something in his voice stopped her from pursuing the issue. He opened the chest and pulled

186

out what appeared to be a wrinkled piece of brown cotton material.

"Blue's other shirt. It ought to fit you. The boy won't mind."

"Who is this Blue?"

"A difficult question. He's someone I found."

"Found?"

"Wandering about in the wilderness. As do we all, in our own way."

He made no attempt at further explanation; despite the echoing loneliness in his voice, Lorelei persisted. "Was Sam with you?"

Preacher shook his head. "I had not yet made Samuel's acquaintance. The boy and I were miles from here, in another woods. He was talking to a bluebird. That's what I called him, Bluebird, since he could not come up with another name. Among the men here the name has been shortened to Blue."

"Does this settlement belong to someone in particular?"

"To those who have need of it, although I doubt there is a name upon any deed. Among us, Samuel settled here first, and we are all his guests. Like yourself."

"You heard me say I was kidnapped."

"That I did. Answer me one question, Miss Latham, if you will. Has Samuel harmed you in any physical way?"

Preacher didn't realize what a complicated question that was. "Not really."

"I would have found anything else difficult to believe. If he brought you here against your will, I feel certain he had no other choice."

Which pretty much put her in her place. By virtue of his having discovered the camp first, the place was Sam's and these were his friends, and if she thought she was going to get sympathy from them when she couldn't get it from Sam, she was very much wrong.

"Thank you for the shirt," she said.

He gestured toward the door. "There's a small stream not far behind the cabin where you can have some privacy. I apologize for the poor accommodations, but we had no way of knowing Samuel would return today and with a guest."

Accepting the status he insisted on according her, she accompanied him around the outside of the cabin to the thick shrubbery at the rear. Pulling aside a tangle of vines, he indicated a narrow trail that would have been visible only to someone who knew it was there. Hat in hand, she followed, dodging the branches and shrubs that partially blocked the way and helped to make the path close to invisible. As she walked, she thought about the strange assembly in the camp.

A former preacher who carried a hoe instead of a Bible; a couple of short-spoken brothers who moved in and out of camp like grizzled ghosts; a mysterious boy who talked to birds. And Sam.

There very well could be others. When they first arrived, Sam had asked about someone named Jet, and there was the Negro she'd caught a glimpse of in the woods.

They were far different from the crowds of men she was used to dealing with at Balzac's, a world

188

away from the planters and workers she met when she visited Catherine and Adam Gase at Belle Terre.

She thought about Catherine and Adam, about Delilah and Ben, about the Gase children and the orphans she helped care for whenever she could. A wave of homesickness swept over her, not the first since she'd left the casino, but certainly the sharpest. For the first time she knew for sure she wouldn't be returning anytime soon.

She couldn't give in to the weakness. To do so would be giving in to Sam. She knew what he was up to, bringing her here to this isolated jungle with its strange assembly of inhabitants, and without a word of explanation.

During the past days he had been her adversary, her almost-lover, even her sometime friend. Because of recent circumstances, the roles had simplified to one. Unless he changed his mind about her staying, the two of them could be nothing but foes.

Chapter Fourteen

Preacher guided her beside a stream so narrow she could jump to the opposite bank if she wished. The patch of grass on which they halted, however, bordered a long, wide spot where the water had pooled against a natural dam of rocks.

"Do you think you can find your way back?" he asked.

She considered the question carefully. Balzac's would easily fit in the land between the stream and the camp, but the overgrown trail linking the two looked little different from the wilderness through which it meandered.

"I think so. If I'm not back in fifteen minutes, maybe you ought to come looking for me."

Alone, forcing herself to ignore the crispness of the air, she pulled off her shoes and stockings, rolled up the legs of her trousers and stepped gingerly into the rocky bed of the stream. The cold water and the sharpness of the stones shocked her; she might as well have been walking on jagged ice.

After a quick look around to make certain she was unobserved, she threw her coat and shirt onto the bank. Staying in the shallows, she made quick work of splashing the water over the exposed parts of her body, then scurried back to the grass.

The borrowed shirt fit her as well as the one Sam had purchased. Tying it at her waist, she stripped off the trousers and underdrawers, stepped back into the water for an even quicker splash, and was again completely dressed in less time than it would have taken her to brush out her hair at home.

Chilled, she sat on the grass to put on shoes and stockings and dreamed of a shampoo with lavish suds and buckets of warm water poured over her hair and trickling down her naked body. Now *that* would be a luxury.

She knelt at the side of the stream to rinse out the shirt she'd been wearing for days, letting her thoughts wander to a few of the things she missed the most—Delilah's sharp comments, a pot of bubbling gumbo, her own warm, soft bed. . . .

Suddenly she remembered Seabreeze; shamefully she realized she had not thought of the fallen horse in days. Over the gurgling of water and the rustle of leaves, she could hear the sound of a bone snapping, the roar of the gun. Sam had made her forget so many things.

"Who are you?"

Startled, she looked up at the gangly figure on the opposite bank. He was no more than a youth, at the most fourteen, in ankle-length trousers and loose shirt, a rope belt at his waist, heavy black shoes without socks on his feet. His face was smooth, fair and freckled, his pale hair cropped short except where it fell against his forehead; narrow, long-fingered hands hung at his sides.

He stood as still as the trees behind him, a faraway look in his brown eyes as if he had forgotten he'd asked her a question.

"My name is Lorelei," she said, sitting back on her heels. "You must be Blue."

"Lorelei," he said softly, then repeated, "Lorelei." He made it sound like a song. The third time he shortened it to Lori and nodded, very proud of himself.

Yes, she thought as she watched an innocent smile break on his face, Preacher was right. Blue was different. She stood to wring out the shirt. "Can you show me the way back to camp?"

He smiled proudly. "I can do that."

Arms and legs flying, he made a great show of jumping over the water where it narrowed back to a small creek; taking her by the hand, he set out, unmindful of the thick brush through which he walked. Lorelei protected her face and hands as best she could as she struggled to keep up with his long-legged stride.

They arrived back at the camp within minutes. Blue ran around the side of the cabin; Lorelei hung the wet shirt on a low tree limb and followed. Sam was standing beside the fire, which had been stoked into life; kneeling close by and erecting a spit over the flames was a broad-shouldered Negro.

"Sam!" Blue cried with delight. With a happy grin on his face, he looked around until he spied Preacher by the pond. "Look, it's Sam."

"Hello, Blue," said Sam.

The boy gave Sam a quick, unabashed hug before running over to Preacher. Sam shot Lorelei a warning look, the first attention he'd paid to her since they arrived. Was he telling her the boy was simple-minded? That she should go easy with him? That's how it seemed to her. How little he knew her or what she understood. She seethed at his insensitivity.

Or maybe what got her was the protective air he'd shown toward the boy when he'd never shown such concern for her. No, that couldn't be right. She didn't want to be protected by Sam. She'd settle for his being polite.

The Negro glanced once at Lorelei, then returned his attention to his work, spearing a skinned animal she couldn't identify onto a long, pointed stick and suspending it over the fire. With his wiry head of hair, strong-featured face, and skin as black as the night, he reminded her of Ben. Would he be as kind as her old friend? As quick to offer assistance and to praise her from time to time?

Of course not. If he said anything to her at all, it would be to declare what a wonderful man Samuel Delaney was and how she should feel honored to be in his presence.

Lorelei looked at the men and then at the boy, who was sitting by the pond, staring at a mockingbird singing high in a tree.

"Could I help with anything?" she asked, directing her words to the entire assembly.

"Stay out of the way," said Sam. No one else so much as looked in her direction.

She made a wide circle around the fire and walked over to Blue. He pulled a small block of wood from his pocket, and then a small knife, glanced back at the bird, then cut into the wood.

Lorelei looked at Preacher, who nodded slowly as he returned to his garden. The twins were nowhere in sight. Even the chickens had disappeared. Feeling conspicuously useless, she knelt to watch the boy.

From time to time he glanced into the tree, then back at the wood as slowly but surely a replica of the mockingbird took shape in his hands. He worked with remarkable speed, paying her no mind. She found herself fascinated by the skill of his nimble fingers and by his eye for detail. She'd seen cruder works of art on sale for high prices in the shops of New Orleans.

Just when the carving looked perfect to her, Blue made several finishing cuts in the folded wings. Returning the knife to his pocket, he carried the welcome-home gift to Sam and placed it in his hand.

"That's a beautiful mockingbird, Blue," said Sam. The boy smiled proudly and took off at a run to help Preacher.

Again Lorelei was left standing like an intruder at a dinner party. Turning on her heel, she strode past the cabin and into the brush, searched until she found a leafy branch that would serve her purposes, then returned to do what she could about her sleeping quarters.

She began by dragging the thin straw mattress off the bunk and outside to the late-afternoon sun. Propping both the window and door open to let in light and air, she proceeded to clear the corners and ceiling of cobwebs. She couldn't keep from worrying about spiders, but she didn't turn up a single one.

In order, she cleaned out the cabinet, swept the hearth and the floor of loose dirt and ashes, inspected the fireplace and chimney to make sure smoke wouldn't back up during the night, and without saying a word to anyone stole a small pile of logs from the stack in the clearing.

She'd been required on occasion to build a fire in the brothel; it was a skill that returned now when she needed it. At last satisfied that her quarters were habitable, she shook out one of the blankets at the edge of the woods, dragged the mattress back inside, and proceeded to make her bed.

When she was finished, she gave thought to going back to the stream for another quick bath, but with the February sun dropping fast, the air was turning too cold even for her. Why not try out the bed? Just for a moment. She could hear stirrings outside. Surely they would call her when it was time to eat.

She lay down on the bunk and concluded that in the muted light the cabin didn't look half bad. The next time she opened her eyes, she was lying in the dark.

She sat up with a jerk, heart pounding, and tried to remember where she was. All the bitter details of her situation came back in a rush. Shivering from the cold, she stumbled in the direction of the door and found that someone had closed it. Fumbling for the handle, she went outside.

In the moonlit clearing she could see Preacher and the twins sitting by the fire.

"Where is everyone?" she asked.

"Samuel's taking a walk," said Preacher. "The boy has retired to his tent." He stood and handed her a tin plate. "I hope you weren't disturbed when I entered to get the supper supplies."

"Not at all," she said. "I must have been very tired." She took the food and, without asking what kind of meat she was eating, wolfed it down and offered her compliments to the chef. "This is delicious. Is it pork?"

"Possum," said Al.

"Oh." Then, "Well, that's no worse than the muskrat I've been served in Louisiana. They kind of taste the same."

"I'm glad you find it palatable," said Preacher. "If you like, you can inform Wash the next time you see him. Which could be tomorrow or next week."

"You're speaking of the Negro?"

Preacher nodded. "A solitary man, Washington Jefferson. His name is the only thing he has told us about himself, but then you will find we are a close-mouthed group. We do not expect to hear any more of your story, and request that you do not expect to hear ours."

She would have had to be deaf to miss the finality in his tone. She looked at each of the men in turn. "I ask only one thing of you. Help me get into the nearest town."

"That would be No Pines," said Al.

"Only place in Dogwood County without a pine tree growing somewhere close. Spelled two words," said Cal.

Al nodded. "When they first got the town going, someone painted the sign running the words together. Trouble was, folks who could read tended to give it a Mexican sound. It come out sounding like a man without his equipment. If you know what I mean."

Lorelei assured them she did.

"The twins mean no offense, Miss Latham," said Preacher. "It's just part of the local lore. As you can imagine in this fledgling country, there's little enough of that."

"I'm not offended. I've seen and heard far worse." She looked at the twins. "What's No Pines like?"

"Never been," said Cal.

"But it can't be far," she said, surprised. She would have gone on except for a warning look from Preacher.

"The town is the center of civilized life in this godforsaken land," he said. "In Texas that means there is a general store for the purchase of the bare rudiments, a jail and livery stable housed in opposite ends of the same building, and two saloons."

"A jail? Does that mean there is law and order? That if a known criminal could be identified, justice might be served?"

"Justice is as rare a commodity in No Pines, Miss Latham, as fine wine in the saloons. I trust you are not thinking of bringing charges against Samuel."

Lorelei remembered her threats to do just that. Empty threats, she realized now, thrown out in desperation against his high-handed way. "If I assure you that I will do nothing to bring him harm, will you help me get to town?"

"I fear that is the one instruction we have been given. Surprising, since Samuel never assumes a superior position, but he has asked us to give you no assistance that would aid in your leaving."

"Then, I'll go alone."

"You would wander in these woods for days, and if some barbarian didn't get you, it is quite possible the wolves might. Or one of the panthers that roam in the wilderness. I'm told they're quite fond of hu-

197

man flesh."

At that moment the air was rent by the scream of a woman. Lorelei jumped. "Who is that? We must help her."

The men remained in place, unmoved. "Do not concern yourself," said Preacher. "It's one of the panthers I just mentioned. They cry out from time to time. You'll soon grow used to it."

Lorelei didn't bother to argue. As she studied the surrounding darkness, a heaviness settled in her heart. She should have known thwarting Sam would be difficult. Despite her demand that she remain in Texas, she seemed just as much his prisoner as ever.

After washing her plate and returning all the supplies to the cabin, she lit the inside fire and went to bed, where she tried in vain to come up with a plan to gain her freedom.

The next few days went much like the first, Wash returning each evening with fish or fresh-killed game, more often than not Sam showing up in time to eat. At first she attempted to confront him, but he simply disappeared in the woods. She concluded he would rather face panthers and ruffians and wolves than talk to her.

Unable to come up with an idea that might alter her situation, she decided that her principal ally right now was patience. She'd threatened him; once he got over it, then they could talk.

In the beginning she was allowed to help with the cooking, but when her stews tasted no better than the ashes beneath the pot, she was relegated to cleaning up after the meal. On her own she started patching the men's clothing, using a needle and

198

thread she found in the cabinet. She felt inordinately proud when they thanked her, and in the evening beside the campfire, she taught her sewing skills to Blue.

From the way Sam came and went and from conversations she overheard between him and Preacher, she knew he was going into town questioning everyone he could find about Bert Jackson. Obviously word of the bounty hadn't spread this far into the woods of Texas, but it was only a matter of time until it did.

One thing struck at her conscience—the worry she was bringing on everyone back at the casino and at Belle Terre. Somehow, without letting Sam know what she was up to, she must get word to them that she was all right.

She caught herself staring whenever he rode into camp, not just because she wondered if he had information to impart, but because he was simply Sam. After all they'd gone through together—after *everything*—she felt a bond with him; she doubted he felt the same.

Still, more than once she saw him staring right back. He'd look away as if he thought of something more important to occupy his mind, but she knew he was pretending. She, too, was pretending; in her case she let everyone believe she was contented with her lot. In reality, she had set up a pattern of exploration around the clearing, extending wider and wider the circle she traveled each morning when she said she was going to the stream.

Always she carried with her a stout tree limb. It was a puny weapon to use against man or beast; but it was all she had, and she was growing desperate.

After a couple of days the rest of the men treated her as though she had always been part of the settlement. Blue especially took to her and in exchange for her sewing lessons taught her the rudiments of woodcarving, but she could never come up with anything that didn't look as though she'd worked on it in her sleep.

On the fourth day, after hours spent exploring a section of the woods and realizing she had explored it before, she reached the end of her patience. When Sam rode into camp in late afternoon, she met him by the corral where he was rubbing down the sorrel. The day had been warmer than the others, the air sweet with the growth of an early spring, and she was determined to try a new ploy.

Planting her feet beside him, she said, "Okay, you win."

He thumbed his hat to the back of his head and looked her up and down. She was wearing her hair in braids now, and his gaze lingered where they fell across her breasts.

"Just what do I win?" he asked.

"A concession from me."

"Hot damn, just what I've been waiting for."

She ignored his sarcasm. "I understand I'm out here because I threatened you. Take me into town and I promise not to claim I've been raped."

"You may be speaking too soon. The way you've been sashaying around camp the past couple of days, you're liable to tempt a man past endurance."

"Don't be crude. The men have treated me with respect."

"I'm not talking about them."

She took a perverse satisfaction from the admission. "So you have noticed me. I thought so."

"Weren't you sashaying just for me? Tormenting me so I'd do something about you?"

"Sam," she said in a rush of hurt, "don't always put me down. I don't deserve it. I've got problems the same as you, only I'm not supposed to do anything about them according to your way of thinking. Everyone sings your praises around here, but they don't know you the way I do." In frustration she kicked at a spindly corral post, which swayed and held. "You're impossible. Forget the concession."

"Look," he said, strained patience in his voice, "I'm not ready to hear any more palaver about what you will or won't charge me with. I've got my hands full trying to prove Jackson set me up with a bunch of lies."

"Maybe I could help."

"How? By going around the county accusing him of being someone else? You'd be known right quick as Sam Delaney's crazy yellow-haired woman."

"That's ridiculous."

"Yep, sure is."

Something about the edge to his voice unnerved her even more. She took a deep breath and started in again.

"Sam, we've come through a lot together. I don't like it that things have deteriorated into threats."

"Then don't make 'em."

"You won't listen to me otherwise."

His eyes seemed to soften, and for a moment she thought he was going to change his mind about fighting her demands. But then the hardness returned. "You're in the way, Lorelei. The sooner you realize it and let me arrange for you to get home, the better off we'll both be."

"And that will be that," she said, speaking out before she thought. "We'll never see or talk to one another again."

He stared long and hard at her, his bark-brown eyes assessing her in ways she didn't understand. "What would be the point?"

The coldness of his rejection sent a chill to her soul, the depth of her reaction puzzling her as much as it hurt. She spun away and set a course for the wilderness. Her pace didn't slow until she was deep in the woods and headed for the stream. Male laughter, which she hadn't heard since she left the casino, echoed among the trees. Keeping to her route, she came upon a surprising sight—Al and Cal cavorting naked where the water was dammed.

They didn't see her at first, so intent were they on splashing water on one another. They acted like boys, not men, which she attributed to the spring-like warmth of the air. The fact that they were naked didn't bother her at all. With their bodies white as slugs, their legs thin and hairy, their stomachs sagging along with various other appendages, they were neither an attractive nor a repellent sight.

Al saw her first. "Lorelei!"

The two men scrambled up the far bank and took refuge behind the nearest bush.

"Oh, come on back to the water. You're not showing anything I haven't seen before."

She turned and crashed into Sam, who stood like a wall in the middle of the path. He stared down at her from beneath the low brim of his hat, a mean and wicked gleam in his eyes.

"For an innocent woman, you seem mighty calm. Sounds like you're used to seeing the men without their clothes."

"Don't be ridiculous," she said with a wave of her hand. "It's just that I used to —" She stopped. Best, she decided, not to explain.

"Go on."

She cleared her throat. Glancing over her shoulder, she saw that the twins had gathered up their clothes and disappeared. There was nothing to do but look back at Sam.

"Let me by."

"Not this time. I came to tell you that maybe I've been a mite harsh in demanding what you will and will not do. I was feeling sorry for you, all pure and abused. Or at least that's the way you've been presenting yourself."

He started walking, backing her up until she came to the grassy bank close by the water. Tossing his hat aside, he shrugged out of his buckskin jacket and began to work at the buttons on his shirt.

"Don't you dare," she said.

"You don't mind looking at naked men. One more shouldn't make any difference."

"But that was just Al and Cal."

"Honey, if you're trying to make things sound better, you're doing a poor job."

By now he'd finished with the buttons and was tugging the shirt free of his trousers. He tossed it to the ground beside his hat and went to work on the belt.

She stared at his chest. It wasn't white like Al's or

203

Cal's, nor was it brown like his hands, but somewhere in between, the skin taut against contoured muscles, sprinkled with wiry black curls and not a sag in sight. His arms, too, were contoured, and she could see the muscles rippling beneath the corded skin as he unbuttoned his trousers.

She swallowed, hard, and forced her eyes to his. "Go ahead and undress. It won't bother me."

His lips twisted into a half grin, but she didn't think he was seeing anything humorous in what was going on.

"And to think Preacher's been hinting that I ought to pay some attention to you. It's not a bad idea. Of course, he had something different in mind."

A flush stole up her neck and onto her face, but it wasn't the rash she'd depended upon for so many years; that seemed to have deserted her as soon as she crossed the Sabine.

He pulled her to his chest and bruised her lips with his. One arm imprisoned her while the other dropped lower until his hand cupped her buttocks and pulled her tight against his thighs; already she could feel the hard swelling of his manhood.

His hunger enveloped her along with his heat; there was no attempt at gentleness, no wooing, no soft words, just mouth and tongue and searching hands and a ragged breath mingling with her own. She panicked, pummeling her hands against his chest, but she might as well have been fighting a storm.

He broke the kiss and murmured into her parted lips, "Keep it up. I like you to fight me."

"I hate you."

His hand caressed her buttocks. "But you love this."

"I hate it."

"Liar."

Even as she denied her passion, she could feel her body grow hot, her breath turn shallow, the blood thicken in her veins. She wanted Sam to do to her what he had done before; she wanted to feel that rush of sensation that put her entire being into a glorious spin. She understood his wanting the same thing.

But it was all so harsh, so ugly with pain mixed in with the pleasure; his hands and arms held her in a cruel embrace, his words hard and brusque.

Trapped as she was by her own yearnings and by his demands, she could not escape. And then she thought of a way.

"I'll do what you want if you agree to one condition."

Something in her voice must have got to him, because he fell silent at last. She took a step backward, away from his arms, and met his hot stare. Her thoughts went back to those first days in the brothel and to the conversation she'd had with Carrie when they discussed a woman's first time.

"If there's tightness and blood—" Her voice broke, but she gathered her resolve. Now was not the time to act maidenly; in truth, she wouldn't know how.

"If you see that I really am a virgin, then you'll let me go into town. You won't make any attempt to keep me from talking to William Jacobs—"

"Bert Jackson."

"Whatever you want to call him. Is it a deal?"

He stared at her so long she thought he must not have heard the question.

"Is it a deal?" she repeated.

"I heard you. The problem is, putting it on a business level kind of takes the starch out of a man."

Such wasn't Lorelei's observation at the brothel, but then Sam wasn't quite like other men.

"I'm bargaining with the only thing I have to bargain with, Sam. It doesn't make me proud."

He reached for his clothes and looked at her in disgust. "You are the single most difficult creature I have ever tried to deal with, Bert Jackson included. Him at least I can figure out."

He turned. She was glad to see him leaving, she told herself. She had to be.

"Where are you going?"

"Back into town. I know a woman there who doesn't try to bargain or make any claims to innocence."

She watched him disappear into the brush. By the time she got back to the camp, both he and the sorrel were gone. Good, she told herself, she'd wanted him far away. She repeated the words several times.

Wash didn't show up that night, and supper was cold beans and cornbread eaten in silence beside Preacher, the twins, and Blue. Lorelei barely touched her food.

They scattered into the woods to their separate tents, leaving her at the cabin. She went to bed early, even though she wasn't tired.

Huddled under the blanket and staring at the firelight playing on the ceiling, she told herself she didn't care that Sam was finding another woman.

She was surprised that he hadn't before tonight.

Something about the night or the mood she was in left her feeling more alone than ever. She knew she had only to call out for help and one of the men would come running. But that wasn't the kind of loneliness she was feeling. Holding the blanket tight, she tried to ward off a chill that didn't seem to have anything to do with the night air.

At last she fell asleep, only to be awakened by the crash of the cabin door. She bolted upright, clutching the blanket as she sat in the bunk and stared at the figure in the doorway. A glow from the embers fell across his lean face, and her heart thundered against her ribs.

"I thought you would spend the night in town."

"Never did get to the woman."

"So you came back here," she said bitterly.

"Had an interesting talk with a man, though. Very interesting." He slammed the door closed behind him and tossed his hat on the chest. Just as he'd done by the stream, he shrugged out of his jacket and worked at unbuttoning his shirt.

"He had a very interesting story to tell. About a woman who runs a casino in New Orleans. A real beauty, he said, fair as an angel, but she deals cards like the devil himself. He hadn't heard anything about a kidnapping, but he did know something about her past."

"Sam, listen to me. I can explain—"

But Sam wasn't listening. Pulling off his shirt, he unbuttoned his trousers. Spurs jingling, he made his way to the bunk, his eyes taking in her loosened hair and her parted, trembling lips.

"Seems she likes to keep all the men at a dis-

Chapter Fifteen

"The deal's off."

Lorelei wished with all her heart she could put more force behind the words.

Sam kept on stroking her throat. "Heart's beating fast. I can feel the pulse under my thumb." The flickering light from the fireplace caught against the planes of his face, and his eyes looked as deep as the night.

The loneliness of earlier in the evening when she'd struggled for sleep seemed as nothing compared to the turmoil tearing through her now. Sam shouldn't be here . . . Sam had to leave, she told herself, but if he really did go, something inside her would harden into a sharp, knifing pain.

She dropped her gaze to his chest, bare except for the dark hairs dusting its contours, and on down to the flat, taut abdomen visible where he'd unbuttoned his trousers. She knew instinctively that lower beneath those trousers Sam would look better than any other man.

Again, her eyes met his. She shifted backward on the bunk, still holding the blanket tight against her body the way she would a shield.

"You frighten me," she said.

"Since when?"

"You *do*." Or maybe, she told herself, the fright came from the way her blood was pounding, and from the tingles of expectation that tremored down her spine.

He laughed, deep and without much humor. "You haven't been afraid of me since I held a gun to your head in the casino. Kinda strange, now that I think about it. A city woman out in the country with a stranger. Not much protection against him except words and tears. I've got to hand it to you, honey. You used them both well."

"I didn't *use* them. No more than I used the rash."

He did not seem to hear. Gripping her shoulders, he pulled her to her knees. She twisted to free herself, but the movement, a feeble gesture, had no more effect on him than her words.

The blanket dropped to the bunk mattress, revealing her nightwear—the petticoat and thin cotton chemise, its narrow straps her only defense against the touch of his strong fingers. With their eyes close to the same level, she watched him study the outline of her breasts. His hands were hot against her skin.

"Lorelei," he said, drawing out her name, "you're a beautiful woman, but you do like to play with the truth. Did you get a good laugh after I left this evening?"

"If that's what you believe, then you've never been more wrong in your life."

"Now, that's what we're about to find out for sure."

She took a steadying breath and caught the scent of town still hanging on him—the whiskey from the saloon and the stale cigar smoke. She could even smell the cheap perfume of the woman he'd gone to see, but then maybe that was a detail dragged up by her imagination. He claimed to have talked with only a man.

"I never was a whore, Sam. Never."

He leaned close to brush his lips against hers. Their bodies touched, and his bare chest branded her with its heat. "Let's get to the proof. Leastways, we'll find out whether I'm the first or not. A ride into town, wasn't that the bet?"

"I'll scream."

"No, you won't." He rubbed her upper arms. "Not unless you get carried away."

Lorelei closed her eyes. Everything was happening just as it had in the woods — Sam touching and talking and kissing, and a heat building up inside her so strong that she was ready to explode. She wanted to rub his arms right back and then let him embrace her and show her what to do next.

Her lips might form words of denial, but every other part of her throbbed with an unmistakable *yes*.

"Whose woman are you, Lorelei?"

Her eyes flew open. "No one's," she said, shaking her head.

"Maybe the question should be whose woman have you been?"

His words came at her in layers of insinuation and desire. Sam did things to her no man had ever dared, and she wanted him to because he was Sam.

For him, it was different. He was taking her because she was available, and because he thought she had lied. A separate kind of heat surged within her, the heat of anger and disgust.

"I told you before, Sam. There has been no one."

"Is it no one or everyone?"

His voice mocked her. She raised a hand to slap

211

him. He caught her by the wrist and jerked her against him, his mouth covering hers as he twisted her hands behind her. She tried to turn away, but she was trapped by a pair of determined lips and by an iron embrace. His breath brushed like hot velvet against her cheek.

She felt his desire burning its way deep inside her, but she also felt his fury; she had dared to fool him, or so he thought, and to arouse him and then close herself to his advance.

Oh, Sam, must it be like this?

With his lips soft and then hard against hers, she knew the answer. There was nothing she could say or do to stop him now. The more she writhed against him in protest, the tighter he held her and the deeper his kiss became.

His will burned into her sanity, withering her last rational thoughts into ashes; from those ashes rose a different woman, one driven by passion and wild hungers. She wanted nothing but to urge Sam on. Holding her wrists in one hand, he thrust his fingers between their panting bodies and tore at her chemise. The cotton gave way as easily as her resolve.

In that moment, with no recourse, no escape, and with every nerve ending prickling with anticipation, she accepted the inevitable, and more, she gloried in the certainty that the all-too-fleeting moment of rapture he'd brought to her in the woods would soon be hers again.

He broke the kiss. She took advantage. "Let go of my hands, Sam," she whispered against his lips.

"Don't fight me." His voice was husky, broken.

"I won't."

He did as she asked, still standing close beside the bunk, and she embraced him with a fierceness that surprised her. She lost control. Knowing nothing about the expected procedure for lovemaking, she let her instincts take over. Was Sam so strong, so demanding that he could propel his thoughts into her mind?

If such were the case, then she truly could not question the wild abandon sweeping over her now. Her hands caressed his shoulders, rubbed against his back and around to the corded, muscled outline of his arms. She reveled in the tight slickness of his skin. Her breasts grew full and eager for his touch, her nipples extended against his chest.

A low growl sounded in his throat, and she opened her mouth over his, thrusting her tongue deep inside him, feeling the rough texture of his tongue; and she answered his growl with a soft cry. His hands stroked her back, trailed down to the base of her spine, then tugged at her petticoat until it was up around her waist, and when he discovered she had nothing on underneath, he growled again and cupped her buttocks, holding her tight against his fullness.

The coarseness of his trousers rubbed at the precise point where she throbbed for him. The throbbing intensified, and she felt a moistness between her legs.

Such strange things her body was doing, and then she remembered a similar reaction to Sam's hand when he'd caressed her to ecstasy. She submitted to the inevitable, thrusting her body again and again against his hardness.

Just as they had before, the sweet spirals began. Sam lifted his head. "We're going to do it right this time."

He backed away. She grew dizzy from the sudden loss of his embrace. Her breath caught as she watched him finish his undressing. Spurs, boots, trousers lay on the dirt floor close by his shirt when he returned his attention to her. It took scant seconds to remove the torn chemise and the petticoat, and then he was lying beside her on the narrow bunk.

She'd had little time to view the strong lithe body that invaded her small bed, too little to see as much as she wanted to of his hunger's swelling evidence, but with even that brief opportunity, she knew she'd been right. Sam looked better than any man she'd ever seen. Never could she look at him as she had others and then casually look away.

She would not have thought the width of the mattress adequate for the two of them, but then Sam was half on top of her, their bodies pressed tight together. In truth they took up little more space than she alone had done.

He slipped an arm beneath her shoulders and with his free hand caressed her breast, lovingly it seemed to her, tenderly as though her body were something precious to him. He bent to kiss the hard tip. The thrill was as much a shock as it was a pleasure. Except for the pressure he'd put between her legs, nothing had ever brought her such satisfying sensations.

She rubbed her hands across his chest; his heart slammed against her fingers. She felt powerful to have caused such violence, and equally powerful because, with all that latent force within him, he kissed her breast with delicate sensitivity.

His hand moved lower to stroke the hair between her thighs, and then lower to the damp valley where she throbbed for him.

"You're ready," he said.

As much as she wanted him, she was suddenly afraid. She gripped his shoulders. "Sam—"

His expert hand guided the parting of her legs, lin-

214

gering along an inner thigh, burning a path higher until once again he caressed her with an intimate massage. With a husky moan, he settled his body between her legs and entered her fast and hard.

Pain caused her to jerk. He grew still, then held her tight against him as he began to thrust inside her, slowly at first, whispering, "It's all right . . . it's good," all the while the strokes increased, and she felt the pain subside and the tentacles of pleasure take hold of her once again.

Lost in the swirls of sensuality, she met his pounding body with her own. Just as she had in the woods, she gave herself to sensation, only this time it was better. This time she was linked to Sam. Tremors shot through her as she reached the peak of pleasure; in no more than a sliver of time, matching tremors coursed through Sam. They clasped one another, each drawing in ragged breaths until at last their bodies stilled. Sam continued to hold her in his embrace, his lips against her hair.

In turn, she held him tight, fearful that if she eased away he would disappear. She didn't want him to go . . . not now, not ever. The crazy notion whirled through her mind, all argument against it blurred by the heat of unwinding passion, and as it faded she willed herself to consider only the pleasure of the moment. For a too-brief time she was successful, the implications of what had happened between them held at bay.

But only for a moment.

Lorelei sighed. Once again he had brought her to a rapture that changed her very nature and altered the deepest convictions she'd held about herself. She was no wiser than anyone else, no more withdrawn from what she'd always considered the darker passions of the human race. With Sam she was all too human; with him she was all too frail. Snuggling against him, her head resting against his chest, she listened to his heartbeat and to the crackling of the fire.

He pulled the blanket over them and shifted his weight to the side, his hand lying against her shoulder, his fingers tangled in her hair. Beneath them, the straw mattress rustled. Lorelei could feel the bloodied stickiness between her legs.

She held very still. Perhaps it would be better if Sam could go away for a while and leave her to cleanse herself and to assimilate her feelings. Regret? Shame? She could summon neither one, not so soon, not with her body still tingling, not with an undeniable feeling of sexual satisfaction curling deep inside.

But she knew that both unwanted emotions would come in time. She also knew that even though he held her in a gentle embrace, the length of his body pressed against the length of hers, she was in some very important ways already alone.

"Lorelei—"

She did not respond.

"Honey—"

A terrible thought struck her. He was about to apologize.

"Is it necessary to talk so soon afterward?" she asked.

"In this case, yes."

"I'd rather not."

"Yeah, well—" His voice drifted into silence.

He began again. "I'm not very good at this."

"Not very good?" Purposefully she misunderstood. "How much better is considered good?"

He kissed the top of her head. "I don't know if you're making me feel better or worse." He paused a

moment. "I'd be lying if I said I understood everything that was going on with you — but I've never
been with a woman who made me feel more like a
man."

Lorelei tried to push away, but in the narrow bunk
there was nowhere for her to go. "I don't want to
hear about your other women," she said, stiffening in
his arms.

"And you don't have any other men to talk about.
I thought that you did."

"I told you there hadn't been any others." The
words came out as a complaint; she regretted them
right away.

"My trouble is I can't always tell when you're
speaking the truth."

"Sam, I really don't want to talk right now."

"Did I hurt you?"

She sighed impatiently. "Anybody ever tell you
you're stubborn?"

"One person especially, and on a regular basis. I'm
holding her right now."

One of the logs popped like a pistol in the fire.
Lorelei jumped, and Sam stroked her shoulder.

"You're safe with me," he said, then added,
"That's a stupid claim, considering what I just did."

She held still and silent, fearful of what Sam might
say next and of what he might not say.

"I guess maybe that man in town was talking about
some other yellow-haired card dealer."

"He had the right woman," said Lorelei. "He just
didn't understand the details of my past."

"Want to tell me about them?"

She considered the question. "Only a few people
know."

He kept quiet, and as she listened to his even

breathing and felt the stroke of his hand, she saw that she very much wanted to let him know a little about herself. Maybe in the telling she could reach a better understanding of herself, and maybe she wouldn't feel quite so alone.

Besides, Sam really was being gentle—almost caring—and he was putting her in a trusting frame of mind.

She started with her father and moved fast to the time when she and Carrie left Boston, including William Jacobs's part in the plan, and their arrival in New Orleans. The months in the brothel she barely touched on, but she could tell from the way Sam held her and muttered an occasional obscenity that he caught on to what she wasn't saying as much as to what she was.

The first years with Catherine and Adam Gase, and then taking over the casino—these she told in greater detail because they were happier times.

"I was hoping to be a big success," she said.

"And then Sam Delaney comes marching in with a gun hidden in his boot."

"I didn't tell you all this to get your pity."

"Good thing because you haven't got it. Truth is I'm proud of you. I'm just not very proud of myself."

"How could you guess I'd have such a background? It's more than a little improbable."

"You won't get an argument from me."

"For a change." She found herself smiling, and then laughing, soft and low but laughing all the same. She'd never had such a reaction before, not when she was thinking about all that had happened to her. Maybe making love had addled her brains.

Sam lifted her chin and kissed her. "You're quite a woman, Lorelei Latham."

218

She felt inordinately proud.

"I guess you were saving yourself for a husband," he went on. "A lot of women do."

The pride and laughter died. "What are you getting at?"

"That maybe I messed things up for you, being so sure of myself and wanting you so much that I saw things the way I wanted them to be."

So he *did* pity her, whether he realized it or not. "You deflowered me, Sam, which in a way I bargained for, but it's not fatal. Don't forget that man in town. Anybody who knows anything about me believes it happened long ago."

"Except that it didn't."

She could sense he was struggling with his conscience, which was something she hadn't known he possessed. If taking her virginity made him uncomfortable, then so be it. She was uncomfortable remembering how she had sworn never to enjoy the occasion. The reality was she had never enjoyed anything more in her life.

"I told you I wasn't a marrying man," he said. "Remember? Could be I didn't know what I was talking about."

The conversation was taking an alarming turn, one that Lorelei had not expected. "Sam—" she began.

"I want you to hear me out," he said. "We fight a lot, but I guess most couples do."

She thought of Catherine and Adam, of Delilah and Ben. "Not all of them. Besides, we're not a couple."

He went on as though she had not interrupted.

"I've been doing some thinking." He brought the words out slowly. "Once I get that title back, the house could get kind of lonely."

And so could a casino bedroom, she started to say. Was Sam really offering her something else? She held herself very still and allowed her imagination to roam. Marriage . . . a home of her own . . . children. She'd someday wanted these very things, only she'd been after a man who respected her. A man who would leave her alone.

On neither count would Sam fill the requirements.

And now that she'd discovered what Delilah had been talking about, she also wanted a man who loved her the way Adam loved Catherine, a man she could love the way Delilah loved Ben. As new as the concept was — and probably unattainable — she accepted it right away.

Which meant she couldn't accept Sam . . . if he ever managed to put what he was suggesting into the form of a question. A few minutes ago she'd been thinking romantic thoughts about his never leaving, but the idea had been vague, her mind as well as her body still heated from his lovemaking. Both mind and body were cooling fast, and she was left with the hollow sensation that came with loneliness, even though he continued to hold her against him.

She eased from his arms and from the bunk. He remained stretched out on his side against the far edge of the mattress, his elbow bent, his upper body raised. She gathered her undergarments from the floor and quickly donned them, pushing aside the longing to cleanse herself from the bowl of water by the door. As she pulled the torn chemise across her breasts, she knew Sam watched her movements, knew he could see the trembling of her hands.

She looked down, and her eye was caught by the firelight reflected in Sam's spurs. Beside them lay his shirt, the buckskin trousers, the tooled-leather boots.

She remembered the way he'd looked in them as he stood in the casino doorway, and the way she'd assessed him as Trouble.

In her innocence, she'd had no idea how much trouble a man could be.

"Lorelei—"

She met his stare, ignoring how the blanket had dropped to his waist to reveal the expanse of his chest and of his muscled arms.

"Don't make more of tonight than it deserves Sam."

"You want me to believe it means nothing to you?"

"If I were to say such a thing, you'd know me for sure to be a liar. It means a great deal. But it doesn't call for a lot of promises that you'd never be able to keep."

She gripped her chemise tightly. "If you don't mind, I'd like for you to go now."

He continued to stare at her, not saying anything, not revealing in the set of his mouth or in his eyes what was running through his mind.

At last he eased from the bunk and reached for his shirt, slipping it on as quickly as he had taken it off. She turned toward the fire, but she could hear when he pulled on his trousers, then his boots.

His spurs jingled, and she turned around. He was holding them loosely in one hand, his arms lank at his sides. His shirt was open and hung outside his trousers. She stared at the bared column of his chest, at the curls of hair still damp with perspiration. Was the sweat from his body or from hers?

Her eyes moved up quickly to meet his, and her heart caught in her throat. What kind of hold did he have over her? Was it truly only temporary?

Of course it was. It had to be.

She forced herself to speak. "There is one promise we shouldn't forget. We had a deal. You owe me a trip to town."

Something flickered in his eyes, but he did not respond. She knew that as much as ever he didn't want her to make that trip. What he didn't realize, even after hearing her story, was that she had no choice.

She shifted nervously, but she could not back down. "I'd like to leave early tomorrow."

Even with his silence, his disapproval filled the room as much as the heat from the fire. But she knew he would agree to take her. In his own special way, Sam was an honorable man.

For some reason the notion brought her close to tears. Stupid woman's tears, coming as they did when she was standing away from him, for once in control.

She blinked the tears away.

"Early," he said.

She nodded.

"You got it."

She tried to see in the sharp lines of his face a sign of the tenderness he'd shown her in bed. There was no tenderness to be seen.

He strode past her and let himself out. She turned in time to see a patch of inky night before the door closed behind him, and to feel a brief rush of cold air. She hugged herself. She'd be with him again soon, she told herself, and admitted the thought gave her a moment's peace.

Early meant she needed as much sleep as the rest of the night offered, and she shifted her attention to a hasty cleansing and then, reluctantly, to the bunk.

Crawling beneath the blanket, she stretched full length on the mattress. She must not think about what had taken place a few minutes ago. She must clear her mind of Sam. But how could she when the warmth of his body still clung to the covers and when each breath she inhaled was filled with the scent of him?

Worse, she could feel the touch of his hand still on her body. Would she ever feel his hands again?

"No," she whispered, again and again, and the word became a litany as she settled into sleep.

Chapter Sixteen

Hearing voices around the campfire early the next morning, Lorelei shook off the drowsiness of the night's wretched sleep and, forcing herself to think only of the journey into town, quickly pulled on her shirt and trousers.

She walked out of the cabin into the dry, cold morning to see she was the last to get up. Sam was explaining to Preacher that she had several things to do in town and he had consented to take her. Listening to his rich, deep voice, she felt all the tensions of the previous night return in a rush.

He didn't look her way across the campfire, an omission for which she was very much grateful, but she couldn't keep from glancing at him out of the corner of her eye. Wearing the usual fringed jacket and buckskin trousers and tooled-leather boots, silver spurs in place, a shock of black hair falling carelessly across his forehead, his face clean-shaven and bronzed from days in the sun, he looked lean and rugged and ready for whatever the day might present.

How dare he look so put-together-right this early in the morning when her hair was a mass of untamed curls, her shirt wrinkled and trousers tight where she

MORE PASSION AND ADVENTURE AWAIT... YOUR TRIP TO A BIG ADVENTUROUS WORLD BEGINS WHEN YOU ACCEPT YOUR FIRST 4 NOVELS ABSOLUTELY *FREE*
(AN $18.00 VALUE)

Accept your Free gift and start to experience more of the passion and adventure you like in a historical romance novel. Each Zebra novel is filled with proud men, spirited women and tempestuous love that you'll remember long after you turn the last page.

Zebra Historical Romances are the finest novels of their kind. They are written by authors who really know how to weave tales of romance and adventure in the historical settings you love. You'll feel like you've actually gone back in time with the thrilling stories that each Zebra novel offers.

GET YOUR FREE GIFT WITH THE START OF YOUR HOME SUBSCRIPTION

Our readers tell us that these books sell out very fast in book stores and often they miss the newest titles. So Zebra has made arrangements for you to receive the four newest novels published each month.

You'll be guaranteed that you'll never miss a title, and home delivery is so convenient. And to show you just how easy it is to get Zebra Historical Romances, we'll send you your first 4 books absolutely FREE! Our gift to you just for trying our home subscription service.

BIG SAVINGS AND FREE HOME DELIVERY

Each month, you'll receive the four newest titles as soon as they are published. You'll probably receive them even before the bookstores do. What's more, you may preview these exciting novels free for 10 days. If you like them as much as we think you will, just pay the low preferred subscriber's price of just $3.75 each. *You'll save $3.00 each month off the publisher's price.* AND, your savings are even greater because there are never any shipping, handling or other hidden charges—FREE Home Delivery. Of course you can return any shipment within 10 days for full credit, no questions asked. There is no minimum number of books you must buy.

GET
FOUR
FREE
BOOKS
(AN $18.00 VALUE)

ZEBRA HOME SUBSCRIPTION
SERVICE, INC.
P.O. Box 5214
120 BRIGHTON ROAD
CLIFTON, NEW JERSEY 07015-5214

didn't want them to be tight, her face most certainly bearing evidence of a misspent night?

She licked her lips and wondered if they still appeared swollen from his kisses. A memory or two of exactly where he had kissed cut into her thoughts. Lowering her eyes, she felt a blush steal across her cheeks. She forced the images from her mind and concentrated on thinking about town.

"It's a long ride," Preacher was saying. His faded gray eyes took in the two of them as they stood on either side of the fire. "You will require an adequate breakfast," he added and gave his attention to turning out a pan of biscuits.

Before she could protest that she wasn't hungry, Al and Cal walked up with an offer to work on the inside of the cabin if she could come up with something for them to do. She couldn't think of anything except maybe the laying of a plank floor, which seemed a bit involved since she knew her stay would end soon.

She thanked them for the offer. While she waited for the biscuits, Blue carved her a bird out of a block of soft pine. She knelt with him by the pond and watched him work, but her mind was elsewhere. She didn't have to be a genius to realize that the entire camp knew things had changed between her and Sam.

How much did they know? Blue was reacting to the tension in the air, but as for the others, she could only hope that if they had heard Sam entering or leaving the cabin in the middle of the night, they'd drawn some inaccurate conclusions.

It wasn't much of a hope. Sam didn't look at her, and she didn't look at him, at least not directly; but from the way they were ignoring one another so shortly before the journey, it was obvious that something was going on. Considering the fact they were a healthy man and woman thrown into isolated proximity, the choices for what that something could be narrowed fast.

Waiting and watching and thinking, Lorelei kept her outside calm, but inside she was as edgy as ever. She could handle being ignored by Sam—she welcomed it in fact—but she also knew it wouldn't last.

How did a man react to a woman after he'd made love to her? How did the woman react to him? Last night, after moments of electrifying intimacy, Sam had tried to play the part of a gentleman; but it wasn't a role that suited him, and he'd dropped it right away.

The only thing she knew for sure was that if he said anything condescending to her, she would either burst into tears or, edgy as she was this morning, rip into him with a spate of brothel invectives the likes of which he'd never heard. Either reaction would be totally irrational on her part; she would hate either one.

By the time they took leave, Lorelei once again astride the sorrel behind Sam, the sun's rays were visible over the tops of the trees, and the day had begun to warm into a pleasant briskness. Sam's attention seemed directed totally to the horse, and her edginess began to ease.

The hour ride, part of it along a deer trail, went through some of the most beautiful country that Lorelei had ever seen—oak and hickory jammed up close together, along with sweet gum and, close to an occasional stream, willow trees thrown in for good measure.

She'd lost track of the date, but it must have been

getting close to March. With a mild winter coming to an end, the trees had begun to leaf out, and she spotted a half-dozen dogwoods already bursting into white bloom. Adding vibrancy to it all were the deer and squirrels that frequently allowed themselves to be seen.

She might have commented on the scenery except that would have invited a response from Sam.

He had the best of the ride, sitting in front where he didn't have to see her the entire time. She took as punishment for her midnight weakness the fact that she had to look at his broad shoulders and at the way his hair curled black and thick against the leather collar of his jacket, and when he glanced one way or the other she couldn't avoid noticing the way his hat rested just above his dark eyes.

Even fresh-shaven, his face had a grim and shadowed cast. He'd been whiskered last night, she remembered. He'd brushed his cheeks against hers; mostly she remembered the way he'd brushed against her breasts.

With her legs spread to either side of him, she remembered, too, the way she'd held him between them. He'd fit just right, his muscled thighs stroking against her softer skin as he thrust inside—

She jolted to the present, calling herself a fool for lingering over the brief moments of pleasure when she should be concentrating on the subsequent hours of regret.

The trouble was that things were truly different between them now, and no amount of rationalizing on her part could alter the fact. They'd shared something important and personal—the most important, personal something a man and a woman *could* share. He had been seeking no more than a brief release, and an end to her claims of virginity. She hadn't been seeking anything, and yet she was the one who was truly changed.

Best think of something else. As they rode along, she tried to see if he was following a particular route that she could find again if she got the chance to leave camp without him. More often than not, they were heading cross-country through dense forests, occasionally crossing narrow streams and stretches of open fields, their general direction into the morning sun.

At the end of an especially long expanse of treeless grass, they topped a rise. "There's your destination," said Sam.

The sorrel bent his head to crop at the grass growing wild on the hill, and Lorelei peered around Sam for her first glimpse of No Pines.

It took up most of the valley before them, which wasn't saying much since the valley was little bigger than the land on which Balzac's sat. Somehow she'd gotten the idea that the town, the center of civilization according to Preacher, would be as beautiful as the surrounding country. She'd been wrong.

Four unpainted clapboard buildings sat two to a side along a street that ran from one end of the valley to another—a distance of a hundred yards at the most. There was not only an absence of pines; there were no trees of any kind, nor was there a blade of grass or a shrub, at least not anywhere close to the inglorious boulevard.

A single-rail corral had been erected behind one of the buildings, which she took to be the county seat's combination jail and livery stable. Inside the corral three horses grazed, one of them a fine-looking,

228

black-maned gray. A half-dozen other horses were hitched to the posts along the street, along with a flatbed wagon in front of what appeared to be the general store.

Other than the animals, there was not a living thing in sight.

The remaining two structures, both of them two-storied, had to be the saloons Preacher had told her about. They didn't look strong enough to withstand a strong wind.

"Here's what you bargained for, Lorelei." Sam shot her a glance out of the corner of his eye. "Hope it was worth it."

She wanted to tell him that for what she had given him last night, a trip into the heart of the Vieux Carré wouldn't have been enough. He'd only say he would get her back to the old part of New Orleans *tout de suite*.

Instead, she ignored his sarcasm. This journey wasn't for an inspection of the architecture of No Pines, Texas; her sole purpose was to learn what she could about Bert Jackson. Sam knew it as well as she.

"Is this the only town in the county?" she asked.

He nodded. "Texas has a long way to go before it's settled, but there are those who claim it's already getting overcrowded."

"Are you one of them?"

"I'm not that much of a loner. If Texas is going to make it as a republic, then it will need people and towns."

"I got the feeling riding in today that there's hardly anybody living in Dogwood County."

"They're scattered, but they're there. Despite the way Bert Jackson's grabbing up everything in sight, there's still too much good land not to bring them running."

"Tell me something, Sam. You've got the money you won off of Frank Knowles. Why don't you just buy another piece of that good land and let the other property go?"

"Because I've found what I want. After Goliad, I set up the camp, but it wasn't what I wanted. Not enough grazing space, mostly, so I scouted around for the perfect site. I found it. I don't need to look anymore."

"That's what I expected you to say. Can't you understand it's the same for me? I've been wanting something for a long time, and I don't intend to let it get away now."

He shifted in the saddle until he could give her a straighter look. "We're not after the same kind of thing."

"No, we're not. You've got your problems, and I've got mine."

Sam stared at her for what seemed a very long time, and she stared right back. He gave no sign he guessed how nervous she was inside. His gaze settled on the half circles under her eyes.

"You look bruised. I don't guess you got much sleep."

"Not much." She stared back defiantly. "I was excited about the journey today."

"Yeah," he said. "I can see how that might keep you up."

They were sitting so close, her thighs practically pressed to his, her mouth so close to his cheek all she had to do was lean toward him just a little —

To do what, kiss him? Would she never learn? Disgusted with herself far more than with him, she pulled her gaze away and stared down at the valley.

"Are you all right?" he asked.

"What do you mean?"

"After the first time and riding straddle the way you are, I was wondering if maybe you might be, you know, a little sore."

"Sam, you've got the delicate touch of a porcupine. I am fine. Wonderful. Perfect. And if I felt like I was sitting on a spike fence, I'd say the same thing."

His face hardened. "Good. I like a woman who doesn't complain."

"I thought you liked a woman with spirit."

"I changed my mind."

She answered him with a sweet smile.

"Your hair's falling loose," he snapped. "Get it back up under the hat."

She'd barely had time to follow his orders before he spurred the horse into a canter down the hill and she was forced to grab on to his coat. The pace didn't slow until they were in front of the No Pines General Store.

They dismounted next to the wagon, and Sam hitched the sorrel to a post. "I'm going for a drink. You've got an hour."

"An hour!"

"You forgot to specify how long you wanted to stay."

"But —"

He was no longer listening, having turned his back to her, his course set for the angled, two-story building across the street. His long stride took him quickly over the rutted dirt road. She was tempted to follow, then decided maybe she could find out more on her own.

Besides, there were probably some women over

231

there who would be all over Sam, even this early in the day, and she didn't particularly care to watch what he would do.

She glanced back to the general store in time to see a man and woman walking out the door. The man was dressed in a rough-woven dark gray suit, boots and a narrow-brimmed hat. The woman, her ample figure clothed in a simple brown chambray dress with a wool shawl pulled tight around her shoulders, stared at Lorelei from the confines of a sun bonnet.

Lorelei smiled. Here was the first female she'd seen since bidding goodbye to Delilah outside the casino, and she stepped forward to greet her.

"Good morning," she said.

The bonnet hid most of the woman's head and half her face, but it didn't hide the cold gaze that slid over the pants-clad Lorelei. The look she got from the man was warmer and friendlier by several degrees but in its way just as insulting.

"We need to be getting t' home, Mr. McElroy," the woman said, tugging at his coat sleeve.

"Yes, Mrs. McElroy," he said flatly as though he said it a thousand times a day.

McElroy tipped his hat and allowed his wife to guide him to the mule-drawn wagon. Lorelei stood still, head high, as they climbed onto the narrow buckboard seat. They headed out of town, and she caught the look he threw over his shoulder at her before his wife garnered his attention with talk. They were too far away for Lorelei to hear exactly what was being said, but she could make out the volume and the pace.

She got the feeling Mrs. McElroy could tell from looking just what had happened last night. Did it show in her eyes, or maybe in the way she was standing? The truth was she did feel a little sore.

Well, she thought as she stared down at her clothing, she'd never been considered exactly respectable—except when she was visiting Catherine and Adam out at the plantation. Everyone there accepted her because her dear friends wouldn't allow anything less.

Still, for the first time in her life she felt as though she truly was disreputable. She didn't like the feeling at all.

She made a quick decision, aided by the pouch of bank notes resting in her jacket pocket, the casino money Sam had returned to her an eternity ago. Inside the general store, under the curious eye of the proprietor, a shirt-sleeved man with mustache and sideburns, she made a few hasty purchases, ordered them bundled as tight as possible since she very well might be sitting on them for the ride back to camp, and announced she would return within the hour.

When she tossed a five-dollar note onto the counter, he responded with a brisk, "Yes, ma'am."

In one way No Pines wasn't much different from New Orleans. Money earned respect.

She strode back outside, looked up and down the street, and decided since she had no reason to go into the livery stable or the jail, she had best choose between the two saloons. She chose the one without Sam.

EDGAR'S WAYSIDE INN, the crooked sign over the door read, and she pushed through the swinging doors. Inside was dark and rank with the odor of stale smoke, cheap liquor and unwashed bodies. With inadequate light provided by a pair of oil lamps, her eyes had to adjust to the dimness.

Directly in front of her at the rear a staircase led to

233

an open hallway on the second floor. To the left was the bar, which was nothing more than a couple of pine boards resting over a trio of whiskey barrels. A mustached bartender in shirt sleeves stared at her as she walked in.

The wooden floor was sticky with spilled drink. As she edged into the room, she had to pry her shoes up after each step. She counted a half-dozen tables. Around the farthest one sat two of the men she'd seen standing outside of Sam's cabin. The other tables were empty.

She spoke to the two. "I'm looking for Bert Jackson."

"Weren't you with Sam Delaney t'other day?" one of them asked.

She answered the question with one of her own. "Are you expecting Mr. Jackson anytime soon?"

The man who had spoken elbowed his companion. "Don't it talk fancy. Trouble is, can't tell if it's a man or woman or one o' those thangs that kinda swings in between."

The second man laughed.

She repeated her question to the bartender. Picking up a glass, he wiped it with a cloth no cleaner than his shirt and kept on staring.

"Come on back here and set a spell," urged the speaker at the rear table.

Lorelei thought over the offer, but she couldn't see any advantage to remaining at Edgar's. Whirling, she looked directly into the cold eyes she'd been seeing in her nightmares for the past six years.

"Oh," she said with a jump.

"You were looking for me?"

Through the wire-framed glasses the man who called himself Bert Jackson studied her just as intently as she was studying him. Was it truly Jacobs standing so close?

"Yes, I was," she said, her heart pounding. "I saw you last week on Mr. Delaney's land."

"*My* land," he corrected. "You have the advantage over me. You know who I am, but who are you?"

He didn't bother to glance at her clothes; he'd had opportunity for that when he was sneaking up on her from behind.

She wished the light from outside wasn't to his back; in the lamplight she could make out his eyes fairly well, but she wanted to catch every expression on his face.

"Shall we sit down?" she said, sidling to one of the tables.

He turned in her direction. "I repeat, who are you?"

"Lorelei Latham."

He gave no sign he recognized the name.

"I mistook you for a youth the other day, Miss Latham. My apologies." He was all courtesy, but then William Jacobs had behaved in much the same way the first time they met.

She took off her hat and shook her hair free. Still, he gave no sign he'd ever seen her before. Doubts assailed her, but none strong enough to make her leave.

"Do we have business?" he asked. Impatience sharpened his voice.

"Perhaps," she said, stalling.

How positive she had been that she would know him immediately if she could only get this close. His voice was the one that haunted her dreams, and he stared at her in Jacobs's mock courteous way, but he was different, too.

"I'm a busy man, Miss Latham. If Sam Delaney

has sent you for some obscure purpose, I wish you would tell me."

"He didn't send me. In fact, he didn't want me to talk to you at all."

For the first time Jackson showed interest in what she said. "And why is that?"

"I told him you reminded me of someone I knew a long time ago, and he said I had to be wrong."

His eyes continued to hide his thoughts. "I'm certain we have not met. Surely I would remember someone as unusual as you." This time as he spoke, he allowed his eyes to take in the complete picture she presented, from slouch hat to dusty shoes.

"It wasn't in Texas."

"Then, it couldn't have been me. I've been traveling through this territory for years."

"I said it was a long time ago. In Boston."

"I regret to say I've never been to that city. Now, if you will excuse me, I'm supposed to meet someone this morning."

Not a flicker. Not a sign. She grew desperate. When he turned, she grabbed his sleeve. At the back of the room a chair scraped against the wooden floor.

She let go of him. "I guess I was wrong."

He dismissed her with a sneer.

"But I was wondering something."

"Yes?"

She searched wildly for a response. "Do you play poker?"

"It is a pastime I occasionally enjoy. Why do you ask?"

"Because I came in here looking for a game."

"Really, Miss Latham, has Delaney put you up to something?"

236

"He doesn't even want me here, remember? See, I'm a gambler, a professional, you know, and I found myself stranded back on the trail aways."

She saw he was listening but not believing. She *did* have his attention, though, and that was all she could ask for right away. Remembering the ruse that had worked so well at the ferry, she edged a little twang into her speech.

"Sam wanted to leave me by the road, but we cut for high card and he lost. That's why I'm here. I thought I recognized you, and then I thought maybe you could help me out. I need a little stake to get me out of this godforsaken county."

"I do not run a charity."

She pulled the pouch from her pocket. The sight drew the pair from the back, who moved up fast to stand beside her. She looked at the three men and at the bartender, who was regarding her with great care. It occurred to her that maybe she ought to be afraid, but she'd been too long in the casino to worry about being the only woman around. Get a man's mind on money and cards, and if a little liquor was thrown in, he'd forget about sex.

"Look, I guess I was wrong about that Boston business. It's been a while. I've got enough money to get a game going, but not enough to get me down to Galveston, where I hear the real action is. Now, how about a little poker?" She looked toward the bar. "You got any cards?"

She could see Jackson's mind working. At last he nodded, and in no more than a minute she was seated at a table with him and his two hired men, her nimble fingers working at a new deck the bartender had provided, the rippling sound of the pasteboards making her feel right at home.

"You sure do like that land of Sam's."

"It's not his any longer."

"He was telling me you own most of the county already."

"Not the best part." His voice was hard, ugly. "At least not until the truth about his false claims came out. I own it now."

"You seem proud of the fact."

"I always get my way."

For a moment triumph lightened his face, long enough for Lorelei to see what Sam was up against. Knowing Sam's determination, she shivered inside at the inevitable clash between the two.

"Never could figure why anyone would put such stock in settling down," she said. "I'm a rover, myself."

"Obviously," he said, giving her a scornful once-over. "Now let's play cards."

They cut for deal; she won and dealt a round of draw poker, folded early, and studied Jackson. His eyes were the way she remembered them, despite the glasses, and she wasn't bothered by his loss of hair. Not even the added girth gave her trouble, not with that voice sounding so right. What bothered her the most was the set of his jaw, the fullness of his lower face, the way he held his mouth. They were wrong.

And if they were wrong, then Sam was right. She'd let her imagination run wild. She closed her eyes.

"Are you going to deal another hand?" asked Jackson. "This game was your idea, and I'm afraid it wasn't a very good one."

She put that same voice back on a dock beside the Charles River. She could hear his words of instruction to Carrie and to her.

She opened her eyes. "Yes—"

"No."

Looking past Jackson, she saw Sam standing in the door only a dozen feet away. "Hour's up," he said. "Time to go."

"It couldn't be."

"Close enough."

"But I'm not done here."

"You heard the lady," said Jackson over his shoulder. "Must you always cause a disturbance, Delaney?"

"Every chance I get." Sam motioned with his head. "Let's go, Lorelei. The air's kind of putrid in here. Smells like something died."

Sam rested his right hand on the handle of his gun. Jackson's hired hands pushed back their chairs.

"Come on, boys," said Sam. "You don't want to cause any trouble. It's only two against one. They're not odds you'd normally choose."

"Three to one," said Jackson, dropping his hands below the level of the table.

"Here I was thinking you'd gone soft and had to hire all of your protection."

"I guess you're right, Sam," said Lorelei brightly. "It's time to go."

A door on the second floor creaked open.

"I wasn't placing myself in those odds," said Jackson. "Allow me to introduce my newest employee." He gestured toward the upstairs hall.

Lorelei's eyes followed the wave of his hand. A man stood in the darkness, light from the oil lamps glinting off the gun he wore at his waist. When he started down the stairs, she got a good look at him. Instinctively she pulled away.

Whip-thin, he was dressed in a gray shirt and trousers, the latter tucked into high black boots, and he carried a black hat in his hand. A black scarf was knotted at his throat.

His face had a skeletal cast to it, sharp bone pushing out against gray skin, dark hair slicked back, his mouth a slash that broke up the gray, his eyes black stones that caught the light.

He came to a halt at the base of the stairway. "Mr. Jackson," he rasped. The sound was inhuman, and Lorelei felt a chill to her bones.

"I heard someone slit your throat, Dun," said Sam.

"A minor inconvenience." Again the rasp. "I had to return the favor."

Lorelei's eyes jerked back and forth between the cadaverous newcomer and Sam, who stood tall and still and, framed as he was in the doorway that led outside, very much like a vulnerable target. Her mouth grew dry, and her heart pounded in her throat.

"You know each other?" asked Jackson.

"I've made his acquaintance." Sam glanced at Lorelei. "Bert's gone and hired himself a killer."

"Dun Straight is not a wanted man," said Jackson.

"Only because he doesn't leave witnesses to testify against him." Again Sam looked at Lorelei, his eyes sending out harsh warnings. "I knew I smelled something dead in here. Now let's go."

She nodded once and wished with all her heart she had gone with him the first time he asked. Pushing her chair back from the table, she started to stand.

The animallike growl that filled the room could only have come from one source. "Can't let you get away with that, Delaney."

This time the gunman's voice was more a hiss than a rasp, and Lorelei froze in place.

Like a snake, Dun Straight slithered silently across

240

the saloon, stopping when he came even with the poker table. His gray features looked carved out of marble as he stared at Sam.

"I've been hoping you'd show up. Been waiting since I rode in last night. Let's settle our problems right now."

Chapter Seventeen

Don't answer him, Sam. Run!

The words screamed so loudly in Lorelei's mind she was surprised she hadn't blurted them out.

Sam held still in the doorway. "What problems are you talking about, Dun?" His stare moved away from Straight down to the seated Bert Jackson, slipping past Lorelei and Jackson's other two hands before returning to the gunman.

Lorelei let out a long, slow sigh. Sam would never run from danger. Especially if she told him to.

Straight's unblinking eyes stared back at Sam, his right hand holding the black hat, his left hand at the side with the gun. "You don't know your place." The raspy voice made the accusation sound intolerable.

Frissons of fear rippled down Lorelei's spine. She sat still in her chair, hands resting on her thighs, only her eyes moving to the two standing men, Straight close at her right and Sam much too far away to the left. What was needed here, she decided, was a distraction of some kind, a little interference. Wasn't there a lawman in this town?

She looked from man to man and then to the others in the room, her survey including the bartender. He'd stopped wiping the glasses to rest his

242

hands at the edge of the plank bar. From the ready-to-shoot hardness in everyone's eyes, she figured herself to be the only one in the room unarmed.

"Let's take this outside," said Sam.

"It makes little difference to me." Straight settled the hat squarely on his head, his obsidian eyes staring at Sam from under the wide brim. His hand dropped closer to his gun.

"Only one problem you might have," said Sam. "I don't plan to turn my back on you."

Straight's answering growl had a feral quality that slammed Lorelei's fear into panic. Sam could face down any man on earth, but right now he was dealing with an animal.

She looked at Jackson. "Aren't you going to do something?"

"Yes." Jackson took off his glasses, held them to the light, then put them on again. "I plan to watch."

Lorelei shifted her attention to the two other men at the table. They glanced briefly at her, then back at Dun Straight, but not before she caught an expression of uncertainty in their eyes. Even being on the same side, they didn't seem to care any more for the gunman than she did.

Straight took a step toward the door, and Lorelei shot to her feet.

"Mr. Straight, I hate to interfere, but Sam and I have to be leaving now."

She felt all eyes on her, Sam staring the hardest of all. For a second no one spoke. She would have given the clothes off her back to have a few of Balzac's guards moving in to help her right now.

"She with you?" asked Straight.

"You might say she's under my protection."

"Then, shut her up."

"Not an easy thing to do."

The look Sam was throwing her had such force that she gave in to his unspoken demands and sat back down, her legs shaking, her breath coming in short, shallow gasps. She glanced once at Straight, who stood within kicking distance, and then down to his gun. It was half-cocked, the percussion cap already in place, guaranteeing him of one quick shot. And he would be using it against Sam.

All she had to do was reach out and grab it. . . . . A risky venture at best that she couldn't work up nerve to take. Somehow she kept her hands steady as she reached for the cards scattered across the table.

"If you two insist on going outside to fight," she said in a high-pitched voice she did not recognize, "then run along. We'll just finish our game." She smiled innocently — and somewhat stupidly — at Jackson. "Whose deal is it?"

"The game's over," he declared.

"Nonsense," she said, swallowing and forcing a deep breath into her lungs. "I haven't won my money yet."

The click of a hammer sounded like a rifle shot, but no one else seemed to have heard. Stark fear swept through her as she glanced at Jackson's man sitting across the table. He was looking at Sam, his eyes focused like a hawk's.

She moved fast, falling to the floor and edging under the table just as she gave her chair a solid kick in the direction of the gunman's legs. She came up hard, putting all her weight into the straightening of her knees, desperation doubling her strength. Her back hit the underside of the table, tilting it toward Jackson's man.

Everything happened at once — a gun roaring at the

same time the edge of the table slammed against the floor, chairs scraping and crashing, men shouting, the shot echoing in her ears. None of it could cover the sound of Sam shouting her name and warning her to stay down.

He asked too much. Peering over the top of the fallen table, she saw a strange tableau: Jackson and his two men crouched on the floor much the way she was, a gun lying beside them, the bartender slowly standing behind the makeshift bar, Straight staring at her, a smoking gun in his hand, and Sam, upright and obviously unharmed close by the table, his pistol pointed at Straight's heart.

She glanced down at the tabletop and saw the gouge where Straight's bullet had ricocheted. She turned a nervous gaze up at the gunman.

She pulled herself to her feet, grateful that her legs could hold her. One look at Sam and she looked down again. The fury in his eyes frightened her more than the chilling stare of Straight.

"Have we got some trouble in here?"

The thin voice came through the open door. All eyes shifted in time to see a bandy-legged little man in woolen trousers and worsted shirt come walking into the saloon, his pale button eyes glancing around nervously, his hands opening and closing at his sides. He was not wearing a gun.

Jackson cleared his throat and stood, brushing the dust of the floor from his dark suit, his men following his lead. "Sheriff Mortimer, just a little misunderstanding."

"Like hell it was," snapped Sam.

Lorelei stared in dismay at the lawman. He didn't weigh much more than she did, and he had a pasty look to his face, as though he rarely ventured into the light of day. Even the badge pinned to his shirt looked undersized and without a shine. A minute ago she'd been hoping he would arrive; now she didn't know why he had bothered.

"Don't want no trouble," the sheriff said, his eyes continuing to shift from man to man, settling in surprise on her. She brushed the hair away from her face and stared back.

"I made a mistake." Straight looked at Sam as the half-whispered, half-spoken words grated from his throat. "Don't count on it again."

Holstering his gun, he walked toward the door, all eyes on him but no one doing anything to keep him in the saloon. He made little sound as he moved, and when Mortimer stepped aside to let him leave, it was as though a shadow had passed from the saloon.

"I should have killed him when I had the chance," Sam said, his eyes pinned on Jackson. "I won't let the opportunity get by again, Bert. Tell him that when you two are discussing strategy."

"Be very careful, Delaney. I have a legal right to protect what is mine. You threaten Dun Straight, you threaten me." He glanced at Mortimer. "You heard him, Sheriff. He's threatening to kill a guest in our town."

"A pest, Bert," said Sam, his voice low and even. "You got that wrong. No crime in killing a pest."

Sheriff Mortimer ran a hand through his short hair. "Don't want no trouble," he said.

Neither did Lorelei. Scooping up her hat and money from the floor, she considered how to make an exit. With all eyes on her, she decided the best way to leave was to stride out the door, head held high, pretending she was dressed in the green velvet gown—fresh as it had been in Carrollton—

and not in a pair of tight britches.

Outside the day had turned as gray as Dun Straight's complexion. Shuddering at the comparison, she gave a quick glance to the blood bay gelding tied to the post in front of Edgar's Wayside Inn. The gelding hadn't been there when she came in, and she assumed it belonged to Jackson. She looked up and down the dirt street; the gunman was nowhere in sight.

With Sam's spurs jangling close behind her, she headed for the sorrel tied in front of the general store. Beyond a doubt, her first visit into town was at an end.

"Lorelei."

The anger in his voice stopped her, and she turned to face him.

"You came within an inch of getting killed in there," he said.

His face was grim, and she could feel his fury and the violence of his nature that he kept barely under control. A damp wind blew, a reminder that winter was not quite done. Her hair whipped about her head, and with a tug on the slouch hat, she hugged herself to ward off the sudden chill.

"I walked out alive, and so did you," she said, regretting the defensive tone of her voice as much as she regretted the harshness of his. He wasn't grateful in the least that she had probably saved his life.

"Sam! Baby! Are you all right?" a shrill voice cried.

Lorelei glanced toward the second saloon. Running straight for Sam was a redheaded woman in scarlet and black satin ruffles, skirt lifted to reveal black stockings and slippers, a stark look of worry on her painted face. Her full breasts came dangerously close

247

to bouncing out of her low-cut bodice as she ran.

Glancing back at Sam, Lorelei thought she caught a look of dismay in his eyes. But she couldn't be sure, not with all that anger hanging on.

"Sam baby?" she asked.

"I'm not through talking with—"

The woman threw herself against him and wrapped her arms around his neck. Lorelei half expected her stockinged legs to wrap around him, too.

Irritation swept over her. It was altogether an unpleasant sensation, and certainly an unnecessary one. Why should the picture of another woman tangled up with Sam bother her?

"Whoa, Francine," said Sam, "back up." His capable hands caught her by the waist and set her on the street.

"I heard the shot," Francine said breathily, her pile of red hair bobbing, "and then I looked out to see that awful man walking over to the stable. He rode into town late last night, and I swear, Sam, just the look of him sent a chill straight through me. He ain't been in the saloon, preferring Edgar's the way he does, and that's all right by me and the other girls."

She paused for air, and Lorelei found herself likewise taking in a deep breath.

"Oh, look," Francine squealed. "There he is."

All eyes turned to the man emerging from the stable door. He was riding the sleek, black-maned gray Lorelei had admired when she first looked down the hill at No Pines. Dressed in gray with black hat and boots, Straight looked right at home on the matching horse.

With his eyes directed up the road, Straight whipped the gray's flanks and took off at a gallop, the horse's hoofs kicking up dirt as he passed Lorelei and the other two, so close she could smell the leather of the saddle.

She glanced at Sam, who shifted his attention from the departing rider to her.

"Take a good, long look at Dun Straight. He's as mean a scoundrel as you'll ever see. And crafty, too."

"I'm not stupid, Sam."

"Sometimes I wonder. You seem proud of the fact we walked out of there, but that was only because he didn't have a backup gun. He won't make that mistake again."

Regret turned to anger as her eyes locked with his. "Jackson's man was ready to shoot you before Straight had a chance."

"You know that for sure?"

"I heard the click of a hammer."

"Sam," Francine wailed. "You almost got shot."

Sam kept his full attention on Lorelei. "He was trying to load it. He wouldn't have had time."

Lorelei gave up. "You just can't believe I can do anything right." The look on his face told her that was the wrong thing to say, and she hurried on. "All right, I'll do something else next time to save you."

"You won't have to. You're not coming back to town again."

"Sam," said Francine, her voice thinning to a whine, "who is this? I ain't seen her before."

Sam's determination rose between him and Lorelei like a wall, but she could do nothing less than stay with her own convictions. "Nothing's settled with Jacobs," she said. "I have to return."

"I'm cold, Sam," said Francine as she tried to hold her skirt down against the wayward wind.

At last Sam looked at her. "Go on back to the saloon. Everything's all right. I'll talk to you later." He spoke firmly to her, but not really harshly, not the way he gave orders to Lorelei.

"But, baby—"

"Now, Francine."

The painted red lips pouted. "Well, all right." She gave a swift, assessing look at Lorelei, taking in everything from slouch hat to trousers to dusty shoes. Then it was back to Sam. She kissed him on the lips, smearing paint on him like a brand, and with a proprietary glance around at whoever might be watching, she flounced back toward the saloon.

Lorelei stared after her, at the yards of scarlet and black satin, at the mound of red hair fluttering in the wind, at the broad behind not quite disguised by the ruffles. She remembered the low-cut front of the dress. Francine was a voluptuous woman. She must also be the one Sam said didn't claim any innocence, the one he'd ridden into town last night to see.

All right, so he hadn't made love to her—at least that's what he claimed—but Lorelei would bet all the bank notes in her pocket that at some time or other he'd known her in the biblical sense.

Feeling dirty and dowdy and misunderstood, she stiffened her spine and turned to face him. Why she also felt like bursting into tears, she didn't understand except that maybe the tensions of the past half hour were getting to her.

"You forgot to introduce us," she said.

"Didn't see much need."

"I don't remember exactly what we were saying. It wasn't anything like thank you, Lorelei, for acting so quickly and bravely in there. No, that wasn't it."

"What you did was dumb."

The ungrateful wretch. She remembered last night . . . the things she had done . . . the things she had

250

let him do . . . the confessions she had made.

"I've done several stupid things lately. Take me back to the camp."

She whirled before he could countermand her order with one of his own. Something like *Wait out here while I have my talk with Francine*.

She tossed an addendum over her shoulder. "I'll need to stop in the store for a package. Since you keep tearing clothes off me, I had to buy some supplies to make repairs."

The return journey was made quickly under gathering storm clouds. Fat splats of rain hit the ground just as they broke through the brush surrounding the camp and rode into the clearing. Before Sam could dismount, Lorelei dropped to the ground and grabbed for the package on which she had been sitting.

Whirling away from him, she bumped into a man she'd never seen before. As tall as Sam and just as lean and tanned, he had a sharper look about him, even though he appeared to be younger by several years.

"Oh," she said, startled.

He tipped his hat, then looked past her to Sam.

"I was hoping to see you, Jet," said Sam.

Jet's dark eyes drifted between Sam and Lorelei, then rested on her. "Were you?"

Lorelei could see he was assessing her the way the men back at the casino were wont to do. Somehow, with the look of approval flashing across his lean features, she didn't feel quite so dowdy as she had in town.

She extended a hand. "Sam forgets his manners

sometimes. I'm Lorelei Latham."

"Howdy, Miss Latham." She caught a drawl to his voice, more pronounced than Sam's.

"And you're Jet."

"That's right."

"Doesn't anyone around here have a last name besides me and Sam?"

"In Texas, it doesn't pay to ask too many questions."

She was suddenly aware of the beginning drops of rain. "We need to get inside."

"All right by me," said Jet.

"She's not available." Sam snapped out the words.

Jet looked questioningly at Sam. "Don't see a ring."

"She's not available."

"You got her staked out for yourself?"

Lorelei felt like a mare at an auction.

"No, Sam *baby* does not," she said, breaking in. "And as for my being available, as he so crudely put it, no, I am not available, not to him or anyone else. Except, of course, in times of trouble when ferrymen want to arrest him or when a gunman wants to shoot him down. Then I am very much available."

She had said more than she planned. Raindrops fell harder. With the package clutched protectively to her bosom, she walked around Jet and strode into the cabin, slamming the door behind her. Let the two men stand outside if they wanted; the choice was up to them.

Sam thought her dumb, did he? At least she knew enough to seek shelter from the rain.

Tossing the bundle onto the bunk, she began pacing the width of the cabin, images flying at her as fast as the rain against the door. Today nothing had gone as she had hoped or even imagined. Jackson, Dun Straight, Sheriff Mortimer . . . *Francine*. They were all a jumble in her mind, and here was another man with a short first name added to the unusual gathering at the camp.

Mostly she thought of Sam. How dare he question what she had done? Had he really expected her to sit at that poker table and watch him being gunned down?

She bent to the banked coals in the fireplace, stirred them with a stick of kindling until the embers sparked and turned to tiny licks of flame, then tossed in a couple of logs. Tonight would be cold. Much colder than last night. And she would be alone.

She shivered and tossed her hat aside, shaking her hair free as she folded her legs under her. Staring into the growing blaze, she saw Sam as he had looked in the doorway of the saloon. Never had she felt such terror, and not for herself but for him. What was happening to her that she could feel such a raw, ungovernable fear? She had acted quickly, and she had acted right. Not that he would ever give her credit.

She liked this anger that was building inside her. It was far easier to understand than the emotions she'd experienced in the saloon. She needed to stay angry with him all the time, but then there were a lot of things she needed to do . . . like keep him out of her bed.

It wasn't likely there would be repeat of last night. He'd taunted her, swearing she would want him again. She was honest enough with herself to know he very well could be right, especially considering the way her stomach tightened and her breath grew shallow every time he came close.

So she had a weakness for him. She also had a

streak of stubborn pride.

There were other matters to concentrate on besides Sam Delaney. Jackson . . . Jacobs . . . who was the man? Finding out was the sole reason she'd stayed in Texas, and find out she would. But it would take time. Just getting back and forth to town presented difficulties, and she needed to talk to him a great deal more.

And she had another pressing problem — letting Delilah and Catherine and the others know where she was; by now they must be going out of their minds with worry over her. She wouldn't be surprised to see Adam and Ben come riding into camp one day, guns blazing. They wouldn't wait for Sam to give an explanation, not after the way he'd behaved in the casino.

If they didn't get him, it was very possible some bounty hunter would find his way to Dogwood County. She didn't like contemplating all the potential enemies for Sam, most of them linked to her.

There was only one course of action possible. She'd realized it when she was back in No Pines. With the rain pounding on the roof, she unwrapped the bundle from the general store and spread her purchases on the bunk. Selecting the items she was looking for and settling down in the glow of the firelight, she got to work.

Preacher came knocking on her door an hour later. The downpour had settled into a light sprinkle as she welcomed him inside.

"I thought you might prefer to eat alone tonight," he said as he handed her a tin plate and a cup of milk. "It's simple fare. Wash and I prepared it in one of the tents."

"Thank you," she said as she took the offering.

He stood by the hearth, his worn suit covered by a

254

long, black coat, droplets of moisture caught in his gray hair and beard. Preacher seldom smiled, and she decided there was something infinitely sad about him.

He had many admirable traits—the way he defended Sam against her criticism and the gentle way he had with Blue, and more, the thoughtful things he did for her, like bringing her tonight's supper. But she knew very little about him. Indeed, she knew very little about any of the men.

"Samuel is a good man," Preacher said suddenly. "You have chosen wisely."

"What are you talking about?"

He turned his eyes to her. "If you prefer not to discuss it, I above all others will understand."

"I don't know what you mean," she said, but in truth she suspected what he was getting at, ridiculous though it was.

"Perhaps you do not care to admit it to yourself, but you have chosen Samuel as yours."

She shook her head in disbelief. "I haven't chosen Sam for anything. I don't even like him."

"I think you do. But then I do not speak of liking him. Your feelings go much deeper than that."

She whirled away and set the food down on the cabinet, her eyes trained on the flap covering the window. "This is preposterous. Sam kidnapped me. He dragged me here. And now he won't listen to what I have to say. He criticizes everything I do, and even when we—"

She broke off, flushed with embarrassment at what she had almost revealed.

"I did not say he was an easy man, or an uncomplicated one. But he is a good man and you have chosen well."

She turned to renew her protest, but the perceptive, certain look on Preacher's lined and bearded face stopped her. Let him believe what he would. He seemed to draw pleasure from it, and she could see that he had little enough of that in his life.

"I need your help," she said, drawing him to the subject that should be uppermost in her mind. "You go to town from time to time, don't you?"

"Not often, but sometimes Blue and I take the mule into No Pines for supplies."

"Is there some way you could send a letter for me?"

He nodded, his gray eyes studying her carefully.

"It's nothing that will hurt Sam. In fact, I'm trying to help him. He wouldn't believe it, but I am."

"We are a fledgling country, but sometimes the post arrives and leaves from the general store."

Hurrying around him, she picked up a sheet of paper from the bunk. "Here," she said, "read this."

"If this is private correspondence—"

"Please. I wrote to my friends in New Orleans to let them know I'm all right. That's pretty much all I said, but I'd like you to look it over in case someone questions what was in it." There was little doubt in her mind who that someone might be.

Preacher did as she asked, then looked up at her with a warm smile in his eyes. "I knew from the beginning you were a considerate lady."

"Thank you, but I'm no lady, and you know it."

"Ah, but you are. A lone woman with all these men, you have conducted yourself with propriety, and you've made them feel at ease around you. You have not made demands for special treatment, you have performed your share of the chores without complaint and indeed have asked for more."

She smiled ruefully. "I've not always conducted myself with propriety."

"In the ways that matter, you have. Most meaningful to me, you have been considerate and understanding with Blue. The boy is a private sort, but he gives his affection readily to those he senses are kind. He has given his affection to you. Witness the bird he carved for you this morning. Yes, you are most certainly a lady of the finest sort."

Coming after all the buffets of her recent past, the words made Lorelei want to cry.

"Thank you," she repeated, this time with sincerity. "You're a good man."

"Not so good, or I would still be in the pulpit."

His eyes took on a faraway cast. A dozen questions sprang to her mind, but she kept silent. Preacher was wrong about her feelings for Sam, but he had paid her great and strengthening tributes. She would not insult him by probing into his private life.

He brought himself back to the present. "I will see that the letter is posted," he said, folding it and slipping it into the envelope she handed him.

She touched the sleeve of his coat. "It might be better if you didn't let Sam know about this. He might take offense, say that you betrayed him, that even if you read the entire letter, it contained a secret message of some kind."

"You must learn to trust one another."

"I just know he won't believe I wrote anything good. Believe me, when I put down those words, I wasn't feeling very kindly toward him, but I had to convince people back home that I have come to no harm."

"A thoughtful gesture," he said, tucking the envelope inside his coat. He nodded good night, then paused by the door.

"You once assured me that Samuel had not hurt you in any way. Have you changed your mind?"

Lorelei took a long time to answer. "You make impossible assertions and ask difficult questions, don't you?" She looked into the fire, her thoughts in confusion. "I don't know if Sam has hurt me, Preacher. I really don't know."

Chapter Eighteen

Sam's tanned, naked body lay sprawled across the satin sheets of the four-poster bed, a double vise of plump arms and white thighs wrapped around him. Tangled red curls covered the pillow propped against the headboard.

"Sam baby . . . baby . . . baby," the woman beneath him cried.

Or worse, he lay spread-eagled on a bed of pine needles in a deserted part of the forest, a red-black stain spreading across his buckskin jacket and matting in the fringe, his once alert brown eyes staring sightlessly up at the only witness to his death, a mockingbird trilling a song that no one heard.

Lorelei squeezed her eyes closed, but the alternating images would not go away.

"No harm has come to Samuel. You must not worry."

The assurance jerked her to the present, to the evening campfire, to the starless cloudy sky overhead. Blue and the twins sat on either side of her. Preacher was handing her a plate.

"Were you talking to me?" she asked. The question sounded stupid, even to her.

"Samuel is a resourceful man," said Preacher.

"You must have faith that he will take care of himself."

She nodded her thanks as she took the food. "Of course he can take care of himself."

And of course she was worried. Sam and Jet had disappeared more than a week ago—the night of the heavy rain, the night Jet had returned—and she hadn't seen them since. She was certain either Francine's bed or Dun Straight's bullet was keeping at least one of them away.

She pushed the meat around on her plate.

"The worry has been in your eyes since the morning of their departure," Preacher said.

Al and Cal both nodded. Blue chewed his dinner and smiled at Lorelei.

Could they all read her so well? She looked around at the gathering. "I'm more concerned about the rest of you."

She enjoyed the look of surprise she got from Al and Cal. "Your beards," she said, gesturing with a piece of possum. "They're shaggier than ever. And you, Preacher. I'd like to trim your hair, too. Even Blue could use a little grooming. It won't take me a minute to get the scissors—"

"No," said Al, shaking his hirsute head.

"Not for me either," said Cal, doing the same.

"We are not given to sartorial splendor," said Preacher.

Lorelei studied them, one by one. "At last you've said something I agree with. Let me know when you change your minds. I'm glad to patch your clothes, and I don't mind giving a haircut or two."

"Most of all," said Preacher, "you are pleased to change the subject, but Sam is a consideration that

260

will not go away. I suspect he continues his search for the lawyer who was hired to represent him while he was gone from the area."

She gave up all pretense at unconcern. "Why on earth would Sam want to find the lawyer? Bert Jackson told him the man drank."

"He was known as a teetotaler when Samuel employed him. We have only Wilbert Jackson's word that otherwise was the case."

Lorelei perked up. *Wilbert* Jackson? You're sure that's his name?"

Preacher nodded. "I read it once on a piece of correspondence waiting for him at the general store." He regarded her closely. "This seems important to you."

"It is," she said. "It most certainly is."

Her mind took off in several directions. Wilbert Jackson. William Jacobs. The eyes, the voice. She tried to keep her excitement down, but everyone, even Blue, could see the animation on her face. She'd like to tell the whole story to them, but that would involve a few personal details she'd rather keep to herself.

To herself and Sam, she corrected, which brought her back to Preacher's announcement. Hurriedly she turned the subject away from herself.

"For Sam's sake, I hope he finds him."

"Sam'll find him all right," said Al.

"Won't quit until he tracks him down," said Cal.

She rather liked this new image of Sam, riding from settlement to settlement far away from Francine and Dun Straight, stopping wherever lawyers congregated in Texas. In New Orleans it was either the courtroom or a casino, but she couldn't begin to guess where it might be in this wild, unsettled country.

The rest of the meal was eaten in silence, and when the plates had been washed and packed away in the cabin, Lorelei prepared a pot of coffee. Offering a cup to Preacher, she said, "When are you going into town?"

"I planned to ride in early tomorrow with Blue."

"Any chance I can go with you?"

Preacher shook his head slowly. "Please do not ask. I have promised to see that your letter is posted."

"I'm not questioning you," she said, resting her hand on his coat sleeve. "That's not why I want to go."

"Samuel expressly asked that we not help you to leave, remember. He has asked little of us since he first shared the camp so readily. In this his wishes must be followed."

The words rolled out in the resonant way Preacher had of speaking, as though he were reading them off a parchment scroll, as though no argument could make him change his mind.

So she wouldn't argue. Dropping the subject, she immediately started making silent plans.

The next morning, with the sky clear after a midnight rain, she was dressed and waiting by the corral when Preacher came out with Blue.

"Lorelei, have you so soon forgotten our conversation last night?" asked Preacher.

"I haven't forgotten. You're not helping me to leave. I'm helping myself. We just happen to be going in the same direction."

"You are determined to do this."

"Yes, I am."

He nodded thoughtfully and set about saddling the mule. When he was done, he turned to face her.

"I cannot allow you to ride; to do so would be to break Samuel's trust. Besides, for all his apparent good health, Blue lacks the stamina of other boys his age. On the journey into town he must go by mule, and I doubt the poor animal could take another rider."

"I understand."

"The walk into No Pines requires at least three hours."

"I've been out on the trail with Sam for days. I'm tougher than I look. If you can make it, so can I."

"You're going with us, Lori?" asked Blue.

She smiled at the youth. "I'm going to try."

"There is no way I can talk you out of this," said Preacher.

"No."

He smiled in resignation. "I believe that Samuel has met his match."

"You must stop trying to pair us up."

"Little effort on my part is required. The two of you have done it for me."

He led the mule out of the corral and helped Blue to mount. Taking the reins, he walked through the brush surrounding the camp, Lorelei close behind. The boy's gangly legs were almost bent double as his oversized shoes rested in the short stirrups, but he didn't seem to feel uncomfortable, not with the awed attention he was giving to every bird he heard in the trees.

At first she, too, found the going exhilarating. The pathway cleared a little, the air was brisk, and under a bright blue sky the early sun glistened off the raindrops still clinging to the leaves.

Two hours later, with her shoes mud-caked, a blister building on her left heel, and the muscles in her calves beginning to cramp, she found herself out of sorts. All those hours astride the sorrel hadn't prepared her for a long hike as much as she had hoped. She kept her complaints to herself, inspired by imagining what Sam would say if he knew what was going on.

He'd smirk over her discomfort and bark a few orders and come up with some complaints of his own. The man had no manners.

Pushing Sam from her mind, she concentrated on accosting Wilbert Jackson in town, maybe getting him in another poker game if at all possible. First she'd check to see if Dun Straight's horse was in the corral behind the livery. Whatever she discovered would guide how far she pushed her quarry.

She had been too direct the first time, blurting out about Boston and having seen him before. Today she'd go for subtlety, chattering on about her experiences in New Orleans, trying to trip him up with an admission of some kind.

More than anything else, she had to decide whether or not he was Jacobs. Having dealt with men often enough, she could tell when one lied.

Thinking about the details of her approach made the next hour go by faster. With the sun high overhead, they at last reached the long, undulating field that led to a distant incline and then down into the small valley where No Pines awaited. With a warning to be careful, Preacher allowed Blue to ride in front while he dropped back beside Lorelei.

"Please accept my congratulations and apologies. I did not believe you would last this far without asking to rest."

"I wanted to," she said, "but lately I've had enough lessons in stubbornness to keep me going."

"Samuel inspires us in many ways."

Lorelei smiled. "I think about all of you sometimes, and I'm reminded of the Ursuline orphanage back in New Orleans. I help out there when I can."

"An orphanage? The twins would be insulted if they knew you considered them children. They were, as a matter of fact, quite embarrassed when you caught them cavorting in the water."

"Ah, they told you. They shouldn't have been embarrassed. It's good for people to be silly every now and then."

"I have never seen you in such a carefree state."

Lorelei remembered the way she'd behaved while crossing the Sabine, with her heavy country twang, her about-to-give-birth moans, her general carrying-on.

"I can act foolish at times."

She fell silent as they continued to walk across the field.

"This comparison with the orphanage—" Preacher began.

"I meant no offense."

"And none was taken. The comparison is not invalid. We are a group of men without ties to the rest of the world. Men whose circumstances have thrown them together in the confines of a small enclosure. Much as orphans find themselves."

"You do understand, don't you?"

He looked past her for a moment, the gray eyes

seeing sights she could not see. His step slowed, and at last he came to a halt and looked at her.

"We are missing much that matters greatly to us, Lorelei, but we have no choice. Otherwise we would not bury ourselves in the country the way we have, seldom seeking company. Samuel offered us refuge. He has helped us each in turn."

"You keep returning to Sam."

"He is a very important part of our lives."

"That seems very strange to me. He once told me he thinks people ought to work out their own problems."

"And he has provided us a place where we can attempt to do just that. I suggest, however, you do not carry this comparison too far and call him our Mother Superior."

Lorelei laughed. "I wouldn't dream of it."

"Perhaps it would help if I told you—"

A youthful cry stopped Preacher from going on. Lorelei scanned the field and the surrounding horizon, but Blue and the mule had disappeared. She and Preacher took off on a run in the direction the boy had been headed. Preacher soon left her far behind and disappeared over the top of the faraway rise. Heart pounding, she prayed he would find the boy safe and sound.

Arriving at the top of the hill, a painful stitch in her side, she came to a sudden halt. Low in the background she could see the four buildings of No Pines; much closer, not more than ten yards away from where she stood, the mule was chomping grass, Blue was sitting on the ground with a dazed look on his face, and Preacher was kneeling beside him to make sure he was all right.

Her attention didn't remain on them long, distracted as she was by the sorrel horse close to Preacher and by the grim-faced rider staring at her with bark-brown eyes.

"Sam!"

He just kept on staring.

Preacher helped Blue to stand and nodded that the boy was all right. "He saw Samuel and became excited. His eagerness to greet him outmatched his ability to remain on the mule."

Blue grinned. "The mule pitched me, Lori. Sam says when that happens, I need to get back on."

"Sam's good at giving advice," she said.

"Blue's good at following it, too," said Sam. "Be better if a few others did the same."

Lorelei bristled. "Preacher wasn't helping me get to town. He tried to stop me, as a matter of fact."

"I wasn't talking about him."

Lorelei took a step forward. "I'm going into No Pines, Sam. I haven't walked all this way to turn back now just because you think I should."

He glanced at Preacher. "You two be all right?"

Preacher nodded. "I became involved in talking with Lorelei and forgot the boy. If anything had happened to him, I never would have forgiven myself."

"Don't brood about it. She has a distracting way about her. We'll see you back at the camp."

"It will be tomorrow, I believe. The boy and I can stay in the room at the back of the store. We've done it often before."

Sam reined toward her. She stopped her forward progress, but she held her ground. "I'm going into town."

Sam wasn't listening. Spurring the sorrel, he came at her in a burst of speed, scooped her up in front of him, and took off across the field. Before she could cry out, Lorelei found herself stomach down across his lap, the slouch hat lost somewhere in the grass, a mass of yellow hair hanging wild on one side of the horse, her legs dangling on the other.

She bounced hard against his spread thighs, the breath crushed from her as they rode across the field. He didn't slow down until they were in the grove of oak and hickory at the edge of the grass. Even then the pace was too rapid for her to do anything more than keep holding on to his leg and pray she wouldn't bounce off.

"Let me down," she finally managed as the blood pulsed in her head. The words came out jerky and weak. Of course he didn't answer.

"I'll fall."

This time he responded by gripping her waistband and holding her down even harder against him. The horse slowed to a trot, and she started jiggling; with the way Sam was put together, it didn't take much imagination to figure out which part of him her stomach was jiggling against.

He slowed to a walk, and the jiggling turned to a slow rocking motion that seemed more intimate than ever. On and on they rode; from her strange vantage point it seemed they were traveling in circles, that the stream they crossed was the one they had crossed not five minutes before, that the water splashing against her face was the same that had splashed before. Viewed upside down, the world was not filled with much variety.

At last he came to a halt in a shaded clearing.

The sorrel's head bent to the grass. Feeling very much like a sack of grain, Lorelei looked the horse in the one eye she could see.

"You belong to a monster."

The sorrel bobbed his head and returned to the grass.

Sam let go of her waist. "Any monster worth the name would beat you within an inch of your life."

She twisted until she could look up at him. "You wouldn't dare."

"Considering the position you're in, that's not the smartest thing you've ever said."

She arched her back, struggling for the leverage that would pitch her toward the side where her feet dangled. He pushed her down again. She felt the hardness of his manhood against her stomach.

"Sam!"

"Surprises me as much as it does you. I was all set to give you a good spanking, but I've changed my mind."

Holding her tight against him with a free hand, he proceeded to squeeze first the right buttock, then the left.

"Oh!"

"Yeah, oh." He stroked from side to side.

"What are you doing?"

"What you don't want me to do. Said it wasn't wise." His hand rubbed along the part in her rear end, then moved between her legs. "Maybe I can change your mind."

"Sam!"

She struggled harder, but his persistent fingers probed onward.

"Stop it!"

Of course he didn't. The sorrel shifted position and continued to crop grass. She forced herself to hold still, but Sam showed no sign of being discouraged as his fingers began to move in slow and steady circles against her, the trousers providing little protection against the pressure of his attack.

She squeezed her eyes closed, tried mightily to hold her breath, to pull her body in on itself, but he was relentless. She felt the familiar throbs, the concentrated fire, the raw hunger rushing through her veins.

Sam groaned once, and she felt herself being lifted into the air by a pair of steady, determined hands. Without knowing quite how he managed it, she was suddenly straddling him on the horse, his enlarged manhood pressed against the throbs that did not abate, his hands stroking down her spine until he could grip her buttocks and hold her firmly right where he wanted her.

This was insane, she told herself, and tried to bring a protest from her throat, but all she came out with was, "Oh, Sam."

She wrapped her arms around his neck, and their foreheads touched. He spoke her name into her parted mouth. "Tell me to stop," he growled, then ran his tongue around the edges of her lips.

"I can't."

He kissed her with total authority, and she ground her swollen breasts against his chest, wanting desperately to force her way through the thick layers of buckskin and wool and rub her nipples against his hot skin.

His hat had fallen, suspended against his back by a leather thong. Holding him tight, she crushed it with her arms. The bulk got in the way of her stroking the flexing muscles of his shoulders and his nape. Too many clothes, she thought wildly, they were wearing too many clothes.

The horse shifted suddenly, sending them both precariously to one side.

"Damn," muttered Sam, then with his usual masculine grace lifted her off him, threw a leg over the pommel and dropped to the ground, still cradling her tight. Before her body heat could begin to cool and the throbs start to ease, he had her stretched out on a cushion of new-grown grass as soft as down, his arms around her as they lay on their sides facing one another, his lips covering hers.

She had never known such abandon as she tugged at the buttons of his shirt, ignoring a ripping sound as she pulled the shirt open and rotated her fingers in the wiry chest hairs. She reveled in the twitch of his skin. Throwing a leg over her thighs, he pinned her against him. She writhed in his expert embrace.

His fingers wound in her hair as he kissed her again and again, his tongue licking her lips and then plunging into the damp warmth of her mouth. She met the invasion with savage eagerness, sucking and then brushing her own tongue against him. Her fingertips played against his taut masculine nipples, and she rejoiced in the rumbles of pleasure that erupted from deep within him.

Everywhere she was on fire for him, from her hungry mouth to her full, hard-tipped breasts, to the throbbing wet valley that awaited with carnal avarice the most intimate invasion of all.

He broke the kiss and the embrace long enough to undress them both. She helped, her eager hands tugging at her clothes and at his until the garments were a forgotten mass of leather and wool tossed to one side.

And then she was back in his arms where she belonged, lips to lips and tongue to tongue, his caress concentrated on her breasts, her own fingers seeking the contours of his arms and chest, moving down the hard length of his torso until she came to the thick hair in which was nestled the part of his body that she had once scorned.

She wrapped her fingers around him, stroked and kneaded and explored the shape of him with nothing more than her hand, and then the hand was no longer enough for her.

She broke the kiss. "I want to see you."

His eyes burned with a feral light. He put scant inches between them, but the distance was enough for her to look at the matted hair at his throat, the firm, subtle shape of his chest, the narrow waist and flat abdomen, the thick black pubic hair, and at last his aroused manhood.

In an instant all of Sam's power and strength seemed concentrated in that central instrument of lovemaking. She wondered how she could have ever rejected anything so magnificent.

"Woman, you drive me mad."

Her eyes darted to his. The light in the brown depths became an inferno. Gently he eased her to her back and ran a palm over her impatient breasts, then stroked in widening circles across her trembling stomach, through golden curls, and along her inner thighs.

All the while, their eyes held, the heat of passion enveloping them like a blanket. "You're smooth as hot silk," he said. "The softest thing I've ever felt."

"Touch me," she whispered.

His fingers did what she yearned for them to do. What sweet, passionate lessons Sam had taught her—magical lessons deliciously learned. Her body pulsed with a total submission even as she realized he was submitting to her will, too. They wanted the same thing, the spirals of ecstasy, the rapture they brought to one another. In this single act if in no other, she and Sam were in total harmony.

The rhythms of love quickened. "Now," she said huskily. "Now."

He spread her legs quickly and slipped deep inside her. This time there was no pain, only a sense of rightness as she embraced him. The thrusts intensified. Working together, they brought each other to paradise.

Chapter Nineteen

Lorelei was a long time coming down from the high to which Sam had carried her. Lying in his arms, the soft grass of an early spring cushioning them both and the mid-morning sun casting down dappled light and warmth through the trees, she listened as his vigorous breathing gradually steadied, and she stared at the rise and fall of his chest with its matted curls of hair.

The urge to kiss those hairs swept over her, but that would be an act of tenderness, separate from the passions that were slowly dying. From the beginning she had met Sam's strength with a strength of her own; even in their lovemaking, after the first overtures, the initial touches and kisses that aroused her, he had not taken the lead.

If she treated him gently now, if he saw her as anything else but formidable, if he knew how tender she could be, he would take it as a sign of her feminine weakness; she could never win an argument with him again.

She closed her eyes against a rush of regret. Why was she thinking of weakness and argument now? Because they were safe subjects. To think of what the past few minutes had meant to her would lead

to the consideration that maybe Preacher was right
. . . that maybe she was developing an attachment
for Sam, a very permanent attachment, that would
only break her heart.

"Well," she said with a sigh.

"Well?" He eased her away just far enough to
look into her eyes. "What does that mean?"

"Nothing. Just well. As in well, we did it again."

His eyes glinted. "More sugar talk from my
honey."

"Please don't call me that. It sounds like you forgot my name. Besides, I'm not your anything."

"Right," he said. He stared down at her, his
brown eyes slipping into their unreadable darkness.
At last he pulled away and reached for the mound
of clothes.

She felt a chill and hurriedly dressed. Sam followed her lead and sat down beside her.

Finger combing her hair, she glanced at his shirt.
"I'll have to repair where the button is torn."

His lips twitched. "I kinda liked you doing the
ripping for a change."

A tiny tremor traveled down her spine as she remembered the state she'd been in at the time. Delib-
erately she avoided his eye. Grasping a clump of
grass in her hand, she wiped at the caked dirt on
one of her shoes.

"I wasn't going to let that happen to me again,"
she said.

"That's what you were telling yourself. I had a
pretty good idea you were telling yourself wrong."

"You're awfully sure of yourself, aren't you?"

"On this subject, it's easy to be sure. You shiver
every time I touch you. That's got to encourage a
man."

She turned to look at him. "So don't touch me."

Their eyes met. "I can't help it. Hell of an admission to make, but looking at you is like putting a spark to gunpowder. We get together, we just naturally explode."

"So you're blaming nature."

"I'm not putting blame on anything. It's just a fact."

She concentrated on cleaning the second shoe. "I think I've got you figured out, Sam."

"Any chance you'll keep it to yourself?"

She shot him a quick sideways glance; then it was back to the shoe. "You told Blue that when the mule throws him, he's to get right back on. The implication was that by doing so, he'd prove he could do it, that the mule hadn't won."

"Hell's fire, woman. Are you saying I mounted you again to show I could?"

"I'm saying that's why you started—"

She hesitated, then saw this was no time for disguising what had happened in genteel terms. "You started fondling me the way you did. Once you had my cooperation, then the rest was simple."

Sam shook his head. "You are the damnedest woman I have ever met. I never know what you're going to come up with next."

"It could be that surprise is my only weapon."

"So why do you need one?"

"Because you keep ordering me around like you're my jailer."

"I see." Sam slowly nodded his head. "I think we've come round to what's eating at you. It's not all this heat and have-to that builds between us. It's what goes on at the other times. You don't want me telling you what to do."

276

"Give the prize to the Texian. He's finally figured it out."

"You haven't wanted my advice from the beginning."

"Advice?"

"Guidance, then. The trouble is when you act on your own, you're forever getting into trouble."

The injustice of his words stung her. Or maybe she was bothered because he was right. Sam had her so turned around, she didn't know which way was up.

Tugging on her shoes, ignoring the pain of the blister on her left heel, she stood and reached for her coat.

"It's my trouble I'm getting into, and it's my life." She started to walk the width of the clearing and back again. "I have to decide for myself how I will live it."

He propped himself against the base of a tree and watched her pace. "You keep up the way you are, you won't live it very long."

Lorelei stared down at him, from the shock of black hair resting carelessly across his forehead, to the torn closure of his shirt, to the narrow hips and long legs, to the tooled boots. He'd already put on his spurs. The silver glinted in a ray of sun.

Heaven help her, she felt a tightening inside just from the sight of him.

She raised her eyes to his. "Do you think you're no danger to me?" She gestured toward the flattened grass where they had lain. "If that's the case, you're thinking with your third leg. And don't look at me like that. I picked up a vulgarity or two in the brothel. They come in handy every now and then."

"Listen to me, Lorelei—"

"No, you listen to me. You're always talking about keeping me out of trouble. A woman can get into a lot more trouble doing what we just did than she can playing poker. What have you got to lose here? Nothing. Not a reputation, not any sense of pride. Men like to seduce women. It's a sign of their manhood."

"Seduce? Ha!"

"You did, in a very unsubtle way, feeling me like that when I couldn't get away. You knew how I would react."

"Yeah. And I was right."

"Don't sound so proud. What happens if I get pregnant? I'm really not stupid, Sam, no matter what you believe. The idea has occurred to me."

He sat forward, and she could see the anger building in him. "I tried to bring up a solution to that little problem," he said, "but you didn't seem to think it was such a good idea."

"Oh, Sam," she said, anguish in her voice, "there's no way I could ever marry you. We'd both be miserable. You knew it even while you were trying to propose."

Tears came without warning, and she turned away from him to stare into the woods. Silence settled between them, and she listened to the wind and to the birds while she regained control. "I've come up with my own solution. I've always wanted a child. A husband sort of came with it, but maybe I was fooling myself that anyone I would want would want me, too."

Hearing him stand and walk toward her, she hurried on. "And don't say I'm just feeling sorry for myself . . . that I'm a beautiful woman with a lot of passion and all those other things that don't mean a thing in the long run. A respectable man has the right to expect a respectable wife as the mother of his children. I have dear friends who know what kind of person I am, but the rest of the world knows too much about the things that have happened to me. And too little. At best I'll always be the notorious woman who ran a casino. At worst I'll be a whore."

"Do you really give a damn what the world thinks?"

She forced herself to face him. He was standing close, towering taller than the surrounding trees. "No, I don't. That's why I could take being an unmarried mother. I'm making money at Balzac's, enough to support a child, and there's enough love in me to make up for a missing father."

"You've really thought this out, haven't you?"

His voice was far too even, far too soft for her comfort. She wanted to stop defending herself, to stop attacking whatever he had to say, but she knew their conversation was not done.

"I've had time to think it out."

"You're way ahead of me, then, but that's no surprise. Now, maybe your having my baby wasn't something I've given a lot of consideration, other things being at the front of my mind; but now I am thinking of it, and I'm not too sure I'll let you take him away."

She stared at him in disbelief. "What would you do with a baby? Get Francine as a wet nurse?"

"Leave Francine out of this."

"If you insist. I'm sure there's someone else you could use instead." Again she was close to tears. "Oh, Sam, this is all talk. I'm not pregnant. I

279

learned a few things about a woman's body at the brothel. Things my father could never have taught me. This is the wrong time of the month."

"If it's just talk, why bring it up?"

"Because we both know that what happened here could happen again. And don't you dare start telling me it certainly will. Neither of us knows for sure. All I'm saying is that pregnancy is a problem for a woman that a man doesn't have to deal with. It's much more serious than playing poker with Bert Jackson and trying to decide if he's who I think he is."

"You have a mighty clever way of bringing things around to the same old subject. You're still not going into town. At least not until Dun Straight's out of the way."

She ignored his edict. There were ways to get around him without a direct confrontation like this.

"Weren't you coming from No Pines when Blue saw you?" she asked. "Is he there now?"

Sam shook his head. "Stable hand says he rode out a few days ago, but he's supposed to be back."

"So let me ride in now."

"No. It's too dangerous."

"You have a stubborn way about you, Sam Delaney."

He settled his hat low on his forehead. "When I'm right."

He whistled for the horse, who had disappeared sometime after Sam helped her to the ground. The sorrel came bounding through the trees. Mounting, he extended a hand.

There was nothing to do but ride with him back to the camp. Still, she hesitated. Something bothered her about what he just said.

"You must have been asking about Straight. Why? Preacher said you and Jet were looking for the lawyer."

"Not any more. We found him over in the next county."

"Drunk?"

"Dead."

"Oh, no. How did it happen?"

"Folks in San Augustine said he shot himself in his hotel room. There was supposed to be a witness who heard him talking about how he was going to do it. Jet's trying to track the witness now."

"And you came looking for Dun Straight?"

"Yeah. I figured there was a witness to the shooting, too. The one who pulled the trigger."

Staring up at him as he sat astride the sorrel, his eyes cold under the brim of his hat, his face lean and lined and solemn, he hardly looked like the man who had brought her to ecstasy such a short while ago. He didn't even resemble the man she'd just been arguing with.

For all his solid grimness, he looked vulnerable. She remembered the way he'd stood in the doorway of the saloon and faced the armed gunman. A strange mixture of warmth and dread shivered through her.

She took his hand and settled herself behind him on the saddle skirt, for once glad to rest her arms at his side and to sit close to his strong back. She'd thought him such a simple man when they first met. He was Trouble and nothing more.

She knew differently now. For all the thousand things that would forever keep them apart, she nestled against him and silently prayed that he would be kept from harm.

Chapter Twenty

Early the next morning Lorelei drank a cup of bitter coffee while the twins gathered eggs from the thick brush close to the corral. From beside the pond, she alternated between watching their efforts and casting casual glances around the perimeter of the clearing. Aside from the squawking hens, there was no other movement in camp.

The task completed, Al stoked the campfire while Cal broke the eggs into the skillet.

Lorelei brought a stack of tin plates from the cabin. "Where is Sam?" she asked as she placed them on a flat rock by the fire. Her voice was not nearly so indifferent as she had wanted.

"Rode out early," said Al.

"Oh," she said. Ignoring a silent self-lecture to change the subject, she added, "Did he say where he was going? Or when he'd be back?"

"Nope," said Cal, who stirred the eggs with a knife, then set the skillet on a pile of banked coals at the edge of the flames.

Lorelei stared into her half-filled coffee cup. Why should she feel hurt because he hadn't told her he was leaving? She'd hardly seen him after they got back to camp yesterday afternoon. Besides, he *never* told her of his plans—not his comings or goings, not his destinations, not his purposes.

Taking the offered plate of eggs, she lectured herself once again against expecting any special attention from him. After breakfast, with the day developing clear and mild, she devoted her energies to cleaning everything in sight — the skillet, plates, cups, cabin, her spare shirt, the petticoat and chemise in which she slept. Even the rocks at the outer edges of the fire got a good scrubbing where burnt food had begun to build.

Next she turned to the twins, who were watching her rock cleaning with a bemused eye.

"No time like now for that haircut," she said. "I'll trim up those beards while I'm at it."

The men looked at one another, then back at her.

"Can't," said Al. "Wild hogs in the area."

"Wild hogs?" she said.

"Yep," said Cal. "Gonna see if we can't get us one. Makes fine eating. Better than possum."

With a speed unlike any she had noticed in them before, they retreated into the woods.

Rebuffed, she returned to the cabin and pulled out the prize item she had purchased in town — a full bolt of blue muslin. For the last few nights, ever since returning from that first journey, she'd examined it, the way a collector might examine a case of valuable coins, thinking about the way she would use it, contemplating the best way to use her sewing skills.

How strange it was to remember her indifferent regard for clothes back in New Orleans; here in the wilderness the muslin took on a value greater than gold.

Removing the buckskin flap from the window, she held the material up to the light. Blue as the

Texas sky, she decided, and even prettier than it had looked to her in the general store. It slipped like soft silk against her stroking fingers. As soon as possible she would get out of the boys' clothes she'd worn for too long.

She set the muslin aside. With the blanket from the bed covering the dirt floor of the cabin, she sat cross-legged in front of the hearth and began cutting the tattered green velvet gown into pieces she could use as a pattern for a replacement dress.

Before she actually cut into the precious material and fitted it to her body, she wanted to be completely clean. For that purpose, she'd bought a small bar of soap. She checked the shirt she'd hung on a tree limb. It was still damp around the collar and hem, but by the time she finished bathing and washing her hair, it would be fine.

In ten minutes she was standing on the grassy bank beside the wide spot in the creek, the surrounding wilderness protecting her as surely as the walls of a house. The noontime sun shining onto the water from directly above was the warmest she'd felt since last October when she'd been out playing tag with young Victor Gase at the plantation. Dropping the blanket she would use to dry herself, along with the clean shirt, she hurriedly undressed and with soap in hand stepped gingerly into the center of the pooled stream.

The cold creek took her breath away. Before she could change her mind about the bath, she went under fast, coming up with her weight on her knees, face held to the sun, hair streaming behind her, the water lapping at the underside of her exposed breasts.

She sat on her heels, bringing the water level to

the top of her shoulders where it could protect her body from the breeze. Gradually she adjusted to the temperature until the easy, undulating waves seemed warm against her skin and the air cool on her face.

The details of her body were clearly visible in the shallow stream, but that was no concern. Here in this isolated part of the forest — except for that first day when Blue suddenly appeared and caught her by surprise — she had always found complete solitude.

Clearing a comfortable space on the rocky stream bed for her bent legs, she scrubbed her hair, scrubbed her body, let the water swirl around her to carry away the residue of the soap, and thought with sudden irony that there weren't too many places she touched that Sam hadn't touched yesterday.

She closed her eyes. Were there no moments of her life when he didn't intrude? Tossing the soap onto the bank, she hugged herself. If he strode through the woods right now, his hat pulled low over those penetrating eyes, his mouth tight and twisted into the almost grin he had when he was set on making love to her . . . if he stood on the bank and began to unbutton his trousers, what would she do?

Gambler Lorelei knew the odds were heavily in favor of her coming out of the water and wrapping her arms around him and telling him he needed to dry every place on her body with his hands. It was a sure thing he would comply.

"Samuel Delaney." She whispered his name into the air. "Sam."

Somehow, sometime, without her realizing it, he had become an obsession with her. Delilah would hoot with laughter if she knew.

And would her dear friend ever find out? Sure to face a thousand questions when she returned to the casino, Lorelei couldn't see herself lying about what had happened between her and Sam. The difficulty would be in making it sound like an experiment to see if she really could enjoy sex, the way Delilah always said she would.

And did she? The water rippling around her seemed to answer the question: *yes, yes, yes.* But somehow it wasn't just the sex that gave her pleasure. She couldn't see giving herself to any other man except Sam.

She held still and let the movement of the stream sway her, arms extended to float on the surface, her clean hair trailing against her neck and shoulders. The wind soughed in the trees behind a cacophony of birds.

And then she heard more than just the water and the wind and the bird songs. Felt more than heard, really. She sensed another presence. Probably just a wild animal, she told herself, which could mean a possum—or a panther.

Her heart quickened; she had forgotten to bring so much as a stick with her for protection, so intent had she been on bathing and then getting back to the blue muslin. She glanced at the bank. Blanket, clothes, shoes—nothing there to help in her defense. Besides, they were well out of reach.

Lorelei told herself to quit being so foolish. Why, she only *thought* she heard something. It might only be—

The wind died and the birds took wing. Over the babble of the creek she heard a paralyzing sound from behind her on the far bank, a hiss of air as though someone was drawing in labored breath through closed lips. The last time she'd heard that particular sound was days ago in Edgar's Wayside Inn.

The vulnerability of her situation overtook her. Naked and sitting in water to her neck, she was trapped as surely as if she were in a vise.

She tried to think, but stark fear froze her mind. Slowly, inch by inch, she turned her head until she could see from the corner of her eye the figure of a man at the water's edge. Her eyes squeezed closed; she forced them open to look at the black boots, gray trousers and shirt, the gun belt and pistol, the black neckerchief and matching broad-brimmed hat, the gray pallor of Dun Straight.

He stared back with flat black eyes.

Thin and colorless, he had an inhuman look to him, a specter against the wilderness. Half-turned in his direction, Lorelei covered her breasts with her arms. She swallowed, wanting to scream but fearful that any cry for help would come out as little more than a pitiful mewing. Worse, she knew there was no one other than the gunman who would hear.

Suddenly she could listen no longer to that macabre hissing. "Get out of here!" she ordered. The words sounded too high, too loud; but her voice did not break, and she hurried on. "I mean it. Run on back to your boss Bert Jackson and tell him—"

A hideous rasping cough stopped her, and she realized he was laughing. The lipless slash that was his mouth twitched, but otherwise his expression did not change.

Slowly—and she prayed imperceptibly—Lorelei edged her right knee across the pebbled bed of the creek until she came to what felt like a large rock.

Abandoning her feeble attempts at modesty, she waved a distracting left hand in the air while she eased lower in the water to pick up the potential weapon.

"I'll scream for help," she warned as she cradled the rock against her thigh.

The dullness of the gunman's eyes took on an ugly glitter as he stared into the water, picking out the details of her kneeling figure.

"Won't do any good," he rasped. "No one's in the camp."

Which meant she had to help herself. Standing, she threw herself toward the opposite bank, scrambling onto the grass, stumbling over the blanket, wasting precious seconds as she righted herself and dashed on shaky, desperate legs toward the brush. She heard splashing, and then a leather-gloved hand clamped around her upper arm, squeezing cruelly, jerking her around.

The fingers bit into the flesh of her left arm as she stared up at Straight.

He gave a quick glance at her naked, shivering body. "You won't die right away," he rasped.

"Sam will kill you."

Again came the hideous laugh. "Hope he tries."

He let go of her arm and grabbed a handful of wet hair, yanking her head back, pulling hard enough to tear the long strands out by the roots. Up close, he stank of stale smoke and old sweat, and a fetid odor she could define only as death.

She raked her left hand across his face, drawing blood; bright red bubbled in fine lines against his gray cheek.

He yanked harder at her hair. "Bitch," he hissed, "you'll pay for that."

She scratched at him again but missed, her hand falling to the black scarf at his neck. She jerked it loose and threw it to the ground, then stared at the ugly, puckered scar that ran from ear to ear across his bone-thin neck.

Freeing her hair, he backhanded her, his breathing coming hard and grating like bricks dragged over coarse sand.

Tasting blood, Lorelei fell backward to the ground. She shook off a wave of dizziness and came up fast to smash the rock against his nose. Blood spurted down to the slash that was his mouth. He howled, the first near-human sound she had heard from him, and she whirled toward the thick brush.

He caught her again by the arm, jerked her around, slapped once, twice, snapping her head from side to side, then whipped her toward the water. Unable to stop her momentum, she fell headfirst into the creek. He bounded after her and dragged her to the opposite bank, tossing her to the ground as he might a piece of kindling.

Head reeling, she tried to rise. He slapped her down again and straddled her, tugging off his gloves and tossing them aside. He lowered himself until he was sitting across her abdomen, the weight of his body pinning her back against the grass, the tip of his holstered gun cold against her skin. Catching her wrists, he thrust them over her head and ran his free hand across her swollen, bleeding lips, then down her throat, catching her by the neck in his steely grasp until she could hardly breathe.

She stared up at him, at the broken, bloody nose, the scratches, the ugly mouth, the flat, cold black of his eyes. Scenes of whores and brutish men flashed across her mind. She remembered Carrie's bruised and broken body. Panic and hate combined to give her strength, and she thrashed wildly beneath him.

He tightened his legs against her, his strength like baling wire. His hand moved down to squeeze one of her breasts. She cried out in pain.

"Lori!" The youthful voice came from across the creek, distant but cheerful, excited.

Blue, she thought. Her hopes soared. Preacher would be right behind him . . . maybe even Sam. She found her breath and cried out. Once again the fingers grasped her by the throat, and Straight glared down a warning filled with hatred and cunning.

She heard the boy crashing through the brush, but she could hear no other sounds that would tell her someone was with him. Her hopes turned to a new and more terrible fear. Straight would shoot down the boy with no more thought than he'd give to shooting a bird.

She fell limp. Straight eased the hold on her throat.

"Go back, Blue," she screamed, barely getting out the boy's name before a bony hand clamped down hard over her mouth.

"Lori!" The sound of her name this time carried a wondering fear, and she was able to see past her attacker. Blue stood on the opposite bank, his usually happy eyes wide and frightened.

Straight glanced back once at the boy. His hand loosened over her mouth, and she bit into the palm, again drawing blood. Again he slapped her.

Blue bounded across the narrow part of the creek immediately downstream from the pooled depths and hurtled through the air toward Straight. The gunman rose to his feet, but the boy reached him before he could draw the pistol. The momentum of his flying body sent Straight falling backward to the ground, the boy on top of him.

Knocking Blue aside, Straight came fast to his feet. The boy wrapped his arms around the gunman's legs. Straight drew the gun.

"No!" Lorelei screamed, scrambling to her knees and throwing herself at him.

Straight held his ground, little impeded by the desperate efforts to stop him. The butt of the pistol crashed against the back of Blue's skull. The boy slumped to the ground. Holstering the gun, Straight aimed the point of his boot into Lorelei's stomach. She fell back, deflecting the full force of the kick, but still a penetrating pain shot through her. Gasping for breath, she clutched her middle and writhed on the ground.

Turning to the still body at his feet, Straight rested the sole of his boot against the boy's back and, with a deep and hideous intake of air, shoved him into the creek. Facedown, Blue floated on the surface.

Lorelei forgot her agony and thought only of the boy. Scrambling across the grass to the water's edge, she grabbed at Blue's shirt. Brutal hands gripped her shoulders and jerked her to her feet.

Straight twisted her to face him. Her body screaming with pain, she flailed weak fists against his chest. The bruising fingers gripped harder. She fought for leverage to bring her knee up in his crotch. Before she could aim, he suddenly released her, his body propelled backward as a tall, lean figure came between them.

"Sam!" she cried out in a rush of elation, ignoring the throbbing of her lips and the burning of her lungs.

Sam's fist crashed into the gunman's already bloodied face. Straight stumbled, caught his balance, then threw himself back at Sam as Lorelei scurried out of the way. The two men fell to the ground, rolling, twisting, fists flying.

Still struggling for breath, she turned to the creek. Wading into the water, she got a firm grip on Blue's shirt and pulled him to the bank. She had no time for the battling men. Besides, Sam was here. He would take care of Straight.

Desperation gave her strength as she tugged the limp body of the boy onto the grass and shifted him to his back. His lips were purple, his skin colorless as she bent her ear to listen for the sounds of his breathing. All she heard were the grunts and struggles of the men.

A new and terrible agony overtook her. Blue was dead. That was all she could think of, and yet the idea was incomprehensible. Tears streamed down her cheeks. She turned to the man she hoped beyond all hope could make things right.

"Sam," she cried out. "Sam."

He sat astride Straight's supine body, fist drawn back as if to deliver a finishing blow. He turned to her cry.

The back of Straight's fist caught him beside the head, and he fell away. Straight bounded to his feet. Before Sam could rise, the gunman disappeared into the thick brush at the edge of the grass.

Sam started after him, hesitated, then with a low growl turned back to her and to Blue.

"Move," he said, and Lorelei scurried out of the

way. Sam flipped the boy to his stomach, turned his head to one side, and straddled him, his blunt hands splayed across the wet shirt. Steadily, rhythmically, he began to press down hard against Blue's back.

Lorelei knelt beside the pair and cursed herself for not warning Blue soon enough, convincingly enough to stay away from the creek. Almost as bad, she'd even been the cause of Straight's escape, but she couldn't give thought to that now.

Blue . . . loving, kind Blue. Clever in his own special way, an artist of the finest sort. She had not spoken to God in years, not since long before she left Boston and even then never to ask for special favors, but here on this wilderness creek bank she closed her eyes and prayed.

The sound of coughing arrested her prayers. Her eyes flew open. Sam continued to press and release, press and release, but the boy's body was no longer still. She saw the water trickling between his lips, the jerking of his back as he struggled to breathe. Slowly allowing herself to accept the possibility he had survived, she hugged herself with sheer joy.

Gradually Blue's breathing grew regular. Sam eased off him and sat beside her in the grass.

"He's all right," she said, her voice little more than a sigh.

"Maybe," said Sam.

"What do you mean?" she said. "He's breathing."

"But he should be coming around by now." Sam fingered the knot at the base of Blue's skull. "What did the bastard do to him?"

Lorelei shuddered. "Hit him with his gun."

"Could be there's damage inside there."

All joy gave way to the return of icy fear, and she

sat back, not knowing what to say, what to do. Every part of her body ached, but no more than her worried heart. She shivered from the air that wafted coolly against her bare skin, and she brushed the damp tendrils of hair from her face.

Sam shifted his gaze to her. "You're cold."

"I'm all right."

His eyes fell to the swollen, cut mouth. He stroked a thumb against the blood, his touch as light as the breeze, then looked down at the bruises already forming on her shoulders and her arms. There would be other bruises, she knew, some deep inside where Straight had kicked.

She watched the way Sam studied her, not with carnal hunger as he had looked at her naked body before, but with a curious kind of tenderness.

"My God," he said, his head shaking slowly.

"I'll be all right."

His eyes met hers. "Did he—"

"No," she said in a rush. "He found me in the water and . . . just hit me. Blue stopped him from doing more."

Sam stroked her throat, stopping against her pounding pulse. His fingers were hot against her chilled skin.

"I should have been here to take care of you," he said.

"It wasn't your fault," she said, but she could see he didn't agree.

In the narrowing dark depths of his eyes, in the tightness of his mouth, in the taut pulling of the skin across his cheeks, she saw the building of his rage. His hand shook against her. All the violence she'd ever sensed in him surged visibly now. It warmed and frightened her with its potency.

"He's a dead man."

"Oh, Sam, I'm sorry. He got away because of me."

"Don't think that way. I had a choice. I could have gone after him. Besides, you'd already done more than your share. He wasn't looking too good by the time I arrived."

"I said I'd never be a victim again."

Their eyes held. "You're quite a woman," said Sam.

Lorelei wanted to tell him he was quite a man, but the words caught in her throat.

He glanced toward the far bank. "Let me get your clothes for you."

"I can manage."

With a nod, he turned to the boy. "If you're sure, get dressed and bring me the blanket. We'll get the boy wrapped up and back to the cabin. Preacher's waiting."

He blinked once, his mouth grim. "Looks like that's what we're all going to be doing for a while. Waiting for Blue to come around."

Chapter Twenty-one

By dawn the next morning, Blue still had not awakened. Having spent the restless, pain-filled night hours on a pallet of blankets in front of the hearth, usually with either Sam or Preacher standing or sitting close by, Lorelei reported the bad news to the men waiting outside.

Every muscle in her body ached, and she felt surely Dun Straight's boot had rearranged something deep inside; but nothing afflicted her like this worry over the boy.

Al and Cal shook their heads sadly. Wash, keeping to the background, looked away before Lorelei could see how he took the news, but the fact that he had remained close by throughout the vigil gave proof of his concern.

Al offered her a breakfast of hardtack and eggs, but she accepted only a cup of coffee. Sipping the dark brew through a sore mouth, she stared over the rim of the cup at Sam. No more than three feet away, he stared right back, his hair ruffled, his cheeks whisker-shadowed, his eyes dark and sunken.

A self-conscious hand went to her own tangled hair. She must look like the wrath of God had struck her—lips cut and swollen, one eye darkened, an ugly bruise across her cheek. And those were just the marks that showed. In the dim firelight late last night, left alone with Blue for a few minutes, she'd made a quick inspection of her body, shuddered once, and decided she would not make that mistake again, not for a long while.

She returned to the cabin and found Preacher continuing the bedside watch. Standing next to him, she stared down at the bunk where Blue lay, his long, thin arms resting on top of the chest-high blanket, his fair hair splayed across the pillow, his eyes closed. He looked so young, so fragile. The best that could be said of his condition was that his breathing was regular.

"The boy didn't talk for a long time after I found him," said Preacher. "Hungry, his clothes torn, his mind only on the birds. He could have wandered off from a band of traveling immigrants, or perhaps he was left behind by a family that did not appreciate his special qualities."

"How cruel," said Lorelei, hugging herself.

"We both know life can be so at times. It is doubtful any of us will ever know the truth about Blue. We can only be grateful that he has shown no scars of any kind from the ordeal. Once he awakens, I expect him not to have changed."

"How long ago was it that you found him?"

Preacher thought a moment. "It must be close to nine months now. Strange how time seems different here in the wilderness."

Lorelei found herself thinking of Carrie. "Why is it that bad things happen to good people?" she asked.

Preacher slowly shook his head. "It was a

question that led me to leave the ministry."

She looked at him in surprise. "You've never talked about yourself."

"I am not a very interesting man."

"If you truly believe that, then you have misjudged yourself. You are more than just an interesting man. You are good. Loyal, and loving, and kind."

"There are things you do not know."

Lorelei would not be swayed. "You speak of the past," she said. "I speak of now. With your garden and your constant attention and care, you work hard to keep this lonely band of men together. I've never heard you utter a cruel or harsh word, and if you can't accept my opinion, accept Blue's. You said he does not give his affection to everybody. But he has to you, along with his trust."

His mouth curved slightly within his long, gray beard. "The woman preaches to the preacher."

She gave him a sad smile. "I'm the daughter of a minister of the Lord, remember? Not a very good minister, I'm afraid. His Church of the Latter Day Puritans was not a church designed to bring solace to the unfortunate. Harsh judgment was much more in his line."

"You speak of a denomination I do not know."

"Papa made it up. He even went so far as to write his own version of the Scripture." She stopped and thought a minute, then looked at Preacher in wonderment. "Do you know this is the most I have talked about him in more than six years?"

"Sometimes talking helps to ease the burdens of the heart."

"A wise observation. You might apply it to yourself." Preacher shook his head slowly. "Samuel says you have an unexpected way of saying what is on your mind."

Her heart caught. "Is that all he's said?"

"He is not a man given to personal revelations."

"I've never met one who was."

Preacher studied her solemnly, his wise eyes moving over her damaged face. "I know little about your past life, Lorelei, but I know that like the others of us here, you have suffered much."

She looked down at Blue and heard herself telling Preacher a few of the particular sufferings, of the journey from Boston to New Orleans, of the brothel and of Carrie, and at last of the kindness she had received during the subsequent years.

"Samuel knows?" asked Preacher.

She nodded. "He's known for a long time."

Preacher touched her hand. "Rest assured that all will be well with you two. I feel this in my heart."

She did not respond, and silence settled over the room as they watched the rise and fall of Blue's chest beneath the blanket. Sam joined them, but the others remained outside.

The rest of the day passed slowly, and the next. Late in the evening, fifty-five hours by Lorelei's estimation since Blue was struck down, he began to stir.

She was standing close by the bunk, Sam at her side. Reaching for his hand, she held it tight as they looked down at the boy.

Blue's eyes fluttered open, closed, then opened once again. He stared up at the rafters of the cabin, then turned to them. "Sam. Lori," he said in surprise, then frowned. "My head hurts."

Lorelei broke into a stupid grin. "How wonderful."

And with Sam's hand gripping hers, she burst into tears.

Blue slept fitfully throughout the night and the next day, but his shifting and moaning were welcome changes from the stillness of his long unconsciousness. That evening, after having gotten the boy to down some of the thin broth that Wash had prepared for her, Lorelei slowly and cautiously ate a tender slice of roasted meat. A portion of the wild hog Al and Cal had slain, it was the first solid food she'd eaten since the assault. With her by the campfire were the twins and Preacher; Sam, restless more than ever, had gone for what he said was a walk.

"Where's Wash?" she asked, casting an eye around the clearing for his dark, broad figure. "I'd like to compliment him on the food."

"Like the rest of us, Washington is a solitary man," said Preacher.

"He spoke last night," said Lorelei. "Did you hear him? When I announced that Blue had awakened, he said 'Praise the Lord.'"

"He, too, is fond of the lad."

"I asked him why he'd never spoken before, and he said because he had nothing to say."

Al took her empty plate, and Cal replaced it with a cup of coffee. Thanking them both, she directed a question to the three men. "Sam rode into town today, didn't he?"

Preacher responded. "You were taking a long-needed rest. He did not wish to worry you with news of his journey. He rode in early and returned late in the afternoon."

"And?"

"The man he sought has not returned to his hotel room in days, nor was his horse in the stable."

Lorelei shuddered, remembering the way Straight had appeared without warning on the creek bank. She could hear the rasp of his strange breathing as though he were next to the twins.

"I had to draw conclusions about what must have taken place today," Preacher continued, "but you can be certain Samuel examined with great thoroughness every room in No Pines. To no avail. Even Wilbert Jackson claimed not to have seen him. This came, I gathered, while Samuel was pressing a gun between his eyes. Sheriff Mortimer was extremely upset."

"Sam seems to have told you a great deal."

"Samuel told me little; but I know him, and I know the men with whom he dealt. He has much on his mind. The loss of his land, the difficulties with Wilbert Jackson, and now this abominable attack."

"These are worries he does not choose to share."

She looked away, the hurt of her body extending into a curious heaviness in her heart. A few minutes later she excused herself to go in for the night. It did her little good to wonder about Sam and his perambulations, but she worried fearfully that he would risk his life in seeing that Straight paid for the attack on Blue and her.

She, a woman who had spent six years thinking about revenge, couldn't bear to think of Sam facing a conscienceless killer for the same reason. She made no attempt to analyze her inconsistency.

Despite her stiff and aching muscles, the night's rest came more peacefully than she'd expected, and Lorelei emerged the next morning to an amazing

301

sight: Al and Cal sporting hair trimmed to their collars and beards shaped close to the face. Even Preacher had been worked over with the scissors. They stood lined up outside the cabin, waiting for her inspection; a handsome crew, she pronounced as she gave them each a hug.

Again, Sam was not to be seen. She reentered the cabin, took out the blue muslin and, by the light of the candles she'd purchased at the general store, got to work.

The next few days passed quickly, with Sam coming and going, casting her frequent looks but saying little, Blue sitting up and then walking, and at last returning to his tent, showing scant evidence of his ordeal. Lorelei worked hard over the muslin, cutting and sewing, keeping her mind and hands as busy as possible, trying not to remember the day of the attack, trying with less success not to worry about Sam. She was grateful that her bruises were fading. Even her middle had ceased to cause her pain.

Jet showed up once, asked how she was and, after a low, solemn talk with Sam that she could not overhear, rode out again.

She told herself that all was as it had been, but there was one thing she could not bring herself to do: return to the creek.

On a moonlit night almost two weeks after Straight had invaded the camp, Sam made a rare appearance at supper, took her by the hand, and announced in his don't-tell-me-no tone of voice that he wanted to walk with her for a while. The feel of his palm against hers, the warm, rough skin, the hint of pulse sent shivers running through her. She had missed his touch more than she would have thought possible.

They headed toward the brush, toward a dreaded path. Lorelei tugged back on his hand. "No, Sam, I don't want to."

He kept on going until they were out of sight and hearing of the others. Taking her by the shoulders, he stared down into her eyes. With the moonlight shining on him, casting shadows across the planes of his face, he looked unyielding, as strong-willed as ever, an invincible force that would not be crossed.

"Remember that mule Blue's supposed to climb right back on?"

"I remember," she said, disappointment edging her voice. "The last time we talked about that, you had just—"

"Lorelei," he said, interrupting. "Take it easy. You've every right to doubt me, but all I want is for you to walk with me for a while."

"I guess I misunderstood." Embarrassed, she made a poor attempt at a smile. "What would you call my condition here in Texas? Gun shy, isn't it?"

He did a better job of grinning. "Know what? I'm back to liking a woman with spirit. Truth is, I always did."

Shivering under the power of that grin, she stared ahead at the shadowed path and thought about where it led. "This isn't at all like climbing back on a mule."

"It's a damned sight worse," he said, his voice once again hard-edged. "That's why you have to do it. Dun Straight came in here like the sneaky bastard he is, and even though he was armed and a hundred times stronger than you, he almost got his butt beat before I ever showed up. Then he ran like a coward. He ran. He's gone. Remember that, Lorelei. He's gone."

"Everything you're saying is true. I just don't want to go back so soon."

His hands stroked her shoulders and down her arms. "You don't go back now, you'll have some more bad memories to carry around with you."

Lorelei knew he was making sense. Would he label her a coward, too, if she didn't force herself to follow him down the trail? She took a deep breath. Maybe he wouldn't, but she would. Reluctantly, she nodded her agreement, and with Sam leading the way, his hand again clutching hers, they walked down the winding, overgrown path to the creek.

After several minutes of silent progress, Sam stopped and stepped aside to reveal a lovely sight, slivers of moonlight reflected on the dark swirling water where she usually bathed. A light, warm breeze ruffled the leaves, and at each end of the pooled deep water, the shallow creek babbled soothingly over the pebbles.

She looked at the wild grass on the bank where they stood, then forced her eyes to the opposite side. No ghost awaited her, no spectral figure in gray and black, no hiss, no rasping laugh.

She rubbed a palm against her trousers. "I guess climbing back on a mule isn't so bad."

Sam turned to look down at her and cupped her face in his hands. For all his gentleness, she remembered another man who had stood this close. Unable to breath, she backed away.

Sam placed himself between her and the water, the moonlight again casting shadows on his face. "I don't want to know what he did, or what he told you he would do. Not if it's hard for you to talk about. No, don't say anything just yet. Listen for a minute."

Lorelei hugged herself and nodded solemnly, letting the sound of his deep voice as well as his words wrap her in a safe and soothing warmth.

"No one ever said I was quick when it came to understanding what's eating at someone else," said Sam with a shrug, "but even I can see where a man's touch might not be high on your list of things you've been missing."

"Sam—"

"Honey, you don't obey too smartly, do you? It's my turn. I won't kiss you, or even hold you too tightly, although you've got to know that you look beautiful to me with that moon shining down making your hair look like melted gold. Never realized light like that could catch in a woman's eyes. Turns them kind of silvery."

"You make me sound like a stack of precious metal."

"And I never thought a smart-aleck comeback would sound so good."

They both smiled at one another, and then the smiles died. This time when he held her face, she did not back away. His lips brushed gently over hers, and she felt comforted.

"Let's sit down for a while," said Sam. "Rest yourself against me, and when you say so, we'll go back."

At that moment Lorelei could think of nothing she would rather do. When Sam pulled a blanket from behind a bush and spread it out on the grass, she knew he'd planned ahead.

Sitting down, he looked sheepishly up at her, and her heart twisted sharply in her breast. "Afraid if I came out here carrying the thing, you'd get the wrong idea."

"I would have."

She stretched out on the blanket beside him and nestled close, his arm a pillow for her head as they watched a thin line of vapor play catch with the stars.

"This really is a lovely place, Sam. Texas is lovely."

She wanted to go on and say that Sam was lovely, too, but she wasn't sure how that would sound. And maybe lovely wasn't quite the word for a lean-faced, long and lithe, tight-muscled man who moved with the grace of a wild stallion, who fought with the fierceness of a lion, and who made love with the passion of a . . . of a Sam. There was nothing or no one else with which she could compare him.

Crickets chirped in the brush, but she gave all her attention to the evenness of his breathing.

"Maybe I ought to tell you what happened," she said.

She started talking before she could change her mind, speaking of the bath she had wanted and of the first warning sound that told her she was not alone.

Shifting closer and turning her head into Sam's chest, she made quick work of the rest, playing up Blue's bravery, playing down her own attempts to stop the attack. As she talked, Sam held her in a warm embrace.

"As it was happening, you know, it was as if it wasn't happening to me . . . as if I were watching Carrie all over again. I was hurt and I was afraid, but it was her hurt and her fear as well as my own."

"Some fear. You were beating him up just fine by the time I got here."

Lorelei spread her hand against his shirt and felt the warmth of his body. "I didn't thank you for saving me."

"Should have been here a hell of a lot sooner. The three of us had come back from town together. Blue was all excited because I was teaching him to ride the sorrel."

"That was kind of you."

"Not kind. Necessary. He'll need to ride when he becomes a man. Anyway, he wanted you to know, and we all figured you were down here. When he didn't come back right away, I followed him." Sam paused, then went on, his voice harder.

"Started to shoot Straight. Never wanted anything so much in my life. But he kept twisting and turning until I was afraid I might get you instead. I remembered how I had grabbed you in the casino. He could have done the same thing. Could have broken your neck." He stroked her arm. "You've had a hell of a life as far as men are concerned."

"It hasn't all been bad."

They both fell silent. With all the ugliness they had been talking about fading fast from her mind, she felt a new kind of tenderness take over. She understood Sam's anger and his frustration on that terrible day. Territory he considered his had once again been invaded by someone connected to Bert Jackson. Two people had been attacked—the gentlest member of the camp and the woman he'd vowed to protect. Bravely he'd rushed to their rescue and had come close to defeating the gunman with his fists alone. He cared for Blue, and he cared for her, at least a little. The evidence was there.

307

"Kiss me, Sam."

He bent his head to hers. The kiss was as gentle as the first time, like the brush of his breath against her cheek. But Lorelei was losing her need for gentleness.

She eased her tongue between his lips, teased it deeper until she could taste the dark, male warmth of him, then pulled away.

"Make love to me. Give me new memories of the creek."

"I don't want to hurt you," said Sam.

"You won't. I'm just about healed."

He tightened his embrace and once again kissed her, this time with more authority.

"I've been aching for you, honey," he said huskily. "Wanting to hold you, but too damned afraid to do a thing. Riding and looking and thinking, and most of all wanting to do this." He brushed a hand against her side and caressed her breast.

"Wanting to feel your softness under my hand. Wanting to feel myself inside you."

"I want you inside me. More than anything in the world."

He whispered her name, and then the talking stopped. Tugging her shirt free of the trousers, he undid the buttons slowly, one by one, letting his fingers burn against her bare skin, teasing with little trails over the rising fullness of her breasts, at last opening the shirt wide.

She watched him as he studied her nakedness, his eyes hot, his lips parted. He leaned close and ran his tongue across a nipple, then gave the same consideration to the other breast. She closed her eyes; behind the lids, black velvet swirled.

She was on fire for him, yet she would not have

hurried him for the world. He kissed her breasts, her throat, her cheeks, her lips, his hands gentle and roving. She felt precious beneath the tender assault.

With equal gentleness he removed her shoes and stockings; unfastening her trousers, he slid them down her legs, along with the cotton drawers she had on underneath. Little cries caught in her throat as she watched him, his tanned hands dark against her pale skin, hungry eyes dedicated to everything he bared.

The last faded signs of a bruise on her abdomen brought a growl to his throat. He kissed the spot, his hands stroking the outside of her thighs. A thousand tremors shot through her.

"Did I hurt you?" he asked.

"No," she answered in a voice that was not her own. "Do it again."

This time his growl took on a lascivious tone, and a small smile of pleasure settled on her lips as he trailed a row of kisses in an arc around her pubic hair. He'd never done anything like this before, and she didn't know how she was supposed to react — except she could not stop him, could not pretend he wasn't driving her wild. And she could not still the arching of her body beneath his lips.

Firm hands parted her legs, and the kisses moved to the waiting softness of her inner thighs. Her trembling fingers reached down to him, but he moved lower, his mouth and tongue brushing against the length of her legs, his hands caressing her feet, his thumbs rubbing against each instep in an unexpectedly erotic gesture. Every place on her body was in flames.

"Sam," she whispered, then again, "Sam. I want to touch you."

He gave no heed to her words, instead retracing the fiery path he'd burned down her legs, this time giving special, sweet attention to the length of her thighs, coming closer and closer to the wild throbbing that only he could still.

He touched her with his tongue, and she slipped into the honeyed madness of ecstasy. As his lips moved in sensitive supplication over that most intimate of places, she closed her eyes and gave herself to him in complete abandon, the black velvet behind the lids streaked with splinters of light, like bursts of stars against a midnight sky.

The rapture intensified. Frantically, she tugged at his shoulders, and he eased upward to let her work at the buttons of his shirt. He helped her strip the clothes from his body. Her hand ventured across his chest, probed for his heartbeat, dipped lower to the thickening hair close to his thighs.

His breathing came in quick, short gasps, and his heat burned into her skin as she explored the wondrous evidence that he was ready for her. It seemed the most natural thing in the world for her to open herself to the joining of their bodies.

He slipped inside effortlessly, as though he had finally come to the place he belonged. Their thrusts were quick and deep, each moving rhythmically with the other, whispered names and sighs flowing between them as they climaxed together, too soon . . . too soon. Holding his hard, hot body in her embrace, reveling in the slowing tremors they shared, she regretted only that the moment of rapture could not extend until forever, even as she realized it was too sweet, too dear, and for all its pulsating power, too fragile to last.

At last they parted, and as he rested beside her, he held her close against his strength, stroking her arms, her shoulders, down the center of her back. She held him tight, unwilling to break the spell that wrapped around them. He might not feel it, but with her it was strong enough for them both.

She loved him. There was no trace of doubt in her mind. For the first time in their lovemaking she had felt more than just the passions of the moment; she had felt a bonding with Sam that would last for all time. She was his woman, unwisely considering all the differences that separated them, but perhaps wisdom was not for a woman in love.

She loved him. Lorelei, the bitter woman of the world who had thought all romance carved out of her in a New Orleans brothel years ago, was deeply, irrevocably in love. Sam was a tormenting rascal, a stubborn taskmaster, a brave hero, a handsome devil, a splendid lover, and sometimes, he was even her friend. She wanted to cry, to sing, to caress him and whisper of the depth and width and power of all the feelings surging through her.

But she was not such a fool. Her love was a private matter, a hidden treasure to hold close and secret, a newborn thing that must be allowed to nurture in the darkness of her heart.

Lying next to him in the moonlight, her naked body pressed against his, she made one request — that there be no talk — and with only the sounds of the night to break the quiet, she studied his strong profile, the straight nose, the stubborn chin, the crescent lines carved at the edges of his mouth and eyes. Lastly, she looked down the long, sleek length of him silhouetted against the night's silvery glow.

Chapter Twenty-two

Dressed in the gown of blue muslin that she'd been working on in secret, her hair worn long in finely brushed waves, Lorelei emerged from the cabin later than usual the next morning. Little more than twelve hours had passed since she had lain beside Sam at the creek.

Alone by the campfire, he pulled himself to his feet and stared at her. She held herself proudly erect, hands at her back, and returned the stare.

She'd finished hemming the gown only minutes before. Free of adornment, it was rounded over her bosom, giving accent to the slenderness of her neck and the gentle rise of her breasts. Full-sleeved, narrow at the waist, and with only a single petticoat to give it shape, it followed the line of her hips and fell long enough to hide her sturdy shoes.

"I may not be able to cook," she said with an edge of defiance, "but I can sew."

Sam's eyes took in the full picture of her standing by the cabin door, a sunbeam shining just on her. "Yep," he said.

Knowing Sam as she did, she took the *yep* as a compliment.

But he wasn't through. "You wouldn't take offense if I said you were beautiful, would you? I recall you told me such things don't matter much."

Her heart quickened. "I wouldn't take offense."

"You're a beautiful woman, Lorelei Latham."

She curtsied, just to show him she knew how. "Thank you, Sam Delaney."

Silently she told him that in his brown buckskins with his skin coppery in the morning light and his dark eyes lit with an admiring gleam, he was beautiful, too.

She shook her head and felt the long curls ripple against her shoulders. "I'm afraid I lost the hat."

"No matter. It wouldn't go with the dress."

"But you're always ordering me to keep my hair hidden."

"Since when do you do what I want?"

"Depends upon what it is," she said, her voice a little breathy.

He took a step forward. "It does, eh? Right now—"

"Lori!"

Reluctantly she pulled her eyes away from Sam to see Blue bounding toward her from the garden, Preacher trailing behind him with hoe in hand.

The boy crashed to a halt beside her, a smile breaking his young face from ear to ear. "Lori," he said again. "You're as pretty as the birds."

"Now, that's as fine a tribute as I've ever heard," she said, giving him a curtsy as well.

"I echo the lad's sentiments," said Preacher.

"Thank you, sir."

In truth, she did feel pretty, which was exactly what she'd wanted. As far as she was concerned, this newly dawned day marked the beginning of a new life for the one-time skeptic who'd been so quick to scorn men. Having accepted the churning feelings of the past few weeks for what they were — a fierce, invigorating, warming love of Sam — she felt feminine and glowing and had wanted very much to let a little of that glow show on the outside.

The light in Sam's eyes told her she had succeeded.

Just what she was to do about those feelings was a matter she would deal with later. Right now she wanted nothing more than to . . . well, than to glow.

She pulled out the packages from behind her back and handed one to Blue. "This is for you," she said. "Open it."

The boy looked from her to Preacher, then down to the package. He tore at the brown paper and held up a shirt that matched her dress.

"I made it while you were getting strong again," she said. "I'll bet you didn't know I fitted it against you while you were asleep."

"Can I put it on?" he asked.

"Later," said Preacher. "We've got a considerable number of chores to perform today." He turned his attention to Lorelei. "That was a kind thing to do."

She shrugged. "You gave me one of his the first day I was here." She glanced around the clearing. "Where are the twins? I made them shirts, too. We're all going to look alike, but I had material left over and didn't want to let it go to waste." She laughed. "Once I got going, I couldn't stop. I even used that green velvet to make curtains for the window."

"Don't worry about looking like anyone else," said Sam. "You couldn't if you tried."

She shot him a sidelong glance and surrendered to an urge to wink.

"Careful," he warned.

"Blue," Preacher said, "we need to return to those garden weeds. They thrive enough to choke out the corn."

Lorelei took the shirt from him and watched as he skipped after Preacher. "He really does seem all right. I look for signs he's remembering ugly things, but I don't find any."

"What about you?"

"I'm fine. No problem with the creek or with anything. I've not forgotten, understand, but the memories don't keep me awake."

She smiled reassuringly, seeing no reason to tell him there were memories of Sam that did disturb her sleep.

"Are Al and Cal out hunting again?" she asked.

Sam nodded.

"For wild hog, I guess. I hope they—"

"Not for hog, Lorelei. They're hunting Dun Straight."

"Oh, no."

"They've been doing it off and on for days. Checking with the settlers and with a band of Indians camped a few miles north. Don't worry. They've traded with the Indians before, and they know how to use a gun."

"Are my thoughts so obvious?"

"Not generally."

"That's a relief. I'd hate for you to always know what I'm thinking."

She looked away from him and gave her consideration to Al and Cal. "What if they find him, Sam?"

"They're just asking if he's been seen. Straight's

a hard man to forget."

"Then, why can't I shake the feeling this is dangerous for them?"

"I told you, they're friends with the Indians, at least as friendly as a white man can get. They trade wild hog and beef for whatever the Indians have been gathering—nuts and chinquapins, for the most part, corn sometimes and bear meat. It's safe."

But Lorelei wasn't satisfied. "What about the settlers? They don't ordinarily trade with them, do they? The twins don't even ride into town."

"You're not going to let this rest, are you?" He hesitated. "Guess it wouldn't hurt you to know. Sit down and have some coffee first."

She settled on a patch of grass away from the fire, spread her skirt around her, and took a cup from Sam.

"They're wanted by the law," he said as he sat beside her.

"I decided as much a long time ago. Or at least that they were running from something. But they're such gentle men. Always soft-spoken. I've never heard them raise a voice in anger, and they're wonderful with Blue. What have they done?"

"Killed a man."

"I don't believe it."

"They confessed to it not long after they wandered into the camp. Told Preacher and me one night. Al did most of the talking, which wasn't much. And they didn't mean to kill him, just knock him out of the way, except that he fell wrong and hit his head."

"Can't they tell the authorities how it happened?"

"It was an authority that died. A deputy sheriff."

Exasperated, Lorelei shook her head. "You are

telling this in the most round-about way, Sam. How could those two men have killed a deputy?"

"This is kind of the way they told us. Back in Missouri they made the mistake of taking some seed that didn't belong to them. Hard times, they said. The plan was to pay for it when the crops came in, but the owner still took offense and had them jailed. Cal's lone contribution was how they almost choked from the air in that closed-in cell where they were put to await trial. They're outdoor men, hunters and farmers."

"So they escaped."

Sam nodded. "The deputy was working alone and got a little careless when he brought them their food. Al said when they saw him lying there and then couldn't get him up, they lit out and didn't stop until they got deep in Texas."

"Where their path crossed yours."

"They got here a short time before I started building on my place. They've been here since."

"Avoiding being seen . . . afraid a wanted poster is out on them," she said.

"Guess that holds true for several of us here."

"Preacher, too?"

Sam shook his head. "The most I can say about him is his title's empty. As to why he left the pulpit, you'll have to hear from him."

"And Jet?"

"Don't know about him for sure myself. And Wash, he's a freedman who lost his taste for being around civilization."

"Don't any of you have families?"

"None, so far as I know. But then you don't either." He regarded her carefully. "Kind of makes you one of us."

318

"Kind of," she said, enjoying a rush of warmth that settled in her heart.

She finished the coffee, set the cup aside, and looked straight at him. There was something she needed to tell him, and she chose to get it over fast.

"I wrote to Catherine Gase, the woman who owns the casino."

A flicker deep in his eyes was Sam's sole reaction. "Should have expected it."

"I knew everybody would be worried about me."

He nodded. "They'd have a right."

Lorelei swallowed, her palms damp, the warmth of a moment ago fading fast. Sam looked so stolid sitting there, so unyielding, as if he expected her to say something that would go against him.

"There was nothing in the letter to get at you in any way, Sam, to punish or accuse you. I told them that no harm had come to me. That they should call off the search."

"You expect them to believe it? Seems to me, they might think you were coerced into writing."

"I put in personal things." She looked down at her hands twisting together in her lap. "About us."

"Thanks, honey. They'll nail my body parts to a tree when they get here."

"No, no," she said hastily, looking back at him. "Nothing specific. I said there were longings, emotions . . . nothing more. But I put it in words that Delilah would understand. She'll know I was writing the truth."

"Who's Delilah?"

"The woman who was helping me at the casino. Catherine's supposed to show her the letter. Delilah's been saying I'd want certain things one of these days." Her words came out slow and forced.

"I wrote that she was right, that I'd decided to stay here a little longer because of you."

"Straying from the truth, weren't you?"

Lorelei shrugged. "Well, I didn't want to write anything about looking for William Jacobs."

"I can guess why."

She ignored the sarcasm. "And while I'm confessing all this, I might as well tell you that Preacher read the letter. Don't get angry at him. I asked him to, so he could tell you that it said only good things."

"No need. I'll take your word for it."

"You know what this means, don't you? There's no more bounty. No way I can bring charges against you. No reason for you to let me stay."

His eyes were dark, his face taut and without expression as he stared at her. "You can't think of one?"

Of course she could. She provided a service for Sam that no one else in the camp could provide. For all the trouble she brought, he hadn't said anything lately about sending her home.

As for her personal reasons to remain, she could think of a thousand, but they all condensed to the fact that she would have no kind of life anywhere else.

Looking away, she stared into the tangled wilderness opposite the small pond. The air seemed suddenly thin, and she grew dizzy as she drew in shallow breaths.

"You won't like my saying this, Sam, but I'm convinced more than ever that Bert Jackson and William Jacobs are one and the same."

"You're right. I don't like it."

"His full name, the one he's claiming now, is

Wilbert Jackson. Initials W.J. Preacher saw it on a letter in town."

"Doesn't prove a thing."

She closed her eyes, then opened them again. Here was the obstructionist Sam that she was used to dealing with. She thrust all her personal feelings aside.

"I've been thinking about the other day when Dun Straight came out here. How did he know where the camp was?"

"Could have followed Preacher and Blue sometime, or even me, getting the lay of the land. He's good at his job."

"And when he showed up, his job was to kill me."

"Hell, Lorelei, you were here and I wasn't."

"Then, why didn't he just ride out and wait until you got back? Besides, he didn't say anything about you, just about killing me."

Her voice grew faint, and she waited a minute before continuing. "One of the first things he taunted me with was that I wouldn't die right away."

"Son of a bitch."

"That's beside the point."

"Which is?"

"That I've figured out why I had to die. When I was in the saloon with Jackson, I told him he looked like someone I'd met back in Boston. He knew I recognized him. Oh, he didn't have any more of a reaction than you usually do when I say something that shakes you up, but he knew, all right. He was afraid I'd tell the authorities as soon as I got to someone with more backbone than Sheriff Mortimer. And he was right."

Lorelei fell into silence, relieved that at least Sam was thinking over what she had said.

"If that's true, then it's all the more reason for you to stay away from him."

"Away from town."

"Away from anywhere he's likely to be."

"And just let him get away?"

"He's not getting away. I've had a confrontation with him a time or two lately. Funny thing, he loves that land he stole as much as I do. Almost makes him human. Almost. I've written to President Houston. Twice. No answer yet. If I have to, I'll confront Houston in the capital, dragging Jackson behind me."

"You're trying to do this legally."

"Only for a little while. If it comes down to it, I'll take back the land by force."

She stared at him in alarm. "But there are so many of them."

"Hired hands. They won't have the stomach for a real fight, not for the kind of wages Jackson is paying. Word is one or two of them don't much care for his bringing in Straight. Could be it was a tactical mistake on his part."

"And facing a bunch of armed men could be a mistake on yours."

"A man has to fight for what he believes in."

"And so does a woman."

"Damn it, Lorelei, I don't want you going anywhere without me."

"But—"

"No arguments on this one."

Nevertheless, she threw a few more protests at him, which he threw right back, and reluctantly she agreed to let him fight their battles for a while. Battles that she sensed would soon be coming to an end.

Long after Sam left, she continued to sit on the grass and to think. It was her curse lately, this thinking, and it seldom brought her comfort. The worst thought right now was that once the battle with Jackson was settled, she would have no reason to stay.

Not unless Sam confessed a wild, undying love for her and a powerful need to keep her by his side until the end of time. As considerate as he'd been to her lately, she couldn't imagine him saying such words.

One thing she knew for certain—she'd make sure she was heading back for Louisiana before he brought up the subject of her leaving. The pride she'd been so dependent on the last few years would have to give her strength until her heart could heal.

That night the twins arrived safely back in camp after a day of futile searching and showed suitable appreciation for the shirts, almost blushing behind their beards when she held them up to make certain she'd made the clothing big enough. Without letting on she knew anything about their background, she gave thanks they were tracking Straight.

When everyone retired to the tents, she asked Sam to stay with her for a while in the cabin. If she had only a short time with him, she wouldn't fritter it away lying in a lonely bunk wondering where he was.

They settled on a pallet of blankets in front of the fire and made love. No talking or arguing, no empty promising, just sweet lovemaking, discovering a hundred little ways to please each other, and finally resting in each other's arms.

"Loving Lorelei," he said as he stroked her arm. "I called you that once before and you didn't like it. Although I meant it."

Sam didn't know how right he was. "I was upset because it was a name my mother called me. I was a . . . gentle child."

He touched her cheek. "You're a gentle woman."

"Not really. I wanted to kill Dun Straight. I tried."

"You wanted to stay alive. Nothing wrong with that."

"I hope not. I'd fight him again." She shivered against Sam. "Sorry I brought him up. Let's not talk of him tonight."

Sam nodded, and for a while they listened to the pop and crackle of the fire.

"I've been thinking," he said.

"That sounds ominous."

"About what you said the other day. About getting pregnant."

"Oh," she said, her voice brittle and small. "That."

"You made it sound important."

"It is. But I'm still all right. There's no reason for either of us to be concerned."

"If you're sure."

"Of course I'm sure."

She wasn't, not nearly so much as she'd been the day she raised the issue, but she couldn't risk his bringing up marriage again, not under the conditions he would be discussing it. As far as taking a chance on having Sam's baby, it was a far more welcome circumstance than separating herself from him, far better than never making love to him again.

Sam's baby—the idea warmed her, but if she tried to discuss the subject as a possibility, the baby's father might not be so thrilled.

She distracted him by running her fingers down his chest and settling a splayed hand against his abdomen. Easing away, she glanced down and saw he was reacting just as she had hoped. She caressed his reaction with gentle fingers.

"I scorned this once." She shifted her eyes to the hard thighs, the flat abdomen, the broad, muscled chest, all of it looking bronzed in the pale light. "I even compared a naked man to a scraped potato." She took a ragged breath. "I was wrong."

"You are a constant surprise to me." His voice was husky and as ragged as her intake of air.

Her eyes met his. Quickly she lowered her gaze lest he see the love that flowed from her to him.

"I try to be."

She bent to cover his lips with hers and in no more time than it took for the tremors of anticipation to travel down her spine, they were once again making love.

She awoke to a gray day. Sam was gone, and somehow she had ended up back on her lonely bunk. She shivered beneath the covers, told herself not to lie abed feeling sorry for herself, not after the wonderful night she'd just experienced, and got up to don her boys' clothes once again.

Emerging from the cabin, she discovered the twins were off searching for news of Straight, Preacher was feeding the chickens, and Sam was down in the corral teaching Blue to ride the sorrel. The milk cow looked on from the far side, a disinterested spectator. Grabbing a cold biscuit, Lorelei went to watch the novice equestrian.

"Lori," said Blue with a broad smile as he sat high on the horse's back in the middle of the corral. He was wearing the new muslin shirt, and she was pleased to see it fit him just fine.

She leaned against one of the fence posts, returned the greeting, then glanced at Sam, who was standing beside the horse, the reins in his hands.

"What happened to the dress?" he asked.

She flipped a braid over her shoulder. "Can't wear it every day."

"Guess not, but it's too bad." He turned back to Blue. "Don't hold the horn."

"I keep forgetting," the boy said.

"You'll remember. I'll just keep reminding you."

Sam spoke in a firm but gentle voice, and he proceeded to show Blue how to hold the reins. At the opposite side of the corral the sway-backed mule stuck his head through the rails and cropped at a stand of grass, and the cow kept on chewing her cud.

Lorelei spent the next few minutes watching the man and boy, occasionally sharing smiles with Preacher, who had switched to tending his crops in the nearby garden. The green shoots of corn stood a foot tall along a half-dozen neatly furrowed rows.

When she heard a horse coming through the brush, she turned, wondering if she might see Jet's dark and lean figure riding into the clearing. Instead of his wide-brimmed black hat, she saw a black-plumed chapeau set at an angle amidst a pile of red hair. Instead of his plain dark shirt and trousers, she saw a scarlet riding habit clinging tightly to the full-busted form of Francine.

"Sam, baby," she said, waving a gloved hand from high on a chestnut mare. She reined to a halt by the fence.

"What are you doing here?" he asked.

Francine licked her painted lips, glanced at Lorelei, then looked back at Sam.

"Why, Sammy," she said, pouting, "the way you ask that, you'd think I'd never been here before." She winked broadly. "And we both know for sure that ain't the truth."

Chapter Twenty-three

"Should I leave?"

Lorelei's heart was pounding, but her smile was sweet as she leaned across the corral fence and waited for Sam to answer. What she'd really like to do was grab the rope hanging beside her and throw it at him. Instead, she stroked one of her braids and added, "I could go sweep out the cabin. If you two want some privacy."

Sam shot her one of his don't-give-me-any-trouble looks, then turned back to Francine. "What brought you out here all by yourself?"

"For heaven's sake, Sam," Francine said in a fussy, high-pitched voice, "help me down before you start pumping me." She fluttered her lashes as she spoke, then looked past Lorelei to the garden.

"Good morning, Preacher."

Preacher gave her a half bow. "Good morning, Miss Hopewell."

Lorelei looked from man to man. They both showed a little surprise to see Francine, but she was the only one who seemed to be feeling dismay. What was there about this camp that invited company? She'd thought it isolated, but the way people kept turning up, there might as well be signs to post the way.

Francine smiled in Sam's direction. "Don't worry about my riding out alone. You ought to know better than—"

At that moment a second horse came into view behind the chestnut mare, a pinto ridden bareback by a young man not much older than Blue. Like Lorelei, he wore his hair in braids, black as night and hanging long against a buckskin shirt. His feet were shod in moccasins that laced against his trousers, and he carried a rifle across his lap.

A half-breed, Lorelei thought, as he nodded at Sam.

"Hello, Michael," said Sam. "Did you have any trouble getting Miss Hopewell out here?"

Michael shook his head, gestured to Preacher, who was obviously no stranger to him, then looked at Blue.

"I'm learning to ride," said Blue.

"Looks like the lesson is over for a while," said Sam. "Let's see if you remember how to unsaddle the horse."

"I remember," said Blue.

The mare shifted and bobbed her head as Francine wiggled her outstretched arms in Sam's direction. "Sam," she said, "are you going to leave me up here all day?"

Lorelei certainly would have, but she was not the one Francine had asked.

"I'll watch the boy," offered Preacher. Dropping the hoe, he opened the gate and took Sam's place by the sorrel.

"I will help," said Michael.

Lorelei backed out of the way as Sam came out of

the corral. Putting his hands on either side of Francine's ample waist, he helped her to the ground. How the woman managed to let her body slide against him all the way down, Lorelei couldn't figure. Practice, probably.

"I'll put on some coffee," she said. "You two must have a great deal to talk about."

"Sam's never been one for talk," said Francine.

Lorelei gritted her teeth and hurried toward the campfire, picked up the coffee tin and dumped enough grounds into the pot to fix a couple of dozen cups. Water from the bucket, coals at the edge of the fire, and within a few minutes she saw the first vapors of steam coming out the spout.

As she worked, she heard snatches of a disjointed conversation back at the corral, Sam asking what had caused Francine to take Michael away from his saloon duties so early in the morning and Francine saying Sam looked so mean that she just couldn't think straight.

The thought occurred to Lorelei that Francine was a little dense, but she also knew that a woman's lack of intelligence didn't matter much to a man when she had a big bust.

Hold on, she warned herself. Even though the woman had apparently been to the camp before, Sam had not invited her today and had not looked openly pleased when she rode into view.

Which pretty much might be his reaction if Lorelei interrupted the two of them in some kind of tryst at the saloon. Or in some compromising situation here at the camp.

The latter thought gave rise to others. Had Sam on occasion taken the enthusiastic Miss Hopewell to the creek and made sly references to why he'd brought a blanket along? Had he stretched out in front of the cabin fire and watched the flickering light play against Francine's white thighs?

He'd made a few comments last night about how that light looked against her skin, and she'd thought it wonderfully poetic; but in the gray of the morning she wondered if perhaps it hadn't sounded merely prepared.

Stop it. Lorelei pulled herself together. Jealousy was an ugliness she'd never experienced before, and she would be foolish to give in to it now.

A rustling of cloth announced that Francine was strolling up behind her. Sam's boots hit against the hard dirt close to the campfire just as a thick black liquid bubbled out of the coffee pot. Without thinking, Lorelei kneeled and grabbed the handle, then just as quickly let it go. Hooking a piece of dry kindling through the handle, she dragged the pot away from the coals and blew on her reddened palm.

"Put some cool water on that," said Sam.

Lorelei stood. "I'm all right. Coffee's ready. Why don't you serve your guest?"

"Sam," said Francine as she rested a hand on his arm, "you never did introduce us."

"Yes, Sam," said Lorelei. "Tell her who I am."

Sam kept his eyes on Francine. "I'd rather hear why you rode out here. And don't tell me again it's because you haven't been here in so long."

Francine pouted. "I thought you'd want to see me. I thought you'd be happy about my news."

"What news?"

Sam stared at the woman, and Lorelei sensed a change come over him, a tension that replaced the irritation. "Does this have anything to do with Dun Straight?"

331

"I've been on the lookout for him, just like you asked, and when I saw him ride in last night—"

"What?" Sam snapped.

Francine laughed nervously and twisted her hands at her waist. Lorelei almost felt sorry for her.

"Now, don't get mad. You said get word out, and Michael volunteered; but I decided to come along, you know, since I hadn't been here in so long. I just wish you'd tell me why you're so set on finding a man like him."

"Straight's at Edgar's?"

Francine sighed in exasperation. "He went in there late last night. That horse of his was still at the stables early this morning."

"Good."

Lorelei swallowed a rising fear as she stepped close to Sam. "What are you going to do?"

"What I have to." He looked toward the corral. "Preacher," he called out, "tighten the girth on that saddle again. I'm riding into town."

"I'm going with you," she said.

He shot her a hard, dark stare. "We settled this last night. You're staying here."

"Sam," whined Francine, "what is going on?"

"You said I wasn't to go anywhere without you," said Lorelei. "I won't be."

"Forget it."

He turned away from the women and disappeared behind the cabin, returning a few minutes later wearing the fringed jacket, leather gloves, and spurs, a hat pulled low over his dark brows, a gun holstered against his hips. Lorelei watched helplessly as he strode to the corral, spoke hurriedly to Preacher and Blue, then mounted. Michael stood to the side, watching in silence with dark, intelligent eyes.

332

Lorelei met Sam at the gate. Gripping the bridle, she looked up at him. He sat tall in the saddle, the lines edging his mouth more visible than ever, his eyes dark as night. Her heart twisted. Why did he always look so vulnerable to her? He was as strong and capable a man as she had ever met.

"Be careful," she said, reaching up to touch the fringe on his jacket.

"Straight's not getting away again."

She nodded and stepped away, and their eyes met for an instant. She tried to tell him with that one look what she could not say in words; but he reined away, and she knew that as intent as he was on getting to town, he had not understood.

He spurred the gelding through the brush, and the wilderness closed behind him. Suddenly chilled, she hugged herself.

"Sam sure does hate that gunman. Guess 'cause he works for Bert Jackson," said Francine, who'd walked up behind her. "Jackson messes everything up. I rode all the way out here and didn't get so much as a smile."

"Sam doesn't smile much."

"He sure don't. But he makes up for it."

Lorelei was in no mood to hear just how. She looked at Preacher and Blue, who had come out of the corral to stand beside the two women.

"Samuel is a capable man. He will not do anything foolish," said Preacher.

"He shouldn't be riding in alone."

"I guess I better be getting on back," said Francine with a sigh. "It's a long ride."

"Yes," said Lorelei absently, then turned to take a good look at the woman, at the scarlet riding habit and feathered hat, at the substantial curves and the pretty painted face with its vacant, long-lashed eyes. Francine Hopewell was part of Sam's life that did not include her.

Lorelei would like somehow to attach herself to Sam and stay there, to shield him and love him and be a part of him forever, but he wasn't the kind of man to allow anything or anyone to get close, not for very long. He'd been kind the other night at the creek, kind and loving, and he'd been the same in the cabin. Maybe there was a little cruelty in that, too, since the loving couldn't last.

But that didn't mean she wouldn't walk over glowing coals to get into town to help him. An idea hatched, and she glanced at the chestnut mare tied to a corral fence post. A sturdy animal, broad of beam and strong of leg, well capable of carrying double.

"How would you like a woman's company riding back?" she said.

"Lorelei, think over what you are about to do," said Preacher.

Lorelei looked at Michael. "Do you have any objections?"

The half-breed's dark eyes narrowed as he slowly shook his head.

"Lorelei," said Preacher, more sharply than before, "are you sure this is wise?"

"It's probably not, but it's necessary." Furthermore, she said to herself, if Miss Hopeless here didn't agree to let her ride double, she would tie her with the rope and steal the horse, hoping as she did so that Michael would show her the way.

"Lori," said Blue, worried, "is something wrong?"

"No," she said quickly, reassuringly, "nothing that Sam can't handle. It's just that he rode out so fast he forgot to take that squirrel rifle he keeps out in the tent. I need to get it to him."

She looked at Preacher. "I really do. I know how to shoot it if I have to, and I've a stake in this, too."

She turned to Francine. "How about it? Shall we go?"

Francine frowned. "Well, I suppose—"

"Good. I'll get the gun."

Before the woman could protest, Lorelei was in and out of Sam's tent—the first time she'd ventured into his domain, but she had no time for an inspection. Gun and loading paraphernalia in hand, she watched as Preacher helped Francine to mount.

Limiting his protest to a worried frown, he gave her a leg up, and she settled onto the saddle skirt behind an expanse of scarlet wool. After another assurance to Preacher and Blue that all would be well, they were off, the pinto in the lead.

Chattering as she went, Francine kept to a slow pace, and more than once Michael had to rein the pinto to a halt while the women caught up. Thinking about town and how much ahead Sam was getting, Lorelei found her nerves stretched to the breaking point. Rather than take to screaming, she turned Francine's chatter to the residents of No Pines and Dogwood County.

Francine proved receptive right away to her questions, once she'd introduced herself as Lorelei Latham, a visitor from Louisiana who was in Texas for only a short time.

"You know," Francine said, "they spelled No Pines one word at first, but it got a Mexican pronunciation—"

"I heard," said Lorelei. "What about the people? There was just a man and his wife the last time I was in town. McElroy was the name."

"Oh, her. She likes to look down her nose at us girls in the saloon, but her old man always stares through those swinging doors like he wants to come on in. He's on the land board, the one that took Sam's title away from him."

"He works for Bert Jackson?"

"Not that I know of. He's owned land out in the county ever since I've been here, and that's more than a year. That don't mean he doesn't let Jackson get his way. So does most everybody. I'm just glad Jackson does his drinking and gambling at Edgar's. Never did like the cold look in his eyes."

"Neither did I," Lorelei said under her breath.

"There's others that come into town from time to time. Hardworking folks that don't judge a girl because of what she does for a living. And there's the drifters. Some of 'em a little rough, but most of 'em just lonely. No Pines ain't a very pretty place, but as things go, a girl could do worse. At least I can get some pretty clothes ordered from the store. Owner takes it out in trade."

Lorelei nodded, half listening now that they had reached the long, sloping plain that led to the hill above the town. A fist took hold of her heart as she contemplated what might await them over that hill.

"What about Sheriff Mortimer?" she asked. "Is he on Bert Jackson's payroll?"

"Oh, no. Jackson wanted him hired, all right, told the town meeting he was just the kind of peaceable man No Pines needed, but us girls knew he was after hiring someone who wouldn't give him trouble."

"And there's no other official in town?"

"Used to be a county judge, but his horse threw him. I guess it's up to the sheriff to call an election, but he ain't got around to it yet."

"Jackson said once he'd like to be judge."

"Hell's fire," said Francine, "let's hope that day don't come."

They traversed the last half of the plain in silence, Lorelei struck with dread and impatience, her mind trying to concentrate on the picture of Dogwood County that Francine had presented. Michael, who'd been riding ahead, reined his horse around and looked past the women, his sharp-boned, young features grim, his dark eyes intent.

"Rider," he said.

Lorelei looked back across the field, but it was a long, tense minute before she saw the figure of a man on horseback. She gripped the rifle in her lap and with a sigh of relief recognized Preacher coming toward her across the spring grass as quickly as the old mule could carry him.

Nostrils flaring as majestically as those of any stallion, the mule halted between the chestnut mare and the pinto.

"Good day," Preacher said, somewhat breathless, his gray hair and beard ruffled, his faded suit dusty from the ride. "Aloysius and Calhoun arrived to take care of Blue. I thought that if Samuel needed assistance, I might be able to help. I've never fired a weapon, but I could provide a diversion of some kind."

"Glad to have you," said Lorelei, and she meant it.

As long as they were stopped, she took time to charge the rifle, both Francine and Preacher and even Michael providing an attentive audience. At last she slid the ramrod back in its fittings beneath the barrel, and they were under way again, the half-cocked gun resting across Lorelei's lap.

Topping the rise, they looked down on the town;

on this gray and gloomy day a small crowd of a dozen or so people had gathered on either side of the main street, but from a distance Lorelei couldn't make out anyone in particular.

"Is there any way we could maybe circle around and come in at the back of the saloon?" she asked.

Michael nodded, and they took off at an angle down the hill. Lorelei could see no sign that anyone noticed their approach.

The saloon where Francine worked was called Buford's, she explained, but the front sign—"as fancy as Edgar's"—was shot down by a drunk a couple of months ago.

The rear of Buford's was a wall of unpainted clapboard with a door in the middle. Michael had already dismounted and disappeared through the door by the time the mare and the mule were reined to a halt. Preacher helped the women to the ground and tethered the two mounts. Rifle held loosely at her side, Lorelei followed the other two inside the saloon.

They entered through a storage area, then came out into a dimly lit room very much like Edgar's; only the bar was a real bar and not just a couple of planks, and the floor wasn't sticky with spilled liquor. A stairway toward the back led to a loft that extended around the second-floor perimeter of the saloon.

"The girls stay up there," Francine explained as she pointed to a bank of rooms above the bar. "The rooms for rent are on the other side."

Lorelei nodded, more interested in the swinging doors leading to the street.

Michael came out of the shadows, rifle in hand. "I wish to help."

"Thank you," said Lorelei. Her conscience drove

her to add, "But it's not your fight."

The half-breed's eyes glittered with the savagery of his heritage. "I help anyone who opposes Jackson and his men."

Lorelei read bitter memories in those dark, glaring eyes. "Just be careful," she said.

He nodded once, then silently headed for the stairs, she assumed to take aim from one of the windows overlooking the street.

She edged ahead of the others and stepped outside. On the porch stood two women dressed in ruffled red taffeta, pretty much the way Francine had been clad when she'd come flying out of the saloon to accost Sam. Beside them was a shirt-sleeved man Lorelei took as the bartender. The women threw quick glances at her trousers and braids, saw the rifle, and backed away.

Directly across the way the owner of the general store leaned against his doorjamb and conferred with a man and two women Lorelei had never seen before. On down from them, several hard-looking men lounged near the stable. Sheriff Mortimer, unarmed, watched the proceedings from the front of the jail.

Sam stood alone in the middle of the rutted road, his hands loose at the side, his attention on Edgar's Wayside Inn. Lorelei stepped off the porch to get a better view of the men standing in front of Edgar's. She recognized two of them as the men who'd gambled with her, two more who could have been out at Sam's new cabin, and of course Bert Jackson, as ever in suit and hat, holding himself in a dignified pose as if he were too good to get involved in a gunfight.

But he would set one up, all right.

Lorelei gripped the gun with sweaty hands as she started walking toward Jackson. The men in the doorway of Edgar's stepped aside, and Dun Straight eased into view. She caught him in profile some twenty feet away, no bigger than a stick figure in the black hat, the gray clothes, a gloved hand close to the gun at his side.

Faded bruises on his cheek, a hump in his nose—he showed signs of the fight by the creek.

Something in the grim look on Sam's face told her he knew she was there, but he didn't look at her, his attention taken up by Straight, who took a couple of steps away from Edgar's, his back to the stable across the street.

"Come on out, Dun. Come out and play."

"Been waiting for you." Straight's rasp sent an icy chill down Lorelei's spine. He, too, saw her, sparing one quick look before returning his attention to Sam. "I'm not turning my back on the woman."

"Didn't know you were so smart," said Sam. Eyes held steady on Straight, he spoke over his shoulder. "Mortimer, think you can watch the men behind me?"

"Don't want no trouble," said the sheriff.

"Not our fight," one of the men beside him said. "Just came out to watch."

Straight stepped off the porch into the street, and the onlookers by the stable eased toward the store, removing themselves from the direct line of his fire. Lorelei watched Sam and Straight and wondered if maybe she shouldn't just shoot the gunman and get it all over with.

From the corner of her eye, she caught the movement of Jackson's arm. She turned the rifle on him.

"It's cocked and ready," she said in a loud and steady voice. "Any of your men interfere and I'm shooting you."

"Now, now, Miss Latham," Jackson said in a placating voice, "there's no need to do anything rash."

"I don't intend to. If I shoot you, I'll do it calmly and very much on purpose. And I'm a good shot. From this distance, there's no way I can miss."

Chapter Twenty-four

The four Jackson men stirred uneasily along the front of the saloon, staring first at Lorelei and her gun, then at the man they were hired to protect.

"Tell them to stay out of this," she snapped at Jackson, the rifle butt balanced against her shoulder as she aimed for his heart.

Jackson's jowly face was flushed, and his eyes darkened angrily behind the thick glasses. "Do what she wants," he growled to the men. One by one they edged backward on the porch.

The principal adversaries in the drama continued to face each other in the street, arms loose at their sides, hands close to their holsters. Lorelei looked from one to the other—Sam lean and muscled, Straight skeleton-thin, and both alert with a deadly intent.

"I don't need help," Straight rasped over his shoulder to Jackson. "Not when I'm facing a man with a woman backing him up."

Sam's eyes roved over the damages to the gunman's face. "Seems to me she gave you a hard time the other day, Dun. Couldn't rough her up, it looks like, without getting a little of it in return."

"That what she told you?" The words hissed out,

an ugly leer tugging at Straight's slash of a mouth. "Didn't happen that way. She came out of the water real fast, naked and glad to see a real man."

The sibilance of his speech heightened the obscenity of what he said.

Sam stared contemptuously at the wraithlike figure facing him. "A real man? Don't you mean she laughed?"

"No one laughs at Dun Straight."

"I sure as hell don't. You beat up women and boys, Dun, and you shoot men in the back." Sam's voice was steady and taunting. "You and Bert ought to get along just fine."

Straight held to the topic of Lorelei. "Your woman likes it rough, Delaney." The grating voice hung on the gray noontime air. "Told her what I had in mind, and she came at me begging for it."

Lorelei had never wanted anything so much as to shift the rifle toward the gunman and fire. The man calling himself Bert Jackson was her enemy, he was the one she ought to shoot, but right now Straight absorbed all her hatred since he was the one threatening Sam.

She'd never met Straight's match for evil—not on the waterfront of Boston, not at the brothel, not in any way close at the casino. She thought of the scar across his throat. Had any of that evil escaped when one of his victims slashed him open, the way foul odors escaped a violated grave?

"Didn't know you were such a talker, Dun," said Sam, cool as ever. "Could it be you're afraid?"

"I ain't afraid of no man."

Straight went for his gun. Lorelei screamed, *"Sam!"* but the roar of pistol shots muffled his

343

name. She lowered the rifle barrel, saw Jackson step off the porch, hand in his coat pocket, and she jerked the gun right back up again, her heart pounding painfully as a rush of terror robbed her of breath.

Her eyes darted to Sam, and she gave a whoop of joy that he was standing. But so was Dun Straight. It seemed impossible that both men could have missed.

Straight swayed, dropping his gun arm, and the weapon fell to the dirt. He swayed again, a hideous smile settling on his face like that of an open-mouthed skull.

He tried to speak, and a trickle of blood ran from his lipless mouth and down his chin. A matching stain of scarlet spread across the middle of his shirt as the emaciated body folded in on itself and crumpled to the ground.

A woman cried somewhere behind Lorelei, and from all around she could hear the rumblings of speech. Holstering his gun, Sam caught her eye, and she forgot all about Jackson, the rifle, the other hired guns and the witnesses, even the body in the street. She forgot everything except that Sam was all right.

Dropping the rifle, she ran forward and threw herself in his arms. She felt him wince beneath her embrace, and her eyes fell to his left shoulder. A red stain seeped through a tear in his shirt and buckskin coat.

"Oh, Sam," she said in anguish.

"Flesh wound, that's all. Bullet must have scraped the skin."

"But it hurts."

344

"No more than a bee sting."

She swallowed and looked up at him, unable to resist brushing a lock of hair back under the brim of his hat. "You're a liar. And thank you," she said, "for doing what had to be done."

"Anytime." His dark eyes studied her. "No timid tears? No trembling in fear? Instead, you thank me. I keep repeating to myself, but you're quite a woman."

She wanted to tell him she wasn't thanking him simply for shooting down a man who had hurt her; mostly she was grateful because he had survived.

"Now," he said, "want to tell me why you rode into town when you promised not to?"

"No."

Before he could persist, she turned toward Preacher, who was standing behind her. "Sam's been hurt. I don't suppose there's anyone here in No Pines who can treat bullet wounds."

"It is my understanding," said Preacher, "that the bartender at Buford's has had practice in such matters."

Lorelei looked past Preacher to the front porch of the far saloon and gestured for help. The bartender left his post by the rail and hurried toward the summons. As he inspected the wound — over Sam's muttered protestations — Lorelei allowed herself to look at the rest of the town.

Most of the onlookers remained at the side of the street; Sheriff Mortimer had circled Sam and Lorelei and was now bent over the fallen Dun Straight, Jackson standing beside him, the other hired hands close by.

Jackson's cold eyes drifted to Sam. "I want Sam Delaney arrested, Sheriff Mortimer. The whole town heard him taunt this poor, fallen man. Called him out. It's a shame and a disgrace when decent folks can't relax without a rascal like Delaney assaulting their safety."

Listening to Jackson's harangue, Lorelei was reminded of his wish for public office. Already the one-time white slaver was sounding like every politician she'd ever heard.

The sheriff scratched at his head and slowly rose up on his bandy legs. Tugging at the waist of his trousers, he cleared his throat, took a quick survey of both sides of the street, and cleared his throat a second time.

"Seems to me Mr. Straight here was doing most of the taunting. Now, don't get upset, Mr. Jackson. Just reporting the shooting the way I saw it."

Jackson's face registered indignation. "I've got men here who saw it differently."

"That may be." Mortimer looked nervously at Sam, then back at Jackson, and Lorelei could see in the set of his mouth that he was trying to do the right thing.

"Can an honest citizen bring charges?" asked Jackson.

"Don't see why not. Truth to tell, I ain't always up on such fine points of law. I *do* know we don't want no more trouble around here than we already got."

Lorelei spoke up. "Sam may have called him out to discuss a few matters, but Straight went for his gun first, Sheriff. I saw it, and I'll bet others did, too."

She looked toward Buford's. Michael had returned downstairs, his gun no longer by his side, and he stepped from the porch and out into the middle of the street.

"I will swear that was the way it happened," he said.

Jackson flicked a scornful look in his direction. "Who's going to believe a half-breed savage?" he asked. "His mother was a saloon whore who left him here a while back. He admits his father was a Choctaw buck."

The comment brought a chorus of protest from the porch of Buford's Saloon. "I saw it, too," said one of the women, her voice indignant, and even Francine got into the act, nodding her head vigorously and setting the feather in her hat to bobbing.

Lorelei felt gratitude for the testimony, even as she admitted to relief that Francine hadn't bounded off the porch after the shooting with a *Sam, baby* cry.

The bartender reported he would like to get his patient into the saloon, where he could wash out the wound, and reluctantly Sam agreed. Walking beside him and feeling a dozen pairs of eyes watching, she asked what would become of Straight's body.

"The town doesn't offer anything fancy like a mortician," said Sam. "Owner of the store doubles as grave digger whenever the occasion arises. Straight'll go into a nameless pit up on the hill."

An inglorious and very much deserved end for the gunman, Lorelei thought. She pictured him lying behind her in the dirt and thought of the black scarf at his throat. Back on the creek bank she'd ripped off one very much like it. How many did he have? Was that his sole legacy, a saddlebag full of scarves to hide his scars?

At one of the tables inside the saloon, the bartender, who introduced himself as Roger, stripped Sam to the waist, gave him a shot of whiskey, and made quick work of cleaning the injured shoulder with a rag and a bar of lye soap. Standing back to give him room, Lorelei suffered each time Roger touched the damaged flesh. As Sam had said, the wound was little more than a scrape, but she knew the lye would burn.

She couldn't look away from the raw redness. Sam's beautiful body . . . she'd like to see Straight die all over again.

Sam winced only once—when a second shot of whiskey was dribbled over the wound.

"Get that liquor to work fast," said Roger as he set the bottle beside Sam's empty glass. He bound the wound with a strip of white cloth Michael brought from upstairs.

"Ought to take it easy for a while," he added. "Thing like this can fester up real bad if you're not careful." He helped Sam put his shirt back on. The white of the bandage showed through the blood-stiffened rip where the bullet had torn the brown cotton.

With a nod to Lorelei, Roger returned to tending bar, leaving his patient surrounded by the women from the saloon. Over her shyness from outside, Francine hovered the closest.

"I'm buying a round for the house," said Sam, dropping his hat onto the table and stretching his long legs out in front of him. His spurs dug into the wooden floor as he signaled to Roger for another glass.

"Sammy, does it hurt?" asked Francine. She rested her feathered chapeau beside Sam's stained headgear and fingered a red curl that fell across her bosom. "If you'd like, you can stretch out in my room upstairs."

"No need."

Francine hugged herself, the clasped arms lifting her ample bosom close to her chin. "Never could stand guns. All that shooting—"

"Have a drink of whiskey and forget it," he advised. "That's what I plan to do."

Sam looked past the satin-clad Francine to where Lorelei was standing. He winked and said, "Care to join me in a little drink of celebration?"

Lorelei's heart twisted. She wanted to excuse herself for a minute, run over to the store and see if a ready-made dress could be bought, and once she was shed of the trousers and shirt, brush out the braids until her hair hung against her shoulders in rich, luxurious curls. All of it would be for Sam, who could call her *honey* as much as he liked.

Instead, she shrugged casually and said, "Good idea."

Francine looked from Sam to Lorelei and back to Sam. Her red lips pushed into a pout, then settled into a grimace of resignation. As if retiring from a field of battle, she retrieved her hat and joined the other two women at their table.

Taking the chair closest to Sam, Lorelei looked for Preacher and found him standing close to the swinging doors. "Aren't you going to join us?"

"No, thank you, Lorelei. I will take advantage of this unplanned visit and purchase a few supplies from the store."

Sam pulled a few coins from his trouser pocket. "Here, buy whatever we need."

Preacher came over just long enough to take the money. He left, and Lorelei stared after him. "Something's bothering him, Sam, and it's not the shooting. He seemed uncomfortable about being in the saloon."

Sam did not respond.

She turned to look at him. "Is it his religion? Does he not believe in anyone's drinking alcohol? I know he's left the church, but that doesn't mean he's abandoned his beliefs."

"I told you before, Lorelei. Preacher will have to speak for himself. Which reminds me—"

Her hands lifted in protest. "Are you going to start in on me again? You might as well get used to my difficult ways, Sam. And every now and then, you might show a little gratitude because I've got them."

"As a matter of fact, that's exactly what I had in mind. It was a brave thing you did, stepping out and facing those men so that I could concentrate on Straight."

"You're actually thanking me?" she said in mock surprise, covering for the rush of pleasure that surely must be staining her cheeks. "You obviously lost more blood than I thought. It's made you light-headed."

"Clear-headed, you mean. We kind of flail away at each other from time to time, but when outsiders try to threaten, we're quite a team."

Lorelei watched his lips as he talked. "You have a point," she said, feeling warm and tingly inside and wanting to kiss him right then and there more than she wanted to breathe.

Sam leaned forward, a lock of hair once again falling across his forehead, his face solemn but showing none of the weariness she might have expected, considering what he'd just been through. Indeed, the gleam in his eyes made him look rather energetic.

Her heart twisted tighter, and she felt a tremor of anticipation in her midsection.

His hand edged toward hers on the table. "Lorelei—"

"Just rode in," a voice boomed out from the doorway. "I heared tell out on the street someone was buying drinks fer th' house."

Lorelei's shiver of pleasure turned to a warning shudder. She stared at the burly man blocking what little outside light came in through the swinging doors. He lumbered into the room, but still his face was shadowed. She could see little more than an outline of him, and hints of the roughness of his clothes, and his whiskered chin.

She also caught a whiff of stale body odor as a breeze wafted in from the street. Whoever he was, he must not have bathed since the revolution came to an end. Others had drifted into the saloon to take advantage of Sam's offer, aligning themselves in front of the busy bartender, but they'd all slipped in quietly without fouling the air.

Taking his place at the bar, where space readily opened up for him, the newcomer turned to look back across the room. For the first time light fell on his face.

Lorelei froze, and her eyes darted to Sam. "Zeke," she mouthed.

Sam nodded once, then leaned close to speak into her ear. "Relax. You wrote the letter, remember? No more charges, no more bounty."

"Yes," she whispered nervously, "but I doubt that Zeke knows anything about the change. If he recognizes you from the river crossing, I don't think your country act will fool him a second time. And it's a little late to make me pregnant again."

"You worry too much."

"And you don't worry enough."

"Who's buying?" barked Zeke. "I'm sure as hell thirsty."

"Sammy is." Francine spoke out proudly. "He just shot down one of the meanest gunmen we've ever seen in these parts, and we're all celebrating. Sam Delaney. Remember the name. He's a real hero."

Zeke's button eyes glanced around the room and settled on Sam. "Much obliged," he said, lifting the glass that Roger had thrust at him. He kept looking. "Ain't we met somewheres?"

Sam nursed his own drink and kept quiet.

Zeke downed the drink and ordered another. "Never fergit a face, I don't." He fell to musing. From the way his brow knitted and his mouth twisted like a corkscrew, Lorelei saw it was hard work.

"We've got a long ride ahead of us," said Lorelei. "We better get started, don't you think?"

"No, I don't."

"Sam—"

"Sam Delaney, was that the name I heared?" Zeke's question rolled across the saloon like sudden thunder. Lorelei wasn't the only one who jumped.

"Delaney," he said to himself when no one answered. "Delaney. . . ."

"It's a common enough name, mister," said Roger, who was wiping a glass behind the bar.

Zeke's face suddenly lightened, as though someone had lit a candle behind his beady eyes. "Sam Delaney. Wanted for kidnapping and robbery." He dropped his empty whiskey glass onto the bar, where it rolled in a circle. Roger caught it just before it fell to the floor.

The saloon grew hushed. Zeke's hulking body edged away from the bar. "You're the fella came acrost the Sabine a month or so ago. Had the woman about t' foal."

He dismissed Lorelei with a quick glance. "Fer damned sure it warn't this skinny little thing. That other one, I'll bet she was the one who's missing."

I'm the one who's missing," said Lorelei, speaking up when she could see Sam was taking the silent route. "Only I'm not missing anymore. The charges have been dropped."

"Wooo-eee," said Zeke, grinning to reveal a mouth of mottled teeth. "Ain't this my lucky day. Free whiskey, and comin' from the bastard's gonna make me rich."

Sam opened his mouth to speak, but Francine chose that moment to get into the action. "What's he talking about, Sam? You kidnapped Lorelei?"

Zeke snapped his stubby fingers. "Lorelei." He divided the syllables as though they were separate words. "Mouthful of a name, couldn't tell how t' say it when I read the poster. Oh, I got me a bounty, all right."

He palmed a gun quicker than Lorelei would have

353

thought possible for a man with such fat hands. "Seems t' me I saw signs of a jail acrost the street. Always pick 'em out first time in a new town. Let's head on over there and see what the sheriff has to say."

"That won't be necessary."

Lorelei shifted her attention to the speaker in the doorway. Bert Jackson nodded at her, then stepped aside. "One of my men overheard the trouble in here. We brought the sheriff right away."

Mortimer, looking more nervous and unsure of himself than ever, edged into the room. Lorelei fully expected him to declare that he didn't want any trouble; instead he tugged at his trousers and said, "Anybody want to tell me what's going on?"

"Got me a runaway thief and kidnapper here, that's what I done," said Zeke, his gun waving toward Sam. "Murderer, too, more'n likely."

Lorelei pushed away from the table and stood. "This is ridiculous, Sheriff Mortimer. As you can see, I'm very much alive."

"Don't pay her no mind. This ain't the woman I seen him with down at a Sabine river crossing," said Zeke. "Musta been more'n a month ago. I'll bet the two of 'em got rid o' her and this 'un is jest usin' her name. So folks'll think she's still alive."

Lorelei shook her head at the convoluted reasoning as Zeke hurried on.

"Word is, Sam Delaney taken a dealer from a fancy casino over t' New Orleans. When I seen him, he had a woman with him about to drop a young'un any minute. Leastways that's the way they were carryin' on. Thought there wuz somethin' funny about 'em, but I wuz feelin' generous-like and let 'em go."

His grin turned to an ugly leer. "Won't make that mistake twice't. There's a thousand dollars on his head, and I mean t' collect."

"Well, well, Sam," said Jackson, shaking his head. "You were very busy in Louisiana, weren't you? Disposing of Frank Knowles, and now kidnapping and theft? You see, Sheriff Mortimer, I told you Sam was a killer."

"But he's not," said Lorelei, her frustration and anger driving her close to panic. "I've written to New Orleans that I'm all right. By now the charges have been dropped."

"Claimin' you're this Lorelei and sayin' you writ home don't make it so," said Zeke.

Lorelei slapped a hand against her thigh. "This is ridiculous."

"Yeah, isn't it?" said Sam.

For the first time since Zeke made an appearance in the saloon, she caught a worried look in Sam's eyes. "Sheriff," she said, "who are you going to believe, this stranger or me?"

"Truth to tell," said Mortimer, "I don't know much about either one of you. As for Sam, it's natural he's gonna deny any wrongdoing. Sure wish somebody here had some proof one way or the other."

"Jes' a minute," Zeke said as he fumbled in his shirt pocket and pulled out several folded and filthy pieces of paper. Thumbing through them, he pulled out the filthiest of the lot.

"Looky whut I got here, Sheriff. Been carryin' it around so long, I plumb fergot about it."

Sheriff Mortimer took the paper gingerly between

two fingers, as though it would bite. Carefully he spread it out on the table in front of Sam. Creased and torn and faded as it was, the words WANTED and on the two lines below KIDNAPPING and ROBBERY could still be read. Worst of all was the name: SAM DELANEY.

A poor likeness of Sam, an artist's sketch, was centered on the page, and below it was what appeared to be a description of the crime. After weeks in Zeke's sweaty pocket, the poster's small print could barely be read, but the last line—REWARD, $1000—was as legible as Sam's name.

"Sheriff Mortimer," said Jackson righteously, "it is your sworn duty to arrest this man."

Sam snapped to his feet, but it was too late. Jackson's men, who'd been filtering into the saloon, already had him surrounded.

Mortimer's short, squat figure blocked Sam's way to the door. "Don't want no trouble, Sam. I took up for you outside, but this is another matter entirely. I've got to uphold the law and put you under arrest."

Chapter Twenty-five

Sam under arrest! Lorelei couldn't believe she heard right.

Gripping the edge of the saloon table, she stared at the determined face of the sheriff, then at the grim visage of his would-be prisoner. The top of Mortimer's head came no higher than Sam's bullet wound, but as the only official in Dogwood County, he held all the power. It was disturbingly clear that right now he was set on throwing Sam in jail.

"This can't be happening," she said to no one in particular. "After all these weeks."

"I'll handle it," said Sam.

How? she wanted to ask.

Fighting panic, Lorelei told herself a long-term jail sentence wasn't a threat; Sam would be cleared eventually, once word got back from Louisiana. Well and good, her more cynical side returned; but that could take as long as a month, and he'd told her early in their relationship that no jail would ever hold him. Unfortunately, he was a man of his word.

She could picture him running, like the twins, separating himself from the land he loved at the same time he brought more-valid charges down on his head. Or worse, he might fight. With Jackson's men hovering, bullets would fly. How many wounds could that lean, tough body take?

Enough! Her mind seized upon a possible solution, and she pulled herself to a stand.

"Sheriff Mortimer," she said, "you are about to make a terrible mistake."

"Maybe," the sheriff replied, his button eyes darting from Sam to her. "And maybe not."

Sam shot her a warning look, but she ignored him, preferring the less-sure expression of the sheriff.

"This morning Sam removed a terrible menace from this town, a man you yourself might have been called upon to deal with."

She noticed the flicker of alarm on Mortimer's face and pursued her point. "You owe him at least a few minutes of time before throwing him into a cell."

"Lorelei—" said Sam.

Edging to his side, she put a hand on his arm and gave him a warning squeeze. "Please, darling, let me handle this. I know I asked for you to keep our secret, but perhaps I was wrong."

She smiled sweetly into his scowling face. "Please," she repeated as she begged him with her eyes. Sam's scowl eased into bemusement. He nodded once and gestured for her to go on.

She turned the sweet smile onto the sheriff. "The truth is that I am Lorelei Latham. I was kidnapped more than a month ago from the casino I managed outside of New Orleans. Well, not exactly kidnapped, but the circumstances were too complicated to go into now."

She looked at Zeke. "Husband," she said in the nasal voice she'd used on the bank of the Sabine, "you want this here young'un borned in Texas, you better get us acrost that there river."

Slack-mouthed, Zeke stared at her. "I'll be damned. You *was* th' wife."

"Right, only I was using a blanket as the unborn infant. Sam and I were afraid you wouldn't believe I was traveling willingly with him, and we resorted to the disguise."

She returned to the sheriff. "You know how weak women are, don't you, Sheriff Mortimer? It didn't take me more than a day or two in Sam's company to fall in love, and it wasn't long before he returned my feelings."

She nestled her head against Sam's arm, careful not to jostle his wound. "We decided to come on to Texas and have Preacher marry us. You've met him, I'm sure. He's a close friend of Sam's, and when we arrived he readily agreed, even though he had not actually preached a sermon in some time."

"Sammy!" squealed Francine from somewhere in the shadowed saloon.

Lorelei ignored the interruption. "We were careless in not speaking up before now, in not letting anyone know, but we didn't think so far away from my home that there was any rush. It was all so new to us, and we wanted to keep it our secret for a while. Or at least I did, and Sam went along."

"A pack of lies," barked Jackson.

"Let her talk," said a man at the bar. "Sounds kinda romantical to me."

"I've written to have the charges dropped but

now—"

She lowered her eyes, then lifted them, having no trouble in letting the worry in her heart show. "Now I see we might have made a mistake. We should have gone right to you the moment we said our vows, so that if someone like this man came along"—she waved airily in the direction of Zeke—"you wouldn't take him seriously."

She gazed lovingly at Sam. "You can't charge a man with kidnapping his own wife, now can you, Sheriff Mortimer?"

Sam's lips twitched as he looked down at her.

"This is a ruse," said Jackson. "A lie. She wears no ring. We have no proof she's who she says. All we have is a poster saying a bounty is on Delaney's head."

"A very old and outdated poster," said Lorelei. "Sheriff, are you going to believe this stranger or will you accept the word of a woman obviously in love?"

Mortimer cleared his throat. "Sam, you got anything to say about this?"

Sam gave a rueful smile to the sheriff. "If there's one thing I've learned in the past few weeks, it's that once a woman makes up her mind to something, a poor old helpless man just might as well give in to whatever she wants."

Lorelei let out a sigh of relief. At least Sam was playing along, even if he didn't much sound like a husband returning his wife's love.

Sheriff Mortimer looked slowly around the now-crowded saloon. "Anybody here got anything different to add? Maybe like some kind of proof?"

"I still say this is all a ruse," said Jackson. "She's

obviously the kind of woman Dun Straight said she is. A woman who will do anything for a man, whatever name she chooses to call herself. She and Delaney have been living a debauched life out at that camp, and she wants to put a good name to it."

"I was asking for some new input, Mr. Jackson," said Mortimer. "You already spoke."

It was obvious that troubles, wanted or not, were giving the sheriff a little backbone, and Lorelei smiled at him in admiration.

"I say we ought to have another round of whiskey," said one of the men at the bar, but the suggestion was ignored.

"Sammy ain't the marrying kind," said Francine. "Leastways that's what he always claimed."

Several of the men snickered, and Francine fell silent.

"I have a suggestion that can clear up the matter."

Everyone turned to Preacher, who was standing in the door. He stepped forward, and the light fell across his features. Even in a suit faded and dusty, he managed to look stately, and there was wisdom and dignity to his gray eyes and gray-bearded face, the kind that demanded respect.

"Miss Latham has told you that I married them already, but as no one here was witness, perhaps I could perform the ceremony again."

The suggestion brought a babble of comment from most everybody but Sam and Lorelei.

"Ridiculous," said Jackson.

"Maybe not," said the man Lorelei had seen in front of the general store. "If Preacher here really is ordained, then we could see that everything is legal and true. I for one am grateful to Mr. Delaney for ridding our town of the likes of that gunman." He shot a glance at Bert Jackson. "He should never have been brought here in the first place."

Lorelei resisted an urge to applaud the man's good sense.

"Of course I am ordained," said Preacher. "A Methodist minister empowered to spread the word of God even here in Texas and to officiate over funerals and marriages alike."

Lorelei was surprised that Preacher could lie so easily. He'd told her himself that he had left the ministry, and Sam had indicated the same.

Jackson tried to renew his protest, but he was drowned out by a chorus of enthusiasm for an immediate wedding in Buford's Saloon. A wedding . . . vows exchanged . . . love expressed. The images pulled Lorelei up short, and instead of being buoyed by all the surrounding eagerness, she felt her impromptu bravery begin to fade.

A wedding . . . a mock ceremony staged to keep Sam out of jail. For all its noble purpose, it could be viewed with only dismay, since the real thing, entered willingly and lovingly by both parties, was what she wanted above all else.

She forced a bright smile on her face as she looked at her supposed husband. "You never did get me that ring you promised, but I guess we could make up for it with double vows. What do you say, darling?"

"You're calling the shots."

Her cheeks aching from the smile, she tried to read what was behind Sam's dark, unfathomable eyes. Weeks ago she'd pretended to carry his baby, and now she was pretending to marry him. She was swept with the bitter knowledge that the milestones that should have been the highlights of her life were one by one reduced to farce.

She looked back at Preacher. "Let's see if we can find a Bible in No Pines and get this over with," she said, all the lightness and romance gone from her voice. "We've got a long ride back to camp."

"Not so fast." Francine bustled between Lorelei and the sheriff. "If we've got to give up our Sammy, it's not going to be to a woman in trousers. Goodness, folks, let's get her dressed decent-like, and then we'll get on with things."

"Right," said another of the saloon women. "This is the first wedding in No Pines since the Republic began, and we got to do things right."

The third woman agreed, declaring at the same time that Francine certainly was a good loser, and over her protests Lorelei found herself hurried to one of the rooms upstairs. The last thing she heard in the saloon was Sam's offer to buy another round of drinks to celebrate the renewal of his wedding vows.

The women went through their spare wardrobes, and Lorelei soon came to realize the bright-colored clothes they were wearing were the fanciest things that they owned. At last, after much arguing and conferring—Lorelei being left out of the conversation—they settled on a pink wool traveling dress that one of the women said she'd worn when she set out from the East a couple of years ago.

"Planned on getting me a good job and maybe a husband, but somehow things didn't work out," she

363

said.

Lorelei could have told her she wasn't alone.

Bathed and with her hair brushed and hanging in loose curls, she donned the dress. A few carefully placed pins to fit the garment to her slender body, and she was ready, the bride fancied up for her groom.

Someone came up with a fiddle, and to the strains of "The Girl I Left Behind Me," which the musician claimed was the only song he knew, she asked Michael to escort her down the stairs.

Jackson stood to the side, his eyes cold, his lips flat, as he viewed the proceedings. Lorelei let her eyes wander around the saloon. The women, augmented by several faces Lorelei had not seen in town before, gathered to one side, and the men to the other, as though they were lined up for some kind of sport.

Preacher stood facing the stairway, his back to the door, an open Bible in his hand. Lorelei could have sworn that hand was shaking, but then she was so tense herself, she could very well be wrong.

To Preacher's left, wearing a bullet-torn buckskin jacket, his hair combed into place, was Sam. She noticed he had taken off his gun.

She also noticed he looked appreciatively at her changed appearance, and she allowed herself a brief, small ripple of pleasure. A woman's weakness, this wanting to be admired, although in her case she wanted to be admired only by Sam.

The fiddle music faded as she took her place beside him, and Preacher intoned the solemn words that ostensibly united them in marriage. The saloon was hushed during the ceremony, the *I dos* quickly said. A quaver worked its way into Lorelei's voice as she spoke from the heart, but no one seemed to notice.

"I pronounce you husband and wife," Preacher said in conclusion, and with tears burning the backs of her eyes, she awaited the formal kiss.

Expecting a light brush of Sam's lips, she was astonished to feel his good arm encircling and holding her close and his mouth, firm and demanding as ever, covering hers for a long and bittersweet time. She held herself stiffly against his warmth and strength, knowing that if she gave in to her desires, she would return the kiss with a fervor that would surprise even him.

He might think that she wanted this ceremony . . . that she was considering it as something real.

A cheer from the crowd went up as Sam broke the kiss and stared down at her with a question in his eye. "I figured we should make it look good," he whispered where only she could hear.

He couldn't have said anything worse, but in that painfully received message he succeeded in drying her tears.

"Be careful, darling," she said as sweetly as ever as she backed from his embrace. "You'll start bleeding again."

Twisting her hands in front of her, she looked for Mortimer and found him standing behind Sam. "There," she said, as though she'd just finished sweeping out the saloon, "I hope that satisfies you."

"Not quite," he said.

"What's wrong now?"

"You two have to sign this." He waved a piece of paper at her. She identified it as a hand-written certificate of marriage.

"Preacher and I came up with it, not having anything more formal from the Republic," he explained. "It's legal, though. Calls for you two to sign it, and then Preacher. I'll sign as witness, if you don't mind."

"I don't mind," she said brusquely.

"All right by me," Sam answered in kind.

Disciplining herself to feel no emotion, she wrote her name beneath his, then watched as Preacher and Mortimer did the same. Staring down at the duly executed document, open and abandoned on the saloon table, she held herself stiff and rubbed a hand over the sleeve of her borrowed suit. The words on the paper blurred, but only because she refused to focus on them.

"I'll need to get this recorded somewhere," said Mortimer as he folded the certificate and tucked it into a shirt pocket.

She nodded once and looked away. Little good recording the marriage between her and Sam would do. As little good as the pledging of their troth.

She stifled a sigh. In a life as crazy as hers, she shouldn't be surprised that the one formal vow of fidelity and love she would ever make would be sworn to in a crude saloon before a preacher with no credentials and would link her with a man who knew the whole thing was a sham.

Except that it wasn't. Everything she had sworn to was the truth. Whether Sam ever knew it, in her heart she would always be his wife.

After a round of toasts, Lorelei went upstairs to change back into her shirt and trousers, and with Preacher riding the mule beside them, they were

366

soon headed up the hill that would lead to the camp. As usual, Lorelei rode on the saddle skirt behind Sam, and as usual she had to fight holding herself tight against his back.

Talk was desultory at best and then stopped altogether. So much had happened since the dawn of this gray day—Francine's announcement back at the camp, the shooting, the arrest. And then the wedding vows. Lorelei wondered which of the happenings occupied Sam's mind the most.

As they crossed the grassy plain on the far side of the hill, she offered to take the reins and let him ride behind her for a change.

"My shoulder's all right," he said, but she noticed a bead of sweat on his brow.

"I'm not so sure."

"Honey, don't take that ceremony seriously. You're beginning to sound like a wife."

Even for Sam, he sounded unusually curt. Her stomach tightened, and for a moment she couldn't speak. Catching a supportive glance from Preacher, she found her temper. "What you mean is, I'm beginning to sound smart."

He had no response, and the three of them settled into a silent ride toward the pink-edged horizon above the western line of trees.

They arrived at camp shortly before dark to find the twins and Blue anxiously awaiting them. Briefly Sam reported the shooting, playing up Lorelei's part more than she thought necessary and leaving out the subsequent activities in the saloon. All the while he spoke, she caught a tenseness about him that she

367

attributed to his wound.

Blue listened to every word and offered Sam a newly carved pine bird. He told Lorelei he'd make one for her the next day.

Al inspected Sam's shoulder. Cal put on a fresh dressing, and both men announced that they could see no signs of festering.

"Knew you'd get 'im," said Al.

"No doubt in my mind," said Cal.

Lorelei kept to the background. If Sam or Preacher had asked her how she was feeling, she could not have answered. The threat of Dun Straight was gone, and for that she should be elated. Sam had apparently been freed from any threat of arrest, and for that she should be relieved.

But then had come the mockery of a wedding. She'd gone along willingly, so why did she feel so upset?

Totally irrational, that's what she was. It didn't help that Sam was acting standoffish and that Preacher kept to the silence he'd adopted on the trail.

After a supper of bear meat and roasted sweet potatoes, she excused herself by saying the day had been long and she would like some rest.

"Please, Lorelei, not until I have said what I need to say," said Preacher from the far side of the fire, his tone so serious that she could do nothing but settle back down on the ground. On this March evening, the air was cool and called for the warming blaze.

With a new moon sending down a pale light, Blue skimmed rocks across the surface of the pool and watched the skittering of the dragonflies. Al and Cal stacked a freshly hewn supply of firewood beside the cabin; Sam stood somewhere behind her, his presence felt more than seen.

"It is time, I believe, to reveal my foolish and quite ordinary story," said Preacher. "Not even you know the full details, Sam."

"It's none of my business, Preacher," said Sam.

"Ah, but I think it is."

He began by telling of his birth sixty-two years ago in Illinois, of his subsequent schooling and call to the ministry, and of his marriage.

"I married late in life, well into my forties. Elizabeth was a good woman. We thought for a while we would not be blessed with issue, but eventually she bore me two fine sons. They were spirited lads, clever and handsome like her."

As he spoke he stared into the darkness, but Lorelei knew he was seeing Illinois and Elizabeth and the boys.

He took a deep breath. "The fever took them. Took them all."

"Oh, no," Lorelei whispered, wanting to rise and take his hand, to hold him close and share his pain.

"Sam knows this much, and it is time for you, too, to know. It's been almost five years now, but I carry the burden of that loss as though it had been freshly laid upon me. I lost my faith and sought solace in the bottle. A too familiar story, and one of weakness. No, do not try to tell me I am wrong. I speak of a life I know well. The life I have lived."

Sam stepped close to the fire, close to Lorelei. She glanced down and saw the tips of his leather boots.

"Preacher," he said, "you're hard on yourself."

"No harder than I should be. I became a wanderer without family or friends, more often than not lost to inebriation. My sojourns brought me to Texas, where I literally and figuratively wandered in the wilderness. The day I found Blue, I was truly more lost than he. He gave me a reason to think of something other than my own sorrows, a reason to thrust the bottle aside. You, Samuel, gave me a home."

He looked down at Lorelei. "And you, dear Lorelei, with your spirit and your goodness and your acceptance of this lonely band of men, you stirred the long-dead affection in my heart. When you spoke of your father, you became the daughter I never had. An old man's foolishness, I know, but it remains a conviction to which I cling."

Lorelei came off the ground, circled the fire, and with tears gleaming in her eyes gave Preacher a hug.

"You've brought me far more than I brought you," she said, her voice tight, her heart filled with love for this sad and wise man.

His eyes twinkled. "I've brought you more than you know."

She backed away. "What are you talking about?"

"I told you that I had abandoned the ministry. What I did not add was that it had not abandoned me. Ordination was not something I could disclaim all on my own."

Lorelei shook her head. "I don't understand."

She glanced across the fire at Sam, who stared back with narrowed eyes.

"Sam, am I the only one confused?" she asked.

"Honey," he said, "if Preacher's saying what I think he's saying, we're both in for a little surprise."

She looked at the twins, who were listening at the edge of the woods. As she returned to Preacher, she caught sight of a shadowed figure back by the corral, but she was too intent on the current puzzlement to wonder at it.

"It's been a long day," she said. "You'll have to spell things out for me."

Preacher nodded. "Of course, Mrs. Delaney. If you believe that is necessary."

Mrs. Delaney. The name hit Lorelei like a shot.

"I'm not Mrs. Delaney," she protested. "It was all pretend."

Preacher shook his head. "It was all very much legal. Believe me, my ordination remains in effect. Forgive an old man's subterfuge, but I felt my actions were called for at the time. And I feel so more than ever as I look at you two tonight. Samuel Augustus Delaney and Lorelei Latham Delaney, I spoke the truth when I pronounced you man and wife."

Accompanied by the creak of leather and the plod of hooves against the packed dirt of the clearing, the figure by the corral took that opportunity to ride through the dark from the direction of the corral. With silver moonlight falling on him, Jet thumbed his hat to the back of his head and grinned down at the gathering, his eyes glinting as he looked from Lorelei to Sam.

"Been listening back there, old buddy. You told me once the beautiful Miss Lorelei wasn't available. She sure ain't, since you've gone and made it legal after all."

Chapter Twenty-six

Lorelei stared blindly up at Jet, but she was hearing Preacher's words. *Mrs. Delaney.* Sam's wife. Her mind raced in a hundred directions. She glanced briefly at Sam, who stood in the dimness across the campfire. He stared right back, but she couldn't tell what he was thinking. In truth, she didn't know what to think herself.

"You're not lying?" she asked Preacher.

"I am not."

"But back in town . . ." She spoke slowly, assimilating her thoughts. The rest of the camp kept quiet. "I thought everything was for show," she said.

"I know," said Preacher.

"You tricked me."

"I did what I saw was necessary."

She remembered the times they had talked together in private. "You said Sam and I belonged together."

"So I did."

"And you must have said the same to him." This more to herself than to him.

Preacher nodded, and a bitter hurt took hold of her as she imagined how Sam must have reacted.

She'd scoffed at Preacher, but only because he said what she wanted to be true. Sam must have laughed out loud—or far worse, he'd turned away in disgust.

She shook off the hurt, well aware of the silence around her.

Her gaze was pulled back to Sam. His eyes remained full on her face.

"You don't sound too happy over the situation," he said. "Remember, we both got tricked."

A sickening knot formed in the pit of her stomach as she saw the situation from his point of view. She'd gone after him back in Louisiana, forced him to keep her in Texas, then in front of a saloonful of witnesses she'd proclaimed herself his wife.

Lorelei rubbed damp palms against her trousers. It all sounded so conniving . . . as though she'd decided back in New Orleans to trap him into being hers. She shuddered to think how close she'd come a time or two to declaring her love.

She forced her eyes from that dark stare of his, looked at Al and Cal, at Jet so high up on the horse, at Preacher so close. With a blanket of darkness surrounding them, they all looked back and waited for her to speak. Even Blue had ceased throwing rocks into the pond and strolled over to the fire to watch and listen. Overhead the stars blinked down as if in mimicry of the men.

"I don't know what to say," she said with complete honesty. "I need time to think."

Sam stood between her and the cabin. Eyes diverted toward the darkness, she skirted the fire, keeping a wide distance from the man she could now call husband, and hurried inside, closing the door against him and the others. Her hands trembled on the knob, and she jerked them to her waist, squeezing the shakiness away, wishing she could deal as easily with her skittering thoughts and her pounding heart.

Mrs. Delaney.

Shivering against the chill that had settled in the cabin, she hurried to the fireplace, stoked the glowing coals, and bent to a stack of kindling and logs. A spindly branch of oak went onto the banked fire, and then another.

Mrs. Delaney. It was a name much wished for under different circumstances, a name that haunted her now.

Tiny flames licked at the kindling, caught and held. She added one of the logs and with her knees resting against the edge of the hearth lifted her hands to the growing warmth.

How should she have reacted to the news? Made a joke of what appeared to be a ludicrous situation? Cried over what was in truth a tragedy? Maybe she should have asked Sam how he felt . . . put him on the defensive for a change . . . made him take over and remove her from the center of attention.

Except that he might have told her what he was thinking, and at the moment she hadn't been strong enough to hear the words.

We both got tricked.

Oh, she knew his thoughts, all right, without his saying more. A man who couldn't bring himself to name a horse wouldn't tolerate marriage, especially an enforced one. It would be as bad as jail. He'd told her more than once he was a man for the single life . . . the last time just before his grudging hint of a proposal an eternity ago.

But he was also a man who would try to make the best of a bad situation, accept the unchangeable, at least for the present, and later see what they could do about making those changes. In this case, that could mean either living apart or getting a divorce.

A cry caught in her throat. There it was, the ugly word that had been hovering at the edge of her mind ever since the truth of the situation became known. Divorce. She'd never known anyone who'd actually gone through the process of ending a marriage, but such an undertaking was well within the realm of possibility. And if any marriage ever deserved to be ended, it was hers.

How many brides, she wondered, contemplated such a future on their wedding day? She stared blindly into the fire. The door opened and closed. Her breath held.

"You had enough thinking time?" asked Sam.

Lorelei had never shown more courage than when she stood to face him. Chin high, eyes meeting Sam's, she shrugged. "All the thinking in the world won't change the way things are right now." She laughed. The sound was shrill in her ears and hung false in the close air.

"Me and my bright ideas," she added. "All I wanted was to get us out of town and back to camp."

Sam kept up his relentless perusal of her, his eyes dark and deep beneath a tousled lock of hair and a thick line of brows, his mouth set, his arms lank at his sides. Breathing deeply, she caught the mingled scents he brought in with him—the East Texas woods, the smoke from the outside fire, the masculine aura that was Sam.

Directing her gaze to the light that danced over the rough-hewn cabin walls, she heard the crack of green wood in the fireplace and the steady measures of Sam's breath as he waited by the door. Her eyes trailed across the dirt floor until they came to the tips of his tooled-leather boots. Slowly she looked up the lean length of him, stopping at the tear made in his buckskin jacket by Dun Straight's bullet.

"You've had quite a day, Sam. How's your shoulder?"

"A horse stomped me once. Feels about the same."

"In town it was like the sting of a bee. Sounds to me as though it's getting worse."

He didn't respond, just kept on staring. Hands twisting in front of her, she said, "The twins think you'll heal all right."

"I'm too ornery to do otherwise."

She nodded. If only he wouldn't keep looking at her that way. . . .

"Correct me if I'm wrong," he said, "but you don't seem any too pleased about what Preacher did."

"What did you expect? That I'd be in here celebrating?"

"Hardly."

He hesitated a moment, looked away, then back again. "We've got ourselves a mess, all right," he said.

"That's just what we've got."

Silence descended, with just the crackle of the fire and the sound of their breathing filling the air.

"You're a tough woman, Lorelei," Sam said at last.

She waved away the hurt of his words. "I've had to be."

Despite her bravado—and against all common sense—she couldn't keep from wishing he'd added her new last name.

Another awkward silence settled between them. "Look," she said, "I'm sorry I couldn't come up with another story back in town. At the time it seemed like the easiest way to get us all out of there without anyone getting in trouble."

"Nothing's easy in this life. It's for damned sure being my wife isn't."

"I'm not your wife," she said.

"According to Preacher, you are."

"In name only."

"Is that what you're thinking? You've forgotten a night or two, haven't you?"

She felt herself blushing. "What we did on those nights occurred before the ceremony. I don't think they count as consummating a marriage."

"I could ask Preacher."

"No!"

Again came the flare in his eyes; she recognized it this time as anger.

"You seem a mite *too* damned sorry about all this," he said.

"No more sorry than you are."

"Which doesn't mean you're not carrying my name now. Could be you're carrying something else, too."

"I told you, Sam. I'm not pregnant."

"Yeah. You seem glad of it."

"Of course I am. And so are you."

He studied her hard. She shifted nervously.

"It's been a long day—" she began.

"I was thinking the same thing. Time we got to bed."

"Surely you're not thinking of staying in here."

"No reason not to. I usually leave, that's true, but damned if I can see why a husband shouldn't sleep with his wife."

She stared at him in dismay. What he was proposing took her by surprise. "But you know we aren't really married."

"There's a piece of paper back in town that says otherwise. Remember I mentioned being ornery? Well, I'm just ornery enough to want my wedding night."

"How romantic of you."

His eyes roamed over her figure, lingering over her hips where the trousers pulled tight and over the stretch of the shirt across her breasts. "Seems romantic enough to me."

"I'd put another name to it." She concentrated on the split in his jacket. "What about your shoulder?"

"It's liable to slow me down a little, but that's not the part that matters."

Heat rushed through her. She glanced toward the door and pictured the scene around the campfire . . . Preacher and Blue and the twins and even Jet waiting for a clue as to what was going on inside. If they weren't exactly standing around staring at the door, they were killing time in their separate ways and seeing if Sam would be tossed outside.

She caught herself. They knew as well as she that once Sam walked through the cabin door, he would be the one to decide exactly when he would leave.

"This is wrong, Sam."

"Why, because it's legal now?" His voice was

hard. "You liked it better the other way? Preacher would call it forbidden fruit."

Her cheeks burned with shame. "That's not what I meant."

"I'm kind of like the sheriff, Lorelei. Just going by the evidence. You asked me in here once before. The only thing that's changed is that now I'm your husband."

She shifted away from his stare and looked into the fire. He was justified in saying what he did; she was too honest with herself to think otherwise, even if he was wrong. Sam wanted his wedding night, nothing more.

She looked back at him, taking in his lean and bristled face, lingering at the hint of black chest hairs just below the hollow of his throat, moving up to his tight lips. Desire ignited inside her. In this moment of honesty, she admitted she wanted him, too.

Sam was most certainly her husband, tonight if not for all time. This might be the one chance she would have to seal the marriage that had already sealed itself in her heart.

Tonight Mrs. Samuel Delaney would make love to Mr. Samuel Delaney because that was what she wanted to do beyond all else. If he was taking her because of lust and orneriness, that was his concern; she wouldn't let his motivations influence hers.

She moved to stand in front of him. "I'm not sure you're as strong as you think you are."

"Let's find out."

She reveled in the husky strain of his voice. Easing him out of his jacket, she stared at the bandage visible through the tear in his shirt.

"What if it starts bleeding again?"

"We'll deal with one problem at a time."

She kept her gaze downward and wondered at her sudden shyness. The blushing bride hardly described her, and yet that was how she felt.

"Maybe you ought to undress me," he said.

Her eyes darted to his, and she caught a familiar gleam in their depths.

"I'll do my best."

Fumbling at the buttons of his shirt, she kept on staring up at him. Wiry hairs tickled the pads of her fingers, and she felt the rise and fall of his chest that marked his even breathing.

She pressed harder against taut, hot skin, leaned close and tasted him with the tip of her tongue. His breath quickened. She spread his shirt wide and trailed her fingers to the edge of the bandage. One of the twins had stretched it over his shoulder and secured the ends under his arm, covering all parts of the wound made by the gunman's bullet.

Brushing her lips over the white cloth — gently as to bring him no pain — she let her love for Sam overwhelm her. The spark that had ignited deep inside her grew into a flame that spread throughout her body. She had no inclination to fight him or this blazing hunger; her only enemy now was impatience.

A couple of tugs freed the shirt from the waistband of his trousers. She slipped the sleeves down his arms, running her fingers over slick, tight muscles, and tossed the shirt to the ground.

"Maybe I can repair the tear tomorrow," she said, then cursed herself. She sounded wifely, not womanly, and she knew all too well which Sam would prefer. To cover her embarrassment, she kissed the hollow of his throat.

He leaned down to speak into her hair. "You keep going this slow and I'll be too old to do either one of us any good."

In another time she might have slugged him in the side . . . but not tonight.

"I doubt that," she said against his chest.

Still, she made quicker work at unfastening his trousers. The pace wasn't fast enough for Sam, and he stepped aside to finish his undressing. She watched his progress with an attention that shut out all else. Her breath caught as she saw his body was ready for hers, but then she had expected nothing less.

He stood there in all his glory and gave her the same attention as she undressed herself. The shirt, the shoes, the trousers and underdrawers, all cast aside. They faced each other as husband and wife, and Lorelei's shyness returned.

She turned from him. Gathering the coverings from the bed, as well as a couple of blankets from the chest by the door, she spread them on the floor in front of the fire.

"There's no need for us to try to balance on that narrow bed. Not with you hurt."

There she was, sounding wifely again . . . organized . . . coolly efficient, when all the while her heart pulsed in her throat and her breathing came in shallow gasps that left her dizzy.

But cool efficiency was her only defense against giving in to the need for confessing how she felt. Sam would not welcome any talk of love; he probably wouldn't believe what she would say, coming so late on this unusual day.

She knelt on the pallet. Suddenly Sam was beside

her, gathering her into his arms. "I'm not an invalid," he growled, and stretched them both full length on the ground in front of the fire, his good arm beneath her shoulders, his other hand caressing her breast. She arched her fullness into his palm and his lips covered hers.

Sam's kisses and the massage of his hands drove all thought from her mind. He stroked her body with thrilling thoroughness, his lips following his hands. She tried to be gentle with him, but soon gave up and followed his lead, touching and kneading and saying with her caresses what she could not say with words.

They spoke in sighs and moans and inarticulate expressions of desire. That night, with the firelight flickering across their naked bodies, Sam was an incredible lover, bringing her to climax again and again with his hand, and once with his lips as she writhed beneath him in mindless ecstasy.

At last allowing her to straddle him, his manhood buried deep inside her, he came to the height of the pleasures she had been exulting in. With his hands cupping her breasts and her bent legs squeezed tight against his hips, she matched his pleasure with her own, then collapsed against him, her lips pressed against his sweaty neck as the tremors slowly stilled.

They held each other without speaking and she sneaked a look at the bandage, which gave no sign that the wound had been reopened. Nestling beside him, she tried for contentment, but she knew his mind was again setting to work as the power of his passion eased.

If she waited patiently, the words of conciliation, of compromise, would fall from his lips. They were married, at least for the time being—she could hear him saying it now—and they would make the best of it by sharing the cabin; and once he worked out his problems with Bert Jackson, which he was bound to do soon now that Dun Straight was out of the picture, then they could see where they ought to go next. How carefully he would have it worked out, almost as though this latest twist in their relationship was nothing more than an inconvenience.

Which was the last thing in the world Lorelei wanted it to be. With Sam she must be the center of his life or she must be gone. Knowing full well that the first was impossible and the second probably scant weeks away, she had to find a defense against the hurt he would inevitably inflict. He kept calling her tough; it was a misconception she would promote.

"That was good, Sam," she said, stealing a line that might have come from him. "Very good. But it didn't seem much different from the times before."

He pulled away and studied her face in the firelight. "What the hell is that supposed to mean?"

She shrugged, wishing she had the loose end of a blanket to cover her nakedness. "Just that a wedding night isn't really different from any other," she lied. She looked down to keep him from reading the truth in her eyes. "Don't get angry. I just meant that they're all good."

"Who's angry?" he snapped.

"You sound it. I'm not asking for a compliment. I'm just saying that for me it was enjoyable. Would you rather hear otherwise?"

He sat beside her and raked a hand through his hair. "Damned if I know what I want to hear."

In the ensuing silence she crawled behind him,

grabbed up her clothes which lay in a nearby tangle, and quickly pulled on her underwear, then returned to sit on the pallet, making sure her body did not touch his.

"You said something in town that I can't get out of my mind," she said as she stared into the fire.

"You listened to me?" he asked.

"I always listen to you. You said something about us not always getting along . . . except when outsiders threaten. In that situation, we're quite a team, was how you put it."

"We are."

"We're also good together in bed."

"I've never claimed otherwise."

"But that doesn't mean that this marriage is anything more than temporary." She caught his intake of breath and hurried on. "You know it as well as I."

He edged away to throw another log on the fire.

"So what do you propose?" he asked when he settled back beside her.

"That we don't do anything rash until word comes from Louisiana that the bounty has been lifted. Then we can see what has to be done. In the meantime, we concentrate on clearing up the mess with Jacobs—"

"Jackson."

"Whoever he is, he's causing trouble. We—or you—get that cleared up. He should be uppermost on our minds."

"You've got it all figured, haven't you?"

"I'm trying to be practical. Don't make our situation out to be anything other than it is, Sam."

"That's one mistake I'll try not to make." He hesitated, then added, "Get some sleep. It's been a long day, and I've got something I need to take care of tomorrow."

"What?"

"Just something I need to check on."

She wanted to pursue the issue, but to question him would sound as though he owed her explanations of his activities. Any real answers from him would show he considered her his wife in a way that didn't involve taking off her clothes.

Smoothing the tangled blankets, she rested under the top cover, but Sam continued to sit with his back to her, his attention directed to the fire. He might as well have been a hundred miles away.

Having said all that she could bring herself to say, she lay in silence. Too weary and too sick at heart for tears, she watched the play of the firelight on his naked skin, wanting to reach out and touch him, knowing she must not. Sam was indeed a man who needed to live alone.

She remained awake long after he settled beside her beneath the blanket. She felt his warmth and his presence, accepting and fighting at the same time the knowledge that one day before long she would have to let him go.

Chapter Twenty-seven

Lorelei opened her eyes early the next day to find Sam already awake. Faint light crept in around the edges of the green velvet curtain at the side of the room, and the fire was reduced to glowing coals; but she could see all too well the shift of his body beside her beneath the covers.

His naked body. Did he awake with an erection? She'd heard from the whores that some men did. What would he do if she lifted the covers to find out? The idea was tempting, but she lacked the nerve. For all the thoroughness of their lovemaking, such a detail seemed too intimate for her to know.

Or too wifely. That seemed closer to the truth.

She lay still and listened to his breathing. No more than a few inches separated them, and she could feel his heat. He made no attempt to speak or to move closer, to give her a good morning embrace. Interest in his physical condition gave way to the acceptance that he wasn't interested in her.

She turned from him, and in silence they arose from their separate sides of the pallet. Hating the awkwardness of the situation, she suspected he was feeling the same.

What did one say to a man in the morning? Before the ceremony yesterday, she might have felt more natural, might have said hello with a kiss, commented on the coolness of the cabin, talked about the upcoming day. But all of that seemed artificial since it did not touch on the topic uppermost in her mind: what was going to happen between them now?

Grabbing up her clothes, she accepted the bitter irony that being married had driven the two of them farther apart.

With their backs to each other, he stoked the fire while she hurriedly dressed, and while she folded the blankets, he pulled on his shirt and pants.

The silence became unbearable. "How's your shoulder?" she asked as she stacked the covers on the bunk.

"Fine."

"Good."

Again silence. She began brushing her hair.

She caught him concentrating on her movements. Their eyes met, but only for a moment, and he focused on adjusting his boots. The awkwardness intensified. Before the ceremony—a phrase that was occurring more and more in her mind—he would have kept on watching, commenting about her hair, saying something provocative and very much like Sam.

This morning, he kept silent and looked away. This morning she felt she barely knew him.

He rubbed at his whiskered chin. "Shaving gear's in the tent." It was the only explanation he gave for leaving. She stared at the door as it closed behind him.

A chill settled over her that had nothing to do with the morning air rushing in to replace him. She wondered if he'd ever spent the night with a woman—really spent the night, not just slept across a campfire the way they had on the trail. In all the times they'd made love, he'd never stayed all night with her. For Sam, a woman, even one he enjoyed as much as he did her, was a temporary distraction.

And she was a temporary wife.

Lorelei hated the hurt her thoughts were bringing. *So stop thinking,* she told herself, and with her hair braided and the legs of her trousers tucked inside her shoes, she strode head held high, out of the cabin.

Dawn was not far past, and for once she was up before the rest of the men. With the sky cloudy and the air heavy with a hint of rain, she made quick work of a necessary trip to the woods, then set about putting on a pot of coffee and gathering eggs from around the corral.

By the time Preacher and the twins joined her, she had the coffee boiled and the eggs whipped for cooking. The thought struck her that she was being very domestic this morning, but she refused to consider why. If the same thought occurred to any of them, they kept it to themselves.

Blue awoke to milk the cow, then took up once again the challenge of skimming rocks on the pond. By the time the clean-shaven Sam joined them, breakfast was served. They ate with little talk, their attention directed to the fire, Preacher speaking occasionally of the progress of his corn, Blue bolting his food and returning to the water, and everyone avoiding the subject of the newlyweds.

The twins and Blue were never much for talk; with Preacher she assumed he'd done what he could to help her and Sam, and now it was up to them to work things out.

Even Jet, who strode in and grabbed a cup of coffee, didn't have much to say. Instead of studying the fire, however, he watched Lorelei and Sam.

At last Sam stood, and she noticed he was wearing his spurs.

"Got to ride into town."

Lorelei bustled about gathering up the tin plates, pretending that she didn't care what he was up to, or maybe that she already knew. Either interpretation of her actions was all right by her.

"Leaving the bride so soon?" asked Jet.

Lorelei wanted to empty the water bucket over his head.

"Need to check on the letters I sent Sam Houston," said Sam. "Should have had an answer before now, but somehow yesterday I didn't get around to asking about the mail."

Jet nodded. "Preacher told me what all happened. For a man intent on settling down to raising cattle and horses, you sure do lead an active life." He smiled at Lorelei. "Not that it doesn't have its rewards."

She felt herself blushing. "So what are you intent on, Jet?" she asked as she stacked the clean plates by the fire to dry. "I can't see you ever settling down."

He grinned, his handsome, youthful face taking on a devilish look. "Can't see it, either. Of course, Sam here's got close to ten years on me."

"Eight," interjected Sam.

"Never was much good with figures."

"You're modest, Jet," said Sam. "I've seen you sit at a poker table for a day and a half and keep up with every card and bet."

"Yeah, well, a man's got to devote himself to something."

Lorelei found looking at the younger man easier than looking at her husband. Jet Rutledge was the one inhabitant of the camp whose background she did not know. For all his lighthearted ways, she knew

389

there was a dark streak in him. She also suspected he was as loyal to Sam as any of the others, despite the fact he came and went like the wind.

With a nod to her—the first acknowledgment of her presence since he'd excused himself to shave—Sam retreated to the corral. She couldn't keep from watching as he saddled the gelding. As far as she could tell, his injury wasn't slowing him down any more this morning than it had last night.

The others scattered to their separate tasks—all except Jet.

"Sam's a lucky man," he said.

She looked at him. He seemed serious enough; he sounded serious, too. All she could say was, "Is he?"

"Don't know if he realizes just how lucky. Maybe I ought to bring up the subject with him."

"Don't you dare!" She forced herself to calm down. "Look, Jet, I don't know if you understand the situation between Sam and me. We had no intention of getting married—"

"At least you hadn't gotten around to it yet."

"We never would have. And this marriage is only temporary."

"Sam know that?"

"Even better than I do."

"Maybe. Maybe not. You don't sound too pleased about the situation."

"There's not much to be pleased about."

She caught a sympathetic look in his eye and returned it with a half smile and a shrug. Somehow she felt comfortable talking to Jet this way, more comfortable than talking to Preacher. But she wasn't comfortable enough to confess what was in her heart, even if she suspected he already knew.

"Did Preacher tell you anything about me? About who I think Bert Jackson might be?"

He shook his head, and she filled him in on the most important details.

"I'm convinced that Wilbert Jackson and William Jacobs are one and the same man. Sam, of course, doesn't agree."

"He takes a little convincing from time to time."

"So I've noticed. Sam won't admit it, but Dun Straight was after me, not him, when he rode out here that day. Jacobs knew I'd recognized him, and he was afraid I would somehow bring the authorities down on him. Someone tougher than Sheriff Mortimer, like a United States marshal. A determined officer with enough credentials could get Texas to cooperate in extraditing Jacobs to face the charges against him in New Orleans."

"You sure there are still charges?"

"If not, I'll bring them myself."

"In that case, you're still a danger to him."

"I most certainly am. I've got too many ugly memories to bury myself in the casino without a fight."

"No wonder Sam's determined to see Jackson gets what's coming to him. He's protecting you."

"No." She shook her head slowly. "At least that's not his main goal. He's after his land. For him that's the only thing that matters."

She turned from Jet in time to watch Sam mount the sorrel. From across the clearing she saw him settle the hat low on his forehead and shift the holster at his side. A rifle rested across his thighs.

As always, he looked strong and handsome, and vulnerable. Her heart went out to him.

Guiding the horse out of the corral, he glanced toward the campfire where Jet and Lorelei stood. He nodded once, slapped reins, and disappeared into the woods. Distant thunder followed his retreat.

"The man's a fool," said Jet.

"No, he's not. He's a loner who knows what he wants. That land is what he's worked for and fought for, and it's rightfully his. He's stubborn and brave enough to challenge the entire county and the Republic of Texas to see that justice is served."

She felt Jet's gaze on her. It was as probing as Sam's.

"Oh, he's right about the land being his," he said. "No argument there. He's just not real sharp in knowing what he wants, and I'm not talking about a deed to some property."

Jet meant well, she thought, but he didn't understand the way things were. She turned toward the cabin.

He continued to speak to her back. "I'm talking about a woman. About you, Mrs. Delaney."

She paused at the door to take pleasure in the name. Fat splats of rain hit the ground around her.

"Your husband might not know it yet," Jet continued, "but you're the best thing that's happened to him in his life."

Early the next morning, with Sam not yet returned and the rains of yesterday gone, Jet once again departed without saying goodbye, and Lorelei threw herself into mindless chores. At noon she returned from the creek where she'd been washing clothes to find Sam unsaddling the sorrel in the corral.

"No letter," he said to Preacher and the twins, who had gathered around him.

Lorelei clutched a bundle of wet clothes to her bosom and walked toward him, stopping halfway to the fence.

"So what are you going to do now?" asked Al.

"Damned if I know. Keep watching and waiting, I

guess. Rode out to my land this morning. Got to give the bastard credit. He's taking good care of it and the cabin."

"I used to teach that no man is all evil," said Preacher.

"Jackson comes close."

Sam lifted the saddle and swung around to rest it on the top rail. For the first time, he saw her. She was close enough to see a glint of pleasure in his eyes. It lightened the rugged lines of his face, but it did not last long.

"Didn't know you were there," he said. "You doing all right?"

Hello, my darling wife, I've missed you, let us go into the cabin and I'll show you how much.

She hadn't expected anything close to such a greeting, but *you doing all right?* fell far too short.

"I'm doing just fine," she said and turned on her heel to hang the wash from the low branches close to the cabin.

"Glad to hear it," he said to her back.

The rest of the afternoon Sam kept out of her way and she busied herself with mending. In the evening, after a dinner prepared by Wash, she renewed the reading lessons she'd begun with Blue a few weeks ago. He'd enjoyed the early sessions spent carving letters of the alphabet out of blocks of pine. She was now trying to show him how the letters went together to form words, but the going was a little slow since he kept asking when he could carve again.

No matter what she was doing, however, she was all too aware of Sam . . . of his movements, his restless pacing around the campfire, the way he neglected his food as he stared into the night. The thought occurred to her that maybe *she* was making him nervous, but she dismissed it right away. Lust and anger were the primary emotions she aroused.

After the dinner plates and utensils had been washed, she excused herself and went into the cabin, leaving Sam and the others to their own company. As she fed the indoor fire, she was surprised to hear the door open and close. Standing, she turned to face Sam. Hair thick and uncombed, eyes narrowed, he kept his distance and returned her stare.

In his dark fitted shirt and trousers and with bristles shadowing his face, he looked as ruggedly handsome as ever. Usually the sight of him brought a tightness to her midsection and a quickening of her breath. But not tonight. He'd abandoned her after their wedding night, ignored her since his return, and now here he was ready to claim his conjugal rights. Like hell.

"How wonderful," she said. "The husband returns."

"Not exactly. I'm not staying long."

"You never do." The words came out waspish, and she wished she could call them back.

"I've been doing a little thinking," he said. "The other night you talked about being practical. That's a good idea. For us both. I know you didn't ask for this marriage, and that we'll be doing something about it before long. In the meantime, maybe it would be better if we just acted as though it didn't exist."

If she remembered the days before the ceremony correctly, that would mean making love as the opportunities arose. Somehow she doubted Sam was thinking along those lines.

"You'll have to spell out what you mean, Sam."

He cleared his throat. "The last time I was in here it was to claim my wedding night. You obliged."

Lorelei felt a surge of hurt mingling with her anger, but she held them both in check. If *obliged* was the way he had seen it, she wouldn't correct him now.

"What I came to say was—" He hesitated, ran his fingers through his hair, and started in again. "What I came to say was that I won't be bothering you again. Not until we decide how we're going to settle all this."

"I didn't know you were such a gentleman, Sam."

He looked at her long and hard. "Neither did I."

She felt a hollowness inside as he continued to stare. If he made the slightest gesture, if the glint in his eye softened, if he gave the hint of a smile, she'd be in his arms in an instant, telling him that he wasn't a bother, that no matter how they settled things she wouldn't give up a single precious opportunity to lie in his arms.

But he kept on staring, waiting for her to say something, and she responded the only way that she could.

"I appreciate your honesty. The situation between us has changed, and neither of us knows quite what to do. What we need is some distance, and some time to think things through."

"Right."

He spoke curtly, at last breaking the stare as he turned toward the door. He paused, glanced back over his shoulder at her, and then he was gone.

She stood a long time staring at the door, wanting to sustain her anger, but unanswered love brought too much pain. A flood of tears burned her eyes. She brushed them away. This unwilling husband of hers just thought he wouldn't be bothering her again; in one way or another, he would bother her the rest of her life.

Chapter Twenty-eight

During the next week and a half Sam was true to his promise: He didn't bother Lorelei by invading the cabin with husbandly demands. In turn, she was true to the promise she had made to herself: She behaved as though she didn't care.

Maybe marriage had killed his desire. She'd heard such a thing could happen.

At irregular intervals he left camp, then returned a few hours or sometimes a day later, always without explanation. When their paths did cross, she detected a restlessness about him she hadn't seen before. He seldom ate, and from the shadows under his eyes she doubted he got much sleep.

More than once she wanted to confront him with demands he include her in whatever he was doing. At the very least he could keep her informed. The tension she saw in his eyes and in his movements kept her from speaking.

He acted very much like a man ready to explode . . . to do something foolish like maybe face Bert Jackson down and forget all about the hired guns that clung to him like manure on a boot.

The way he was keeping to himself, he wouldn't

have her to back him up this time. And so she told herself to be patient.

"You must understand Samuel," Preacher told her one night.

"I think I do."

"You have heard he was at that tragic struggle in South Texas?"

"Goliad? Yes, I heard. What has that got to do with how he's behaving now?"

"This week marks the first anniversary of the massacre. No doubt the memories are much on his mind."

Lorelei felt a rush of sympathy for her husband, and a tremor of hurt because he hadn't confided in her. To do what she could to help him, she sent Preacher into town with another letter to Louisiana, this time asking specifically that word be sent to No Pines about the canceled bounty. Until she got word Sam was cleared—or until he opened up to her—she must content herself with watching and waiting, never two of her most successful endeavors.

The longer he kept himself from her, the weaker her sympathy for him became. One week and six days into their marriage she arose early to find him once again saddling the sorrel in the corral. He must have ridden in late, after she'd gone to bed, and here he was leaving. Her patience snapped. She was the one to explode.

Striding to the fence, ignoring the stares of the men by the campfire, she threw open the gate and halted in front of the horse.

"Where are you off to now?" she said, hands on hips. "You ride in and out of here as though this were some kind of wayside inn. As though we were all strangers. And don't you dare tell me not to sound like a wife. I'll sound like anything I please."

He dropped the stirrup he was adjusting and, thumbing his hat to the back of his head, looked sideways at her. "I've been wondering when you'd get around to speaking up."

"You deal with me only when you don't have a choice?"

He turned to face her straight on. His eyes were shadowed, his visage gaunt. Her anger drained away, and she felt a renewed sense of the power he held over her. Regret took charge. Here she was yelling at him when she wanted to stroke his face, to kiss him, to hold him close and offer what comfort she could.

"I'm dealing with you the only way I can right now," he said. "I promised to keep my hands to myself, and that's what I've done. If you think it's been easy, think again."

She got a swift image of those blunt, tanned hands on her. Regret turned to longing. She wondered if that was what he wanted. Whenever he so desired, he could play her like a harp.

With great effort she got control of herself. "I just want to know what's going on, that's all. Talk to me once in a while. You don't have to touch me to do that."

But, she wanted to add, a little touching wouldn't hurt . . . and a lot of it might make them both feel much better.

Settling his hat back low on his head, he returned to the stirrup. "I've been looking for soldiers who fought with me. Putting up posters, asking around."

"You found no one?"

He shook his head. "And I've been trying to track down Jackson's background. No luck. He showed up in No Pines months ago with money to spend and nothing to say about his past. Except for money, what I know about him fits half the Republic."

"So what are you going to do now?"

"I'm on my way into town. Haven't checked by the general store in a few days. Maybe I've heard from President Houston by now."

"What did you write him?"

"Everything that happened with Frank Knowles and Jackson and the board. Described the battle at Goliad as best I could remember it, to prove I was really there. I'm hoping Houston will read the truth in the letter."

"Can he change the board's ruling? The court didn't."

Sam made a final adjustment to the cinch and took up the reins. "Old Sam'l is the hero of the Republic these days, even if he does take to the whiskey too much. They've gone so far as to rename the capital after him. He can do just about anything he likes."

"Then, you've got hope."

Again he looked at her. "About the land? Yep, I've got hope."

He shifted a little and kept on staring, solemn and gaunt, his body taut as wire, the buckskin jacket still ripped where Dun Straight's bullet had torn through. His hat rode low over dark, unreadable eyes, and the lines of his face, coppery from the springtime sun, seemed deeper than ever.

He looked altogether endearing. She swallowed hard to keep from telling him so.

"Don't do anything foolish, Sam," she managed.

"That's a tough order to obey."

"Take it as a suggestion, then."

She touched his sleeve, and he dropped the reins.

"Damn it, you're a hard woman to ignore."

He pulled her into his arms, and his mouth covered hers, the brim of his hat brushing against her cheek. She melted against his embrace, her lips parted to welcome a deeper kiss. Sam responded. His rough, invading tongue stirred a hundred familiar passions. She wanted to taste his dark masculinity forever.

The kiss deepened, and then it was over and he was standing apart, his hands on her shoulders, his eyes burning down at her. Lorelei thought her knees would buckle and send her to the ground.

"Wait for me, honey. I'll get back when I can," he said, dropping his hold on her. "During the past couple of weeks, I've been doing a lot of thinking. We've got things to discuss."

She nodded once and stepped back, hugging herself as she watched him mount. He stared down at her; then without a word he reined toward the corral gate. As she had done so many times before, she watched him leave, but this time with a new kind of regret. He'd called her *honey*. He hadn't done that in a long time, and she wanted to tell him how much she liked the name.

She waited impatiently the rest of the day. Airing out the bunk mattress, hanging the blankets on the trees, washing, mending, going over words with Blue—nothing kept her mind away from Sam for very long. Something in the way he had kissed her, the look in his eye when he'd said they had something to discuss, maybe just the way he had held her so tenderly—she didn't know what it was, but for the first time since she'd admitted her love for him, she had hope that he felt a little of the same.

The next day she donned the blue dress, brushed her hair five hundred strokes, and waited. By midmorning he still had not returned, and she was close

400

to panic. No matter how much she lectured herself on the absurdity of that panic, she could not get rid of it. When Jet rode in, she caught him before he could curry his horse.

"I need your help," she said as calmly as she could manage.

Jet broke into a grin. "I've been waiting for you to say that."

She brushed a strand of hair from her cheek. "I'd like a ride into town."

He looked around the corral, gave a brief glance to the mule and the cow, then came back to her. "Where's that husband of yours? Damned fool to leave a wife as pretty as you practically on your wedding day."

"We've been married two weeks, Jet." *And slept together once,* but that was none of his business.

"Two weeks today? That makes it an anniversary. What you need, Mrs. Delaney, is a man to treat you right."

She most certainly did, but only one man would do.

"I know you've been out riding and the thought of another trip must be terrible. I know I shouldn't be asking."

"But you are. Must be mighty important to you."

"I've got supplies to buy. The twins are making me a spinning wheel and loom for a wedding gift. I thought about seeing if there was some cotton on sale."

"And that's why the rush."

She shrugged. "Maybe it's not the only reason. Sam told me he'd be riding right back, but he hasn't and I'm worried."

A thought struck her. "Did Sam ask you not to

help me leave? He's asked everyone else."

"What's your old man doing? Keeping you prisoner?"

"Of course not. He just wants to keep me from getting into trouble." *And to keep me out of his hair.*

"Yeah, I'll bet. Let me take care of old Barbara here"—he slapped at the horse's flanks—"and get some grub for myself. Then we can leave."

She felt a rush of relief. "That's very generous of you."

"Truth is, I haven't ridden all that far the past few days. Been with a widow woman a few miles from here. I visit her place from time to time."

The news did not come as a surprise. Jet had a charming way about him, and a lonely widow out in this wilderness could easily welcome him into her bed.

Lorelei left to prepare a meal, then changed into her trousers once again. Her hair she left hanging loose. She offered to ride the mule, but Jet insisted she ride with him.

"We'll make better time," he said as he pulled her up behind him. His eyes glinted. "We've got to get those supplies."

He made fast work of the journey, shaving a quarter hour off Sam's best pace, but then he had a wilder riding style. Lorelei had to hold on tight to keep from falling to the ground. They moved so quickly through the woods she barely had time to notice the lush springtime growth that had blossomed during the past few weeks, the flowering dogwood and redbuds, the wild flowers, the sweet-smelling grass.

No Pines, unfortunately, had not benefitted from the season. As they rode down the hill and along the lone rutted street with its sparse clapboard buildings on either side, she saw that nothing had changed since the day of the wedding ceremony.

Sam's horse was grazing in the corral behind the stable, a sight that did not bring her much comfort.

Jet tethered Barbara in front of the general store and helped Lorelei to dismount. She hurried inside to confront the proprietor.

"Sam Delaney?" he asked, scratching his head. "Ain't seen him today."

"What about yesterday?"

"Oh, he was in here then, all right."

"Did he have a letter?"

"Yep, he sure did. Matter of fact, I got one here for you, too." His mustache twitched. "Addressed to Miss Lorelei Latham. Guess your folks ain't heard about the wedding and all."

She fought impatience as he looked through a cluttered drawer behind the counter. At last he brought out an envelope. "Big responsibility, handling the mail of the United States of America and the Republic."

She tore into the letter. It was from Catherine Gase. Everyone was fine, she wrote, and greatly relieved to hear she was all right. She'd had to send for Adam and Ben, who were out organizing a search for her through the swamps. Delilah sent her love and said something about knowing what was really going on over in Texas. She attributed it to a pouch of voodoo she'd sewn into a cape. Catherine assumed Lorelei would understand.

She went on to say the children were fine, the girl growing fast, the boy asking for his aunt La-la, which was the way he pronounced Lorelei's name. And of course, the bounty had been canceled and all charges against Sam Delaney dropped. But that didn't mean

Lorelei wouldn't have to answer a thousand questions when she returned.

Lorelei held the letter to her bosom. For the first time in a long while she realized how much she missed everyone back home. But she missed them in a different kind of way from how she'd be missing Sam.

If she had to leave. Again came the glimmer of hope, and she asked the proprietor where she might look for her husband.

"Over at Buford's, I suspect. He spent the night there."

She started. Somehow she'd pictured him sleeping in the room at the back of the store, the way Preacher did when he stayed in town overnight. Pushing aside her uneasiness, she thanked the man and hurried outside to find Jet leaning against the rail.

"Everything all right?" he asked.

She folded the letter and tucked it into her trousers pocket. "I've got proof that the charges against Sam have been dropped." She looked at the saloon. "I'm supposed to find him over there."

"Why don't you let me get him out here for you?"

"You don't have to protect me, Jet. I've been in there before. It's where we were married."

Besides, she thought to herself, she wouldn't find anything disturbing inside. She trusted Sam.

Before he could say more, she hurried toward the porch of the saloon. Francine's shrill laughter, echoing over the hum of gruff male voices, stopped her at the swinging doors. Cautiously she went inside and, stepping away from the shaft of outside light, waited as her eyes adjusted to the dim interior.

Dark figures stood at the bar, and she could pick out a scattering of men at the saloon tables. Michael, the young half-breed who had stood beside her on her wedding day, stopped halfway down the stairs.

"Sammy, you need to be spanked."

A sickness hit her in the pit of her stomach as she turned toward the voice.

She had no trouble seeing Sam. He was seated with his back to the door, his hat resting on the table in front of him, his long legs stretched out and crossed at the ankles.

Francine, ruffled and painted, stood beside him — no, leaned against him was a better way to put it. Leaned and mussed his hair. Lorelei's trust faded fast, and she realized how weak it had been.

Sam pushed her hand aside and muttered something Lorelei couldn't hear, but she was just as glad. Sam and another woman. The phrase echoed in her head.

Francine caught sight of her and pulled away from Sam. "Looky who's dropped by."

Sam glanced over his shoulder. "Lorelei."

A hush settled over the saloon. He straightened and turned completely. "What are you doing here?"

What, indeed. For a moment she couldn't breathe, couldn't think. Sam and another woman. Why was she so shattered? Why was she even surprised?

All the torment of the years was nothing compared to what she was going through now, but she couldn't give in to it. Using the strength those years had given her, she stood straight and spoke loud and clear.

"I came by to let you know that I heard from Louisiana. The charges have been dropped. I thought you'd want to know."

Before he could respond, she was out the door and striding toward the general store, where Jet awaited. Shame burned through her. How foolish she must appear, the abandoned wife come in from the country

405

to find her husband with a saloon woman. And just when she'd allowed herself to think things might be all right.

To complete her shame, she caught sight of Mr. McElroy and his pinch-faced wife watching from a wagon tied by Jet's horse.

Sam caught her in the middle of the street, his hand grabbing her by the arm and whirling her around to face him.

She stared up at him with a hate that was pure and powerful. "Let me go."

"No."

"You're hurting me."

"I'm not letting go until you listen to me for a minute."

She wouldn't allow herself the indignity of a struggle, or the disgrace of tears. "Go back inside, Sam. You don't owe me any explanation of what's going on with you and Francine. We both know our vows were a lie."

"Not for me. Not when I found out they were for real."

"Does that mean you won't cheat on your wife? Even when you don't want her?"

"Who said I didn't want you?"

She laughed bitterly. "Oh, come on, Sam. We both know how things are between us."

"We're man and wife."

"Ah, Mr. Delaney," a man's voice interjected, "you do like to twist the truth."

They both turned to see Bert Jackson walking toward them from Edgar's Wayside Inn. A second man, dressed in a similar black suit, followed close behind.

Sam dropped his hold on her arm. "Stay out of this, Bert."

"I just hate to see the little woman labor under a misapprehension." He stepped aside and gestured to the second man. "Allow me to introduce James Hockley. He's an attorney from San Augustine who had some very interesting information to impart concerning this marriage of yours. I assumed your supposed husband had told you, Miss Latham. Apparently I was wrong."

"Let me deal with this, Bert," growled Sam. "It's none of your business."

"Told me what?" asked Lorelei.

"Why, that your marriage was not legal after all."

"Not legal? How could that be? Preacher is ordained, and we signed a certificate."

"Perhaps Mr. Hockley should explain."

He stepped aside. The lawyer, a short paunchy man with graying hair, took his place.

"The Republic of Texas is still in its formative years, you understand, uh, Miss Latham, is it not? Several laws necessary to a civilized country have not yet been put on the books. In some cases it is an unfortunate oversight; in others, there is no immediate harm."

Lorelei wanted to scream that he get to the point, but she'd dealt with lawyers before. Anything she said would only drag things out.

"It would seem," he went on, "that there is no statute legalizing marriages. Some counties have chosen to recognize an ordinance passed last January by the provisional government, but that ordinance has been challenged in court. Other counties, Dogwood included, have elected to wait until a more proper ordinance has been passed."

Lorelei had little difficulty sorting through all the information the lawyer threw at her. "Are you saying

Sam and I aren't legally married?"

"According to the ruling of this county, that is exactly right."

"But who had the authority to make such a decision? Surely not the sheriff."

Jackson cleared his throat. "You have been absent from No Pines for some weeks, Miss Latham. Since that unfortunate day when a man was killed right here in this street, an election has been held. I am now the judge of Dogwood County, there being no one who cared to step forward and run for the post."

"Maybe," said Sam, "because the election was called and held during the middle of the week when most men were at work on their farms."

Jackson ignored the comment. "It is my ruling that the January ordinance is invalid. Your marriage is not legal. I might add that Mr. Delaney has known for some time."

She looked at Sam. "You knew this?"

"I said we had something to talk about."

"You called us man and wife a minute ago."

"Only a technicality keeps it from being true."

"I don't understand, Sam. Why on earth would you want to keep me as your wife?"

"Perhaps I can suggest why," said Jackson. "You may not be aware that a married man receives twelve hundred and eighty acres from the state, twice what he gets as a single man. I can only assume Sam wished to keep you ignorant until he could make the marriage legal. You know yourself how much land means to him."

"I can explain, Lorelei," said Sam. "But not out here."

Turning to face him, she forgot everyone else. She stared right into his eyes, saw determination and sincerity, but knew the latter to be false. It had taken her a long time to accept the inevitable without any reservations, but accept it she did. Too much evidence mounted against him—the distance he'd kept between them, the dalliance with Francine, and now this.

She looked past him to the shabby saloons, to the rutted road where they stood, and at last back at him.

"We're not married. We're married. We're not married. We've both been jerked around, Sam. Admit the fact we're getting out of this more easily than either of us imagined possible."

"I don't want out of it. And land has nothing to do with how I feel."

She was through listening to him. "It might seem an indelicate moment to mention this, but I don't plan on having another chance. During the past few weeks while you've been riding around and keeping secrets from me, I found out for sure that there's no little Samuel on the way."

"I'm supposed to be glad?"

"I don't care how you feel. The best thing you can do is leave me alone. I came into town today because I was worried about you, but I'm not worried anymore. And don't you worry about me. Since I'm not your wife—and of course wasn't last night when you stayed in the saloon—you should have no compunction against returning to Francine. I assure you, I don't care."

"You've got your mind made up, haven't you, honey?"

"Don't call me that."

She dug into her pocket and pulled out a half-dozen folded bank notes. Peeling off the top two, she stuffed them into Sam's hand.

"A long time ago you said I would have to pay my

way. Consider this a payment on whatever I owe. As soon as I get back to Louisiana, I'll send you the rest."

She spun on her heels and headed for the general store, hating as much as anything else that she had no place else to go.

Jet stepped in front of her. "I'll get you back to the camp if that's what you want."

"I guess so. Give me a minute to myself."

She moved on past him.

"Sam," said Jet behind her, "old buddy, I think the lady means what she says. And if you're feeling the way I think you're feeling, you've got yourself in one hell of a mess."

Chapter Twenty-nine

Slapping leather, Sam rode toward the southwest along the deserted wagon trail. He was six hours from No Pines, six hours from Lorelei, six hours from the worst few minutes of his life.

Goliad had been bad, but bad in a different kind of way. In that slaughter he'd witnessed human cruelty of the worst kind; but there had been human bravery, too, and he'd been able to fight back against an armed and visible enemy.

Today there had been no lance-wielding Mexican soldiers to battle, no San Antonio River to cross. Today, struggling against accusation and judgment, he'd lost his wife.

He leaned low across the neck of the sorrel, the rush of early April air stinging his cheek. Leather creaked, and the gelding's hooves pounded rhythmically against the hard dirt, but Sam knew only the tight-gut frustration that had grabbed hold of him back in No Pines.

The scene wouldn't go away—Jackson and that San Augustine lawyer talking in the middle of the street and Lorelei turning pale, her chin high, those wide eyes proud and hurt at the same time. When he'd seen how she was taking the news, and how she was pushing him away, the frustration had gotten mixed up with anger.

In that instant he could have whipped everyone in the town, taking them on at once, but he wasn't worth spit against a slender, blue-eyed blonde with fire in her eye.

"Leave me alone," she'd said.

She asked the impossible. He hadn't been able to leave her alone for very long since the early morning on a muddy Louisiana field when he'd pulled her up on the sorrel and headed west.

She must have read what he was thinking because she'd made fast tracks for the store. He'd gone after her, and right there between the sacks of grain, with Jet warning him to let her go for the time being and the McElroys crowding inside to get a better view, he'd cornered her.

Told her she was making a big mistake, that she was falling into Bert Jackson's trap, that the mixup in their marriage could be cleared right up.

She'd whirled on him like a creature from the wild, her mane flying loose, her eyes fired with fury. She'd been magnificent and maddening both. One got him as much as the other, and he'd wanted to shake her until she came to her senses.

He saw now that maybe that's what he should have done, but at the time he'd depended on words.

"I'm taking you back to camp, Lorelei, where you belong."

"I'm not your property, Sam. I'm not your wife." She'd thrown the words at him like stones.

He'd tried changing tactics, tried telling her about the letter from Houston . . . at least the one from his intermediary, whatever the hell that was. Since its arrival that morning, he'd been working on what to do. She hadn't been in a listening mood.

Sam was a fool when it came to Lorelei Latham. "I love you," he'd shouted just as she slammed the back door of the store behind her. It hadn't been the best of times to declare himself.

She'd locked herself in that little room at the rear, and when he'd tried to kick it down, Michael had shown up and told him to stop.

Since the half-breed had been holding a rifle at the time, he got some attention. Hell, everyone was on her side. Preacher, the twins, even Jet. And the kid from Buford's, where she thought he'd been philandering.

Everybody was against him except Francine, but that didn't amount to much. She'd already caused him enough trouble, pestering him and then objecting when he told her to go away, leaning against him, trying to get him hot. And all the time Lorelei had been standing at the door and watching. No wonder she'd gotten the wrong idea about what was going on.

Francine had held some attraction for him a few months ago. Last night, when she'd come knocking on his door, he couldn't remember why he'd ever been interested. Telling her to go away had come easy.

The next day in the store the situation had been turned on him. He was the one knocking. It had taken a while, but with Jet frowning in the background, Michael waving a rifle at him, and Mrs. McElroy smirking in satisfaction, he'd finally got the message. Lorelei wanted nothing more to do with him.

Sam had been forced to concede the battle, but he'd be damned if he would give up the war. He'd learned a little bit about women through his bachelor years, and a lot about Lorelei during the past couple

413

of months. She wouldn't have thrown such a fit over Francine and over the news about their marriage if she didn't care just a mite.

If her caring was in any proportion to her rage, she cared for him as much as he did for her.

Problem was, shouting "I love you" through a locked door wasn't the way to court her. Drastic means were called for, and that was why he was on the road. He had a long way to go and an impossible task to take care of when he got there, but he couldn't see any other way to make things right.

Jet and Michael had promised to watch over her until he got back, but that might not be for several weeks. Needing to shorten the journey as best he could, he left the wagon trail and spurred the sorrel on a cross-country route.

Riding hard, Sam made it all the way to the Trinity River, where he made camp. The next day he crossed the Brazos at San Felipe, and on the third he hooked up with the Atascosito Road, a primary artery that ran from deep in Mexico to Nacogdoches.

Here was a different kind of country, flatter than he was used to, with fewer trees and farms. Compared with some of the trails he'd been on the past few days, the Atascosito itself was crowded. Every mile or so he passed a half-dozen riders and men on foot, or a wagon carrying families and piled-high goods, or big-wheeled, oxen-drawn Mexican carts. Some travelers nodded in greeting, others kept their eyes straight ahead, but none of them went for their guns or jumped for the bushes at the side of the road the way they had the last time he'd been this way.

The third night out of No Pines, lying under the branches of a cottonwood on the western bank of the Colorado, he pulled out the letter from the capital.

Light to read by wasn't necessary; he knew the important words by heart.

"You state that the testimony before the Dogwood County Board of Land Commissioners concerning your lack of war-time service was perjured, but no evidence accompanies your claim. As President Houston's intermediary, I must inform you that your request for a review is herewith denied."

The letter went on to say that Sam could appeal the decision when the Republic's central land office opened June 1. By June Lorelei would be gone. He had a plan for that title, a plan that would keep her with him. He couldn't wait for June; he'd already waited too long.

Life had seemed a hell of a lot simpler a year ago; all he'd had to worry about then was a five-thousand-strong Mexican Army and a little dandy of a dictator who fashioned himself the Napoleon of the West. Head propped on his saddle, Sam stared up at the stars and remembered exactly how things had been.

Already in love with the land from visits before the war, he'd decided Texas was a cause worth fighting for. Six hundred and forty acres were offered for joining General Sam Houston's forces, a motley assemblage of several hundred farmers and lawyers and rascals that didn't deserve the name Army.

He heard talk about a band of men already fighting the Mexican dictator Santa Anna in the South Texas town of San Antonio de Bexar; their fortress was a mission known as the Alamo, the Spanish word for cottonwood.

Men whose names were known back in the United States were part of the battle—Jim Bowie, William Barrett Travis, Davy Crockett. They were names to stir a man's blood.

"Let's get a little of that action," said a young adventurer he'd met in a Harrisburg saloon. "Frank Knowles is the name. Late of Louisiana, but a Texian now."

Knowles had a slick look about him, a heavy whiskey thirst, and a tendency to hang on to a poker hand when he ought to fold. He made Sam uneasy, but he was also suggesting a journey that was already on Sam's mind.

"Sounds good to me," said Sam, and instead of joining Houston's troops, they packed light provisions and headed west. It was a decision that was to prove near disastrous.

With unfriendly Mexican patrols in the area, they kept mostly to the wilderness, avoiding settlements and open stretches of prairie, always riding hard. Occasionally they passed farmers fleeing toward the east with their families, loaded wagons rumbling over the rutted trails.

"They're a-comin'," said one homesteader when Sam asked him why he was on the road. "We stay, they'll kill us in our beds."

They were nearing San Antonio when a rider, coming up from the south, crossed their path. Reining in his lathered horse, he identified himself as James Bonham, a courier from the Alamo who'd been sent down to Goliad with a message for Colonel Fannin to bring help.

"Things are bad," Bonham said, catching his breath. "Santa Anna's got thousands of troops, can't guess how many, and we're under two hundred. They've got us surrounded. I'd advise you two gents to head south and report to Fannin. The presidio down there is about as strong a fortress as you're liable to find."

"So why are you heading back?" asked Sam.

Bonham wiped a sleeve across his face, leaving a trail of dirt mixed with the sweat. He looked past them toward San Antonio.

"Fannin and his men started out with me, but after they'd crossed the river the officers consulted and voted to head back." He spat in the dirt. "I've got friends up ahead who deserve to know the help's not on the way."

Sam saw the fervor in Bonham's eyes as he spurred his mount. The courier knew he was riding to his death, but still he rode on. Struck by the man's bravery, Sam was torn between riding after him and following his advice.

"Let's ride south, Sam," said Frank. "Maybe we can do some good at Goliad."

At the time Sam thought maybe his companion wasn't so interested in doing good as he was in protecting his hide. But he had to admit Frank was suggesting the wiser course, and they changed directions.

They got into Goliad close to dusk. Built close to the San Antonio River, the town wasn't much, mostly a collection of brush jacales and mud and stone houses, all of them empty except for a few mongrel dogs. Just out of town was the presidio, a stone-and-lime structure built high on a rock hill right on the Atascosito Road.

Sam made a quick survey of the garrison. In the northwest corner, protected by artillery, was the chapel; extending south and east high stone walls enclosed the parade grounds. Sam took pleasure in the sight of those walls; they'd go a long way in holding off the marauding Mexicans.

A patrol approached them. "We're here to fight," said Sam, and he and Frank were immediately taken to the camp headquarters.

Fannin himself welcomed them. A West Point man, he sat stiff-backed before a spread of maps.

"We'll need all the men we can get," the colonel said when he heard why they'd come. "Sent two patrols down south to Refugio to help out the people there. That leaves me with fewer than four hundred troops. Don't get me wrong. This fort is strong, and the men I've got, most of 'em southerners, look like a ragtag bunch, but they're fighters. We'll whip Santa Anna's fancy pants troops if he rides this way."

Four hundred against thousands? Sam wasn't so sure of success, but over the next few days he and Frank threw themselves into the drilling that Fannin was so fond of. When word came about the fall of the Alamo, a gloom settled over the fort. Slaughtered down to the last man was what the runner said. Travis, Bowie, Crockett. All dead. Sam remembered the brave courier James Bonham who'd ridden to his death. He wondered how many men marching beside him today would be lost in the Battle of Goliad.

But there never was much of a battle, and none at Goliad. Days after receiving an order from Houston to march to Victoria, Fannin at last led his troops out. In a field ten miles east he ordered the oxen to be unhitched from the wagons and allowed to graze. Ahead was a timber line marking Coleto Creek; there they could find some protection in case the Mexican troops showed up. They never made it that far.

The Mexicans came, all right. The fighting was fierce and brief. The larger numbers won out. After Fannin negotiated a surrender guaranteeing his men safety and nourishment, they were marched back to the presidio. The wounded were crowded into the chapel, the others on the parade grounds.

Santa Anna sent orders countermanding the terms of the surrender. A miserable week followed, with little food and water. On Palm Sunday, March 27, 1836 — a day Sam would never forget — those who could manage to walk were divided into three companies and marched out of the walls. Sam and Frank were among the first to leave; he estimated their division at one hundred and fifty strong.

Their route took them toward a ford of the San Antonio River. Word was they were headed down to Copano, where they would be put on boats and released. A half mile out came the order to halt, and then the order to fire. By then they could hear fire back at the presidio, where the wounded were being slain.

Sam headed for the river. Frank was close behind.

A hundred men must have fallen in those first few minutes, and most of the rest soon afterward in the mad scramble that followed the initial volley. Sam and Frank were among the few who made it to the river and across; all around them men fell, victims of shot and bayonets.

Lying in the tall grass, Sam came close to death when a Mexican soldier came at him, lance drawn. Sam leg-tackled him, and brought him down in time to see Frank scurrying away. Grabbing the fallen lance, he straddled the Mexican and brought the weapon down hard against his gullet, then watched his enemy choke to death. It was his lone skirmish in the war.

Heading for a line of timber, Sam searched for Frank, but he wasn't to see him again until months later, when he showed up in a No Pines saloon.

"After we parted," Frank claimed, "I headed south toward Copano. Thought maybe I could get into battle, but spent most of the time dodging patrols."

Sam took him at his word, having done much of the same.

"Remembered you telling me how pretty this country is," Frank went on. "You're right. Plan to get me some of this land for myself."

But that was all later, long after the days of near starvation as Sam hid out in the brush, avoiding detection by the Mexican patrols, slowly making his way east to catch up with Sam Houston's troops. Without water or weaponry, he was in a sorry state. To slake his thirst he sucked on Turk's head cactus; his main source of food came from the abandoned carcass of a deer.

Two days after the meat was gone, Sam had a stroke of good fortune. Sneaking up to what he took for an abandoned jacal, he surprised a Mexican peasant woman. Middle-aged and squat, she was tending to a patch of corn at the rear when he came around the corner of the brush hut.

"Madre de Dios," she cried as she lifted her crude hoe. Her brown, flat face was wide with terror, but that didn't stop her from advancing on him.

Sam set to using what little Spanish he knew, backing up as he spoke, hands raised to show he was unarmed. He never knew what made her trust him, but eventually she lowered the hoe, communicating through gestures and words that others of her people showed up from time to time. Sam was best off away from the hut.

That night as he crouched in a nearby field she brought him a dinner of tortillas and beans, and the next night she did the same. When Sam felt strong enough to take up his journey once again, she provided him with a small store of food. Her name was Consuelo; that was all he ever knew.

He made it all the way to Harrisburg, at least what was left of the village after the Mexicans burned it to the ground. He rode on to the San Jacinto River, but he was too late for the brief battle in which Sam Houston's Texians had defeated a far superior force. Santa Anna, known as a ladies man, was reputed to have been occupied in his tent in amorous pursuits during the unexpected attack, but Sam never knew if that was just rumor or fact.

As a veteran of Goliad, he'd claimed his six hundred and forty acres. Then Frank showed up in Buford's Saloon.

The land board met soon afterward, and his one-time fighting companion testified that Sam had never made it to Goliad, had run away when word came about the fight at the Alamo.

No documents remained to show that Frank lied, and Sam had started his search for other survivors. Failing, he'd gone after Frank. On this journey, with far more at stake than the land, he was searching again.

After a restless night spent on the bank of the Colorado, he made a fast trip down to Goliad. The town didn't look much better than it had the day he'd first arrived and reported to Fannin; with no one remaining at the presidio from a year ago, he was forced to turn east. The next few days he passed by scattered settlements and isolated farms, keeping to the route of last spring.

Two weeks after he'd watched Lorelei slam the door against him, he found what he sought — a lonely jacal where he'd once found help.

At first he didn't see anyone about, and then an old *campesino,* crook in hand, came around the corner and stared at him with worried eyes, his wrin-

Chapter Thirty

Late on April 21, 1837, Sam arrived in Houston, the capital which had been built on the site of the burned-out Harrisburg. It was two days after he'd found Consuelo and one year to the day after the Texians defeated the Mexicans at the Battle of San Jacinto.

The city was mostly crude buildings and tents and log structures, none built to last. They'd been thrown up along Buffalo Bayou to accommodate the seven hundred residents. Tonight hundreds more had crowded in to celebrate the anniversary.

Roisterers, singly and in groups, lined the streets, singing off-key, off-color songs, waving bottles as they might flags. Riding past them, Sam decided they were celebrating for him.

He picked out a sober-appearing gentleman.

"Where might I locate President Houston?"

The man stood in front of a brightly lit inn. "Inside, my good sir, enjoying a well-deserved late-night supper." He cleared his throat. "It's invitation only, I fear," he said, hiccuping and giving rise to the suspicion he wasn't as sober as he looked.

Sam patted his buckskin jacket. "I've got my invitation right here."

Dodging the formally dressed butler who stood in the hall, Sam went toward the sounds of laughter coming from a door to the side. He slipped in unseen. The room was centered by a long table, on each side of which sat a half-dozen men and a third that number of women; a brightly lit chandelier sparkled overhead, its candlelight reflected in the glasses of champagne below.

Houston's large, square face and penetrating eyes were easy to target at the head of the table. He was big all over to match his face, and he wore a rich silk velvet suit that made him appear all the more formidable.

Sam started for him. A hand on his arm brought him to a stop.

"This is a private party, sir. I must ask you to leave."

Sam stared at the hand, then up into the eyes of the butler he'd slipped past at the front door. "I will in a minute. I need to see the president."

A few heads turned.

"That is impossible," said the butler. "If necessary, I will summon help."

Jerking his arm free, Sam spoke up loud and clear. "You'd better send for a battalion. It'll take that to stop me."

Excited talk sprang up around the table as Sam began striding toward his goal. A half-dozen men materialized from the side of the room. They surrounded Sam before he could make any move to evade them. More hands clamped down on him, and he struggled to get free.

Houston cleared his throat. It was a sound to quieten them all.

"Let the man speak."

The words came out slightly slurred, and Sam took that to mean the president was in the same condition as most of his constituents on the street.

Sam nodded to his president. "I was at Goliad, sir. I'd like a word with you."

Another man at the table spoke up. "You wouldn't be Samuel Delaney, by any chance?"

"By chance or by design," Sam said with a shrug. "You wouldn't happen to be the intermediary who wrote me not long ago?"

"I told you all that I could in the letter."

"You told me sh—" Sam caught himself, but he could see by the amusement in Houston's eye that the president got his meaning.

"Goliad, eh? There are damned few who lived to make that claim." Houston stood, threw down his napkin, and downed the contents of his wineglass. "I'm done here, Mr. Delaney. Let's confer back at my office."

Limping slightly, Houston walked around the table, past Sam and the guards still close by him, and out the door. Watching his progress, Sam remembered that Houston had been shot in the leg while charging Santa Anna's troops.

Outside, Sam mounted the sorrel and followed Houston's carriage to an unpainted, two-story frame building two blocks away. He gave the president time to enter and settle himself before following him inside.

They met across a cluttered desk in a room opening off the foyer.

"Sit down," said Houston, gesturing grandly as he took his seat in a leather-bound chair behind the desk.

"I'd rather stand, if you don't mind."

Houston opened a bottom drawer, pulled out a bottle and two glasses, and poured them each a drink. "Here's to the Republic," he toasted.

"To the Republic," echoed Sam.

Houston emptied his glass, and Sam did the same, then launched into his story before the president, a well-known raconteur, could come up with another topic.

He started with the day he decided to fight for Texas and ended with the journey back to Goliad, leaving out mention of Lorelei and the trip to Louisiana except to say that he'd reason to believe Frank Knowles died there not long ago.

Houston nodded as he spoke, then reached for the piece of paper Sam handed him.

"This is Consuelo's statement which swears that I was a sorry specimen of a man when she saw me creeping around her home a few days after the battle. That I spoke of the massacre. That I accepted her help. It's in my hand, since the woman cannot write, but between her broken English and my pitiful Spanish I took down what she said. That's her X at the bottom, but if that's not enough, I'll see what I can do about getting her here in person."

The president set the letter aside. "Unnecessary," he said solemnly. "You've given a powerful description of what you've gone through. There's suffering in your voice that only remembrance could bring. And besides," Sam Houston added as he reached for the bottle, his eyes twinkling, "would a man named Samuel lie?"

At last taking a chair, Sam accepted the second drink. The liquor warmed him and loosened his tongue.

"As long as we're talking suffering, Mr. President,

there's something else I might bring up. I got married a short time ago."

"Say no more. Women can bring comfort and joy to mankind, but more often than not they plague us into our graves. It's no secret I've had trouble with a wife or two."

"My trouble is not with Mrs. Delaney, Mr. President. I like her just fine."

With the two of them sipping and talking, Sam told the hero of San Jacinto and the president of the Republic about how he and Lorelei had met, about how he'd been forced to bring her to Texas and eventually how they'd been tricked into a marriage that was ruled illegal just when he'd decided he was damned lucky to have her as his wife.

Even leaving out the part about Jackson and Jacobs, which he figured might be a mite too much even for the receptive president, he'd never had a more attentive listener in his life. By the time he rode out of town early the next day, he was carrying a letter ordering the land board to convene and give him back his title, a certificate declaring the marriage legal, and a special gift from Houston himself.

The latter was wrapped in leather inside one of the saddlebags. It had been a gift to Houston from an eastern gunmaker named Samuel Colt.

"Got to trust another Samuel, now don't we?" the president had said.

The gun, called the Paterson Colt for the New Jersey town where it was made, was a .36 caliber five-shot repeater pistol and was without a doubt the most peculiar weapon Sam had ever seen, lacking a trigger guard as it did. When the shooter pulled back on the hammer, the trigger dropped down ready for use.

Best thing about it was a man could fire five shots

without reloading, which offered a distinct advantage over the single-shot cap and ball weapons Sam was used to carrying. Houston didn't swear it was accurate or wouldn't explode after a firing or two, but Sam figured the Colt was worth trying if he got the chance.

By mid-afternoon of the following day Sam was back in camp. He rode in tired but confident, planning on waving both the letter and certificate at Lorelei, telling her that he had regained title to his land but was willing to set it aside and ride back to Louisiana with her if that's what she wanted. He'd mean every word.

In the clearing, a crowd awaited him: Preacher and Blue, the twins, Jet, and Michael from town. But no Lorelei.

"Thank the Lord, Samuel, that you have returned," said Preacher.

Dismounting, Sam picked up quickly on the solemn looks the men wore. He got right to his real concern.

"Where is she?" he asked.

"Jackson's got her," said Jet.

Sam whirled on him. "What?"

"At least that's what we think. She stayed in town after you left. Said she had to figure some way to leave, that this Jacobs wasn't so much of a worry to her after all. She figured you'd take care of him, anyway. Michael and I took turns holding watch. I was the one got caught from behind last night."

He rubbed at his head. "Came to and found out from the sheriff that someone had broken into the back of the store. She was gone."

428

Sam listened without interrupting. Wild fear took hold of him; he held it in tight, trying to think through what Jet was saying.

Michael spoke up. "I know where she is, Mr. Delaney. I rode out here just now to report."

"Speak up," said Sam.

"I tracked her to the place you built south of town." Hate glittered in the half-breed's eyes. "Bert Jackson scorns my father's people, but his efforts to hide his tracks would not fool any brave."

"You got any idea if she's hurt?"

"I heard her talking inside the cabin; but I couldn't make out the words, and I don't know who was with her. Her voice was strong as if she was arguing with someone."

"I'll bet she was." Sam reached for the sorrel's reins.

"There are men on guard," said Michael. "I counted three, and I know that after the gunman died in town, two others rode away. That leaves one guard and Jackson himself unaccounted for."

At the most five men, Sam figured. And five shots in his new gun. He'd make every one count.

"Rest awhile, Samuel," said Preacher. "You look half-dead from your journey."

Sam shook his head. "Later, when my wife is safe." He looked at the sun halfway down the western sky. An iciness settled over him as he thought of what he must do.

"Got a few more hours of daylight left," he said. "Say your prayers, Preacher. By nightfall Bert Jackson will be dead."

Chapter Thirty-one

Sam spotted one of Bert Jackson's hired guns riding patrol in the thick timber at the north rim of his property. Protected by brush, he watched the man ride at an angle toward him through the trees, his pace slow, a rifle across his legs. His eyes moved constantly from side to side.

Dismounting, Sam covered the sorrel's nose to muffle a whinny at the approaching horse. Twenty-five yards, twenty, ten . . . the gunman rode on, his hard-bitten face grim beneath a stained, wide-brimmed hat.

Sam drew the Colt. He had no compunction against shooting from ambush, but he didn't want the sound of gunfire to announce his presence to whoever was in the cabin with Lorelei.

At the last minute he stepped into the path of the oncoming horse and aimed the pistol at a spot between the gunman's eyes.

"Halt right there," he ordered.

The rifle came up.

"Try it and you're dead," said Sam.

The gunman looked down the long rifle barrel at the Colt. "What the hell is that?" he growled.

"Lower the rifle or you're liable to find out."

430

Slowly the rifle lowered.

"Now get rid of it."

The gunman blinked in hesitation.

"Now!" Sam barked.

The gun went down at the same time the man's hand went behind his back. He came up with a pistol, half-cocked. Sam pulled back on the hammer, and the trigger slipped down from its recessed notch.

The Colt bullet caught Jackson's man just above the eye and sent him backward over the rump of the horse. He fell to the ground and lay still; the horse took off at a gallop through the trees.

Sam's first thought was regret over the gun blast; the second, that he'd have to adjust to the Colt's pulling up and to the right.

"Delaney!" The shout rose above the echo of the gunshot. Sam whirled to see the grinning face of a second gunman, this one on foot, a rifle carried carelessly in the crook of his arm.

Slowly the gunman took aim. "Looks like I got me the man who took down Dun Straight."

"Looks like you don't."

Sam fired. Blood spurted from the hole in the gunman's throat; a look of surprise was etched on his face as he slumped to the ground.

A rustling sounded in the timber behind Sam, and he whirled. A dark figure on horseback emerged from the trees. Jet grinned down at him.

"That's some fast shooting, Sam. Didn't even see you reload."

Sam relaxed. "What are you doing here? I thought I asked everyone to hold back while I checked things out."

"The twins are doing just that. I can't answer for Michael. He disappeared right after you rode out."

"And you of course just had to follow."

"I'm the one who was supposed to keep all this from happening."

"You were outmanned."

"I figured you would be, too." Jet glanced at the two still bodies on the ground, then at the Colt pistol. "Now I'm not so sure."

Sam glanced at the weapon. "A gift from President Houston. I'll tell you about it later. Right now we've got to worry about just how many men were alerted by the gunfire. And just where those men might be."

A second figure on horseback emerged from the timber behind Jet. Michael rode beside them and nodded.

"Anyone else gonna join us?" asked Sam.

The young half-breed rested a hand on the knife strapped to his waist. "I came upon one of Jackson's men. He won't be bothering you, Mr. Delaney."

He spoke with the voice and power of a man.

"Sounds good to me," said Sam. "You sure are showing an interest in all this."

"Mrs. Delaney asked that I stand beside her during her marriage."

Sam could hear the pride in the words, and he understood. Indians didn't draw much respect, but Lorelei had welcomed Michael's friendship. Openly, where the whole town could see.

Love and fear for her shook him. She was a woman above all women; if she'd have him, he would take care of her the rest of her days.

He didn't doubt he'd save her today. Two down here, and a third taken care of somewhere back in the woods. That left maybe one more gunman and Bert Jackson.

William Jacobs, he corrected. Lorelei had been

right. Jacobs had known his disguise was found out, and he'd taken prisoner the lone witness against him. As best Sam could figure, she was being held hostage to keep him at bay. Jacobs would have been a hell of a lot better off heading farther west using another name.

Sam whistled for the sorrel, which came at a trot out of the trees. Mounting, he looked from Jet to Michael. "Follow me, but hold back when I say. The three of us ride up to the cabin and there's liable to be some crossfire before I can do a little negotiating."

Michael's dark eyes narrowed in disapproval. "These men are not to be trusted."

Jet spoke up. "Sam knows what he's doing. If he wants us to hold back, that's what we do."

Sam rode out ahead. When they came to the stretch of open field leading up to the hilltop where Sam had built his home, Jet and Michael halted in the shadows of the trees. Sam skirted around until he was coming toward the front of the cabin. He rode past the lake and through the tall spring grass, always keeping his eyes on the cabin door high on the hill. A thin ribbon of smoke rose from the chimney into the late-afternoon sky.

He kept the sorrel to a steady walk, one hand on the reins, the other holding the Colt at his side. He was fifty yards from the cabin when the door opened. A rifle barrel emerged.

"Stop right there, Delaney."

Sam didn't recognize the voice.

"I've got a deal to make," he yelled back.

The rifle belched fire, then disappeared. The shot came close enough for Sam to hear the zing.

The sorrel skittered, but he held tight to the reins and kept on riding up the hill. When he'd halved the distance to the cabin, he raised the Colt and fired once into the air.

"You heard the shot, Jackson. I'm not carrying another weapon, and I'm not reloading. Now come on out where we can talk."

Slowly the gap in the doorway widened; again he could see nothing but the rifle tip, the barrel, the hands holding the gun. At last the shooter stepped onto the porch. Sam reined to a halt. Holstering the gun, he pulled a piece of paper from his pants pocket and waved it in the air.

"Tell Jackson I've got something here for him. But first I want to know my wife has not been harmed."

Jackson stepped out from behind his hired hand. His eyes scoured the landscape.

Sam rode a dozen yards up the hill. "Your boys won't be riding in."

Jackson eyed him narrowly behind the wire-framed glasses. "Why is that?"

"They've quit their posts."

"So that *was* gunfire I heard. I'll have you charged with murder."

"You already tried that with Dun Straight." Another half-dozen yards. Only a few feet from the porch, Sam glanced at the gunman. "Ought to hire better men."

"Let me take him," the man growled.

Jackson shook his head and kept on staring at Sam. "What makes you think I've got your wife?"

"You've got her, all right. A long time ago she figured out who you really were, maybe did a little talking to the sheriff during the past week or two, maybe mentioned she'd be conferring with the New Orleans authorities before long."

"You're speculating."

"I know my wife."

"If such is the case, and mind you, I'm not saying it is, but if you were to be correct, why wouldn't I just kill her? Why hold her hostage?"

"To draw me out here and get rid of the two of us at once."

"I'd have little to gain. I have a position in the county now, and of course I have the land."

"The two of us dead, and you'd have peace of mind. That must be worth something, even to a man without a conscience." A wave of impatience swept over him. "Let's get on with this. I've come to bargain."

"Bargain?" Jackson smiled as he brushed at his suit coat, looking for all the world like nothing more than a newly elected county judge. "You're not in much of a position to bargain."

Sam's fingers itched to grab for the Colt. "Maybe not, but I'm doing what I can. This isn't a situation I would have chosen."

"I've a mind to hear you grovel, Delaney."

"As I said, I'm doing what I can. Now, how about I get a look at my wife."

Jackson tugged the edges of his coat over his paunch. "She's an ill-tempered sort, but I suppose she makes up for it in bed."

"Sam!"

Lorelei's cry came from the cabin. Sam started, then forced himself to settle back down. She'd put a healthy volume to the cry, which gave him encouragement.

"Fool," snarled Jackson at his man. "I thought you gagged her."

"The bitch must have worked it loose."

435

A black cloud of rage swept over Sam. "You hurt her?"

"I'm the one got bit," the gunman growled.

"Enough of this," said Jackson. "You mentioned having something for me."

Again Sam waved the paper. "A letter from President Houston giving me rights to this land."

"You've been busy. Houston himself, you say."

"That's right. You let her go and I write across the bottom that I give up all claims to the title."

"You take me for a fool. This land means far too much to you."

"The woman means more."

"Sam!" Lorelei's voice came out of the cabin stronger than ever. "I love you." And stronger still, "Now go away!"

"How touching," said Jackson with a smirk.

Ignoring him, Sam stared at the darkness of the open doorway and pictured his wife bound up inside listening to everything he said. She'd picked as poor a time as he had to declare herself, but he was glad she'd spoken up.

Except where it came to the marching order. He wasn't quite ready to leave.

"Let's get on with this," he said. "What do you say?"

"But what of the ridiculous charges that I'm somebody called Jacobs? I believe that's what she said."

"She's also admitted that you don't look like him. Just the voice is the same. And she hasn't seen him in almost seven years. I don't think a judge anywhere is going to pay attention to a woman giving that kind of evidence."

"I truly hate to do this," said Jackson, nodding at the gunman beside him. "Truly I do since you seem to appreciate all this beauty as much as I."

The gunman grinned and took aim.

"You won't get away with killing me, Jackson."

"Oh, I believe I will. It might be necessary for me to leave, but as you must have figured out from listening to your wife, I'm a man who knows how to survive."

Sam caught a whiff of smoke. Gray curls of it seeped around the edges of the shuttered front windows and rolled out the door.

He came off the horse fast, shouting "Fire!"

The two men jumped to the ground in front of the porch, Jackson adjusting his glasses as he hurried down the slope. They drew abreast of Sam, and he went for the Colt. The gunman took aim. Sam shot him through the heart.

Jackson reached for his pocket. A pistol had barely cleared before Sam fired again. This time the gun fired low, and he caught Jackson in the gut.

Jackson dropped the weapon to grip his middle, but Sam was already at a run. He was on the porch by the time Jackson's body hit the ground.

Smoke filled the cabin, flames licking at the back walls. He found Lorelei on the floor near the hearth, her arms bound behind her, legs tied at the ankles.

Lifting her into his arms, he ran for the door. She coughed against his shoulder. He cradled her close and made tracks down the hill. She was still coughing when he came to a halt by the lake. Jet and Michael rode at a gallop out of the woods as he lowered her to the ground, whispering her name over and over. He waited until the coughing eased before cutting the rawhide that bound her. He rubbed at the redness of her wrists, and then she was back in his arms.

She threw her arms around him and held on tight. "I did a stupid thing, Sam, kicking the logs like that. I thought I could distract them with the fire." She shuddered against him. "I was so scared."

He stroked her shoulder, kissed her tangled hair, and held her close. She was wearing the blue dress she'd made weeks ago; but it was stained and torn at the shoulder, and somehow that made Sam angry all over again.

"I know, honey. They must have terrified you."

She eased away and stared up at him. He caught the light of indignation in her eyes. "I wasn't afraid for myself, Sam. I was afraid for you."

"Sounds like you're all right," said Jet as he looked down from high on horseback.

Lorelei smiled up at him. "I couldn't be better."

He reined away and rode up the hill toward where Michael was kneeling beside Jackson's body.

"That's quite a gun you've got there," Jet called out over his shoulder. "I counted five shots."

"Yeah, quite a gun. It's going to do a lot of damage once word of it spreads." Sam stared up at the two still figures hunched on the ground in front of the cabin. "A lot of men died today," he said, more to himself than to Lorelei.

She nestled tighter against him. "You tried to end all this another way. You've been looking for evidence against Jackson, and you would have found it, too, and taken care of this in court if it hadn't been for me."

Sam pushed her back and stared at her soot-stained face. "You're blaming yourself for what happened? Good God, these men were the kind to end up like this sooner or later. You better start forgetting them right now. Especially Jackson. You've carried his

438

memory around with you for too long as it is."

She nodded once and managed a smile. "He admitted to being Jacobs. His face looked different because of false teeth."

"I'd already decided you called that one right."

"Glad to hear you admit it." She looked on up to the burning cabin. "Oh, Sam, I'm so sorry. Your home is gone."

Stroking her hair, Sam kept on studying his wife's beautiful, smudged face. "We can rebuild it. It needed a woman's touch, anyway."

"But—"

He kissed her, forcing himself to make it short. "I love you."

She reached up to touch his cheek. "I heard you in town before you rode out."

"I wondered if you did. And if it made a difference."

She held him tight. He was surprised that after all she'd been through, she had so much strength. "It tore me apart. I didn't know what to do. I was so sure I had things figured out."

Sam kissed her again. "I hope you've got them figured out now, Mrs. Delaney."

"I'm not Mrs. Delaney."

"Can't get out of it. I've got a piece of paper that says you are. A certificate declaring our marriage legal and binding."

"Signed by Houston himself, no doubt."

"Of course."

She frowned. "The other letter, the one about your land. Does it really say what you told Jackson?"

"Yep."

"You were willing to give up the land for me?"

"That's why I went and got the letter in the first

place. I needed something besides words to get your attention."

"Oh, Sam," she said, tears in her eyes. "I've been such a fool."

He didn't argue, figuring that this was the last time she'd make such a statement and he ought to enjoy it for a while.

She pulled away from him, and he helped her to stand. Brushing the tangled curls from her face, she looked up and smiled.

"I must look terrible."

"I wouldn't say that. Remember that first time I saw you in the casino? You had your hair piled up and some fancy dress on and a ribbon at your throat. You were a beautiful woman, but, honey, you're more beautiful right now. And those better be tears of happiness in your eyes, because I don't think I could stand to see you cry."

"Oh, they are, Husband, they are. Now, put your arms around me, and give me a sweet, welcoming kiss. I need a little more convincing that you're really home safe."

Sam was happy to comply.

Epilogue

Lorelei stood in the high grass next to the lake and watched a heron circle overhead, its wide, white wings stark against the afternoon sky.

The sight was beautiful, a touch of sweet Texas magic. Blue had taken recently to carving herons, and he was doing a wonderful job in capturing the essence of the bird's soaring flight. The boy kept improving with his works. Already she'd sent a dozen examples to Catherine Gase, who reported back right away she found a Vieux Carré gallery eager to sell the artist's entire output.

Blue didn't understand quite what that meant, but Preacher had assured her he would work on his young charge until he did. When money from the sales started coming in, every dollar would be put aside for Blue's living expenses.

"The lad is going to be able to take care of himself. As he grows older, he will appreciate the security. I won't be around to take care of him forever."

Lorelei refused to listen to such talk. At this very minute Preacher was in No Pines supervising the building of the county's first church, and he was already starting to talk about a school.

He wasn't the same man Lorelei had met just over

a year ago. Not that he wasn't just as wise and caring, but now he was quick to smile, and he had a spring in his step that she'd never seen in camp. She'd even heard him humming a hymn or two while hard at work on the church.

Blue, his designated assistant, was helping with the furniture when he wasn't carving birds.

Lorelei had to smile when she thought of the changes coming to No Pines. There was a new county judge, the lawyer James Hockley who'd moved down from San Augustine, and she'd heard talk about adding a justice of the peace for out in the county. A church, a school, a system of courts, and a couple of houses going up on the hill . . . it would be civilized yet.

The saloons hadn't changed. Francine Hopewell had moved to a similar establishment in Nacogdoches, but two other women had taken her place.

Bending to study a wild buttercup that grew in the midst of the tall greenery, Lorelei felt a pinch of her trousers across her middle. She wouldn't be able to wear them much longer, not with the baby on the way. Sam didn't like her to wear them now, but she felt comfortable in them when she was helping with the building of their new house.

He indulged her by not complaining. He was indulging her a great deal lately, and she was loving it. He even went so far as to compliment her cooking, which she didn't think was improving despite Wash's instructions.

Oh, but Sam Delaney was a loving man. He liked to tease her about the rash he'd brought out the first few times he kissed her.

"Now," he'd say, "you break out if I don't."

She would always admit he was right.

"Lorelei!"

Sam waved at her from the top of the hill.

Returning the wave, she started toward him. They met halfway, and he encircled her in his arms. Behind him loomed the spacious three-room log cabin that was replacing the burnt shell of his first home. Only the puncheon floor needed completing, along with a few pieces of furniture Sam didn't think she could do without. Including a cradle and a rocking chair.

"How are you feeling?" he asked.

"I'm fine. The same as I was a half hour ago when you asked. Just thought I'd walk for a few minutes. The air is so sweet. A perfect April day.

"The second anniversary of the fight at San Jacinto. They'll be celebrating in the streets of the capital."

"I'd rather have a more private celebration."

Sam growled. "I knew I was right to marry you. This is our anniversary, too, in a way. A year to the day after President Houston signed a certificate making you an honest woman."

"It didn't take a piece of paper to make me honest. I'd decided that whatever the Republic of Texas chose to accept, I was your wife. I just didn't think we would be able to occupy the same house."

"Or the same country. Admit it, honey. When I got back from the capital, you were still determined to leave. And you would have, too, except—"

"Let's not think about that time, Sam." She buried her head against his chest and held tight. There was such a solid feeling to Sam. She liked to hug him this way. It gave her a sense of rightness with the world.

She played with the buttons of his shirt. "Do you

want a boy or girl?"

"Makes no difference."

"We'll need to pick out names."

"I've got a few in mind for your consideration."

She pushed back to look up at him. "You certainly are agreeable."

"I'm still not used to being a father."

"You won't be for another five months."

He rested a hand on her abdomen. "Only a technicality. Our baby is growing strong."

A horseman approached from the rear, and they turned to watch as Jet rode around the edge of the lake. He reined to a halt beside them.

"You got a letter from Missouri, Sam. Thought you'd want to read it."

Sam took the offered envelope and scanned the contents. He grinned at his wife. "Aloysius Harrison and Calhoun Harrison have been sentenced to six months for escaping jail."

"I guess that's good news," said Lorelei. "They went back not having any idea what would happen to them."

"They went back," he corrected, "because they'd vowed to Preacher they would if you got away from Jackson safe. And their situation isn't so bad. They're to serve the time by helping erect a more secure facility for housing the county's criminals. They figure they'll be out in the open air more than they'll be in their cell."

"Aren't you forgetting something? What about the murder charge?"

"That's the really good news. The deputy was only knocked out. He was so ashamed of letting them get away that he said if they wouldn't brag about it all over town, he'd forget all about it, too."

"And the original charge they'd stolen planting seed?"

"Dropped. Al and Cal will be back in Dogwood County before next spring. They're planning on buying some land and setting up a farm."

"That's wonderful." Lorelei looked up at Jet. "With Preacher and Blue in town, and Wash and Michael helping us out here, that takes care of everybody but you, Jet. You're still dropping in when we least expect you. Still keeping your thoughts private and your background to yourself. When are you going to settle down?"

He grimaced. "Never. I'm happy for you two, but I'm a loner. You know I'm not one to turn down a little nighttime comfort, but I don't need a particular woman to make me happy. I can get along on my own."

"You just haven't met the right woman yet."

Jet laughed, shook his head, and with a lift of his hat spurred his mount on past them and over the hill.

Lorelei smiled to herself.

"What's so funny?" asked Sam.

"I listened to myself just now and remembered that someone said almost the exact same thing to me the day you walked into the casino."

"Delilah? It sounds like her."

Sam had met Delilah and Ben and the Gases six months ago when he'd taken Lorelei for a brief visit back to Louisiana. This time they had gone by wagon down to Galveston, then to New Orleans by ship. Lorelei had financed part of the journey with a little card-playing one of the nights, but Sam, having to stand guard to keep all the men from crushing around her, said that since they really weren't hurting for money, she better not do that again.

445

She promised she wouldn't, but he didn't seem convinced.

Lorelei thought of the success Delilah was making of Balzac's, and of her happiness over her former charge's marriage to Sam. "Delilah was always pointing out I was independent because I hadn't met the right man."

"And you took one look at me standing in the door and thought, hot damn, Delilah, you were right."

"Actually, I decided you were Trouble. With a capital T. And, honey"—she liked to throw the name at him—"I sure was right."

He scooped her up in his arms and headed for the cabin.

"I can be trouble, all right," he said, nuzzling her neck. "I'm going to settle you down in that new bed I just built and show you exactly how much."

FEEL THE FIRE IN CAROL FINCH'S ROMANCES!

BELOVED BETRAYAL   (2346, $3.95)
Sabrina Spencer donned a gray wig and veiled hat before blackmailing rugged Ridge Tanner into guiding her to Fort Canby. But the costume soon became her prison—the beauty had fallen head over heels in love!

LOVE'S HIDDEN TREASURE   (2980, $4.50)
Shandra d'Evereux felt her heart throb beneath the stolen map she'd hidden in her bodice when Nolan Elliot swept her out onto the veranda. It was hard to concentrate on her mission with that wily rogue around!

MONTANA MOONFIRE   (3263, $4.95)
Just as debutante Victoria Flemming-Cassidy was about to marry an oh-so-suitable mate, the towering preacher, Dru Sullivan flung her over his shoulder and headed West! Suddenly, Tori realized she had been given the best present for a bride: a night of passion with a real man!

THUNDER'S TENDER TOUCH   (2809, $4.50)
Refined Piper Malone needed bounty-hunter, Vince Logan to recover her swindled inheritance. She thought she could coolly dismiss him after he did the job, but she never counted on the hot flood of desire she felt whenever he was near!

Available wherever paperbacks are sold, or order direct from the Publisher. Send cover price plus 50¢ per copy for mailing and handling to Zebra Books, Dept. 3716, 475 Park Avenue South, New York, N.Y. 10016. Residents of New York and Tennessee must include sales tax. DO NOT SEND CASH. For a free Zebra/Pinnacle catalog please write to the above address.